Blue Heaven

Blue Heaven

a novel

ELAINE KAGAN

Alfred A. Knopf New York 1996

THIS IS A BORZOI BOOK
PUBLISHED BY ALFRED A. KNOPF, INC.

Published in the United States by Alfred A. Knopf, Inc., New York,
and simultaneously in Canada by Random House of Canada Limited, Toronto.
Distributed by Random House, Inc., New York.

Owing to limitations of space, all acknowledgments
for permission to reprint previously published material
may be found on page 353.

Library of Congress Cataloging-in-Publication Data
Kagan, Elaine.
Blue heaven : a novel / Elaine Kagan. — 1st ed.
p. cm.
ISBN 0-679-43598-0
1. Family—United States—Fiction.
2. Women—United States—Fiction.
I. Title.
PS3561.A3629B58 1996
813'.54—dc20 95-37591
CIP

Manufactured in the United States of America
First Edition

for Milly and Jewel

ACKNOWLEDGMENTS

For their patience, support, and steadfast involvement, thank you to Razel Ronne, David Freeman, Eric Lax, Carole Smith, Eve Kagan, and Deborah Kagan.

For their profound and vital contributions, thank you to Iva Rifkin, Milly Zeff, Isadore Zeff, Earl Goren, Miriam and Ruben Goren, Louis Kalmes, Henrietta Kling, Eleanor Kean, and Harry Kraal. Without their gifts, this story would not be.

For sharing their technical expertise, thank you to Ted Witzer, Bob Mills, Jeffrey Fiskin, Dr. Michael Bush, Dr. Louis Fishman, Captain David Thompson of the Los Angeles Fire Department, and Ray Simmons.

John Cassavetes,

Tonto, always,

and of course, Bob Gottlieb.

Matthew watched them silently as they faced each other across the table. Amanda smiled tentatively and extended her open hand to Kate. Kate hesitated a moment, and then took the hand wordlessly, her eyes never leaving Amanda's face. He had the feeling something passed between them in that moment, something almost tangible passed between them as Kate took Amanda's hand in her own, a love, an understanding, something he could not quite fathom, something like . . .

He shook his head.

Something like a legacy, he had thought.

"Eat your potatoes, son," he said.

Evan Hunter, *Mothers and Daughters*

MONDAY

Gilliana

"Gillian, I'm leaving."

He's come up behind me. I'm in Clare's room putting her folded warm laundry back in her chest of drawers. She's not home; it's the third day of Christmas vacation and she and three other hysterical teenage girls have escaped high school and are running around some mall.

I smell lavender. There are sheets of lavender-smelling liner paper on the bottom of her drawers. Lavender and Cheer and Downy, that's what I smell. And dog. Murray the dog. He's lying on the rug by the foot of Clare's bed. He rolls over on his side and sticks his paws way out in front of him, stiff, like Sonja Henie skidding to a stop on the ice.

Sonja Henie . . . God, what ever happened to Sonja Henie? Is she alive?

Maybe she's reincarnated as Murray the dog. I look at the dog—and, as if by magic, he flexes one of his paws.

Wait a minute . . . this could be something. A dog with skates and a Norwegian accent. A Norwegian bark. Yah-roof? Yah-sure-roof? No, it's too much. It's too much, Gillian.

"Gillian?" Chris says again from the doorway.

So what have I got here? I have Sonja Henie and Murray the dog . . .

"Gillian?"

Damn. Don't bother me, I'm working on something here.

"What?" I say, without turning. What fresh hell is this?—that's what Dorothy Parker said every time her phone rang. I do not say this to Chris.

"Hey, Chris," I say, closing Clare's pajama drawer, "bring me home a celery, would you? I was gonna make tuna salad and our celery up and died."

"Gillian . . ."

"Christopher, it's only a celery, it's not like I asked you to bring me a charlotte *russe."*

They ought to have drive-through markets like McDonald's or the bank—you drive through, pick up some milk, a loaf of bread, a celery, maybe two celeries, and zip, you're on your way. It could be very trendy, very L.A. I hate L.A.

I let go of Clare's socks lovingly and pat them into place in her top right drawer. I'm still holding a stack of her sweatshirts in my left arm. Her room is flooded with sunshine; it faces east and in the late morning it's practically yellow with light. It may be December and nearly Christmas but this is L.A.—the sun never stops. You could die here pining for grayness, for a thunderstorm, a downpour—you could make chili or maybe beef stew, you could listen to Mahler or throw yourself off a cliff . . . actually, here you couldn't throw yourself off a cliff, you'd have to drive yourself to the cliff and then throw yourself off—here you don't go anywhere without your car.

Of course, all this yellow light in Clare's room is beautiful, I have to admit. Yellow-gold light and pale-blue walls, and everything else is white.

"I want it calm, Mom, peaceful. I want it like an island in a dream. Like a Monet," she says to me, smiling. Clare is even more beautiful than this yellow-gold light.

But that was three summers ago when she and I still talked. She was fourteen then; now she's about to be seventeen and I'm not worth talking to. It seems that *now* I suddenly know *nothing* about life. That's the way she talks to me, in sentences where certain words have extraordinary emphasis and meaning, as if they're coming out of her mouth in italic type—and all of them are spoken with high drama and enormous attitude. *"I said I would, didn't I?"* or "You *know* I don't *eat that,"* or "I *tried* to call, there weren't any *phones*." And, of course, the big one: *"Everybody else* is going; what is your *problem* with this, *Mother*?" I have also graduated to Mother, I used to be plain old Mom. A hundred years ago I was even Mommy. Ah, the good old days.

But three summers ago when I was still Mom, Clare still talked to me and that's when we painted her room, the summer before she started high school. Actually, we didn't paint it—Phillie the painter did, but Clare picked the colors from the tiny squares on the brochure he brought her from the paint store. "Fountain blue" was the name of the color she picked. A pale lavender-blue like a morning sky. She was starting high school, she didn't want a "baby" room anymore. We packed away her dolls, stored the toys in bags clearly labeled with Magic Markers, and gave lots of things away. I know that the whole experience upset me much more than it did her. She was happy not to be the "baby" anymore, I don't think I was so happy to pack the "baby" away.

So fountain blue covered the sparkling rainbow she and her daddy had painted on her wall, and fountain blue covered the glue where she'd stuck her stickers, and fountain blue covered the big purple block letters where she had spelled out "C-L-A-R-E" when she was three. I didn't mind that she'd written her name on the wall but Chris got all pissed off. I thought it was kind of daring to be so bold at three. I couldn't write my name on a wall until I was at least thirty. Maybe thirty-five. Actually, I've never written my name on a wall, but I am considering it.

Anyway, white antique lace replaced the patchwork quilt, pristine white pillowcases with ivory edges went over the Marimekko red and blue shapes, a white woven-cotton throw was tossed on a white-and-pale-blue couch (very Monet-ish), white shelves went up and I painted an old-fashioned wooden dressing table white with a white-on-white sheer billowing skirt, and Clare's "grown-up" room emerged—a white refuge, a white cotton ball in the sky.

"Gillian?" Chris says.

As I turn, I see my face in the mirror above Clare's chest of drawers. I look okay. Not bad for forty-seven. Great for forty-seven. What the hell is forty-seven supposed to look like anyway?

I look at Chris in the doorway.

"I'm leaving you, Gillian," he says to me.

"Hmm?"

I try to decipher his expression. Determined, joking, angry—what? After all, I know this man for twenty years; I should be able to figure out his face.

No clues. He's just standing there. With a regular face.

And then he frowns.

Aha! A clue.

"I'm leaving you," he says again.

I laugh. I'll be funny. I'll change his mood. I mean, he couldn't be serious. After all . . . we're married for eighteen years.

"You mean like the cartoon in the kitchen?" I say.

We have a cartoon from an old *New Yorker* taped to the kitchen wall. The woman is sitting at the breakfast table with a pot of coffee in front of her; she's wearing a dress and pearls and has one leg crossed over the other at the knee, a cup is poised in her hand. The man is standing in a suit and tie and hat with an attaché case in his hand; he's surrounded by suitcases. She's looking up at him and her eyes are wide. His mouth is open, he's the one who's speaking. The caption reads: *"Well, goodbye, Emily. It's May 19th. You may remember my having mentioned some time ago that I was going to leave you on May 19th."*

I'm trying to remember who cut it out and taped it to the wall. I did. I thought it was funny. But he thought it was funny too. He laughed. I remember. We laughed together. Didn't we?

I look at him. "Huh?" I say. "Like the cartoon?"

"Don't be funny, Gillian," Chris says to me.

"I'm not being funny, I'm asking you."

I lie. I am trying to be funny. It just isn't working. Maybe it will never work again. Maybe I'll be a straight man for the rest of my life. That would not be good. They pay me the big bucks to be funny. Well, the medium bucks. And it's to be funny for somebody else. To write funny for somebody else so they can get the laughs. And the big bucks.

"I can't do this anymore," he says. "It's killing me. I just can't do it."

He's serious. He's dead serious. I see it now. And I don't move. That's the funny thing. I absolutely do not move.

I think I'm going to move but I don't. I think I'm going to throw the sweatshirts in the air and pole-vault across the room. Grab him, smack him, kiss him, spit on him, hug him, shoot him—something—but I don't. I hold on to the sweatshirts like a life raft, the way the lady in the cartoon holds on to her cup. Emily, her name is Emily, the lady in the cartoon. Well, goodbye, Emily. I'm leaving you, Emily.

It occurs to me that Emily was one of the names we were thinking of for Clare. I never thought of this before. My God, what if we would have named her Emily—would her fate have already been Scotch-taped to my kitchen wall?

"Don't you want to wait until May 19th?" I say to him.

I know that he knows what the caption on the cartoon says as well as I do.

"Please don't be funny, Gillian. I asked you not to."

"Okay," I say. "What should I be?"

After all, I'm amenable. I don't have to be funny. I can be something else. I think.

He looks at me.

"Huh, Chris? What should I be?"

"Well, I guess the truth is . . . I really don't care."

That's what he says to me. Quietly. He doesn't even use his pompous tone, he just says it plain. "I really don't care." And then he turns in the doorway of our daughter's "grown-up" room and walks off down the hall.

And I stand there.

I don't move.

I look at the dog, golden sunshine stripes cut across his fur. I look at my boots, I feel the soft sweatshirts against the skin on my arms.

You're leaving me?

Wait a minute. I thought we had an agreement here. You be the thinker and I'll make the jokes. You be the smart one and I'll be funny. Wasn't that it? Look what an original couple they are. Chris and Gillian, the brain and the laugh.

And what about for richer and poorer? And what about in sickness and health? And what about, we can do this, you and me?

What about all the Thanksgivings and all the birthdays, suitcases dripping with history? What about I know you're allergic to vinegar and could secretly poison you with a Caesar salad? What about I know your only tickle spot, that you get seasick, that you love to sleep late and hate pistachio nuts?

And what about growing old together? Huh? What about that?

What does that mean, "I don't care." I'm forty-seven years old here. You don't care about any of it? What does that mean?

Wait a minute. Is that what Rhett Butler said? I don't care?

No. No, wait a minute. He said, I don't give a damn. "Frankly, Scarlett, I don't give a damn."

That's what I'm thinking about? Rhett Butler? What am I—crazy? That's a movie, Gillian. This is a real life. This is not a routine, Gillian.

What does Clare say to me? Get a grip. Get a grip, Mom. I clutch her sweatshirts to my breasts. I look at the mountain outside her window. I look at the books on her shelves. I look at the picture of me and Chris on the table next to her bed. I look at the doorway where Chris stood.

Why am I standing here? I'm married to this man for eighteen years.

Why am I standing here holding on to my daughter's sweatshirts? Why am I not moving through the doorway and down the hall?

Wait a minute. Rhett Butler was in a doorway when he said it. He was . . . wasn't he?

He was. I'll be damned. He was in a doorway and he said it and then he shut the door and walked off into the fog. You could see he was in a doorway because you could see the fog behind him before he shut the door.

I look at the doorway where Chris was standing. No fog. Just sunlight and wood floors.

And Chris didn't shut the door either, the way Rhett Butler did. He just turned and walked away into no fog without shutting the door.

Of course, you need a certain amount of swagger to shut the door. A certain amount of pizzazz. You have to be a dashing man to say something like I don't give a damn or I don't care or fuck you, Gillian, and then shut the door. I'm leaving you, and shut the door. A man needs swagger to do that, a man needs black eyes and black hair and a mustache to pull that off . . .

Chris doesn't have a mustache. He doesn't have any swagger. He's an intellectual, for crissakes. He's a *summa cum laude. Summa cum laude*s don't have swagger, everybody knows that.

I stand there.

A mustache. Black hair and a mustache.

I stand there, I don't move.

Jesus.

My father had a mustache.

My father had a mustache *and* black hair.

Bingo.

I stand there. I don't sit on the edge of Clare's bed. I don't get dizzy. I don't cry. I don't vomit. I don't do anything.

I just remember.

I don't want to remember; it's not the thing that I would pick to do at this particular time in my life. I should be running down the hall to stop my husband, I should be flinging myself across the front door to save my marriage, I should be carrying on like a maniac in front of the closet before he packs. But I stand there.

And I remember. I can't help it. It overtakes me. Like a puzzle—no, not like a puzzle, not in pieces—more like something in soft focus, like a movie that's in soft focus and then the guy back there fiddles with the controls on the projector and it's suddenly sharp.

But that isn't right either.

It's like whipped cream. You know, the way you make whipped cream. You have the cream in the bowl and you're whipping with the beaters and the beaters are cold and the bowl is cold and you're whipping and you're whipping and it's still cream floating around in the bowl and then suddenly it's not. It takes form, it stiffens up and it's . . . Jesus . . . it's whipped cream and you're watching it. It's just stupid whipped cream but it happens right in front of you and you're amazed. That's how the memory comes in. Like whipped cream.

I walk in and I hear them. Or do I hear them and walk in? Where was I? Sleeping? Do I have on pajamas? I don't know.

Look down, Gillian. What are you wearing?

I see nothing, I don't know.

I only know I walk in and I see them.

She's crying. My mother is crying. He's yanking things out of a closet and jamming them into a suitcase.

It smells like fish. How could it smell like fish? What am I—crazy?

She has on dress-up shoes. She does. Dress-up high heels with a housedress. *With a housedress?* Come on, Gillian. No, I see them. High-heeled dancing shoes. Why is my mother wearing dancing shoes in the middle of the day? I don't know.

Is he yelling?

No. My father is not yelling.

He says he's leaving.

Where is he going? On a trip?

She's crying. Why is she crying if he's only going on a trip? What's the big deal? It's just a trip.

She says don't go. Why shouldn't he go if it's only a trip?

He turns and walks away. He's going toward the door.

I run. My mother doesn't move but I run and grab his leg.

"Let go," he says to me. Is that what he says? "Let go of my leg, Babe." That's it. That's what he says. Babe, he always called me Babe. I love him so much I can't see straight and he says, "Let go, Babe."

I've got my fingers clenched tight on his gabardine trouser leg and he's pulling my fingers off. Little-girl pudgy fingers with red nail polish so I would look like her.

"Don't go, Daddy." Do I say that? Yes, I say that.

She says that. "Don't go, Jule," she says, but she doesn't move.

She doesn't move.

I'm standing here holding the sweatshirts and I remember clearly that my mother doesn't move. My mother stood there next to the sink. I stand here next to the bed. *She doesn't move. I'm not moving and my mother doesn't move.*

She's crying.

I'm crying.

Is he crying? No. No, I don't think so.

No.

He's prying my fingers off his pants leg.

Please, Babe . . .

And . . .

. . . he's out the door.

Boom.

He's out the door? That's it? That's the whole thing? What is this? This isn't whipped cream.

Try, Gillian. Come on. You can remember. Try.

Where is she? Does she come to me? Does she hold me?

Where am I? Do I crumple to the floor in a little heap? Do I yell and scream? Do I kick my feet? After all, I'm only six years old, I could scream if I want.

I don't know. I don't remember. I really don't remember.

My hair is in pom-poms. A ponytail on each side of my head. Pom-poms, my mother and I called them. *That's what I remember?* That my hair is in pom-poms? What am I? A moron?

Where's the whipped cream? I still have cream here floating in the bowl. This isn't good enough. I can't get it. It won't stiffen all the way.

Oh, I don't have it and I won't get it. That's the real truth. I'm not going to get it by myself. I'll have to ask her.

I move. Finally. I don't take a step or anything, I don't do anything big. I just bend my knees and sit down on the edge of Clare's bed. The dog lifts up his head, looks at me, and puts his head back down on the top of my boot.

I'll have to ask her. It's all too blocked. The beaters aren't cold enough. The date on the cream carton is too old. And I know then what I have to do.

I don't know why it should be now. Or what it has to do with me and Chris. Or what it has to do with this marriage. It makes no sense.

After all, I didn't do what she did, I didn't do what my mother did. A nice Jewish girl is not supposed to marry an Italian guy. I know that, even being half-Jewish I know that. And certainly not a dashing, handsome Italian guy with a topcoat and a pinky ring and a flashy smile—everybody knows that you're not supposed to do that. You marry some gorgeous Italian guy who says I love you and then before you know it, he says fuck you and he walks away through a doorway and takes a powder with his mustache and his black hair and you're standing there in a kitchen smelling of fish looking at your kid.

I touch the beautiful white antique lace coverlet on my daughter's bed. I run my palm across its silkiness. I know that I will always be eternally grateful to whoever is up there that Clare is not home.

I close my eyes for a second.

They were dress-up shoes, the shoes my mother was wearing the day my father left. I do remember that. They were red lizard high-heeled ankle-strap dancing shoes. I can see them on her feet. I have no idea why she was wearing them but I can see them now as if she was here standing on Clare's rug.

They used to go dancing, Mollie and Jule. It was a big thing with them. I remember the "coming in to kiss me good night" part. Old Spice and Camel cigarettes, his black mustache grazing my nose as he gave me a kiss.

"G'nite, Babe," he'd whisper low to me.

And then her cool lips replacing his, her perfect long red nails with the white moons touching my cheek.

"Good night, my sweetie," she'd say, "good night and sleep tight . . ."

"And wake up in the morning nice and bright," he'd say with her from the doorway, and then he'd wink at me in the bed. Wink at me. My God.

"C'mon, honey, let's go." His cuff links would catch the hallway light as he straightened his tie.

"I'm coming, Jule, I'm coming," and she'd tuck the blanket in all around me, stroke a curl back from my cheek.

A cloud of Zibelene, the rustle of taffeta and they'd be gone. I would lie there in the dark except for the glow from my Hopalong Cassidy nightlight, praying that I would grow up fast to experience such romance for myself.

Dancing. Suits and ties and gardenias. Highballs. Rhinestones. Fedoras. Short rustling cocktail dresses cut on the bias. Cuff links and ankle straps.

But I didn't marry that.

Oh, I played with it all right, I ran around with it, I did my share; but I knew those guys weren't for keeps.

The ones who looked in your eyes and said all the longed-for words but were gone by the morning light. The ones who were gorgeous in a dinner jacket but wouldn't be caught dead holding your head over a toilet when you were puking your guts out with the flu. The ones who could dance like Fred Astaire but couldn't listen when you had something to say. Those weren't the forever guys. I knew that, so I didn't marry one of them.

I didn't marry my father.

I didn't do what Mollie did.

I married reliable. I married plain—straight-arrow and steadfast—plain without the nuts. I married *summa cum laude.* A guy who checks the stock market, not the morning line. A guy who drinks cranberry juice with maybe just a *little bit* of vodka if it's *really* a *special* occasion, not a guy who throws back a couple of V.O.s neat with a water chaser every night. I married a guy who doesn't appreciate off-color remarks, not a guy who winks. Christopher William Hall couldn't figure out how to make a wink work if you gave him a million bucks. He's an Episcopalian, for godsake. So, what's happening here? What does he mean, I'm leaving you. Episcopalians don't leave you—Episcopalians aren't supposed to go anywhere.

I look at the gold wedding band on the third finger of my left hand. Plain. No diamonds. No sparkles. There isn't even an inscription on the inside.

I didn't even wear a wedding dress, for godsake. Not a real wedding dress, not a *white* wedding dress. He was so busy not wanting to make a fuss, not wanting it to look like it was a wedding, it practically looked like a business lunch.

I mean, I wore rust. Okay? Rust. I'll give you that it *was* silk jersey and it *was* expensive, but it was *rust.* I'd never worn rust before. I've never worn rust since. What kind of a wedding is it where you wear rust? Certainly not dashing, right? Certainly not something that you think is going to be laden with *Sturm und Drang.* Certainly not something where somebody's going to say I don't care and leave you and walk down a hallway with or without shutting the goddamn door.

I'm angry. Of course I'm angry. Who wouldn't be angry if out of nowhere your husband comes up and says he's leaving you?

I move my foot a little and the dog picks his head up off my boot and looks at me.

No, I'm not angry; if I was angry I'd be throwing the sweatshirts, not holding on to them as if they were some sort of life raft. I'm not angry, I feel more like I've been hit with a stun gun . . . that's it . . . rendered senseless . . . like I've been anesthetized . . . frozen . . . with fear.

I have to go home and see my mother.

Sitting in the golden light on the edge of my daughter's bed clutching her sweatshirts, I know. I have to go home to Kansas City and ask Mollie about the day my father left. About that marriage. About why. I have tiptoed around this discussion before but never really . . . I never did really get into the real whys. I don't think I ever really wanted to know.

There was a piece of me that just wanted to add it to the list of me as if it was nothing at all: I like cheeseburgers, I didn't finish college, my father walked out when I was six, I can play the saxophone, I hate asparagus . . . you know . . . like it was nothing. Uneventful. No big ting, mon, no problem at all.

But now I have to know.

I have to go home and find out why my father left.

I move the wedding band around my finger with my thumb.

I'll find out. And I'll feel better. It'll give me a clue.

And then I'll think about Chris.

And why he's leaving.

Tomorrow.

I'll think about Chris tomorrow.

Oh, Jesus. I did it again. It's you and me, Scarlett.

That's when I start to cry. I laugh first that I could even think this thought and then I start to cry. The dog immediately stands up and puts his paw on my knee. He's very attached to me and hates it when I cry.

"It's okay, Murray," I say, sobbing, "don't worry, puppy, I'm not a straight man yet—I've got a good thing going here about me and Rhett and Scarlett, I just haven't quite figured out the end."

Clare

My mother's going to Kansas City to see my grandma. Like out of nowhere—you know?

Something happened. I don't know what it was but it was big, and neither of them is talking about it; my parents, I mean. Or if they're talking about it, they're certainly not talking about it to me.

I went to the mall with Lisa and Jenny, and when I got home everything was changed. My mother didn't look at me. She said she was going to Grandma's but she didn't look at me when she said it. Not that I need my mother to look at me or anything, but, I mean, you know, she's always looking at me and I'm never looking at her, and then all of a sudden she's not looking at me. You know? I mean, I knew something was up.

And she didn't say she wanted me to go with her. That's really strange. Not that I wanted to go. I mean, I love my grandma and grampa and all, but did you ever go to Kansas City? It's like time stopped in their house. It's like you're walking around in slow motion or underwater or something, waiting for something to happen, waiting for the time to be up so you can leave.

So I said to her, Do you want me to go with you? Not really wanting to, but knowing she'd probably say yes and how it would really be a nice thing for me to do because it is my Grandma Mollie's birthday on Christmas Day and she is gonna be eighty years old and all, and who knows how long she'll be here and she's not well besides, but my mother didn't say that. She said she wanted to go by herself. No, she said she *needed* to go by herself. Needed was what she said. And she was quiet, you know, reserved—like she was doing an imitation of my father or something, not like she was herself at all. I mean, my mother is verbal, you know? And she's funny—not my kind of funny, but she is funny. And she's big—I don't mean big physically, physically she practically looks anorexic; I mean, she's not, but, you know, she's really thin—but she's big, like in her actions; I don't know, I guess you'd have to say she's passionate. Like, my mother throws things. You know? I don't mean at anybody or anything, but she's highly volatile, if you know what I mean. Like when it all gets to her she could just pull a bunch of books off a shelf or something and crash them to the floor. I guess it makes her feel better. It used to scare me when I was little, but I don't even think twice about it now. You just hear a crash from somewhere and you go right on with what you're doing. And she talks sometimes and you're absolutely sure that she's angry—as if you did something really ghastly and she's really pissed off, but then she says she's just speaking emphatically, that she's not angry at all. I don't know. I mean, she says *I* have attitude, I think *she* has attitude.

But, whatever happened with them, there was no attitude and no voice-raising and no book-throwing or anything like that. She was just sitting on this little couch they have in their bedroom; it's just this little flowered couch under a window, but she's very attached to it. She absolutely loves this couch. She says she spent her whole pregnancy on it. When she was pregnant with me, I mean. She was pregnant one other time but she had a miscarriage. I'm the only kid they had that made it. Anyway, that's where she sat when she was pregnant with me, on that flowered couch, that's where she thought about me, she says, or did whatever you do when you're pregnant. And now sometimes she sits there when she's thinking something through, you know, like something in her head she's working on—she's a writer, my mother. She doesn't write books or anything like that. She writes comedy for this guy to do. He's a real asshole. You've probably seen him, he's on television and all—Andy Minkoff, he has his own show. You've seen him, right? Everyone thinks he's a big deal, but they don't know. I mean, I've had to *eat* with him, you know? He's really disgusting. Anyway, she writes for him. That's what she does.

My dad does this stock shit, something with stocks and financial consulting and all. I mean, he's some financial wizard or something, and a genius at math. I mean it, it's disgusting. You should see him look at my homework. I mean, he can just look at logic or trigonometry or even calculus and like do it in his head. I'm not kidding, in his *head.*

Anyway, I got home from the mall and I was late, of course, and I hadn't called. I knew they'd be pissed. I meant to call, but Lisa had left the boots she'd bought in the MAC store where we were trying on lipsticks, so we had to go all the way back there to get them and she was hysterical the whole way that somebody might have picked up the bag with the boots, and then by the time we got back to the car, I forgot. I wasn't driving, Lisa was. Anyway, I got home and I was sure I was gonna get it, you know, 'cause I didn't call and I'd said I'd be home by three and it was after five, but the house was like dead silent. I mean, there was nobody waiting there to yell at me, you know?

So I say hello, but nobody answers me. And I go upstairs to my room and it's like I have this feeling that my mother is in the house, you know, so I go into their bedroom and she's sitting there on that little flowered couch she loves. She's sitting there in the dark. I mean, there's not a light on anywhere and it's dark. You know, this may be California and all, but even here when it's supposed to be winter it gets dark—like in December at four. And it's twenty past five so it's dark. And I have this sudden outrageous thought that hits me—like, oh my God, she couldn't be pregnant, could she? I mean, really, it's ridiculous. I mean, my mother is old—not old, but you know . . . and I say *Mother* three times before she even looks at me and then she says, "I'm going to Grandma's tomorrow." And I say, "What's up?" I mean, I think to myself did somebody die or something? Of course, I don't mean my grandma or grampa, because she would have told me that, but you know there are lots of other relatives there that could have died and it has to be something big because we were supposed to go to asshole Andy's ranch in Aspen for Christmas, we had the tickets and everything. But she said no, everybody was fine, she just had to go. Needed to go, that was what she said. And that was all she said. Nothing else. I mean nothing. She just sat there.

And I stood there and then I had to say *Mother* again, maybe three more times before she finally said "What," and that's when I asked her if she wanted me to go with her and that's when she said no. And then I asked her where Dad was and she said she didn't know. And I stood there a while. I did turn the lamps on, on either side of their bed, but she didn't say anything to me so I left. She was just staring off into the air. So, you know, I left.

I have no idea what's going to happen now. I mean, if Dad and I will still go to asshole Andy's ranch for Christmas without her or what. Let's face it, my father doesn't really fit in with that group—he's not what you'd call funny. I mean, he's an okay guy and everything, and really terrifically smart, but he's much more comfortable listening to classical music or discussing something terribly difficult, you know, like deciphering Chaucer or somebody or figuring out the Louisiana Purchase or the theories of Marx, than sitting around with a bunch of Hollywood phonies telling jokes. I mean, the people that will be at Andy's house at Christmas could not discuss Marx. Possibly the Marx brothers, but certainly not Marx.

Anyway, it's fine with me if we just stay here. Absolutely fine. I didn't want to go in the first place. I mean, I certainly didn't want to leave Scott.

TUESDAY

Gilliana

"So what do you want to know, sweetie?" my mother says to me in my daydream on USAir.

"Well, what happened, Mom? How did it turn bad? What happened with you so that my father left? Why is it happening to me? I didn't marry the same kind of guy you did—why is it happening again? What is it—hereditary? Is it in our genes? Like the mole on my left shoulder that's just like yours? Like the way we have good arms even though we don't exercise? What is it, Mom? What did I do wrong?"

And she tells me. Everything. She tells me about her and my father and what happened. She tells me about me and Christopher and what happened. She explains it all perfectly and I understand it and *none of it is my fault.*

That's the way I have it all written out in my head as I sit on the airplane. Especially the *none of it is my fault* part.

I pour the last few drops out of the miniature Smirnoff bottle into my plastic glass.

But some of it has to be my fault, right?

I look out the window.

No, shut up, Gillian. Be quiet. Listen to your mother, she knows. I hear some of the dialogue I've made up in my head as I watch the little squares of brown-and-tan farmland getting bigger.

"You did everything right, sweetie, you did everything you could, and it's not your fault."

"Oh, that's good."

I turn in my plastic glass, smile at the stewardess, and we begin our descent.

Of course, nothing turns out the way we plan, does it? Well, not when you're dealing with my family, it sure doesn't.

I took a limousine to the airport. Christopher asked if I wanted him to take me, but I said no; other than that, no words have passed between us. He came home last night because when he called, Clare answered, and she told him I was going to Kansas City this morning. I assume that's why he came home—I don't know if that's the reason or if he would have come home anyway because I couldn't bring myself to ask. What could I say?—I thought you were leaving me—what are you doing home? He slept in the guest room. It's the first time that's happened since we're married, and the funny part was that I didn't know where to put me in the bed—on his side, on my side, spread out across the middle, my legs open like a nutcracker, touching my heels to either side—and I wanted to go into the guest room and tell him how funny that was, sit on the side of the guest-room bed and maybe even take his hand while I was telling him and then we could have laughed.

Is that what it is? That somewhere along the way things stopped being funny? That I stopped making Christopher laugh? Is that the part that's my fault?

Well, maybe we just need some new material here . . .

I hold on to the table and try to take a breath. Well, we've certainly got some now.

My mother folds a dinner napkin; it's a white linen dinner napkin, a match to the other twenty-three that sit on the dining-room table in front of her. Fine Irish linen, hand-rolled hems, ribbons and flowers dance along the border in white-on-white; a perfect napkin, to say the least. She has never used all twenty-four of them for a dinner party that I know of, only for buffets. She's folding this one into pleats, accordion pleats. She's also whistling "Harvest Moon" between her teeth.

My mother has two whistles—the one she does between her teeth and the beautiful one. The beautiful one is like what John Wayne did in *The High and the Mighty,* or whoever it was who was really doing it, but John Wayne was puckering his mouth. She whistles as good as Ukulele

Ike did when he was Jiminy Cricket. Better, even. But now she's doing the one between her teeth.

She is not wearing red lizard high-heeled ankle-strap platform dancing shoes. She's wearing pink leather wedgie scuff slippers with thin white anklets and gray polyester pull-on slacks with elastic at the waist and a blue sweatshirt my friend Carole Rose sent her from California from a TV show she was working on years ago. *"Cagney & Lacey"* it says in big yellow script letters on the blue across my mother's chest, *"Cagney & Lacey"* and a New York policeman's badge. So much for cocktail dresses cut on the bias, so much for the promising swish of taffeta, so much for romance today.

In four days it will be Christmas and my mother's birthday. I have arrived just in time. Happy Birthday, Mom and Jesus. Mollie will be eighty years old this Christmas—she doesn't look it, she looks, maybe . . . sixty-eight, tops.

She finishes the last fold in the napkin and looks up at me and smiles. A radiant smile, beautiful—big and wide and full. I smile back, I can't help it.

It occurs to me that I can't sit here much longer, I may go off like a Roman candle and shoot out of her hot dining room into the cold December sky. Pieces of a small brunette woman exploding across dead, brown winter Kansas fields, my elbows and breasts and teeth falling on parked cars and people all dressed up carrying red-and-green packages, like tinsel falling on a Christmas tree. Or maybe I'll just sit here and scream.

We gaze at each other for a second, my mother and I, her brown eyes looking into mine, as if this all was okay, as if it all was fine. But I am not deceived by this bit of normalcy, I know what's coming next. I've been watching and I know. She will see the napkin. I wait.

She sees the napkin. From the corner of her eye she sees the napkin, sees it folded there, caught in her hand. Her eyes widen. It's a complete surprise to her, this napkin, a shock. She has been betrayed by a piece of white linen.

She shakes her head vigorously in disapproval, she yanks the perfectly folded folds apart, she unfurls the napkin and flaps it up and down in the air by the side of her chair. The frown lines pull together and deepen between her eyebrows. She's angry, my mother. I would even go so far as to say she's pissed off. She would never say this, of course. "Pissed off" are my words, not my mother's. "Pissed off" is much too off-color to come out of Mollie's mouth.

She bends forward and squints at the napkin. She gives it a dirty look. She surveys it. She purses her lips. And then with great drama she yanks it firmly down and across her knees. She spreads the cloth back into a square and tries to force the creases out, she rubs at them, smooths them, tugs at the white cloth's edges trying to make the wrinkles go away. She's agitated now, she breathes heavier as she pulls at the napkin. And then because of some sign that I can't decipher, some something that I can't see, she stops. Suddenly.

It's fixed. It measures up. It passes the test. I don't know why—only she knows. And she allows herself to begin again. Painstakingly she refolds the napkin. In and out go her fingers, in and out to make the pleats. Carefully, so carefully, she measures and checks and rechecks the edges, making sure the pleats are precisely the same. In doing so, she relaxes, her shoulders lower, the frown lines ease back into place, and she resumes her teeth-whistling rendition of "Harvest Moon."

I taste blood in my mouth. I have bitten a nice little hole in the center of my bottom lip.

I realize I could make a lot of jokes here. This situation is ripe for jokes, bubbling over with good stuff—more than enough material for a guest shot for Andy on Letterman, enough left over for a special or two. But I'm not laughing. My heart hurts so much I can't seem to get my breath.

I have been watching my mother fold and refold this napkin for approximately *two hours and a half.* This reality is so devastating to me that I suddenly realize my daughter's need to sometimes speak in italics. *Two hours and a half.* Ever since my plane got in, ever since my stepfather picked me up and said he would have brought Mollie with him but she had a little sniffle so he thought it wouldn't be such a good idea, what with it being so cold outside and all. How 'bout that? "A little sniffle." Let me tell you, Lewis, this is not a little sniffle. This is not a big sniffle. This is completely outside the sniffle category.

For some reason, Lew decided not to tell me that my mother was this far gone, that she had deteriorated this much . . . because I just saw her in the summer . . . didn't I? No, wait a minute . . . I was going to stop on my way back from New York but I didn't, did I? No. I haven't seen her since . . . since last February . . . is that right? Sure . . . no . . . wait a minute . . . didn't I see her in February? No, it wasn't February, it was before Thanksgiving . . . My God, is it a year and a half since I've seen Mollie?

How could that be . . . that it's been over a year . . . and they didn't come to us last year, did they? Why didn't they come to L.A.?

My God . . . I don't know, I don't have the slightest idea why they didn't come to L.A. last year. Why don't I know?

I've talked to her on the phone, though, every week, right? Well . . . nearly every week . . . every other week for sure . . . of course I did. I talked to her, I talked to him . . . but mostly it's been him, hasn't it? . . . That's right, mostly I've talked to him . . . There's always some excuse . . . she's in the bathtub . . . she's outside with the dog . . . My God . . . where was I? Is this what's been going on here? Where have I been?

I haven't asked Lew why he didn't tell me. I haven't said one word since I came in and sat down and tried to talk to her. I haven't done a thing except watch her fold. With my mouth shut. No words from Gillian. Gillian the Silent. A new one for me.

"What are you two doin', Gillian?" Lew says, walking into the dining room. He's got a salami sandwich with him, half of it on a plate and the other half in his hand. There's a bite missing. I can't see that it's salami but I can smell it, that's how I know what's in between the slices of rye.

I look up at him but I don't answer. I can't. The words are stuck somewhere behind the blood on my tongue. That's when I realize that his eyes are more sad. When I look at him. They've been sad since this whole business with my mother started, but now they're practically unbearable to see. I didn't think such a thing was possible—anybody's eyes getting more sad—but somehow this amazing man has accomplished this feat. It is in his sad eyes that I find my voice.

"You're not supposed to be eating salami, are you, Dad?"

He shrugs. "What's the difference?" he says to me.

The man definitely has a point. After all, look what we're dealing with here—let the man eat whatever he wants.

He takes another bite of the sandwich as he crosses behind my mother, puts it back on the plate, and gently pats her shoulder.

"How you doin', Moll, sweetheart?" he says to my mother.

He speaks loudly and distinctly, as if she has suddenly gone deaf instead of suddenly gone "gone." I smile, because I have tried this approach myself. I threw a few questions at her with the volume right up in her face when I first arrived. Nothing.

She looks up from the napkin. It's clear she's delighted to see him. She's thrilled. She lights up. She gives him one of her best smiles, one of the big ones like the one she gave to me. She smiles at Lewis, her husband, her third husband, the husband she has lived with for thirty-some-odd years. She says nothing, but she certainly smiles. And he smiles back. Then she lowers her head back to the napkin and continues with her work.

Without lifting her eyes from the linen she's folding, she lets "Harvest Moon" slowly die between her teeth. Her body inches a little toward mine from her chair, I can smell her Bellogia; they don't make Zibelene anymore. She nudges my arm gently with her elbow and I think I hear a sound that resembles a quiet giggle under her breath. And then in a conspiratorial whisper to me, as if we were girlfriends, she says, "Oh, you're right, Dell, look, he's smiling at me, he's gonna ask me to dance."

My heart stops.

My mother doesn't know who I am.

My mother thinks I'm Dell, her best friend.

Dell, who has been dead for at least twelve years.

It is at this precise moment that it is clear to me that my mother is gone. I look at this woman sitting here across from me and I realize that she may have Mollie's face and she may have Mollie's hands, and Mollie may be in there somewhere, behind those brown eyes smiling at me, behind that gentle face, and inside those beautiful hands, but the odds are I won't get her back again. The odds are my mother is gone.

Mollie

Mollie sits still in the chair and holds on to the napkin. Her face is soft and lovely and a smile touches her lips as her eyes close. She may appear to be in her dining room in Kansas City four days before Christmas and her eightieth birthday, but she isn't. Inside herself she is on a riverboat on the Mississippi outside of St. Louis; she is twenty-seven years old and it's a blistering hot day in June.

Another scorcher, the third one in a row, a record-breaker even for St. Louis since it was just the very beginning of summer. The thermometer on the top of the *Globe-Democrat* tower read 101 degrees and it was already suppertime.

The sign at the end of Wharf Street read:

THE ADMIRAL

Free Parking
Free Air-Conditioning
Free Water
Free Band
Free Dance Floor
Fare: One Dollar

The Admiral had been a railroad transfer ship named *Albatross* out of Vicksburg, Mississippi. She was bought by a company named Streckfus in 1937 and turned into what Streckfus called "the finest river boat pleasure craft in America." They advertised her as low-priced entertainment for families and romantic couples; they actually wrote "romantic couples" in her brochures.

She would leave Wharf Street at the St. Louis riverfront and steam down to the Jefferson Barracks Bridge, turn around and go back, and turn around again. She would turn around and turn around, again and again and again. Every night except Monday and twice on Saturdays and Sundays—in the night and in the afternoon. For four and a half hours while she steamed back and forth on the Mississippi River, you could drink a lot of free water and dance on the free dance floor to the free band. Germany might have invaded Poland and taken Belgium and the Netherlands and France, bombs might have been falling on England, but Pearl Harbor hadn't happened yet and America wasn't marching; they were still dancing on that Saturday night in June.

The Admiral was 374 feet by 92 feet, she was allowed 4,400 passengers and it seemed that at least half of them were packed into the ladies' room on the upper deck.

Mollie Kramer bent and adjusted the seams of her stockings and then turned around with her back to the mirror and looked over her shoulder to make sure they were straight. It was hard to get a piece of mirror space, there were so many girls. She had Dell's purse and her purse under her arm, and both their sweaters in case it got cool. There was not much of a chance of it getting cool; it was predicted to stay hot until Tuesday, but you had to carry a sweater just in case. And gloves, she had both pairs of their white cotton gloves. She set everything down neatly on the counter and opened her purse.

A fat blond girl in a red polka-dot dress that was way too tight for her got pushed by a woman turning around to leave and the fat blond girl fell against Mollie—grazing her cheekbone with a hairbrush.

"Oh, I'm so sorry, excuzzze me."

"It's okay."

"Are you all right?"

"I'm fine," Mollie said.

"Ya sure?"

"Really. I'm fine."

"It's so crowded."

"Uh-huh."

The door to a stall opened and three women charged at each other to get in.

"Hey, watch it!" Dell said, coming out of the stall fast. "Jeeze," she said, pushing in next to Mollie at the mirror, "it's a zoo in here."

She opened her white clutch purse and dumped the contents out on the counter.

"So, as I was saying," she said, picking up her comb and running it through her cropped straight brown hair, "he was looking at you."

"He was not, Dell."

"He was looking at you, he was watching you and he's gonna ask you to dance. Take it from me, kid."

"Don't be ridiculous," Mollie said, "I'm going with Benny."

"So? What does he care?"

Mollie opened her lipstick tube and rolled up the color. "Enny wd kiii im," she said, her mouth opened wide in an oval as she filled her lips in with a rich, deep red.

"Huh? Whatja say?"

Mollie smoothed some of the color around her upper lip with the extended little finger of her right hand.

"I said Benny would kill him."

"Oh, yeah, sure," Dell said, "Benny, the big killer. Benny couldn't kill a dead horse. The only thing Benny could kill is you, 'cause you let him push you around."

"Shhh," Mollie said, giving Dell a look.

"Wait, I'll tell ya, if that slob even touches you again, I'm gonna come over there and punch *him* in the jaw."

"Dell . . ."

"Anyway, like I was sayin', himself is gonna ask you to dance."

"Hey, excuse me," the fat blond girl said, leaning in close to inspect Mollie's mouth, "what color is that? It's gorgeous."

" 'Bravo,' " Mollie said.

"It's gorgeous," the fat girl said.

Dell looked at the fat girl, the fat girl smiled at Dell.

"Don't you think it's gorgeous?" she said to Dell.

"Gorgeous," Dell repeated flatly.

"It's so hard to find a true red, don't cha think?"

Dell didn't answer.

The fat girl smiled at Mollie. "Whatja call it—Bravo? That's so sophisticated . . . gosh. I always wonder who thinks that stuff up, don't you?"

"Let me see, Mollie," Dell said, holding out her hand. Mollie handed Dell the tube of lipstick.

The fat girl watched as Dell applied the red color to her mouth. "It's got too much orange in it for you," she said to Dell.

"Oh, really?" Dell said to the fat girl. "You think so, huh?"

"Well, it's just my opinion," the fat girl said, shrugging, "but it looks much better on her. Your skin is far too pink."

"No shit," Dell said.

"Well, exxxxscuzze me," the fat girl said dramatically. She moved away from Dell, gathered her things, gave her dress a couple of tugs, and pushed her way through the crowd to the exit door.

"Dell, you didn't have to be so rude," Mollie said.

"Well, I certainly don't have to listen to some fat cow tell me my skin is too pink."

"All right, all right."

"Anyway, I'm supposed to be rude, I'm from New York." She made a face at Mollie in the mirror and Mollie laughed. "So, he's gonna ask you to dance."

"Well . . ." Mollie said. She fluffed at the dark waves in her hair.

"And he's Italian."

"He's *Italian?* How do you know he's Italian?"

"I know. I asked Nat."

"You didn't! What did you say?"

"I said, 'Who's the guy at the bar who's givin' Mollie the eye.' "

"Oh, God. You didn't!"

"Of course I didn't, silly. I just said who is that, since it was clear the guys know him."

"Who knows him?"

"Nat and Benny, they know him; they played ball with him in Forest Park."

"Benny knows him? You're kidding."

"Nope."

Mollie pinched her cheeks until they got a little color in them.

"You want my rouge?"

"No, thanks."

"Soooo?" Dell said.

"What?"

"Don't cha want to know his name?"

"I don't care."

"Oh, yeah, sure you don't. His name is Julius Ventimiglia, he's single, and he sells shoes."

Mollie looked at Dell in the mirror. Dell winked.

"Cut it out, Dell," Mollie said, and giggled. She picked up her purse and gloves and sweater. "Come on, let's go."

"Moll?" Dell said, taking a last look in the mirror.

"What?"

"Tell me the truth. Is my skin too pink?"

"No, silly, it's perfect. It's ivory with a sweet touch of rose."

"Oh, swell," Dell said, grabbing her stuff off the counter and linking her arm through Mollie's. "That means pink, right?"

There are moments. You don't know that they'll wind up being the big ones until afterward, after you've walked through them and they're gone. And when you're young, when you start out, you have a whole different concept of what they'll be; you think they'll be the ones that are linked to special occasions, the ones that can be captured so beautifully on a Hallmark card.

For instance, your graduation from high school with your whole life out there in front of you and everyone wishing you well. Well, the morning I graduated from high school my mother was dying and the woman who was supposed to be helping us nurse her in the house—the woman who later became my stepmother, which is, of course, another story—but who hated me already, made a nice, fresh pot of hot coffee and poured it all over my white graduation dress. Not a Hallmark card. Not exactly a Kodak moment, my daughter, Gilliana, would probably say to you.

Or when you get married—you imagine yourself standing in front of all those people, trembling, in a long white satin gown and a white veil, your arms filled with white cymbidium, and you watch him coming down the aisle toward you and you look at him through the lacy tulle and you know—he's the one. The only reason I married Larry was because my mother was nearly dead from tuberculosis and she wanted so desperately to see her only child get married that I did. Larry was ten years older than me and he was a real nice guy, but I didn't know if I loved him, I'd never gone with anybody else. I didn't know anything, I was only seventeen. My mother died two months later. Larry and I stayed married for four years, but it was never right. That much I knew for sure. He wasn't the one.

So I got a divorce. A divorce in those days was a terrible thing. A nice Jewish girl didn't get a divorce. It was a *shandeh*—that's what they called it. In English it means, like an embarrassment, a scandal, a shame. And my father—who really had no room to talk, considering what he did with that *courveh*—which in English is what we used to call "a lady of the evening," but much worse—anyway, considering what he did with her, the *courveh*—while my mother was dying, and he married her yet—my father had no room to talk, but he told me but good anyway.

And I did it anyway. I knew if I stayed married to Larry my heart would die. That's how I felt, so I got a divorce. I became a *shandeh*.

By the time I was dating Benny, I figured that I was never going to get any of those moments they have on the Hallmark cards. I was divorced and I was twenty-seven, I was working as a bookkeeper in a dress factory, I was on my own. I knew it wouldn't be Benny; I tried to pretend that he was a nice guy, but I knew in my heart he was a louse. He'd even given me a nice smack in the face once to prove it. It was only once, but once was enough, and I shouldn't have even seen him after that, but he was all over me trying to make up. Benny tried to act like he was going to take care of me after the night he smacked me, like he was some big tough guy who was going to protect me, which, if you thought about it, was all backward, since the only person I needed protection from then was him.

It was a Saturday and we were on *The Admiral*. Me and Benny and my best girlfriend, Dell, and her husband, Nat. Dell and I worked together at Carlee in the office. Carlee was a dress manufacturer that made fancy dresses, not evening dresses but not for work either, kind of in between. It was a really hot day, the third one in a row, which was one of the reasons I'd said I'd go, I didn't want to stay cooped up in a hot apartment; the other was Benny was begging me, and I decided this was going to be the last time I would see Benny and I would tell him on the boat with Dell and Nat there for protection.

Dell and I had been to the ladies' room and when we got back inside the Grand Ballroom, Nat and Benny had landed a little table right near the dance floor. Benny handed me a whiskey sour with two maraschino cherries in it, one red one and one green one—he knew I loved maraschino cherries; it was part of his "I'm going to take care of you" routine.

I took a sip of my drink and then Dell said something funny and we all laughed and that's when it happened. We were just sitting there, the four of us, just like that, and the band was finishing up a song and you'd think I would remember what song it was but I can't right now. Of course I remember what the next song was, because that was the one we danced to, but I don't remember the song that had just ended when the moment began. I had picked up the toothpick with the cherries on it, the toothpick had a little frilly yellow paper thing on one end, and I was about to pop the red cherry in my mouth; it was actually touching my lips and I could smell the cherry juice and the whiskey sour on my lips and my hand was cold from the ice cubes in the glass, and he came up and he was behind me so everybody else saw him first. And he said, "Excuse me, Mollie, may I have the next dance?" And I turned my head and he was standing there right next to my chair, right next to me. Smiling. I'd seen him before, I'd seen him looking at me from across the dance floor when he'd been standing at the bar. Then he said something about how he had asked Benny if he could have a dance with me while Dell and I were gone and Benny had said okay, and so could it be this one, or something like that. I don't know exactly how he said it, I was looking at his eyes, in his eyes. They were brown, very brown, and his hair was very black and his mustache was very black—he had a mustache—and with all that thick black hair he looked something like Clark Gable. Not exactly, of course, because he looked like himself, but a little bit like Gable. Clark Gable was very popular then.

He bent down a little and held the back of my chair.

"That cherry is the color of your lipstick," he said, smiling, and he extended his hand. I was so taken aback that I took it; I don't know why but I took his hand, this stranger. I didn't say a word to Benny or Dell or Nat, I know that. And I stood up. And I ate the cherry, I know that too, the red one. He took my hand and I stood up but we didn't walk to the dance floor. Maybe that was what did it—made it the first of my moments, my first Hallmark card.

We didn't walk to the dance floor because he took me in his arms right there at the table and he danced me onto the dance floor. I was chewing the cherry . . . I was . . . and we were dancing and I could smell his aftershave, my nose was up against his chin, and his hand was on my waist, his fingers spread across my waist and my back and his other hand was holding mine, and in a low voice he said in my ear, "I'm Julius Ventimiglia, Mollie," and I didn't even look up at him but I knew. He was the one.

Clare

Well, we're not going to asshole Andy's. We're staying home instead. Praise Allah.

Scott's on his way over. We'll probably go to the movies or just hang out, I don't know, it doesn't matter to me.

My grandma is really bad, my mother said when she called. I mean, my grandma doesn't even know who my mother is. My mother, of course, did not give me this information, my father told me, my mother wouldn't tell me anything even if she was being held at gunpoint, I promise you. I talked to my Grampa Lew and he sounded awful. I mean, he was trying to sound okay, you know, trying to be perky for me, but I could tell. He's probably dying inside. I mean, how could he live without her? They've been together for practically a hundred years.

I don't know if I could ever be with one guy for that long. I mean, not that I don't love Scott and all. I don't mean *love* him. I mean, I love him but I don't know if I'm in love with him, you know?

Of course, my grandma was married three times, she had two other husbands before my grampa, which was pretty advanced for her day. But she's been with my Grampa Lew forever, since my mother was my age, you know.

Anyway, he was humming on the phone, my grampa, like everything was okay. He hums. He doesn't know he's humming. It's so sweet. Really.

He hums even when you're the one talking and he's listening on the other end. I mean, he hears you, it's not like he hums loud or anything, it's just quietly to himself. Hummmm hummm humm hmmmm, kind of like that, like a little tune but not one you ever heard of or anything. Not that I would know the same tunes they would know or anything. It's just this sweet kind of random humming. He's so sweet, my grampa.

There are lot of stories about his humming. Of course, the whole world knows them because my mother wrote about them in all those monologues for asshole Andy to do in his act. I mean, can you imagine? He tells all these things about his father, but he's really talking about my grampa, you know? It makes me so mad. How could my mother do that? It's so disloyal, you know?

I always watch everything I say in front of her and everything I do. Really. I mean, I could say something and the next thing you know *I* would be part of one of asshole Andy's stupid routines. My mother would use anything, you know—anything!

I can tell you the best story about my grampa humming. You've probably heard it, of course, but it was adjusted for Andy. I mean, I know all the real details, I've known them since I could practically walk, because the whole family repeats this story every chance they get. Especially at gatherings like Thanksgiving or Passover . . . I mean, we celebrate everything. I don't know what I'm supposed to be. My mother's half-Italian and half-Jewish and my father is extremely Episcopalian, so what does that make me? I don't know. A Capricorn, right? That was a joke.

Anyway, it was the night before this big Jewish holiday. Yom Kippur. You've heard of Yom Kippur, right? It's where everybody atones for their sins. It's actually much more practical than the Catholics—the Jews do the whole thing in just one night and one day. Anyway, in Yiddish the night before Yom Kippur is called "*erev* Yom Kippur," so that's always the way the story starts. You know, like you're sitting around with the family at my grandma's house and somebody will say, "Hey, remember when Lew had the store and the black guys robbed him and Mollie *erev* Yom Kippur?" And everybody laughs. I mean, they all know the story already so they're already laughing, but they tell it anyhow.

My grampa had this little dry-goods store—I don't know why it's called dry goods except that's some term left over from long ago, I guess. Anyway, it was this little store with clothes for everybody, you know, but cheaper, like a Kmart or something, but sweet, like a whole family could go there and get shoes and jeans and stuff, but it was really little. So these two African-American guys—of course, in my family nobody would say "African-American," they'd say "black"—anyway, these two black guys came into my grampa's dry-goods store one evening, maybe thirty years ago, right before he was going to close up to go to the synagogue for services the night before Yom Kippur, right? And he and my grandma are all dressed up ready to leave, they're the only people in the store, and the black guys come in to rob them. So they take my grandma and grampa into this little back room where my grampa piles up all the extra stuff, you know, jeans and shirts and stuff, and they tie their hands behind them and put tape across their mouths and throw them on the floor. I guess they were pissed off 'cause Grampa didn't have enough money in the cash register or something.

Anyway, this is the part in the story where my grandma usually interrupts to remind everybody how nervous the guys were, the robbers. Actually, the one without the gun was yelling at the one with the gun, who was pointing the gun at my grampa's brain, and he's yelling, "Shoot the motherfucker! Shoot the motherfucker!" And the gun is shaking. When my grandma tells the story and she gets to that part, she says "Shoot the motherfucker" very quietly, like she doesn't know what she's saying, like it's a foreign language or something, you know? Anyway, the whole time this screaming thing is going on between the two black guys, my grampa is humming. He's like looking into my grandma's eyes, 'cause they're lying on the floor across from each other, lying on the cold concrete with their hands tied behind their backs and tape across their mouths, and he's looking at her and he's humming. Don't you love it? Humming. With a gun at his head. A shaking gun, right? Humming. It's funny, right? Anyway, then comes the best part of the story. The black guys are going on and on about whether to shoot my grampa or not, and this causes whichever one of them who has it to drop my grandma's gigantic wedding ring. I mean, it's huge, you know? All these diamonds and everything. And they've taken it off her finger, right? And she's only wearing it in the first place 'cause she's all dressed up to go to synagogue for Yom Kippur, right? So, the jerk who drops it doesn't know he dropped it, but my grampa does. And he rolls over on top of it, covering it with his body on the concrete. I mean, like he's Arnold Schwarzenegger or Bruce Willis or somebody. I mean, with his hands tied behind his back and tape over his mouth, my little grampa—I mean, he's like five feet seven, you know—he scooches over on top of the diamond wedding ring right under the noses of the two black guys and the shaking gun. Humming. Right? He saves my grandma's wedding ring with his body. But he never stops humming. I mean, it's funny, don't you think? But also sweet. I mean, I think it's terribly sweet and so romantic. Looking into her eyes and all . . . I don't know.

They have this great thing, you know? I mean, that's why I don't know how he'll live without her. And somehow it's worse that he would have to watch her be like "not there," you know, than like actually be dead. I can't imagine loving somebody the way they love each other and then watching the person disintegrate, their brain and all. I mean, she loves him so much and she doesn't even know who he is. God.

Anyway, so my mother, I guess, has to figure out what to do with her. Like she may have to put her in a home or something. I can't imagine. Have you ever been to one of those? I had to go with my cousin Sarah Jane once, to see her Aunt Pauline . . . I practically died. I mean, they have people tied to their chairs, with sheets and stuff. I mean, little old ladies who used to be young and now they're tied to their chairs with pillowcases because they don't remember how to sit up. God, it's so degrading.

I mean, my grandmother had a life, you know? She had three husbands and one daughter and me, a granddaughter, and she worked and all—she was a bookkeeper or something—and she was this fabulous cook until she forgot how to do it.

She actually forgot. It was pathetic. We were in Kansas City this one time and, you know, my grandmother was not only this superb cook but she did it all really beautifully, set the table with the wineglasses and flowers and everything, and so we were making like this really simple lunch, just for her and me, just sandwiches, bologna sandwiches. And she couldn't do it. She couldn't figure out how to make a bologna sandwich. My grandmother, who could make this eight-course gourmet meal, you know, like some famous French chef, and she's standing there at the sink with a slice of bologna in one hand and a piece of bread in the other, just looking at it. I practically went crazy when I saw that. Really, it just blew me away. God.

And she used to be so funny. She was actually funnier than my mother. Really she was. Not jokes, I don't mean jokes, I mean the way she saw stuff, her take on life, you know? My grandma saw things a certain way, like she just took it all with a smile. Not like my mother, you know? I mean, my grandma probably never threw anything in her life. She just had this wonderful way of seeing things, it's such a waste. She was a real person, you know? She did things. She lived.

But it's even more than that. It's like, I was thinking about how here I am, sitting and waiting for Scott to get here, and I can't wait to see him, to just look at him, you know? And my grandma did that. I mean, at some point in her life she was just like me, you know, young, and with her whole life ahead of her, waiting for some boy to come. Maybe her first love—you know, the way I feel about Scott—maybe my grandma did this too. It just kills me.

I mean, look at what life does—one day you're waiting for this boy to come and the next thing you know they could be tying you to a chair. God.

Gilliana

I stand and look at my face in the mirror above the chest in the guest bedroom of my mother's house. I see my face, Mollie's face, Clare's face—all three look back at me. Three sets of brown eyes, three sets of big movie-star lips, three okay noses, and three foreheads with three lines from side to side. Three crying faces.

None of these faces has an answer for me.

What happened to my mother? . . . How did this come to be? . . . the disappearance of Mollie . . . lost somewhere inside her body. If we could get Perry Mason on the case, he could go inside her body and find the real Mollie and bring her out. Or the Royal Canadian Mounted Police; wasn't that their motto—We always get our man? Do you think they do it for women too? Or are those Canadian guys with the funny hats and boots sexist?

Okay . . . I can see it: Andy sits across a desk from a large Mountie wearing a funny hat. "Do you think you can find Mollie?" says Andy. "Describe her," the Mountie says . . .

Oh, good, Gillian, make a bit out of it, that will certainly help everyone.

"It's too late for bits," I whisper to the mirror and I sit down.

I sit on the edge of the bed and look out the window. I stare at the brown bare winter limbs of my mother's peach tree until they blur into the sky.

Of course, there were clues. Clues and moments. The moments of Mollie's near demise. Signs, trumpets . . . neon signs lit up as bright as Broadway, as big as the billboard where the cardboard Marlboro man blows out the smoke. But I didn't want to see them. Not me. Not for a long time.

Little things. A moment here, a moment there. Now you see it, now you don't. She would forget what she was talking about in mid-sentence —that was actually going on for a long time; she'd just stop right in between words, she was talking to you and then boom, there'd be silence. And then she would look at you and smile, as if you were the one who had been talking and she was being polite, waiting to hear what you had to say as soon as you got your thoughts together. And you'd smile back at her and the moment would pass and then somehow there was nothing you could say about what had just happened. I mean, what could I say to her anyway—"Mom, you just stopped talking in mid-sentence, you're slipping through my hands like rice."

Not me, cookie. I was too afraid.

The other thing was that sometimes if she gave you a wrong answer it was funny. Sometimes really funny. I mean, you had to laugh—physically, you had to laugh, you couldn't help yourself. And that became my way out. Instead of getting terrified over these horrifying little moments, I decided I would just take them as comedy instead. Much easier for Gillian. Mollie was always funny, anyway. Mollie, my darling, delightful Billie Burke-ish mother, could now really be good for a laugh. Twelve laughs, twenty-seven laughs. I could even write about her. I could turn these hideous, horrifying little moments of hers into jokes, into material. Rich, delicious material that would make Andy laugh, and if I could make Andy laugh, he could make millions laugh. I decided I wouldn't let these moments of Mollie's scare me; I would let them be my barrel of riches instead.

The first time I had to admit to myself that there was really something wrong with her was the incident with the refrigerator, and the only reason I happened to even be in on that was that I'd come home, back to Kansas City, for Clare to see Mollie and Lew. And the leaves. Clare was two years old. She wasn't a terrible two, she was a delicious two and she was into everything—she wanted to taste it or see it or smell it, hold it in her arms—a baby lizard, a big yucky bug, a piece of fur, dirt, sushi, a stranger's purse—it didn't matter—whatever it was, Clare wanted it. And I didn't want her to miss the leaves. After all, it was October. There are no leaves in Los Angeles in October, none that fall down, that is. There is no autumn, no oaks and maples turning red and amber and gold; it doesn't exist. There is only green in Los Angeles. Green leaves that go on forever, born of trees that have no souls. In my humble opinion, of course.

There are lots of leaves in Kansas City, and in October they fall down. The place is loaded with leaves and trees—big, lush, spreading, stunning trees. Across some of the wide streets they even reach out and touch branches with each other over the tops of the cars. I took Clare home to run in the leaves.

We piled them up everywhere—in the backyard, in Swope Park, in Loose Park, where we took her to feed the ducks. It was heaven. She would run through the piles with her little arms up in the air, running and laughing and jumping and screaming with delight. And it was contagious. I also did some running and screaming, and so did my mother. Three zany females chasing each other through the leaves. I'm sure if anybody saw us they were jealous, we were having too much fun for them to think we were nuts. It was on one of those glorious October days of leaf running and screaming that the thing with the refrigerator occurred.

We got home from Loose Park, Mollie filled up the house with spaghetti-sauce smells, I gave Clare a bath, Lew walked around humming and tinkering . . . We ate: garlic and tomatoes and olive oil getting mixed up with baby powder and shampoo. Clare took turns sitting on all three laps, making sure to drop noodles and sauce on each of us. She loved my mother's spaghetti. So did I, I still do. Of course, Mollie hasn't cooked like that in years, but back then my mother cooked as if she was Italian. You'd never know she was born Jewish; you'd think she'd just gotten off the boat from Sicily.

I put Clare to bed in her powder-blue jammies with the feet on them, all cuddled up tiny in the middle of the guest-room bed, this very bed that I am now sitting on.

We did the dishes, the house was safe and quiet, and we went into their bedroom to do the rings. The rings are a ritual. Mollie has a passion for jewelry and especially rings; a sizable collection of them sits in her jewelry box on top of her chest of drawers. She wears different rings every day, and whenever I'm home we go through them. I try on each one and show her how the big ones don't look good on me, don't work on my squatty hands. I don't have my mother's hands. She has beautiful fingers with long, perfect oval nails. I have short squatty hands with little stubby nails. It doesn't matter what I do, I could eat enough gelatin to choke a horse—actually, they make Jell-O from horses—horses' hooves, don't they? Why do I think I know that? Anyway, whatever I do, my nails don't grow. I am cursed with my father's hands.

The reason I had to go through the rings with her whenever I was home was so she could make sure I knew who got what when she'd be gone. Of course, the "gone" we were talking about then meant dead, not the "gone" that she is now.

We did this routine every time I came home since I left when I was twenty-four. When I was twenty-four, Mollie was only fifty-seven. She certainly wasn't about to "go," but she was always a firm believer in "God-forbids," and you had to be prepared no matter what.

"Age has nothing to do with it, Gilliana, you never know when I may be's a dead duck."

My mother calls me Gilliana, which is my real name; I never use it, I never saw myself as a Gilliana, I just see myself as a Gillian. Anyway, that's how she always said it—"be's a dead duck." So, whenever I came home we'd go through all the rings so I'd know what to do with them when Mollie be's a dead duck.

"Your cousin Chava wants that aquamarine but don't give it to her, the topaz will do her fine."

"But, Mom, this thing is too big for me."

I lift my hand with the huge aqua stone surrounded by diamond baguettes on my second finger. "It's awful on me, look."

"I don't care. You keep it. Give it to the baby when she's big."

What can I say to that? The pale blue-green stone shimmers on my finger. I imagine Clare's little hands getting big. Maybe she'll be lucky and she'll have her grandmother's hands instead of mine. I slide the ring off and hold it.

"I bought that aquamarine for your mother in Bermuda," my stepfather says. "Cost a goddamn fortune," he says, humming as he turns down the spread on their big bed.

Lew hums. All the time. He's been doing it for so long he doesn't know he's doing it. I want to tell you about the humming, but not now. I want to tell you about the refrigerator, the refrigerator is what's on my mind.

"A goddamn fortune," he mumbles as he staggers past us with the big bedspread in his arms.

He was wearing his pajamas already; it was only ten past nine. Lew goes to bed every night at nine-thirty and gets up at five. I have no idea why. It's another ritual. Hell or high water, in bed at nine-thirty and up at five. His pajamas were beige sea-island cotton and they'd been ironed. Perfectly. With creases in the pants.

"Just give Chava the topaz. Okay, sweetie?" my mother says to me. She takes the aquamarine out of my hand and puts it back in the jewelry box.

"God. Poor Chava will have to make do with the humble topaz," I say. I'm kidding, of course—the topaz is the size of the Grand Canyon.

"That's a goddamn fine topaz," my stepfather says. His voice is slightly muffled. I turn. He's in the bed by now, but he's got the covers pulled up over his head so their little poodle who's jumping around on the bed can't lick his face.

"Lewis," my mother says, "that's enough with all the goddamns."

"Well, it is a fine topaz," he mumbles from under the blanket. "Where'd we get that goddamn topaz anyway? Mexico?"

"Lewis!" my mother says, and he laughs. Then we laugh with him. Mollie grins at me.

What she doesn't know that I know is that she not only irons Lew's pajamas but she also sometimes warms them. She sticks them in a low oven for a few minutes so when he gets out of the shower and puts them on they won't be cold from the drawer. Do you see what I mean about comedy material? Look what I've got going for me here. Did you ever hear of warming anybody's pajamas? You didn't, I know you didn't. I can't imagine warming anybody's pajamas, not even Chris's, but then, maybe I should have warmed Chris's pajamas, maybe then everything would be okay.

And then Lew tells us about the Sears man.

"The Sears man is coming tomorrow to bring the new refrigerator," he says from under the blanket. "I forgot to tell you."

Mollie lights up. "Oh, isn't that wonderful? What time?"

"Early, the first stop, between eight and nine."

That's it, it's not a big deal, just the announcement—the Sears man is coming, hoorah, hoorah.

We put away the rings, Lew says good night, she gives him a kiss, we turn out the light and go down the hall together. We check the baby together, my mother and I. We look at her from the doorway, watch her sleeping like a little angel surrounded by pillows in the big bed. Mollie touches my hand and we smile at each other. All's right with the world. I go into the kitchen to make myself a drink, I carry it back with me into the living room and turn on the TV. I leave my mother in the kitchen, puttering around, doing whatever she's doing, happily puttering around her kitchen, perfectly fine. *Perfectly fine,* as Clare would say. My mother was *Perfectly fine.*

I watch something on the television, I don't know what, some inane movie or something, something moronic. I drink my drink, I sit there. And then it hits me, I don't hear her. It's very quiet in the kitchen. What's she doing in there?

I get up from the couch and go into the kitchen. No Mollie. How could that be? You can't get out of their kitchen without walking through the dining room and the living room where I was sitting in front of the TV.

This is ridiculous.

"Mom?"

The kitchen is spotless. You can still smell spaghetti sauce; it's such a happy smell, spaghetti sauce, a comfort smell, like everything's okay, fine and safe. But smells can be a deception. I have never trusted the safe smell of spaghetti sauce since then.

"Mom?" I call out again, like a moron. It's a little kitchen, for godsake.

And then I see that the refrigerator is pushed away from the wall on one end. I walk over and look behind it. My mother is lying on the floor behind the refrigerator with a wet rag in her hand. Her eyes are closed and she's on her side, curled up the way she does in the bed. She's lying there like she's asleep.

"Mom?"

How can my mother be sleeping behind the refrigerator? She was too tired to go to her bed? What is this?

I kneel down beside her.

"Mom?"

For an instant I think she's dead. I'm stunned. I reach out and touch her hair. Long dark hair, dark like mine, only always long and pulled back into a bun, a beautiful bun, like a ballerina or a rich lady, a bun at the nape of her neck.

She opens her eyes and smiles at me when she feels my hand on her hair.

"Just give me five more minutes, Gilliana," she says, and she closes her eyes again.

My heart slams around inside my rib cage.

"Mom, please—what are you doing back here?"

"I'm cleaning," she says in a whisper. She keeps her eyes closed but she's still smiling.

"Mom, I'm going," I would say to her from her bedroom doorway, on my way to school. And she'd smile at me with her eyes closed. "Oh, that's good, sweetie, have a good day. In five more minutes I'll be up, just give me five more minutes."

"Sure, Mom," and a car would honk out front and I would run with my books under my arm, banging against my hipbone.

She loved to sleep five more minutes; it was always Mollie's favorite thing to do.

But she was behind the refrigerator this time, she wasn't in the bed.

"Mom, please, what are you doing?"

I'm on my knees now next to her.

"Mom?"

She opens her eyes and looks at me.

"Oh," she says quietly.

That's it. That's all she says. Just oh. And she looks at me. Neither of us says anything for a second or two.

And then she sits up. She just sits up with the wet rag still in her hand; it's not as if she's woozy or anything, she just sits up.

"Well, that's better," she says.

"What's better?"

I want to scream. I want to scream and run through the leaves some more. I don't want whatever this is to be happening.

"Well, I wanted to clean back here," she says, "so when the Sears man comes it wouldn't be too dirty when he takes this old clunker away." She pats the refrigerator with her rag.

"Mommy, you were sleeping."

Mommy. I call her Mommy, it just slips out of me. I want her to be the Mommy and make this go away.

"I was not, Gilliana, don't be silly, I was cleaning the floor."

"You must have fainted or something . . ."

"Gilliana, stop this, I'm fine."

"Mom, you were unconscious, or sleeping or something . . ."

"Please," she says to me, "I'm fine." She picks up a little pile of dust with her wet rag and she stands up. Just like that. She stands up and I'm still on my knees on the floor.

"Come on, sweetie," she says.

I look up at her. She's fine. *Fine?* How could she be fine? She was just sleeping behind the refrigerator. I sit there with my heart banging. I don't know what to do.

"Gilliana, come on now, help me push this back and we'll set the table for Lew."

She sets the table for his breakfast every night. It doesn't matter what time it is, it doesn't matter if there's been a tornado, the table gets set. A bowl for his cornflakes and a spoon, the knife to cut the banana, a beautiful cloth napkin folded under the spoon and the knife, the toaster, a little glass for his juice, a cup and a saucer for his coffee—all on a pretty placemat just so.

My mother was just dead behind the refrigerator and now she's gonna set the table? God, please help me here.

"Sweetie, come on now. Get up."

She gives me a look like "that's enough of this silliness" and she turns and walks away with her rag and her pile of dust. And I don't know what to do, so I get up and push the refrigerator back against the wall and wash my hands and pour myself another vodka and watch Mollie set the breakfast table for Lew.

My mother was unconscious behind the refrigerator. I knew that. She was not having a nap with a wet rag and a pile of dust. I knew that too. My mother was not having "five more minutes." What my mother was doing was having one of her first of probably over a hundred silent strokes—that's what they call them—sweet name for something so deadly, huh? Silent stroke. A silent stroke that made me want to scream. Of course, I didn't know that's what was happening, I didn't know anything then. I didn't want to know and she refused to discuss it, so both of us played dumb and what I did was, so that I could stand it, I turned it into a routine. A piece of standup. Actually, my best piece, the one that turned it around for me and Andy, the one that made Andy hot, like Steve Martin with the arrow through his head. Remember that? Well, Andy did a routine about *his* mother sleeping behind the refrigerator and *his* mother warming *his* father's pajamas while *his* father hummed, and people laughed until their tears came down.

Even Mollie and Lew laughed.

Everybody laughed but me.

That was fourteen years ago, when Clare was only two. This horrible business with my mother has been going on for fourteen years, but that time was the first real sign, Mollie sleeping behind the refrigerator, Mollie taking "five more minutes"; that was when the red flag went up, that was the first time my heart stopped and I was really afraid.

Clare

Multiple infarct dementia. That's what my grandmother has. I had to look it up. Not recently, of course, but when I was old enough to notice that every now and then she was a little off. Not loony, exactly, but you know? Kind of just not there the way she was supposed to be. So I ask my mother and she says, "Multiple infarct dementia," and I say, "Right," you know . . . so I look it up because it's not the same as Alzheimer's. That, at least, she tells me.

"Multiple" is the regular multiple, you know, as in more than one, or many, that I know. So I start with "infarct," which is "a necrotic area of tissue resulting from failure of local blood supply," so then, of course, I have to look up "necrotic," which I had never heard of, which turns out to come from "necrosis," which is "the pathologic death of living tissue in a plant or an animal." That I can figure out. Right? I mean, I'm not a moron. The blood didn't get to the tissue so the tissue died. Okay.

But wait, it gets even better; listen to this one: dementia—"irreversible deterioration of intellectual faculties with concomitant emotional disturbance resulting from organic brain disorder." I already knew "concomitant"; it means occurring concurrently or at the same time, right?

So look what we've got here. The blood isn't getting to the tissue so the tissue can't live without blood so the tissue has to die, but look where the tissue is—it's in her *brain*. Right? And then look at the word that can really chill you—"irreversible"—you see that?—"irreversible deterioration"—that means it's over, irreversible, unable to be reversed . . . finished . . . done.

That's what's been happening to my Grandma Mollie all these years, pieces of her brain have been dying that couldn't be fixed—multiple infarct dementia, that's what it is. Can you believe that this could happen? I mean, to a person? I mean, God, how do people handle this shit?

So then I asked my doctor, I was there filling out camp forms—you know, you have to go and fill out all those stupid forms before you go away to camp and they make you have another tetanus shot and another blood test and all that shit before they even let you in—and I nonchalantly asked her; she's a woman, my doctor—actually, she's my pediatrician, I haven't made the switch yet, even now that I'm going to be seventeen, but this was years ago, when I asked her, a couple of years after I had been in Kansas City that Christmas when the stuff had gone down between my grandma and me.

So, get this, I asked her as if I hadn't looked it up yet, you know, as if I hadn't known that there was something wrong with my grandma's brain or her blood flow to her brain's tissue. I wanted to see how she would tell me—to get her to say it in layman's terms. So she goes: "It's a lot of small insults to the brain, Clare."

You believe it? That's what she called it. *Small insults.* Well, I guess so. I don't know how she thinks she can get off calling the death of brain tissue *small insults,* and I wanted to punch her because it was my grandmother's brain tissue we were talking about, but I didn't say anything, I just let it go. I mean, I'm not really interested in having a real discussion about anything with my doctor. She's okay and all, but it's not like she's my close friend, and why should I divulge private information to her about my grandmother? It's weird about doctors, don't you think?—I mean, they know all this stuff about you, it's written all over your chart, your heartbeat and your blood pressure and how much you grew since last June, but what do they really know? Nothing, right? Anyway, I let it go.

The stuff that happened with me and my grandmother was when I went there one Christmas vacation. I was eight years old and my grandma was seventy-two, but she certainly didn't look it. I mean, none of the women in our family look their age, which is a blessing, I guess, when you're older, but so far, for me, it's been awful; everybody always thinks I'm younger than I am. I hate it.

We were going to the Plaza to have lunch together, just her and me, you know, like a date. My folks were in Kansas City too, but they went off to do something with my grampa so Mollie and I could be alone. Anyway, they left first and she and I got all dressed up, I mean, we were supposed to be getting all dressed up to go to this fancy restaurant on the Plaza for lunch—the Plaza is a really nice area in Kansas City where they have the really good stores and all—it's not like a mall, it's all separate like a neighborhood but very charming with sort of Spanish architecture and red tile; I have no idea why it's Spanish, being in Kansas City, but it is—so, anyway, I took a shower and I put on my burgundy velvet dress, which I really loved, and these dress-up shoes I had then that had little tiny heels on them, not really but sort of, you know—I was only eight—and then I kind of wandered into her bedroom to talk to her while she was in the bathroom putting on her face and we're talking, but I hadn't really seen her, I mean I hadn't looked at her, at what she was wearing, until she came out.

I was going through her jewelry. My grandmother has this extraordinary jewelry collection—tons of gorgeous stuff—so I'm looking through some rings and stuff and she says, "Why don't you wear some pearls, Clare, they'd look beautiful with that dress." And I say that I don't have any pearls, and she says she means some of her pearls, she's got every size of strand conceivable, from under your chin all the way down to your waist, and I say I'd love to, I mean, they're beautiful, my grandma's pearls, and she says, okay, she'll get them for me and she comes out of the bathroom smiling at me, you know, because she loves me and I'm her only grandchild, and I love her and she's all excited that I want to wear her pearls.

So, she looks great, right? She's all dressed up from head to toe, and my grandma is quite a dresser. She has these really slick clothes and she's petite and she always looks really cool, you know. So she's all dressed up. But the problem is *she's all dressed up all wrong.* It's about 12 degrees outside, you know, Christmastime, with snow piled up everywhere, and my grandma is wearing white. I mean, summer white, like what you wear in Hawaii or somewhere, tropical-island clothes: these stunning white soft-linen flowing summer pants and a beautiful white-and-black summer kind of gauzy short-sleeved blouse and white sandals with a small stacked heel and open toe—Chanel, I think, or one of those guys that's really chic, I don't know.

So I look at her. I don't say anything. I'm dumbfounded, you know?

"Let's see," she says, pulling all these Chinese satin bags out of her drawer, "we need something that hits you right about here," and she touches my neck right below where you swallow, where that little indentation is in your throat. She's got beautiful hands, my grandma, with beautiful red fingernails that are always perfect. When I was little, she would scratch my back if I asked her—I mean, for hours. You could lie on the couch and watch TV and put your head in her lap and she'd just scratch and scratch. Most of the time I would fall asleep, it was so great.

Anyway, she takes all the satin bags with her and sits down on the foot of her bed. I follow her and sit down next to her. She opens each bag and lets a strand of pearls fall out of each bag into her lap.

"Grandma . . ." I finally say.

"What, sweetie?"

I didn't know where to start. Of course, you have to remember I was only eight years old at the time and I was really shocked, you know, by the fact that she was wearing summer clothes in the dead of winter, and so it just came out . . .

"You can't wear that."

"What?"

She looked down at her clothes.

"Don't you like this outfit, Clare? I thought it was very smart. Of course, I was concerned about the pants, I can't stand women who don't dress their age . . . do you think they're too youthful for me?"

"No, I love the pants, Grandma, it's just . . ."

She stopped going through the pearls and looked at me.

"What, sweetie?"

"Grandma, you're wearing summer clothes and it's winter outside."

She looked down at herself again, at what was on her body, as if she was seeing it for the first time.

"Oh," she said.

"You can't go out to lunch in that, you'll freeze."

"Oh," she said again.

That was it, just oh, and she frowned.

"Well . . ." she said, and it was like what I said before, you know, just a little off—not loony or anything, but just not right—not like she was supposed to be.

Of course, I didn't know at the time that her brain was being insulted even as we spoke.

Mollie

"Vos trachtstu? Iz nisht genug far dir, du host aine get? Itzt vilstu a Talyaner farharetn?"

My father was yelling at me. In Yiddish. What was I thinking? It wasn't enough I had a divorce? Now I wanted to marry an Italian?

A *Talyaner*. My first Hallmark card was a *Talyaner*.

"What was it?" Gilliana, my daughter, asks me. "What was it about him?"

What was it? His eyes? His face? His hands?

Jules was handsome, very handsome. Is that what it was? Who can explain such things? He was the one, that's all. Dell said to me once, "I know, kid, you don't have to explain it to me, it's how I feel about Nat . . . any room he's in, that's where I gotta be."

Any room he's in, that's the way it was with Jules and me. It didn't matter what we were doing as long as we were together. I could watch him read the paper, he could watch me paint my nails. It was the same with him as me.

How can you explain such things? Sometimes I think young people nowadays try to understand too much, they should just enjoy and stop trying to figure everything out.

We got married. My family was unhappy and his family was unhappy. We were happy.

There was a long list of people besides my father who told me not to marry Jules. Not because he was Italian, but because he was a gambler. "And he'll never change." That's what they all said. Benny, Tamie Markinson—who was Jule's first wife and my cousin Chava's friend—and my cousin Chava, and her husband, Howie Karpf, and my boss, Augie Pellerino, and even Jule's best friend, John Padrelli, and more. They all told me. It was a very long list.

"I'm not doing that anymore, honey, that was my past," he said to me, smiling, "past tense, before you, you know?" he said, and he kissed me.

The list meant nothing, the list evaporated from my head. Who could worry about a list, who could worry about gambling, I had to find a dress.

I wore rose. I wore white when I married Larry because it was the first time, and I wore rose when I married Jule. The dress had stitched-down pleats and puffed sleeves and a crushed soft leather belt a shade darker than the dress. The dress was silk jersey and cost more than three weeks' salary at Carlee, and that was wholesale, Dell and I got it down in the garment district where we worked. We found shoes the exact color of the belt, high-heeled pumps with an open toe and a closed back. My corsage was lily of the valley and my lips, of course, were "Bravo," the perfect red of a maraschino cherry, the red Jule loved.

We went to City Hall—the two of us with Dell and Nat and John Padrelli and his girlfriend, Angeli. No family. We figured it was better that way. We got married at City Hall and went to the Chase Hotel and danced and spent the night. It was very expensive, the Chase Hotel; that was our whole honeymoon, one night and breakfast there. It was all we could afford.

It was perfect for me—it was everything.

I got married.

And then I got pregnant.

And then the Japanese bombed Pearl Harbor.

And just like that—boom, boom, boom, I was going to have a baby and America went to war.

They didn't take Jules right away, they took the younger boys first. They didn't take him for two years.

We named the baby Sandra Lee for my mother, whose name in Jewish was Surahleah. She had my mother's name and my mother's hair—a rich, deep auburn red—but her eyes weren't brown like my mother's, her eyes were blue. We could never figure out who she got the blue eyes from; Jules used to tease me that it was the milkman.

We had her for eight months.

We had each other and our baby and everything was good. Better than good, it was like a love song, like a poem on a Hallmark card.

And then she died.

Out of nowhere.

It started on a Sunday, a cold Sunday afternoon, cold and clear in February. "February the bad," Jules called it after that. Look how some things you can remember no matter how long it is, some things you could never forget.

We met the doctor on the pediatrics floor of Barnes Hospital. I was wearing a brown suit and a coat and a hat with a feather, a chocolate-brown hat with a beautiful brown-and-green feather on the brim in front. The baby loved the feather, it made her laugh.

It was going to be nothing, a simple nothing. But it wasn't. It was something; something terrible, you could see the look in the doctor's eyes. They took her away from me and then everything went fast like when they speed the film up and the people run around as if they're in a cartoon.

Something about a transfusion, something I didn't understand, something about her kidneys. Something they told me but I didn't understand. Gilliana would tell you I blocked the name. I don't know. We didn't know from blocking back then, or maybe they just didn't have a name for what was wrong with her in those days—they didn't know so much in 1943. Her little kidneys just fell apart, that's all. She was fine and she was laughing in her daddy's arms, and then she was white, icy white. I could practically see through her in the taxicab, I could see her little blue veins under her white skin.

"It's gonna be all right, honey. It's nothing, it's a cold."

Jule was nearly as white as she was, trying to smile at me, his eyes big and wild.

"But she doesn't have a fever, she doesn't have a stuffed nose. Jules, look at her. Jules, what's the matter with her? *Julie, please!*"

I was crying and he was yelling at the taxi driver to go faster, his knuckles pressed hard against the seat, his hand bent into a fist, hitting the back of the seat. His other hand was wrapped around my back, his fingers clutching me around my waist, holding me so tight, he was so scared, I had a bruise there later, he held me so tight and hard, a purple-and-yellow bruise that lasted until March.

We went to the hospital in a taxicab, we didn't have a car. We didn't have anything. We had each other and a little apartment on Gambleton,

6114 Gambleton on the second floor. We had each other and an apartment on Gambleton and a beautiful baby with my mother's red hair and we took her to the hospital on a Sunday and by Tuesday we didn't have a baby anymore. Our Sandra Lee was dead.

Gilliana is always pushing at me to tell her what happened and how and why.

"After all, Mom, she was my sister," she says to me.

As if I could tell her. I couldn't tell her because I didn't know. Even before I started to forget things, I didn't know.

She just died, my Sandy. What difference did it make how?

She died.

And we buried her.

At Hevre Kadisha. We buried her in a Jewish cemetery because I wanted her where my mother was and Jules never said a word.

In a little coffin in a little grave. I didn't even know they had such things. All I knew was I couldn't breathe and Jules and I had to hold on to each other and look into each other's eyes in order to stand up and walk around.

She died on a Tuesday and we buried her on a Wednesday. We didn't know what hit us. We stood in the gray cold by her grave until someone pulled us away, I don't know who, but they moved us to a car and drove us home.

I remember thinking I left my baby in the ground. I couldn't get over that. And I remember how many steps there were to climb up to the apartment on the second floor. Eleven. And I remember her crib, her empty crib. Look what I remember—me, who doesn't remember anything.

They told me later, the doctors, that she wouldn't have lived to be a teenager, her kidneys would have failed. I never understood why they told me that—did they think it was gonna make me feel better? She didn't even live to be a year.

And in May Jules got the letter. He was drafted.

Just like that. What did America know about what was happening to us? What did they care?

He went to the draft board to try and get an extension so he could stay with me a little while, and the man told him he had two months, two months to clean up his affairs. "His affairs," the man at the draft board called it; I never knew a dead baby could be called "affairs." Look at the things you learn in life.

I knew Jules would die. I knew it. My mother was dead and my baby was dead and I knew that God would take Jules too. There wasn't anything he could say to me to comfort me, I was sure he would never come back. And if that happened, I would kill myself. I didn't tell him but I had it all figured out.

"I'll be back, Mollie, I promise you. I love you. I'll be back. Please, Mol. I'll be back."

Sure, Jules. Okay. You'll be back.

I didn't believe it.

They sent him to Fort Ord in California, someplace called Salinas, for boot camp, and I moved into my mother- and father-in-law's house. I had to. I wasn't about to go live with my father and his *courveh*—we weren't even speaking—and I had nowhere else to go. Nat had gone into the Navy and Dell was living with her folks. That's what people did back then, they went home. So I went to Jule's mother and father.

Most of the time I had no idea what they were saying; they spoke Italian or broken English-Italian and I was lost, but it didn't really matter to me, I didn't want to talk to anyone anyway, I had nothing to say. I was just waiting. They would ship Jules overseas and he would get killed—they would send me the telegram:

> DEAR MRS. VENTIMIGLIA, WE ARE SO SORRY TO INFORM YOU
> THAT YOUR JULE HAS BEEN BLOWN TO BITS.

And then I could kill myself. It was all I could think about, I was just waiting to get it over with, that's all.

My mother-in-law finally got to me but it wasn't with words, it was with food. Sophia taught me how to cook. It didn't take any language, it just took doing it. I couldn't make an egg right until Sophia, and then I was making noodles, all kinds of noodles, hanging them out to dry over the backs of Sophia's wooden kitchen chairs. In a month I could cook like an Italian. I was the only Jewish girl who didn't know how to make chopped liver or stuffed cabbage because my mother was too sick and died before she could teach me, but I could make cacciatore or osso buco as good as my mother-in-law. I think the real reason Sophia taught me to cook was so I would eat. She made me taste as I put in each ingredient and that was her way of knowing that at least I'd put some food in my mouth that day.

I spent a lot of time at the cemetery. I would take Jule's letters with me and read them to the baby in her grave. I couldn't help it, she was my link to him and I had to go there. I think that's why Sophia and Alfonzo gave me the money to go to New York, because they thought I was losing my mind. I probably was. Nowadays they would have sent me to see a doctor or, better yet, a support group. Now they have support groups for everything; there's probably one for women who have to bury an eight-month-old baby and then send their husbands off to war, they probably have that, they have everything else. They probably did a show about it on "Geraldo," but in those days you just made do, you lived with it until you got to the other side and you were better or you went crazy and that was that, they took you away.

Jules had finished basic training and the Army was shipping him out, only not from California but from Fort Dix in New Jersey. They were sending the boys by train, cross-country, and Sophia and Alfonzo gave me the money to take a train from St. Louis to New York to see Jule before he went overseas.

I don't know how we figured out what train would get me there at the right time or how we knew which day. I don't remember how we knew any of it or who made the plan. I only know they bundled me on in St. Louis with enough food for a platoon.

All I could smell was olive oil; egg and zucchini and cheese fried with bread that Sophia had made for me for the trip, wrapped tenderly in the St. Louis *Post-Dispatch,* the oil melting through the newsprint, running the words together in a blur.

I was in the seat for a day and a night and a day until I got to New York.

I was supposed to get off the train and stand right there, right on the platform, I was supposed to stay put so Jules could find me in the crowd.

And he did.

And we had one hour together.

One hour. On September 30, 1943.

Uniforms, I'd never seen so many uniforms. And duffel bags. Against the benches, against the walls, against people's legs, duffel bags piled everywhere.

Soldiers and sailors and marines and coast guard. Mothers and fathers and husbands and wives. Babies and children and grandparents and friends. Everywhere. I'd never seen so many people in my life.

Kissing.

Everyone was kissing in front of everyone. Strangers kissing in front of strangers.

Hugging. Holding on tight until the end.

Handkerchiefs waving in the air, a man calling out track numbers and train numbers on a loudspeaker that you couldn't understand; a loudspeaker echoing and blaring but you couldn't understand the words, like he was yelling at you from inside a big tin can.

Goodbye, darling.

Write me, honey, write me every day.

I promise, baby, I promise.

See you, Mom.

Take care of yourself, Dad.

That's all I could hear, snatches of other people's conversations. Pieces of people's hopes and dreams.

Say goodbye to Daddy, sweetheart.

Say hello to Daddy, sweetheart.

This is your daddy, sweetheart—say hello.

Jules was pulling me fast by the hand through the giant rotunda of Grand Central Station in New York, I was trying to keep up with him, my high heels clattering on the marble floor; he was smiling at me and I was following his smile through the crowd.

Don't forget to write, son.

Send me cookies, Mom.

So long, Joe.

And, my God, Mother, look, there he is—my God, there's our boy.

I heard everything.

Men scuffling their feet on the marble, their hats in their hands; women crushing their sons to their breasts until they had to let them go.

Crying. So much crying. People were crying everywhere.

And the ceiling was twinkling; I looked up and they had painted the galaxies on the ceiling, stars were twinkling down on us from inside.

"Wish, baby, make a wish," Jules said, and I made a wish and blew it into the air with my lips.

"Come back to me, Jules, please come back to me."

"I'll be back, honey, I promise. I'll be back before you know it, before you can say boo."

Holding me and kissing me. Lifting me up in his arms, my feet not touching the ground.

"I love you, Mollie, I love you. I'll always love you."

I'll see you, honey, and take care of yourself, baby, and I love you, sweetheart. I love you, sweetheart, everywhere.

One hour. That's all we had.

We sat on a wooden bench and Jules ate a hot dog and had an orange drink. Our eyes never left each other. I couldn't eat my hot dog, I just held it and watched him. I was sure I'd never see him again—I tried to remember everything. His smile, his frown, the way his eyebrows nearly came together in the middle, his mustache, his thick black wavy hair, his brown eyes and his lashes, his hands, his fingers—wide and stubby—the bones in his face, the width of his shoulders, the hardness of his chest up against me, his ribs pushing against my breasts as he held me tight, lean and hard, his kiss, the way it felt with his lips on mine, the smell of him, the taste of him, the touch—I tried to remember it all. Me, who can't remember, I tried to remember it all.

The yellow of the mustard bled through the tissue around the hot dog and the fingertips of my white cotton gloves turned gold on my left hand.

They wouldn't let us go with them, walk them down to the train. They kept us barricaded behind a gate. Women bunched together, crying, stunned, waving at a blur of khaki and blue. Goodbye, goodbye. Holding on. And then letting go. Fingers touching, parting.

Goodbye, baby.

So long, honey.

I'll be home soon, kid, you'll see.

He kissed me hard one more time and he turned and went; he pushed the empty paper cup from the orange drink he was holding into my hand, whispered "I love you, Mollie" in my ear, and turned and walked away into a sea of other men. I stood there with the other women and watched my husband disappear.

I stood there for the longest time, and when I realized he was gone, really gone, I couldn't believe I'd seen him at all. It wasn't until I realized I was holding the paper cup that it all seemed real. Maybe because it said "Orange Julius" in writing on the paper cup. It said "Orange Julius" and I'd just sent my Julius off to war.

I walked back through the rotunda and waited by the track for the train to St. Louis to leave. I didn't see the other people anymore, I only saw Jule's face.

I never stepped one foot outside of Grand Central Station. Gilliana always asks me, "Mom, how could you not step outside? Didn't you want to see New York? The Empire State Building? Times Square? Anything?"

What did I know? I didn't want to see anything except Jule's face. I never stepped one foot outside Grand Central Station, I never breathed one breath of the city of New York, and the only souvenir I took with me was a crumpled paper cup.

WEDNESDAY

Gilliana

I went through a lot of my mother's things today when we got home from the doctor's. Purses—shelves and shelves of purses in her closet, all in perfect condition, all like brand new and some of them from so long ago that when you bought them then, they came with a mirror and a coin purse already inside—now the only thing you get inside a purse is the price tag.

And gloves—you have never seen so many gloves—black satin ones with tiny black bugle beads hand-stitched in designs along the tops, black leather and white leather, short ones and long ones and ones with fur inside and navy and gray and cotton and lace. She could have opened a glove store, my mother.

And hatboxes filled with letters from people I've never heard of and pictures of people I've never seen. And people I have seen; lots of pictures of Dell and Nat, his arm around her, her gazing up at him—in his sailor uniform during the war, in a suit and tie and her in a cocktail dress at some party; she's actually got a martini and a cigarette in her hand and is wearing a hat with a *veil.* Dell and my mother in white bathing suits about to fall out of a rowboat on a lake somewhere . . . terrifically young and beautiful and laughing . . . When Dell died twelve years ago, she had a heart attack, one big fat huge heart attack that hit her when she was in the middle of doing one of her favorite things. She was in a department store in St. Louis called Famous Barr parading around the shoe department while Nat read the paper in a chair; she was giving a pair of black suede pumps what she called a test run. "You put on the shoes and walk around in them for at least five minutes, Gilliana, you hear me?—*five minutes*— don't do like your mother does, she falls for them, gets them home, puts them on to go out and they kill her but she wouldn't take them back if you gave her a million bucks." She winks at me. "Would ya, Mol?" she says to my mother, and they both laugh. I have never bought a pair of shoes without walking around in them for at least five minutes before I fork over my credit card.

I study a photograph of Dell and me in front of a blooming peach tree in somebody's backyard. Maybe I'm five years old and the two of us are wearing look-alike dresses and standing posed the way fashion models do at the end of a runway before they turn around, a hand on each hip and both feet at right angles, holding our chins up and sucking in our cheeks to make cheekbones just like real models except we're both looking at the camera cross-eyed.

I never thought about it before, but it occurs to me—Dell was the first comedian in my life. I stand there, overwhelmed.

I flew to St. Louis for Dell's funeral. "She didn't even know what hit her, Mollie," Nat said, holding on to my mother, "she was parading around in those shoes and then she was on the floor—I thought she was making a joke."

"Well, that's how I want to go, Lew," my mother said at the house afterward. "Fast, so I don't know." Lew said he'd see what he could do.

Fast. Now that's funny.

We can put her in a home, the doctors said. That would be easier, they said. They gave me and Lew the alternatives. You could keep her at your house with round-the-clock help or you could put her in a home, which, of course, would be easier. Easier for who?

I looked at this guy, this expert whizbang of a doctor, and I could see George Segal and Ruth Gordon singing behind him. "Never put your mother in an H-O-M-E, never put your mother in a hooomme." They're giving it the old "one-two" from *Where's Poppa?* right behind the doctor while he explains how Mollie will continue to deteriorate. In detail. She will know less and less until she knows nothing at all, and when he got to the diaper part I stood up; actually, I believe I catapulted out of the chair.

My beautiful Mollie of the red high-heeled ankle-strap shoes, my dancing, cut-on-the-bias, elegant mother, the Marcella Hazan chef of the Midwest, the impeccably groomed, calm, smiling, stunning homemaker who could make brunch for fifty and never raise her voice and sew bugle beads perfectly in a tiny row and hem your new skirt and let you stay up late with her, eating pumpkin seeds and watching TV, and make you laugh and tuck you in and listen to your woes and teach you how to pack a jacket so when you took it out it wasn't creased and do the triple time-step as good as Ginger Rogers and play poker like a shark and type more words on a single postcard than a linotyper with *The Washington Post* and hide brownies and snowball cookies in your duffel going off to camp and put your hair up in pom-poms and send you out into the world telling you you could have it all—that very same mother was going to forget how to chew and swallow and go to the bathroom and stand up. Not necessarily in that order. Not necessarily fast or slow. It could happen tomorrow or take years, the doctor said. There was no way to know, the doctor said. It would be at her own pace, the doctor said. I wanted to punch him, I wanted to kick him in the balls, I wanted to scream.

I said, "Excuse me, please," very politely to my stepfather and the doctors—there were three of them—smiled graciously like the lady that I am, walked out of their posh offices, down the hall, into the elevator, pushed "L," walked across the lobby, out the door, into the parking lot, and screamed. People looked at me but nobody did anything.

It was snowing. I didn't notice it right away, I was too busy screaming but then I realized the stuff melting on my face was snow. Eventually I went back upstairs to listen some more. I told Lew I'd been to the ladies' room.

Lew says he won't put her in a home. Never. Okay, that's fine with me. Now there's two of us who won't put her in a home. Never. So we'll get help—how much could it cost? Everything we have, right? So I'll write faster. I'll try to remember everything funny that ever happened in this family. Maybe I'll just stay here and do research right in my mother's closets and drawers.

She watched me today while I went through her things. She sat in a chair in her bedroom and watched me, smiling. She had no idea what I was doing, she had no idea the things were hers. She either sits in a chair where you put her or she lies in the bed. She's very obliging. Of course, she also can't always remember how to walk, so the odds are she won't go anywhere; you know she'll be there when you get back.

Can I do this? Can I make jokes about Mollie not remembering how to walk? How can I do this? How many jokes will it take to pay for "round-the-clock" help? How much screaming?

I was going to knock a few things off a few shelves when we got back from the doctor's just to feel better, but I couldn't; after all, this is my mother's house. I took a walk instead and then I had a bath and then I had a nice big vodka. It was only four o'clock but I decided it was okay. It may have been only four o'clock in Kansas City but it was five o'clock in New York, definitely time for a cocktail; the shank of the evening, Dell used to say.

Mollie whistled while I went through her things, she whistled and watched me. And smiled. Old songs, songs from the forties she was whistling, songs from the Second World War. And I sang. I know all the words; after all, she used to sing them to me over and over, she sang with the radio on when I was little all around our apartment—while she dusted, while she cooked, did the ironing, braided my hair. Today she whistled and I sang. We were great. We could have gone on "The Ed Sullivan Show" . . . He's dead, isn't he? We could have gone on Ed Sullivan with Sonja Henie, right? Oh, God.

Listen to this:

> *Oh, give me something to remember you by,*
> *When you are far away from me, dear . . .*
> *Some little something meaning love cannot die,*
> *No matter where you chance to be.*
> *Though I'll pray for you, night and day for you,*
> *It will see me through like a charm,*
> *Till your return, dear . . .*

Some lyrics, huh? "Some little something meaning love cannot die, no matter where you chance to be." What could that be? A charm for her bracelet? A photograph with an inscription? A book? A glove?

Not a cartoon on a kitchen wall, certainly. Surely not that.

What do I have? What are my little treasures tucked and locked into my bureau drawers? My little "somethings" meaning love cannot die . . . Well, I do have some things from Christopher, some sweet things, dear things, besides a lot of apology notes. Specifically, some postcards he sent me when he was in Japan on some business thing and I was home very pregnant with Clare; he made these little childish drawings of me pregnant that he drew in between his tiny script, very *un*-Christopher-like, very dear. I cried when I got them, I carried them around with me in my purse for years. There were drawings before there were cartoons. There always are, I guess.

But Christopher wasn't my first; I was nearly thirty when I married Chris.

I have nothing from my first. Not even a photograph, just memories.

Tom Johnson.

Freckles. Lanky. Blue eyes. A lopsided smile. Long skinny legs. Funny. A crew cut. A fake front tooth from a fight after a basketball game. A wife. Two children. Oops. That's not supposed to be in the list, right? Maybe I should have kept a photograph of his wife and kids; he had one in his wallet, as I recall. But, of course, he'd left them when he had me. Left them, was leaving them, was about to leave them, was in the process of leaving them, any minute now, Gillian, I'm leaving them . . . I'm separated, I'm nearly separated, I'm in the process of separating . . . going, going, going . . . but never gone.

Two years of splendor, two years of magical hours and moments meeting Tom Johnson on the sly. Planning our lives together when he'd be free. It would have been smarter planning our lives together when he would be's a dead duck. That, at least, was possible. Leaving, on the other hand, was not.

Tom Johnson, the first of my unattainables. The first of my broken hearts. Just ask any shrink, they'll tell you—a daughter of a disappearing father will search for disappearing men.

"You think you can type this for me?"

"I don't know, you'll have to take a number." I didn't look up from what I was already typing; my fingers went faster on the keys.

Type? I could type faster than the speeding bullet that Superman could beat and I could take shorthand and I could file and I could do everything there was to do in an office, everything that Mollie told me I had to learn to do, in case I had to have something to fall back on in case of an emergency. An emergency to Mollie was that I would never find a husband and have to earn my own living for the rest of my days.

"What is this, a deli?" he said. "I'll have two jelly doughnuts, a tuna sandwich, and a typed report. Please."

I looked up. He was standing in front of my desk, smiling. His jacket was off, his tie loosened and pulled to one side, his top shirt button undone, and his sleeves rolled up.

"Well, I did like the 'please' part," I said.

"So you'll type it, Gilly? Really, I need it bad."

"Who said you could call me Gilly?"

"Jim Mayer calls you Gilly."

"Yeah, but he asked me first and I said he could, and besides, he's my boss."

"Okay." He grinned real big and I could see his funny front tooth. I had a sudden impulse to stand up and run my hand along the top of his crew cut but I didn't.

"Miss Ventimiglia, do you think you could please type this for me today? Huh? 'Cause I have to take it to Len Barhyde or he's gonna fire me and Miss Scott went home with the flu and if I try to type it myself it won't be done until Thursday of next year. Please. Did you notice I said 'please' twice?"

Freckles, blue eyes. So cute.

"Jesus, Johnson, you know, you're a pain in my you-know-what."

"But you'll do it?"

"All right, I'll do it. Leave it there."

"I love you," he said, putting the pages down gently next to my right elbow on my desk.

"Really," I said back, deadpan. "That's nice."

"So can I call you Gilly?"

"Absolutely not."

"Someday?"

"Never."

"We'll see, Miss Ventimiglia, we'll see. I'll be in my hole of an office if you can't read my writing or need me for anything. Anything at all, Miss Ventimiglia."

"Shut up, Johnson," I said, laughing.

"I didn't say you could call me Johnson," he said, and walked down the hall.

We were off.

It was 1967. I was twenty-one. And still a virgin. The only one in existence then, I'm sure. I don't know how it happened, or how it hadn't happened, but it hadn't. There hadn't been anyone at college, I'd been close but no cigar. There just wasn't anyone that seemed right to me, no one that I wanted to do it with, no one that even came close. I was still perfectly intact—well, maybe not perfectly but pretty much so, a few jabs here and there but nothing for real.

It was ghastly. It was embarrassing. I was the only one of my friends, no matter what they were doing—married, engaged, going with somebody, running around—they were all deflowered. I was the only one. A pariah. A dinosaur. A disgrace. I was even taking the birth control pill in expectation, I was so upset.

We worked for an advertising agency called Jasper-DePensa in downtown Kansas City on six floors of a big office building at Fifteenth and Baltimore. We were in walking distance of lots of restaurants, department stores, bars, and fashionable hotels. Very convenient. We worked together, had lunch together, and had drinks together every Friday after work, a crowd of us. Sometimes during the week, too, but Fridays for sure. We were a great group. We worked hard and we liked each other. The secretaries were all female and all single, the executives, salesmen, writers, copy guys, and what-have-you were all men and mostly all married. You get the picture, right?

Mix two cups of young, attractive, eager women with two cups of young men "on the rise," already bored with their tired wives and screaming toddlers, add six tablespoons of work in common to talk about, three scotch and waters—with or without a twist—and stir. Somebody's got to fall in love. Yield: a moving train bound for the end of Gillian Ventimiglia's virginity. Oh, boy.

And I fell for him, I was crazy for him. Hook, line, and sinker, also the rod and the tackle box, the bait, the works. I don't even know how it happened; it must have been something about his crazy tooth or his grin, his crew cut, or maybe that he made me laugh, or maybe, even better, how he laughed at me—I don't mean at me, I mean he thought I was funny. Tom Johnson was the first person besides my mother who thought I was funny. Maybe that was it. Or his freckles. I'm not sure which. Probably his freckles. Freckles are a rarity in Jewish-Italian families; there's hardly a freckle to be had. Needless to say, I had all his freckles, and before I knew it no one called me Gilly except for Tom.

Saturday mornings. No matter what times we had together, we always had Saturday mornings. Mollie went to help Lew in the store, went *with* him, in *his* car, no chance of her returning home unless the store burned down. I still lived at home, you see. And Mr. Johnson told Mrs. Johnson that there was this new thing at work—the "Saturday morning breakfast staff meeting" or something like that. Of course, I didn't know Mr. Johnson was still living at home; Mr. Johnson told me that he was separated and staying in a spare room at his cousin's house until all the details were worked out. I guess I should have thought that sounded fishy but I didn't. I was in love. And besides, he wasn't making enough cash to keep her and the babies in milk and diapers and also pay for an apartment for himself too. It made sense to me that he would stay at his cousin's and how could he take me to the cousin's? He was still married. See? It made sense. Okay, it didn't make sense but I bought it. You let some blue eyes and a bunch of freckles make love to you for four hours without stopping and see if you can tell the wheat from the chaff. Or from the fishy, for that matter, too. He came over to my mother's house every Saturday morning. He came and I came and we came . . .

"I'm on my way."

"Where are you exactly? I want to picture it."

"I'm at Forty-fifth and Main at the phone booth behind Roy's and Ray's. You want me to bring you a doughnut?"

"Absolutely not."

"Some onion rings?"

"It's nine o'clock in the morning. Who could eat onion rings at nine o'clock in the morning?"

"A Danish?"

"Now you're talking, Johnson. Blueberry. I'm going to take the blueberries and the icing off the Danish and put them on you."

"Cut it out, Gilly." He was laughing. "I'm getting a hard-on in this phone booth. I won't be able to get out."

"People will think you're a pervert."

"You're the one who's a pervert, look what you want to do with the innocent blueberries on a Danish."

"You better hurry up and get here. I'm running around naked and it's cold in this house."

"I'm on my way—why don't you put on a robe till I get there?"

"I can't, I'm working on my dance."

"What dance?"

"The one I'm gonna do for you, the one where I wear only boots and tassels, that I'm gonna do for you up on the kitchen table as soon as you get here."

"Tassels? Did you say tassels? Jesus, Gilly, I can't get out of the phone booth, I'm trapped."

We did it everywhere. All over my mother's house. Darling Mollie, who never discussed sex in any way, shape, or form, who blushed at off-color remarks, did not appreciate dirty jokes and was adamant about my not using "bad" language—Mollie would have died instantly. If poor Lew even made the slightest indication that they ever "did it," she practically collapsed on the spot. Mollie would only discuss *romance,* never sex. Meanwhile, we were doing it on her dining-room table, against the wall in her upstairs hall, on each of her living-room chairs, over the arm of her favorite chintz sofa, and all over her kitchen floor. She thought I was taking an oil-painting course at the museum on Saturday mornings and here I was making love all over her house. Or was it sex? Or was it romance? Sometimes it's hard to know the difference, or maybe it's only hard for me; maybe I was confused right from the start.

Clare

Scott wanted to do it yesterday. I mean, not as soon as he got here or anything but soon enough. I keep thinking about it, like my every waking moment, you know?

I don't know why I didn't. I could have. I wanted to. My dad wasn't home or anything, but I don't know, it just didn't seem right, the timing and all. I mean, what if he would have walked in?

Some of my friends have done it, but not that many. Everybody's like this really big talker, you know, but when you're really right in the middle of everything and, you know, it really could happen—well, then you have to stop and think. I mean, how do I know he's the one? I love Scott and all, and he's perfect for me and I am sixteen, practically seventeen, but you could also look at it and say I'm only sixteen. You know? It works both ways. And once I do it, then that's it, it's over—right? It's the end of everything. It's also the beginning of everything, but it's also the end. I don't know. I mean, who are you supposed to discuss this stuff with? Your mother? Really.

My friend Amy, she's my best friend since we're four or something—well, she would die if I did it, she thinks it's foolish to do it before you're like at least twenty when you really know what you want to do. But that's so intellectual, if you know what I mean, so planned, so unspontaneous. Of course, sometimes it's too hard to think. Like, you know that there's

AIDS and all and you're supposed to be careful, but really, who's going to stop and think about AIDS when some guy has his hands all over you and you can't breathe and you want to do it as much as he wants to do it and who could stop to think about anything, much less protection? I mean, really, do the grown-ups who talk about how you have to protect yourself, do they think that they would have been able to stop and put on condoms when they were sixteen and young? Give me a break. Please.

Anyway, we didn't do it. I said I couldn't in my mother's house. I mean, this is where I was a baby, you know? Where I grew up and took my first steps and all. I mean, I had the chicken pox in this bed, it's not where I want to get laid. Not for the first time anyway. I think I'd like something a little more romantic.

Scott acted like he was mad at first, but he really wasn't; he was just disappointed, you know? Besides, I pointed out to him that he certainly wasn't ready to do it at *his* mother's house, so why would I want to do it at mine? So we ordered a pizza and watched MTV and, of course, my father came home like ten minutes later. Right? I mean, God, can you imagine?

You know, I was thinking, it must have been much easier in the olden days—not when they didn't have cars or anything, but like when my grandma was a girl. You didn't have sex until you got married and that was that. No discussion, no anything. Of course, I guess you did if you were a slut, but other than that you didn't. And there was no AIDS then, there was no "anything," as far as I know, except things that could get wiped out by a strong antibiotic. The worst thing that could happen to you if you had sex then was that you could get pregnant and then your parents could kill you, but not some disease. I don't know, it's as if now teenagers have sex, but with the privilege comes all these built-in horrific conditions. It's like the more we discover, the better it is and the worse it is, all at the same time.

Anyway, Scott is so sweet . . . really he is. I mean, I love him, I just . . . well, I don't know.

Mollie

Mollie sat in the corner of the rose sofa in the sunroom of her mother- and father-in-law's house. It was eleven in the morning and the room was flooded with light. It was a corner room off the living room with windows on all three sides; Sophia had each windowsill filled with potted plants. It was Mollie's favorite place to sit.

She sat with her legs tucked under her, pink wedgie slippers side by side on the Persian rug in front of the sofa, steam rising from a cup of coffee on the table by her arm. She wore a pink chenille bathrobe over a man's torn white undershirt. A letter sat in her lap. A letter of thin, fragile pieces of paper that folded and became its own envelope.

She opened the letter and read it again, smiled, held it to her chest, sighed, folded it back up, and slipped it into the pocket of her bathrobe.

She smiled again, turned to look out the windows, and began to weep.

Dear Mollie,

I love you. I miss you like hell. I got two of your letters yesterday and one from Mom. I've read them at least thirty-eight times.

Everything's okay here. Jimmy Doogan, that's the guy I told you about from Georgia, the one with the accent that's so thick you can't understand what he's saying most of the time, well, it turns out his brother's in the Navy and knows Nat. What do you think of that? They were in basic together. Small world, huh?

I miss you, honey. I think about you all the time. I look at your picture and I think about us together. Don't worry. I'll be home soon and we'll be together. Just like in that song we like, right? Don't know where, don't know when, but we'll meet again. Right?

Don't worry, honey. I'm fine. I love you with all my heart.

Your,

Julie

My darling Julie,

I'm in the sunroom on the couch. The kids are coming home from school but the little boy across the street has the chicken pox and so he's watching his friends come home and waving at them from his window and they're waving back. It's so sweet.

It snowed last night. It started yesterday and went on all night so this morning it was deep and the sun came out and everything glistened. I went out early and it was quiet and still. I stood on the front stoop and realized it was deeper than my galoshes but I jumped in anyway—it was the only way to get to the mailbox. I sent you three letters. I miss you so much. I'm wearing all your shirts. Your mom and dad think it's funny, they laugh when I walk into the kitchen in the morning wearing your clothes.

Now they call me tesorina, *your mom and dad. Isn't that sweet? Actually, I'm beginning to understand quite a bit of Italian. Boy, will you be surprised when you get home.*

I dream about you every night and think about you all day long. Please be careful, my darling. I know it's terrible where you are even though you never tell me or mention bad things but I know. Please be safe. I love you, love you, love you,

Your,

Mollie

P.S. Tesorina *is a "little treasure," just in case you didn't know. So there. I love you, darling.*

P.P.S. I'm also sleeping on your side of the bed. Where all the power is, right?

What I didn't tell him was that I was also wearing his Old Spice and using his comb. I was doing everything I could to keep him close to me; the sleeves of his shirt against my arms, the smell of his face on mine, my cheek on his pillow, my back on the sheets on his side of the bed. I fell asleep at night with his arms around me. I would lie there until I could feel them around me, his skin against mine, his hand on my hip, his breath in my hair. It was only then that I could close my eyes.

And in between the letters I would play the records, over and over, actual records of Jule talking to me from somewhere over there. They were made by the Red Cross and they were scratchy and skipped and hopped around on the turntable but I could hear him, and just hearing him gave my heart a little peace. First would come the announcer, a man with one of those resonant radio voices that boomed: "Hello. This is the American Red Cross bringing you your husband from overseas."

And then Jule would say, "Hi, honey. It's me."

And then he'd ask how everybody was and to say hello from him and how he was fine and everything was okay—I'm sure they told them what they could say, what they were allowed to say because of what was supposed to be kept secret, but it didn't matter to me what he said as long as I could hear him. And he'd always end with: "Okay, honey, I gotta go now . . . but I'll be home real soon. Okay? Take care of yourself. I love you. I love you, Mol."

"I love you, Mol, I love you, Mol, I love you, Mol," the record would say, echoing out of the Victrola across Sophia's living room.

He was somewhere in the European Theater; I didn't know exactly where; they didn't tell you anything.

"E che vuol dire? Teatro Europeo? E che è questo teatro?"

What theater? My father-in-law was banging his spoon on the kitchen table. What kind of people make this name, a theater? They think this is a play? Men killing each other? What kind of people make this name, a theater?

There was no way to explain it, I didn't understand it myself. I didn't understand most of it. I tried to imagine Jule marching and singing in step, sitting in a foxhole, why they called it a foxhole, what it looked like, how big it was. I tried to visualize him sleeping in a tent, on a cot, on the ground, eating out of little cans, C rations, he called them; he made a lot of jokes about how all the boys bet on what kind of meat was inside. He said even sometimes when they were eating it they still didn't know. I imagined little sardine-like cans that rolled up across the top.

I could imagine some of it but not the worst of it. I couldn't imagine Julie with a gun. Shooting a gun. Killing someone. I couldn't imagine that.

Dear Mollie, my sweetheart,

We actually got four days out of here. Me and Al Goldberg from New York and a guy I haven't told you about named Tommy Schneider who just got transferred in. Anyway, we got a four-day leave and wound up in this beautiful town in Belgium called Liège.

The best thing was we met this really nice couple and their three kids and they wound up having us all to dinner. He's a dentist. We had a great time, they were really swell and she took all our addresses and said she would write you and Al's wife and Tommy's mom. He's not married yet. He's only twenty-three and really green from Chicago.

I miss you a lot, honey. But yesterday I felt like I'd won the Daily Double at Cahokia Downs—we got back and there were four letters waiting from you.

I love you, Mollie. I promise you, honey, that once I'm home and out of this mess I'll never leave you again. Never.

You said in one of your letters that there were buds on the trees outside Mom's sunroom. I promise you, honey, we'll have a million springs together, a million buds to watch open. Just look up at the moon 'cause it's the same moon I'm looking at and I'm sending you all my love.

Your,

Jule

P.S. Their names are Helene and Willy Cole, the people in Liège.

He had two furloughs—one in June of 1944 for sixteen days and one in March of 1945 for ten days. That was it. The hardest thing about having him back was knowing he would have to leave again and the hardest thing about having him leave again was knowing he might never come back at all. I tried to appreciate the hours and the minutes but, at the same time, I was counting them off on my fingers until I'd have to let him go, so as good as the furloughs were, they were awful in a way. He would never let me go with him—wherever he and his buddies would meet when their time was up, the bus station or the train station or in the front of a hotel—it didn't matter where, Jule wouldn't let me go. "I want to picture you right here in my head, honey, standing just the way you are." So we said good-bye in front of the house; me all dressed up in a dress and high heels and lipstick as if I was going out somewhere, wearing something pretty so he could remember me pretty if he got shot. That's what I would think later—if they shoot him, he'll remember me in this blue dress as he dies. I'm sure Sophia and Alfonzo watched him go from the windows but I stood in front alone. I'd hold on to him until the car would come, another soldier in a uniform, three soldiers, four . . . someone driving them back, someone else whose heart was breaking. I'd hold on to him and he'd kiss me in front of the whole neighborhood and get in the car. He'd lean out the window and wave until I couldn't see his hand anymore and then I'd go inside.

Dear Jule darling,

Dell came over today. Nat left yesterday and she was blue. He'd been home a whole month. I was so jealous—not really, you know I love them, I just wish it could have been us. I saw him three times while he was home, he looks tired but okay. He didn't talk a lot about where he's been or what he's seen—I guess there's nothing to say. Anyway, your mother and I gave Dell a big spaghetti lunch today to cheer her up. With wine!

I miss you so much. Last night I was listening to records and your mom and dad were in the room with me and the sweetest thing happened. Your daddy got up and did a little bow in front of me and asked me to dance. Jule, it was so sweet. He was very elegant and danced me around the room like we were at a ball. Now I see where you learned to dance. I was so touched.

You better watch out because when you get home I will never let you go. Not to the store or to get a pack of cigarettes or anything. I'm going to hold on to you like glue.

I love you, darling. Please be safe. I'm looking at the moon and wishing on it to bring you home to me soon.

I love you,
Mollie

P.S. He danced with your mother too and it was so beautiful I cried, she still had her apron on.

P.P.S. I've gotten three letters from Helene in Liège. Maybe someday when this is all over I'll be able to meet them too.

P.P.P.S. Did I tell you I love you? I do.

Your, M.

He came home on December 4, 1945, at four-thirty in the afternoon. He was discharged and shipped back to the States and sent directly to Jefferson Barracks in St. Louis. I knew approximately when he would get back but not exactly, they didn't tell you that. I only knew it would be sometime during that week.

I was taking a bath. It certainly wasn't the way I would have planned it but none of those moments are, the ones you think will be perfect. Of course it was perfect because he was home, but it wasn't the way I'd planned it in my head. I wouldn't have been in the bathtub, I would have been all dressed up standing out in front of the house waiting for the car to drive up. It wasn't like that at all.

Sophia and I had been cleaning all day, cleaning the house as if it was dirty. It wasn't, it was spotless, but we were cleaning anyway. For him, for when he got home, she wanted everything to shine. She was in the backyard doing something, I don't know what. It was cold and gray but there wasn't any snow on the ground. Alfonzo wasn't home. It was around four-thirty in the afternoon and getting dark outside. There was a cake in the oven and the whole house smelled like cake, sweet and warm. I was in the bathtub. I heard the front doorbell ring and I heard Sophia go to the door—the back door slam, her footsteps across the kitchen linoleum and through the house on and off the rugs and the hardwood floors.

"I go, *tesorina,*" she called to me, and mumbled something else in Italian I didn't quite get.

But then I didn't listen anymore. I was shampooing my hair when he opened the door to the bathroom. The mirrors were all steamy when I turned my head.

"Hello, honey," Jules said from the doorway, as if he'd just been down at the corner drugstore and not coming home from a war.

"Hello, honey, I'm home," he said from the doorway, standing so handsome in his uniform, with his hat in his hand. I think both of us started to cry at the same time . . . and then somehow he was in the tub with me and . . . then, well . . . it was a good thing I didn't drown.

Gilliana

Mollie found my birth control pills. That was the beginning of the end of Tom Johnson and me. It had been going on for two years. It's not like I was a baby, I was twenty-three years old and typing my fingers to the bone and earning money, but I was still living in my mother's house and things were different then in the late sixties, early seventies, and especially in Kansas City. Nice Jewish-Italian girls might have been making love without getting married in New York or in Los Angeles, but if they were doing it in Kansas City they weren't telling anyone. And they certainly weren't doing it without getting married if Mollie was their mother, that's for damn sure. There was no way Tom Johnson could marry me—after all, lest we forget, he already had a wife. Nothing had changed on the separation front. I loved him with everything I had and only wanted to be with him, and I actually let it go on believing it would happen, that someday he would be mine. This was the beginning of a long run of dumbness on my part.

The confrontation between Mollie and me was nearly the end.

Very dramatic and probably funny, but certainly not so at the time.

"What are these?"

She was holding the little round plastic container of birth control pills in her hand.

"Huh?"

I was floored. Panicked. Like a seven-year-old caught stealing with his hands in his mother's purse—only it was my mother's hands in my purse. Of course, we never got to that part, the part about why she felt it was okay to go into my purse, we never got to that.

What could I say?—they were vitamins? The funny part was she really didn't know at first, she'd never seen a container of birth control pills before. But she knew by the time she confronted me. She'd taken the name down and called the pharmacist to find out what they were. She knew "but good," as she would say.

"Gilliana, what are these?"

I stood there. The look in her eyes was a sure clue not to tell her I was secretly dying of leukemia and those pills were the only thing keeping me alive. The look in her eyes also told me that she already knew damn well what they were. It wasn't until I became a mother myself that I realized the full beauty of this trick. You ask your child something when you already know the answer—the force and power behind this knowledge nails her to the spot.

"Clare, did you do your homework?"

I already know when I ask this that she has some French left.

"Clare, do you have my black T-shirt—you know, the good one with the little buttons at the nape of the neck?"

I have already seen this very same T-shirt lying in a crumpled heap on her bedroom floor.

"Gilliana, what are these?" my mother asked.

"My birth control pills," I said back. I saw her eyes, there was no way to avoid it, I was caught.

"What do you think you're doing?"

"What do you mean?"

"Don't do that to me, Gilliana, you know what I mean."

I wanted to be funny. Let me tell you, I had at least a million snappy answers to her questions that would have made 'em roll in the aisles.

"I'm protecting myself, Mother, so that I don't get pregnant."

Good girl, Gillian, very grown-up answer, very good.

"Where are you all the time when you say you're going out with all these friends of yours that I've never met?"

Bingo. It was clear this was more than just a packet of birth control pills we were discussing here.

"I'm with my friends."

"What friends?"

"Friends . . . I don't know, people from work . . . I've told you."

Not so good. Weak, Gillian, not up to par.

"What friends?"

"Friends, Mother. What do you mean, what friends? Do you want their names?"

Be careful, Gillian, don't get nasty.

"How come I've never met any of these friends?"

Good, she let the name remark go.

"What?"

"How come I've never met these friends? How come they never come here?"

Oh, they do, Mother, every Saturday morning, they come and come right here. Shit. Watch yourself, Gillian, watch yourself, you could lose it all.

I inhaled and gave it my everything. "I don't know why they don't come here. It just seems strange, I guess, since it's your and Lew's house. It's not like I have my own apartment, you know. I'm awfully old to be living at home. Maybe I should get my own apartment, maybe it's time."

"So you can do what you want with your friends? And these?" Holding out the little packet of birth control pills at me.

"No."

"It's one friend, isn't it, Gilliana? All these friends is really one. One man. Isn't it?"

"No."

"Don't lie to me."

Oh, God, please help me here. How much does she really know?

"Gilliana?"

I looked at her.

"It's one man." I sighed.

"He's married, isn't he?"

I didn't move.

"Gilliana?"

She must know. How could she know? There's no way she knows. Lie, Gillian. Go ahead. You can do it. Lie, she couldn't possibly know.

"Gilliana? He's married, isn't he?"

Oh, God. Help me.

"Isn't he?"

The ever-trusting Mollie, looking at me, her brown eyes just like mine.

Oh, God, I can't.

"Yes, he's married," I said.

She went white. As she raised her hand to her face, the birth control pill container slipped to the rug.

"Oh, my God," she said, "I didn't know. I just couldn't understand why you wouldn't have brought him home."

We stood there looking at each other.

"I don't know what to say to you," she said, and left my room.

This conversation made an indelible mark on my brain. It's probably the reason I don't ask Clare what she does with Scott. I hope I know and I think I know, but I don't really know for sure. Not a hundred percent. Just the way my mother didn't know. And maybe I don't want to know—remembering, always, the look on my mother's face.

I moved to L.A. I had to get out of there. My mother knew all about Tom Johnson, and Tom Johnson would never marry me and I would never find anybody else in Kansas City and that was that. I just couldn't picture myself getting an apartment there, making curtains out of marked-down flowered sheets, framing Georgia O'Keeffe posters from the museum to put on the walls, finding wonderful old pine pieces at yard sales and taking shorthand at Jasper-DePensa for the rest of my life. I could see doing that somewhere else but not in Kansas City; if I had to do it in Kansas City I would die. It was like a revelation to me—I didn't belong there, I had to go.

It was either New York or L.A., and New York seemed a farther stretch. After Kansas City, that is. Something about New York seemed more weird and dark and frightening after flat plains and corn by the side of the road and people who said, "Come back soon now, ya hear?" Somehow I didn't think people there talked that way; somehow I couldn't see my twang falling into place on Broadway or down in the Village or in any of those other exotic places people talked about that were in New York, which, of course, I'd never seen. Somehow I thought I'd never make it from the East Side to the West Side without getting at least raped or kidnapped—maybe even pillaged. The truth is I was too chicken to move to New York so I moved to L.A.

First I said goodbye to my girlfriends; that part was easy. They were all either married, or engaged, or going with somebody—somebodies who were available, of course, somebodies who didn't have a Mrs. Johnson waiting at home for them. Most of them were married with little babies, so the idea of flying off to Los Angeles to do anything instead of trying to think up interesting things to do with the meat loaf and wiping endless amounts of spitup off their shoulders was enticing to them. More than enticing; actually, most of them would have dropped their husbands and babies in the trash can and jumped on the plane with me, but women didn't do things like that back then. After all, it was 1970—my girlfriends were supposed to be the lucky ones because they were married already; I was supposed to be the poor old maid. They were supposed to be the happy ones; I was supposed to be running away with shame. So how come I was the one who was excited and all lit up and they were the ones who looked like they'd just come down with the flu? Needless to say, it was very confusing to all of us.

Then I said the two big goodbyes: goodbye to Tom Johnson and goodbye to my mother and Lew. I thought the goodbye to Tom Johnson would be the more dramatic of the two goodbyes, but I was wrong.

"I'm moving to Los Angeles."

"Why?"

"Because I can't stand this anymore, because you're never going to marry me, because you're never going to leave her and I'm sick of meeting you at my mother's house on Saturday mornings or in the dark in the parking lot of Jasper-DePensa in the backseat of a Dodge."

Silence.

"Are you?" asks I, in a little voice.

"What?"

"Ever gonna leave her?"

"I guess not," answers he, in a voice even littler, and that was that.

Goodbye.

Except for a lot of lovemaking, which was, of course, a big part of the goodbye. But that was the biggest part of everything we did—lovemaking and laughing, that was me and Johnson right from the start. The part that was shocking was not that I loved him—because I did love him; the part that was shocking was that I thought that first sweet love could last. That I could have married him and stayed in Kansas City and been happy forever in a little house with a white picket fence and a peach tree, standing in the backyard in a halter top basting barbecue ribs with beer.

I thought I would never get over him, and then I got to California and very soon I'd forgotten to think about him for a *whole day* and then for a *whole week* and then for two weeks and on and on. That funny front tooth and those freckles could always bring a smile to my face, but the ache from leaving him disappeared pretty fast—that was what shocked me. Of course, it was my first dance with love. My first dance with falling-in-love and lovemaking, which, when they're all rolled up into one dance like that, can make for more drama than a fucking tango. Maybe it should be a rule that the first person you do it with cannot be someone you love; maybe things would have been less confusing for me if they wouldn't have been overlapping like that. Do not tell my daughter what I just said.

The goodbye to Mollie was quite another thing. She didn't exactly stick her head in the oven, but it was clear—me moving alone to California was not her first choice. The only thing worse would probably have been me marrying Tom Johnson or me getting a brain tumor and dying in her arms. Maybe worse, maybe a toss-up; I'm not sure which.

"I'm moving to Los Angeles."

"What did you say, sweetie?"

Of course, I'd already gotten a job there. A job in a place called Pasadena working for some guy who'd gone to school with a guy I knew at Jasper-DePensa who'd called the guy in Los Angeles and told him how great I was and this guy said he was gonna have an opening for a secretary in his office in about two months—some lucky girl was quitting to get married and stay home to try her hand at interesting things to do with the meat loaf. I had no idea who the guy was; even worse, I had no idea where Pasadena was. Both big mistakes.

"I'm moving to Los Angeles."

"Don't be silly."

"I'm not being silly, Mom, I'm moving to Los Angeles. There's nothing here for me."

"What do you mean, nothing? What are you looking for that they don't have here?"

Be careful, Gillian.

"I need a life, Mom."

"You can't have a life here? What is this you're living? Not a life?"

"No. I don't think so."

"Why not?"

"I don't know. It has something to do with Tom Johnson and everything, something about that being over, something to do with getting out of here to someplace bigger where there's more opportunity."

More opportunity? What the hell does that mean? What am I talking about?

"What do you mean, more opportunity? To do what?"

"I don't know, Mom."

This is great, Gillian. You sound like a baboon.

My mother wiped her hands on her slacks, brushed her palms against the sides of her slacks at her hips. She was standing at the sink drying a mixing bowl. It was the only thing in the drainer, but she would never let anything drip-dry, she had to dry it with a dishtowel as soon as it got wet. I, on the other hand, only dry dishes when I don't have enough room in the drainer. I could let service for twelve drip-dry, including the pots and pans and crystal, if I had the space.

"Why all the way to California? If you don't know what you're going to do, why do you have to go all the way there?"

"Because what's the point of moving unless I go to New York or L.A.?"

"I don't know. That's why I'm asking."

"I don't know, Mom. I just have to go."

She frowned. "I don't like it."

"I can't stay here."

"Why not?"

"What don't you like, Mol?" Lew says, coming into the kitchen. He opens the refrigerator door and stands there looking in.

"What are you looking for?" my mother asks him.

"I don't know."

"You want some juice?" she says, frowning.

He squats down and pushes a few things around on a shelf.

"Lewis, what are you looking for? We're gonna eat soon."

"Uh-huh," he says, shutting the door. "So, what are you girls doing? Having a heart-to-heart?" He puts his hand gently on my shoulder and pats it a couple of times.

"You want a sandwich?" she says.

"No, I'm okay."

"He's hungry," she says to me.

"I'm fine," he says.

"He's hungry—I know when he's hungry," she says to me.

"So? What's going on?" Lew says, looking at the two of us.

"She's moving to California."

"Who's moving?"

"I am, Lew," I say.

"Well, that's exciting."

Thank you, God, thank you, thank you, for Lew.

I smile, Mollie doesn't. She gives him a look.

"I don't like it," she says.

"Well, I wouldn't think so, she's your baby, Mol."

Her eyes fill up. "That's right," she says.

"But she's twenty-three, sweetheart, you have to let her go."

"I'm twenty-four, Lew."

"My God, that's even worse," he says, deadpan.

I love him. He's trying to make her laugh. He's my hero for life.

"I don't care if she's twenty-four, I don't want her to go all the way to California."

"We'll visit her. They have airplanes, Mol, we'll go bother her there. We'll stay in her apartment and you can redo her drawers." He puts his arm around her.

"That's good, Mom, you can even dry the dishes as soon as I wash them when you come. Okay?"

She looks at me.

"Before I even put them on the drainboard," I try.

"Come on, Mollie," Lew says. He kisses her on her cheek.

"I don't want to come on," she says. "Why does she have to go so far away?"

"Why?" he says. "Would it make a difference if she moved to Chicago? It's still a plane ride away."

"We could drive."

"Okay, we'll drive to California."

"It's too far."

"Mollie, come on. Gillian's gotta go. Why do you want to make it more difficult for her?"

"I can't help it—I'm a mother, that's what I do."

Lew and I fall apart laughing. Eventually, Mollie joins in. Let's face it, it was a very funny line.

So I moved to California. I said goodbye to my girlfriends and Tom Johnson and my mother and Lew and I went. I didn't know why I was going. I never knew why, that's why I couldn't explain it to her. Let's face it—who in their right mind would move to Los Angeles unless they had a gun pointed at their head?

Mollie

A life—that's what I thought we were having. A regular life.

The alarm goes off and you make coffee while he takes a shower. The baby sits in her high chair laughing and banging her spoon on the tray. Your husband puts on a suit and tie, eats some toast and two eggs over easy, kisses you goodbye, and goes off to sell jewelry. You dust and scrub your little apartment until you can eat off the kitchen floor. The baby goes down for a nap and you listen to the radio while you iron his shirts, the cuffs and collar starched just so. The baby gets up and you dress her and feed her lunch, sweet mashed peas out of little jars, applesauce with no lumps, and pieces of hot dog she drops on the floor. You push her to the park in her stroller and talk to the other mothers about teething and recipes. You go home and she plays by your feet with your measuring spoons while you make stuffed shells at the sink. You take a bath and get dressed for him—not in a dress, but in something nice. You put on lipstick and stand at the window waiting; the apartment smells like supper when he comes in the door. He kisses you hello and holds you, he looks into your eyes and you know he loves you. The baby squeals with joy and holds out her pudgy arms to him, he picks her up and swings her over his head in the air in the living room. You can hear her laughing as you stir the sauce. He washes up and reads the evening paper, you eat supper together and give the baby a bath, you tiptoe away from her crib as she falls asleep. You talk about the day. You pay bills. You make plans. Maybe you go to the movies and a neighbor watches the baby; maybe if it's summer and it's hot out, you sit on the front steps or in the backyard, maybe you take a walk or go for a ride, maybe you drive to the Pevely Dairy and watch the fountain change colors while you eat a hot-fudge sundae in the car and listen to the ballgame on the radio. Maybe if it's winter, you sit at the kitchen table and eat chili and play cards. If it's Saturday and he's not working, you do things together, you go to the grocery store and push the cart together and buy something silly that you can't afford, maybe a rib roast or double lamb chops with little frilly paper panties on their ends. If it's Saturday night, you get dressed up and go dancing, maybe buy a fifth of good scotch and go dancing with Nat and Dell or John Padrelli and one of his girlfriends at the Jefferson Hotel. If it's Sunday, you go to Sophia and Alfonzo's house and eat too much for Sunday lunch. Or maybe you watch Jules and Nat and the boys play softball in the twilight in Heman Park. Or you sit on the front stoop while the baby sleeps in her crib in the apartment and you watch your husband rake the red-and-orange leaves that fall from the maple tree into a big pile in the middle of the yard. You watch the muscles move in his arms. He smiles at you. You're wearing a sweater and the air is crisp and you smile back at him as the wind blows your hair across your eyes. Days, weeks, months . . . you're happy, or sometimes you're sad, there are good days and there are bad days, there are ups and there are downs . . . but mostly it's a blur and the years pass. You love him, you love the baby, you love your life.

A life, that's what I thought we were having—a married couple with a baby, having a life . . . But what did I know? For over three years that's what I thought we were having—and then I went to buy the lamps.

Jules had come home from the war three and a half years before. We had stayed with Sophia and Alfonzo for four months until he got on his feet and then we got a place of our own, a tiny place that we rented from a cousin of Alfonzo's, Vinny Ventimiglia. On the Hill it was what they called a "shotgun" house, so named because it was said that if a bullet was fired into the front door, it could zip through the three rooms and right out the back door without hitting anything on its way. It was over on Shaw and of course still on the Hill; you didn't move off the Hill if you were Italian. I was the only Jewish girl making toasted ravioli in the neighborhood; I was the only Jewish girl in the neighborhood at all. And for Sophia that was fine. She accepted me as her daughter. I think it had to do with

Sandy, that we had lost her. Sophia had delivered three babies before Jule was born and all of them had died. I think that was our connection, that and our mutual love for Jule, but Sophia and I never talked about feelings or matters of the heart. It wasn't something she did; I don't even think she did it with Alfonzo and she certainly didn't do it with me. As far as Alfonzo was concerned, I could cook, so I was okay. He said I was "a good kid"; that was a high compliment coming from Alfonzo.

Jules got a job selling jewelry for his friend Arnold. They were overseas together a part of the time in France until Arnold got wounded and they sent him home. He walked with a little limp but other than that he was fine. Arnold was taking over his Uncle Sherman's jewelry store and he gave Jule a job; it didn't matter to Arnold that Jule knew nothing about selling jewelry.

Jules was home and he had a job. We were fine. But I couldn't believe it. I watched him all the time—I watched him eat, I watched him shave, I watched him sleep, I would have watched him go to the bathroom if I could have. It was hard for me to stop watching him, I couldn't believe he was really there. It was hard for me to let him go anywhere without me—I was afraid that something bad would happen and I would never see him again.

And then I was pregnant. And like so many other things in life, it wasn't what you'd expect. Every minute that I was happy was perched on a teeter-totter with a minute of seeing Sandy dead. Back and forth I went, up and down with joy and dread, and when the baby started to move inside me it was the worst time of all. I guess because those signs of life made me know that it was for real. A baby would really come out of me and then what would happen? Would it be Sandy all over again? Would she die on her eight-month birthday? I tried to put it out of my mind, but minds are hard to talk to; you tell them to stop it and then when your head is turned the bad thoughts start in again. In a way, it was better when I started spotting; it was as if the shoe that was hanging over me finally fell on my head. I would lose the baby—that seemed right—you shouldn't ask for too much; it was enough I got Jules back, who said I could have a baby too? But Gilliana was not Sandy, she was tough right from the start. I didn't miscarry and I didn't lose her, she held on tight and was born defiant; they told me she didn't even cry when they pulled her out, she just looked the doctor right in his face.

September 7, 1946, my Gilliana was born—nearly nine months to the day Jule came home from the service; he teased me that we should name her Harry Truman Ventimiglia in gratitude, but I told him I thought a girl's name was more appropriate so we named her for Sophia's sister who was still in Sicily—Gilliana Ada Ventimiglia, six pounds seven ounces, twenty inches long, and as brown as a baby monkey. And ugly. I know that's a terrible thing to say and of course she didn't stay ugly, she turned beautiful, but when she was born she was a little ugly. You could see it in people's eyes when they came to look at her in the hospital. "Oh, my goodness," they'd say, "would you look at this baby . . ." and then there would be no more words. They were speechless. I knew what was going on. Her hair was dark brown and way too long for a newborn baby, her eyes were dark brown and too big for her face, her skin was olive, dark olive, certainly not pale and pink and white. She didn't coo, she screamed in anger; she wasn't a bundle of softness, she seemed to be all elbows and knees; she didn't close her eyes and melt into your shoulder like a sweet angel, she wiggled and squirmed and tried to turn her head to see what was going on. I didn't care, I loved it. It was such a relief to me that she didn't look like Sandy that I thought she was the most beautiful baby that had ever been born.

So I thought my life had turned around. That since God had taken my mother and Sandy from me, He would let me keep Julie and Gilliana. As if human beings can make bargains with God. I should have known better already; after all, by then I was thirty-five, but thirty-five was much younger in those days, if you know what I mean. In 1949, thirty-five was probably the same as twenty-two is today. Jules came home from the service and for three and a half years I lived in a dream world because I thought we were having a life. And then I went to the bank to take out the money to buy the lamps.

There were two of them, one for either side of the sofa. They were in Lambert's Furniture Store, on the second floor. Fine white creamy porcelain bases with hand-painted green ivy leaves twisting around. A thin dull gold rim on the bottom of the bases and green felt underneath so they wouldn't scratch your tables. Ivory silk shades and dull gold finials in a teardrop shape that you screw on up at the top to hold on the shades. I didn't know those things were called finials, but the salesman, Mr. Kinney, explained that to me the third time I was there. I'd been watching the lamps since January, the first time Jules and I saw them in the store. It was pouring outside and freezing cold and the rain was about to turn to snow.

"Jule, honey, maybe we should go home before it gets too awful outside." I was running my hand across a silky mahogany tabletop. He didn't answer me and I looked up. "Julie? Whatcha think?"

"Hey, honey, look at these," he said, stooping over to turn on one of the lamps.

They had them plugged in like it was a real living room and not Lambert's Furniture Store. Like you could sit down and live there and never go home. Plugged in and sitting on two end tables on either side of a three-pillowed blue-and-green brocaded couch.

"They're from England," he said, smiling. "Aren't they beautiful?"

They were beautiful. They were the most beautiful lamps I had ever seen.

And I'd been watching them ever since, waiting for them to go on sale. And now it was Memorial Day and the lamps had been marked down at last. $39.50 apiece. That was a lot of money then, $39.50. For the two of them, with tax, it was nearly a hundred dollars and that was more than Jule and I had ever spent on anything. Most of the furniture we had then was leftovers, discarded pieces from other people in the family. But Jule was beginning to make a pretty good living. We even had a car; it was just an old Packard with tape on the windows and newspapers on the floorboards, but it was ours. We called her the "Cockameena Special"; Jules said the car was definitely a girl, he said you could tell when you drove her, the way she handled on the road. Not as good as me, he said, but still a girl.

I wanted those lamps for him. I wanted them for me. I wanted to surprise him. I wanted to see his face when he walked in one night and they were sitting on the end tables by our couch, lit up like in Lambert's Furniture Store.

I'd been saving. More than saving, I'd been scrimping and saving, dribs and drabs, pennies and nickels from the food budget. I cut out coupons and scoured the papers, I would walk blocks and blocks to get something on sale, I even went on the streetcar once with the baby because a grocery store way far out of our neighborhood had Gerber's on sale. I didn't buy stockings, I put nail polish on the start of every run. I saved the tiny scraps of soap and pushed them together to make a bar. I searched Jule's pockets and under the pillows on the couch. I saved every cent I could get my hands on and hid it in a little coin purse under the towels until I'd have enough to take to the bank. Little by little I did it and now they were on sale. I had $361.17 in that savings account.

I wanted to bide my time, I wanted to see if they'd mark them down some more, but then Mr. Kinney told me about the lady who'd been looking at them and how she'd come back twice. About how she had a very expensive blue silk suit on with shoes and a purse to match. About how she'd held the lamps quite lovingly and explained to him in minute detail how they would go so perfectly in her living room. About how she was going to tell her husband about them and would probably be back that afternoon.

Gilliana colored on deposit slips while I waited in line at the bank.

"Hello, Mrs. Ventimiglia, how are you today?"

"I'm just fine, Mr. Thurman, how are you?"

"Fine and dandy," he said, smiling at me. "The world is good."

"It certainly is," I said, handing him my withdrawal slip. "I need a hundred dollars, please."

"Of course, Mrs. Ventimiglia," he said, turning to go to the cabinets where they kept the files, "I'll be right back."

I was smiling; I could see Jule's face when he saw the lamps, how happy he would be. And I would make steak and peppers, his favorite, and buy a bottle of wine. I was smiling. I remember. I watched Gilliana make a stick figure with a red crayon, a person with a too big head.

"Hi, Mommy," she said, looking up when she felt me watching her.

"Hello, my baby," I said back.

"Well, now, we have a little problem here, Mrs. Ventimiglia."

He wasn't smiling, Mr. Thurman.

"We do? What kind of a problem?"

"Well, not anything earthshaking, just a little problem," he said, and he tried a weak smile but he couldn't quite do it, so he cleared his throat instead. "Ah, uh, it seems, that, uh, that account has been depleted."

"What?"

Gilliana pulled on my skirt and I looked down.

"What, baby?"

"I need green," she said, her hand out.

I handed her the whole box of Crayolas and then looked back at Mr. Thurman.

"What?" I said again.

"Depleted, Mrs. Ventimiglia, all the funds withdrawn."

"Withdrawn? How can that be? I didn't withdraw them."

"Well, no, I see that here, I definitely see that, you certainly didn't, did you."

We looked at each other.

"And so?"

"Excuse me?" he said.

"And so how could the account be depleted?"

"Look, Mommy," Gilliana said, holding out the deposit slip. "You and me and Daddy. Mommy, look."

Three stick figures: Jule the biggest, and all in red, me middle-sized and turquoise, and Gilliana in the middle, multicolored, with a big purple smile in the middle of her green circle face.

"It's beautiful, sweetheart."

"Can we go now?"

"In one minute, just give Mommy one more minute, okay, my sweetheart?"

I noticed my hand was shaking as I held on to the Crayola drawing on the deposit slip. I looked at Mr. Thurman.

He blinked and tried his smile again.

"I don't understand, Mr. Thurman."

"Your husband, Mrs. Ventimiglia. Your husband depleted the funds."

"My husband," I said, standing stock-still.

"Yes, ma'am," he said, "you see here"—he turned the ledger around to show me—"right here . . . Julius Ventimiglia . . . You see?"

Julius Ventimiglia, it said. Julius Ventimiglia had withdrawn all of it, three hundred and sixty-one dollars and even the seventeen cents.

I stood there.

"Well, then," Mr. Thurman said, and tried his smile again.

I looked at him.

"Yes," I said and I stood there. I didn't know what to say. I had to go home.

"Are you all right, Mrs. Ventimiglia?"

"Of course, Mr. Thurman. I just . . ."

"You must have forgotten," he said bravely. "It happens all the time; husbands put in and wives take out, wives put in and husbands take out . . . hard to keep track . . . happens all the time . . . I've even told my wife, Margaret, you must keep track, dear . . . I tell her all the time . . ."

"Of course," I said. I reached down and picked up the baby. She put her arms around my neck.

"Can we go now, Mommy?"

"Goodbye, Mr. Thurman," I said.

"See you next week, Mrs. Ventimiglia," he said, and raised his hand to his forehead as if he was tipping his hat. He had given up trying to smile; by then he looked more like someone had just died.

It's a blur to me how I got home, but I do remember one thing—I was very frightened. I knew that I had lost more than two English lamps; somewhere along the way I was afraid I had lost much more. I had no idea then, of course, that I had lost it on the ponies. Ponies, hoops, and bookie joints—who could know about such things?

Clare

I cut this thing out of the paper once when I was at my grandparents'—not Mollie and Lew's house, but my other grandparents, my dad's parents, Marilyn and Kent's house back East. They live in Connecticut—Wilton, Connecticut, in this big white wooden clapboard rambling house set in the middle of this great lawn. I'm not kidding, it's like living in some National Park, you know? And they want you to think that it's very laid back but it's really very la-de-da-ish. I mean, they actually have a croquet set set up on the side lawn, and they actually refer to it as "The Side Lawn." You see what I mean?

Anyway, I was losing my mind there for two weeks one summer; three summers ago actually, when I was fourteen and supposed to be at this camp where I used to go, which is also in Connecticut, but not near their house, but eleven of us got kicked out of camp that summer for smoking marijuana, so I was sent to Marilyn and Kent's house before I was sent home. I never figured out if that was supposed to be the punishment or what. I mean, to sit around and watch a bunch of old people in powder-blue golf pants drinking cocktails and smiling with too much lipstick on and playing croquet and trying to talk to you about your life when they don't have a clue who you are—that's punishment to me. It's not like I don't like Marilyn and Kent, but they're not like real grandparents, you know? I mean, there's no cookie-baking going on there except by Cynthia, the cook, and served by Beverly, the maid. I'm sure Marilyn has never even been in the kitchen except when it was somebody's day off and she was hard-pressed to find vermouth. When you go there it's not like going to Mollie and Lew's house—it's more like stepping into the pages of *The Great Gatsby* or something. My mother says when she goes there it's like being in an Arrow shirt commercial. I mean, I don't even call them Grandma and Grampa, I've called them Marilyn and Kent since I could talk.

Anyway, you should have heard the discussion Kent had with me about smoking pot; you would have died, it was so hysterical. I mean, what does this elegant seventy-eight-year-old *very* straight man know about smoking pot? He's probably never even seen pot; he's probably never even seen anything, he's so super-straight. For all I know he wears his golf pants to bed at night and she wears her lipstick.

"That marijuana can lead to terrible things, little lady, things you might not be able to stop."

Really, can you have a serious discussion about smoking pot with a man who calls you "little lady"? Give me a break. Everything he knows about smoking dope he probably learned from watching old black-and-white movies about jazz musicians way back in the fifties. And he's having this discussion with me while he's drinking a martini, right? Probably his third martini before dinner. I mean, let's talk about using substances to get away from our regular lives, okay? Thank you very much. Anyway, as my Grandma Mollie always says, Kent and Marilyn are fine people, but if you have to have a discussion with them you should be sure to do it before the cocktail hour, because after that they're sloshed. That's her word—"sloshed." Great word, isn't it? I love it. Sloshed.

Anyway, I was going mad there with boredom one afternoon; everyone had gone into town to buy fresh scones or something and I was sitting on their screened-in porch listening to the bees buzz and I picked up this little local newspaper and I was browsing through, catching up on the "Big News" in Wilton, Connecticut, when this thing caught my eye and it really got to me, so I cut it out. I keep it in a manila file folder that I hide special things in under the rug under my bed. I'm not about to let my mother find it; that's all I need is to hear my personal things come out of asshole Andy's mouth on HBO one night.

It's an advertisement or whatever but from the death page, the obituaries, right? I know, The Obituary Page. What a word that is. I actually looked it up; it's medieval Latin. Did you know that? Can't you see some guy in a toga and sandals saying, "Well, let's call it an obituary, Emperor. I thought that word up earlier this morning while I was watching the lions eat the Christians."

Anyway, listen to this—this is what it says:

MAUSOLEUM FOR TWO
MOUNTAIN VIEW I
ROSE HILL MEMORIAL PARK
TOWN OF PUTNAM VALLEY
$8,700 914-555-6644

Amazing, huh? Mausoleum for Two. That's what got me. I mean, it's so tragic, isn't it? How would somebody know if they bought it that they would both die at the same time? Well, of course, they wouldn't—I mean, you have to buy them that way and then one person dies and gets buried there, and then when the other person dies they get buried there too. But what about the years in between, and what if the one who's left marries somebody else?

Like, what if the guy dies first and everybody thinks they really loved each other but secretly she hated him because he was a real dick to her and then one day she marries somebody else she really loves and then later she dies—so where do they put her? With the first guy? Or does the second guy buy another mausoleum for two and he buries her there, and then when he dies, he gets to be buried with her and they're together? But if that's what happens, then what happens to the first guy—he's just left all alone waiting—right? I mean, not that he didn't deserve it, but it still gets to me. I mean, it's the thought of it, you know. I envision all these rolling green hills across America covered with mausoleums for two that are only filled with one person on one side. It's so, I don't know . . . so uneven to me, so lopsided and pathetic, so sad.

I mean, look at my grandma and grampa. Not Marilyn and Kent 'cause they've only been married to each other so they wouldn't have this problem; I'm talking about Mollie and Lew, because Mollie was married three times and Lew was married two times, so what would happen there? I mean, luckily, I guess it will all work out, because her first husband was just this young thing; I don't mean him, I mean the marriage—over really fast and no kids or anything, but her second husband was my real grampa, my mother's father. Jules Ventimiglia, or, as my mother refers to him,

"Black Bart." Not that I ever met him or anything, but from what I hear he was not exactly what you would call a gentleman, you know, but they were married for a long time and they did have my mom and all. So what if they bought a mausoleum for two and he's buried in St. Louis somewhere waiting there for her? I mean, not that she's dead yet to join him, God forbid, but you know . . . and Lew was married to this lady named Bess before he was married to my grandma—she had cancer and died years ago and, from what I hear, she was really a wonderful person and she's buried somewhere too, right? That's what got me thinking about all this. I mean, here Mollie is so sick and it doesn't look good for her and I got to thinking about Lew's first wife and where was she buried and what if she's lying in Kansas City somewhere waiting for Lew? I mean, where's he's gonna put Mollie? With Bess? You see what I mean?

It's like when you go to the cemetery and you see a headstone and there's a name on one side with the date of birth and the date of death and then on the other side there's the other one's name and the date of birth is there and then a dash and then a blank because the person is still alive. They're actually waiting to put in the date of death. I mean, doesn't that get to you?

I guess what's really getting to me is the commitment thing. I mean, how do people make a commitment like that? How do they know that things will last? They don't. Nothing lasts. You already know that going in. You love somebody and then it's over—it's not like you don't know that. Look at me—I love Scott. I do. But what if I wake up when I'm thirty-four and I look at him and I don't. What if he has an affair with someone? What if he leaves me? What if I look at him one day and he doesn't turn me on? You know, my mother listens to country music and I always tease her about it, how sappy it is and all, but there's this one song that I've heard, like sometimes when I'm stuck in her car with her going somewhere and she says, Let me just hear this song, Clare, and what can I do, it's her car. Anyway, there's this particular song, I mean, I know it's really stupid but I actually wrote down the words because they got to me. I have them in the manila file folder too. Listen to this.

Do you still get a thrill when you see me comin' up the hill? Do ya?
Do you whisper my name just to bring a little comfort to ya?
Do you still like the feel of my body lyin' next to yours?
Well, I guess what I'm askin' is, do you still love me?

Mollie

Jules Ventimiglia retied the red ribbon in his daughter's hair.

"There you go, Babe, you're all fixed."

She turned and faced him. "Can we go to the ponies now, Daddy?"

Fat Solly Rubinek laughed. "Your kid likes the ponies, huh, Jules? That's some kid you got there."

"Not those kinda ponies, Solly, the ponies at Kiddieland, she means."

"Oh, yeah . . . I forgot about them ponies . . . Sure, the ponies at Kiddieland, I know."

Gilliana slid off Jule's lap. She held her doll in her arms and looked up at the fat man on the ladder writing numbers on the blackboard. "They go in a circle."

"Yeah," he laughed again, "just like our ponies, kid."

"But you always get to go right by your daddy again, they don't go anywhere but around."

"Well, that's good," Solly said.

"Oh, yes," Gilliana went on, "I can't get lost that way and I can see Daddy the whole time." She smiled at Jules and he winked at her.

"I used to take my kid to Kiddieland," Fat Solly said. There was a change in his voice that made Jules look up.

"You did?" Gilliana said, smiling at the fat man.

"Yeah, sure I did, Saturdays I used to take him sometimes when Cahokia was closed. Sure."

"But you don't anymore?"

"Oh, well, he's big now, kid. He kinda outgrew it, you know."

"Oh. I still like it, but I'm only four."

Fat Solly laughed. "Well, you're a pretty hot number for four, kid, let me tell you. No disrespect, Jules."

"Where's your little boy now?"

"He's all grown up, Gilly," Jules said, interrupting, "he . . ."

"It's okay, Jule," Solly said, "I'll tell her. He got sent up, kid, he's in Joliet for six more years, six come October, that is. Unless he gets time off for good behavior, but knowing my kid, that won't be the case."

Gilliana looked at the big man on the ladder; she studied his face. "Is that a bad place, Joliet?"

Fat Solly laughed. "Well, I don't think it's no picnic . . ."

Morris Lapinsky flew in from the back room with a bunch of papers flapping in his hand. His face was red and sweaty. "What the hell's goin' on, Sol, you're behind on Saratoga and the Phillies are down by two. What the hell's goin' on here?"

Fat Solly turned back to the blackboard and began writing. "Shit, I'm sorry, Moish. I—"

Jules stood up from where he was sitting and took Gilliana's hand. "It's my fault, Moish, we got to talking . . . sorry."

"I'm runnin' a business here, Jules."

"I know. Sorry."

Morris looked at Gilliana. "That's a nice ribbon you got in your hair today, *Miss* Ventimiglia."

Gilliana giggled. "Thank you, Mr. Lapinsky."

"And how's Miss Sweetie Pie doin' today?"

Gilliana looked at her doll, "Oh, she's better, thank you, she still has a runny nose but no temperature." She held her little hand on the doll's bisque forehead and looked up at Morris. "See?" she said. "Cool as a cuke."

"Is that so?" Morris said. He gave Jules a grin.

Jules smiled at his daughter; she sounded just like Mollie when she checked Gilliana's head for a fever.

"So," Morris said, looking at Gilliana intently, "you ready for your Clark Bar?"

"Yes, sir."

"Well, go get it, then."

"You mean, I get to go behind the counter *all by myself?"*

"Yes, ma'am," Morris said, "I think you should get to today since you got that nice ribbon in your hair and all."

"Thank you, Mr. Lapinsky." She dropped Jule's hand. "I'm gonna get my Clark Bar, Daddy, okay? Hold Sweetie Pie for me. Then can we go?"

"Sure, Babe."

"See ya next Saturday, *Miss* Ventimiglia," Morris said.

Gilliana smiled at Mr. Lapinsky, handed Jule her bisque doll with the soft cottony red hair, and ran from the back room of the bookie joint that fronted as a candy store on DeBoliver Boulevard. Jules gave Morris Lapinsky the fifty dollars he owed him from the third at Belmont, said goodbye to Fat Solly, and took his daughter to Kiddieland.

I didn't know about it for a long time and when I found out, it wasn't as if Gilliana told me, it came out in another way. We finally got a television set. It was a big deal to have a television set then and we had waited a long time to afford one, and then Jules walked in one night with a 12-inch Dumont that was up on wheels that you could move around the living room. I practically fell on the floor, it was such a surprise.

Every Friday night on the television in those days, the fights were on, and so every Friday night Sophia and Alfonzo came to our house to watch the fights. They weren't really fights, they were boxing matches, but Alfonzo called them the fights and he loved them. Sometimes they came over for supper beforehand, but mostly they came after supper for coffee and cake. Alfonzo and Jules would watch the fights while Sophia and I would watch them watch, all of us sitting around the television set.

Gilliana bounced back and forth from Jule's lap to her grandpa's lap, to me and her grandma, out to get her doll, back with something else—in and out—back and forth—she played on the floor right next to us, she ate cannoli on a doily from the bakery box, and Sophia gave her coffee with a lot of milk and sugar in a flowered china cup, like she was a "big lady," she said. She got to stay up late with four grown-ups who loved her inside-out. Gilliana loved Friday nights and she loved the fights, everything about it.

"To look sharp," she sang with her grampa, "every time you shave . . . to feel sharp, la da dee da dah . . ."

I don't remember them but she knew all the words, the baby, and Alfonzo sang right along with her in his thick Italian accent, both of them speaking simultaneously with the announcer as he said, "The Gillette

Cavalcade of Sports brings you boxing live from Madison Square Garden in New York City."

"Che vuoi? Pantaloncini bianchi o neri, topina mia?"

"Don't call me a mouse, Grampa. I'm not a mouse."

"Okay, okay, I don' call you no mouse . . . so, what do you want, joyamia, *bianchi o neri*? Eh?"

That was how they picked who they would root for, the color of the men's boxing trunks, the black ones or the white ones, Gilliana and her grampa would pick every Friday night. It was years later that it dawned on me that the satin trunks in person were probably in colors: red ones, blue ones with yellow stripes, all kinds, but it was a black-and-white television in those days and so the trunks were either black or white and that's how they made their decision, the *bianchi* or the *neri,* they carried on every Friday night.

The night I found out was actually a lovely night. Sophia had come over in the late afternoon with Alfonzo and he took a nap on the couch while we made her special shrimp and broccoli and then polenta with butter and cheese and then a cake, a wonderful yellow cake that had hot milk in the recipe. Alfonzo got up and he and Sophia had a little glass of wine and Jules came home and he had a V.O. and water and I had a whiskey sour that Jules made me in a shaker and we ate supper and it was delicious and then Sophia and I did the dishes. We were going to have the cake with coffee while we watched the fights.

"Hello, my love," he came up behind me and put his arms around me while I had my hands in soapy water up to my elbows in the sink. He kissed the back of my neck and nuzzled my ear. In front of his mother.

"Jules . . ."

Sophia laughed and said something in Italian that I didn't get, and then they both laughed.

"What?" I said, laughing too. "What did she say? What did you say, Sophia? Tell me."

"No, it's too dirty," Jules said, laughing, "my mother has a dirty mouth today."

"What dirty? I don' say nothing dirty, Julius, you jes' make it dirty in your head. You jes' like you father."

"What did you say, Sophia?"

"I tell you later," she said to me, and smiled and lowered her eyes. She put down the dishtowel she was holding and left the kitchen.

Jules turned me around to him and kissed me. My hands were all sudsy and I held them out, away from his shirt.

"What did she say, honey?"

"I'll tell you later," he said in my ear. "I'll *show* you later."

"Hey . . ."

"Come on, honey, the fights are gonna start, Pop wants you to come in."

"What does he care? He knows I don't watch them, I don't like to see men punching each other like that, you know that."

"I know that but come in anyway. Come on." He kissed me again and held me close to him, his body pressing against mine. I held on to him; I couldn't help it, I put my wet soapy hands on his back and held him tight. We'd been married then for eight years and I still felt the way I did right from the start, maybe even more so. I always felt that way about Jule, I wanted him and that was that.

They picked the white trunks that night. The man was black but his trunks were white. Of course, in those days, nobody said a "black man," you still said "colored" back then. They picked the colored man with the white trunks and in the fourth round he hit the white man below his belt. I wasn't paying much attention but Alfonzo said that this was a very bad thing. The referee reprimanded the man, and his manager came into the ring and the other man's manager came in and there was a heated discussion, and I guess the colored man said he wouldn't do it anymore and they went back to their corners and rang the bell and the fight began again.

I cut the cake into squares and put a square on each of the flowered china plates. Gilliana was on Alfonzo's lap and Alfonzo was yelling at the television for the colored man to do a good job now. I spooned the cream we had whipped with marsala wine on top of each square of cake except the square for the baby; I put plain cream on hers.

And then the colored man hit the white man again, but this time he hit him in his kidneys, something Jules called a rabbit punch, and that was a very, very bad thing.

Alfonzo stood up. "Summova bitch!" he was yelling. He was very upset and excited, and Sophia told him in Italian to calm down. Gilliana was watching her grandfather. The white man's manager and the other men who stood in his corner with him jumped into the ring and the colored man's people jumped into the ring and the referee was in the middle of it and they were all yelling at each other, and then somebody must have said the wrong thing to somebody because out of nowhere the colored man hit the white man hard in the face, he punched him very hard right between his eyes at the top of his nose and the white man fell over like he was dead—even I stood up, it was so awful—and then the white man's manager jumped on top of the colored man hitting him and then, as they say, all hell broke loose.

Everybody was punching everybody and other men were trying to get the white man out of the ring on a stretcher and Alfonzo was yelling in Italian at the colored man that he was a no-good so-and-so and worse, and Jules was yelling in Italian at his father to take it easy, and Sophia was yelling in Italian at both of them to stop it, and the baby said loud and clear in English, "He better not do that, that bad man, or they'll send him up to Joliet like they did Mr. Solly's little boy. Right, Daddy?"

"What, sweetie?" I said. I had the bowl of whipped cream in the crook of my arm; it was cold up against my skin.

"Joliet, Mommy, that's where they send bad boys, they send them *up* to Joliet."

She said it in the proper vernacular, my four-year-old daughter. She said it perfectly because she knew how to say it perfectly because every Saturday morning she went with her father to the bookie joint.

"What do you mean—the money's gone?"

"I just got in a little over my head."

"What does that mean?"

"Just what I said, I got in a little too deep."

"How much do you owe them?"

"Not so much, Babe."

"Oh, God, Jule . . ."

"No, please, don't do that . . . it's not so bad, really, honey, I don't owe them that much."

"What is that much?"

"What difference does it make?"

What difference and how much, and how much this time, and why is there another "this time," and when will you stop it: this time, next time, never. How long would it take me to realize the answer was never? The answer would always be never, I just didn't know.

* * *

"You promised."

"I promise now, Mol, please, I won't do it again."

"You promised last time."

"I love you, Babe, please don't cry."

"You promised, you said it was over."

"I'm sorry. I love you, Mollie, I'm trying. God, I'm trying."

He was trying. He was trying and I was crying and the years went by. On and on since the lamps in Lambert's Furniture Store, the beautiful white porcelain lamps with the hand-painted green ivy leaves. Lies and promises. On and on and over again. A basketball game in Boston, a football game in Chicago, the Rose Bowl, the playoffs, a racetrack somewhere back East called "the big A," which I found out later was in New York and called Aqueduct. Promise and lies. The money I'd saved to buy new dishes, the money I'd saved to buy a new carpet for the living room, or even a new suit for him. Ponies, hoops, and ballgames—as the years went by I learned. It didn't matter what it was, the only thing important was the odds and the bet. Only, this time it was different.

"How could you take her there?"

"It's not such a bad place."

"Oh, Jule, please don't say that, you know it's a bad place."

"I know . . . but . . . I mean, there's nothing going on there, just guys playing cards and you know, they track the odds . . ."

"I don't want to hear, don't tell me . . ."

"Mol, please, I love you."

"She's only four years old."

"They're nice to her there, the guys, they're crazy about her . . . they . . ."

"Who's crazy about her? Hoodlums? That's where you take your daughter on Saturdays? To hang out with gangsters . . . to know about sending people *up* to prison?—oh, my God . . ."

"Please, Mollie, don't cry like that—please, honey, I love you so much, please don't."

I made myself believe that he would change this time. This time would be different because of the baby, because he'd taken the baby there and he felt so bad about it, so embarrassed and ashamed that he would change. That Jules would give up gambling, that Jules *could* give up gambling, I made myself believe it could happen this time.

And that's not all. I not only made myself believe it but I did something else that I never told a soul. I went to the Catholic church and had a talk with Mary. I did. I went to St. Ambrose on Wilson Avenue and had a talk with her and lit her a candle. Can you imagine? Me, a nice Jewish girl. My father would have had a heart attack and a stroke to boot.

And not once, I went there lots of times. At first I was afraid the priests would notice me, that somebody would say something or tell someone, but nobody did anything; they left me alone. Somehow it made sense to me that I should go there, that she would understand, Mary, that she was a mother too; after all, the holiest of all mothers, no matter what you believed—none of the mothers in the Old Testament could hold a candle to Mary—not even Sarah, who bore Abraham's son Isaac when she was already ninety, or Miriam, who was the sister of Moses, or Rebecca or Leah or Rachel or even Deborah, who they called the mother of Israel—none of them seemed right, and besides, it was Jule's faith and Jule's church.

And then, after the first time I went, when I really stopped to think about what I'd done, it made perfect sense to me. After all, Mary was Jewish. Mary was Jewish and she was a mother and a wife like I was; she would understand more than anybody. So Mary was the one I prayed to, to save Jules from the gambling. Mary would fix it, I decided.

So? What can I tell you? About that, I was wrong.

Gilliana

It's six-thirty. I feel like it's the middle of the night and it's only six-thirty in the evening.

I'm washing the dishes. Mollie and Lew are watching television. I take that back—Lew is watching television. Mollie is watching some show of her own. We ate already, even though it was ridiculously early. He said he was hungry.

Mollie did eat most of her dinner, I'll say that for her, which was very difficult for all three of us since she doesn't really know what to do with the food. How to get it in her mouth is what I'm really saying, how to chew it is what I'm saying, *how to eat* is what I mean. I drank most of my dinner; this is only the fourth time I have seen this eating disaster and I'm not quite used to it yet.

I think Lew and I are in as muddled a limbo state as Mollie is, but I feel that Lew's waiting for me to make the first move. Maybe because he's been carrying this secret, keeping her slow descent such a secret from me, and now that I know, now that it's out of the bag, it's as if he's off the hook; he can let me bear the burden for a while. I don't mind, I love Lew.

Of course I love Lew. I am so tired I feel I could ooze down from the chair, ooze down and melt into a puddle . . . Well, of course, one can melt here, it's Kansas, after all. I'm melting, I'm melting . . . I wonder if you need a house to fall on you to melt . . . no, wait a minute, it was water, wasn't it? That's what killed the main witch, not the house falling on her; Dorothy doused her with a bucket of water. Damn, where is that Dorothy when you need her? Probably with Ed Sullivan and Sonja Henie, with all my luck.

Oh, look at this, I'm crying in the dishwater. Laughing and crying. Well, what's the difference, Gillian?

I have no idea what to do. Inside my head are floating questions. I can actually see them—words with question marks at the end typed out in my brain like shreds of ticker tape or slips of fortune-cookie paper drifting around.

Can he take care of her alone? No. That one I know the answer to.

Can I stay here and help him? No. I can stay a little while, but not indefinitely. I can't move back to Kansas City and live with Mollie and Lew; I'm a grown-up, I have a life, I have a daughter and a husband to take care of . . . uh-oh, a husband . . . do I have a husband?

Wait a minute . . . don't do that now, Gillian . . .

Damn, where was I? Help . . .

Help . . . that's right . . . that's where I was . . . good, Gillian . . . can we afford live-in help? I don't know. Lew can't, that's for damn sure. What do they have? Social Security and a couple of IRAs?—I don't even know what they have.

Why don't I know? Am I a bad daughter that I don't know? Don't change the subject, Gillian. Stick with the priority questions we have going here, don't fuck around.

Can we afford it? I don't know.

I have to call Christopher, don't I?

Oh, boy. I have to call Christopher . . .

Yes indeedy, oh yes, I do . . .

I find myself staring at Joe and Dorothy LaPaglia's kitchen window across the way from my mother's kitchen window, but their café curtains are drawn tight. What are they doing in there at six-thirty in the evening with their shades pulled so close and no sign of light? They're the same age as Lew and Mollie—have they already gone to bed? What time do they eat their supper?—three-thirty in the afternoon?

I was trying to remember what happened to those postcards, the ones Christopher sent me from Japan when I was pregnant; I was trying to remember when I stopped carrying them in my purse. Did they just get too old? Turn yellow like a page from a leftover newspaper? But postcards don't do that, do they? Maybe the edges frayed, maybe I put them away in a drawer somewhere to preserve them because the edges got frayed. What drawer? Where?

Or did I somehow just have the gall to lose them when I changed purses from summer to fall? How can something be so important and then it's not? Why can't I remember what happened to the damn postcards?

I fold the dishtowel into squares and lay it on the dish drainer.

What I do remember was a time when Christopher and I were first married and I got this awful food poisoning from a rotten clam, so awful that I had a fever of a hundred and two and was hallucinating in between bouts of losing everything from inside me from every place where it could come out and shaking with cold or sweating with fever, and during all of it Christopher read to me, sat quietly by the side of my bed and held my hand and read aloud from *The Chronicles of Narnia: The Lion, the Witch and the Wardrobe,* and the white lion and the snow queen came alive in my room, walked right out of my closet as if they had been in there all the time. And if it wasn't a white lion and a snow queen, don't tell me because that's how I remember it and I don't want to know. The snow queen wore red lipstick and looked very much as if she was related to the evil stepmother who sends the woodsman to kill Snow White, I think maybe even her sister, and the lion had huge paws and was so white he was sparkling, and this was all taking place in my bedroom, that's how real it was, that's how magical and beautiful he made it, Christopher . . . snow piled up high against the bed, drifts of snow and icicles hanging around off the chair and the curtains and even off Christopher, little snowflakes on his eyelashes and his hair, and me squinting at the shadowy closet door through my fever-eyes while he read . . . but that's stuff that only happens when people are sick, right? Married people don't sit around reading to each other from children's books after they're married a while . . . do they?

I look at the dishtowel over the drainboard and move it to the left side of the sink and put it where my mother does. Did.

Oh, God. My mother. I have to get help for my mother, that's where I was . . .

And where do I call to get this fantastic help? A service? And where do I look in the phone book? Under the "People Who Come to Help You When Your Mother Has Lost Her Way" section?

And how will I know if it's any good? How will I know that whoever the help is who comes to take care of my mother will like her? How will they see through her little body and know there's an extraordinary woman locked in there? How will I know that who I pick won't let her drown in the bathtub or choke on a chicken bone?

I sit down in a kitchen chair and take a sip of vodka. This whole thing makes me want to sleep.

I look at the clock. Ten minutes to seven. In Los Angeles, it's only ten minutes to five. I have two hours to wait until I can call Christopher if I want to talk to him when he's at home. Two hours . . .

And then I can say, hey, Christopher, before you leave me, you got a few minutes?—I have a few things here I need to discuss. Do you have any ideas about what I should do with Mollie? And . . .

Well, I'll be goddamned . . . what was the other one? . . . Oh, right, I know—how the hell could you be leaving me now, you jerk, when my mother is the way she is?

I stand up and walk back to the window.

I can't think about this now. I can't. Don't think about what's happening with Christopher, Gillian, keep your priorities where they belong. Mollie. Mollie is your number one priority at this particular time.

Maybe I should take a nap . . . No, that's ridiculous, I hate naps . . . I didn't even nap when I was pregnant . . .

And anyway, Christopher had no way of knowing that the week he picked to leave me would be the same week Mollie took a dive . . . poor old Christopher, what shitty timing, what rotten luck. Of course, if he wouldn't have said he was leaving I wouldn't have come home, and if I wouldn't have come home I wouldn't have known that Mollie was on her way to becoming a mere shadow of her former self. Oh, that's good, Gillian, a mere shadow . . .

Oh, please.

I take a sip of the vodka and look out the window at my mother's side yard.

"The land, Scarlett, you've always got the land."

I smile at the window. If I could just go back to Tara, maybe I'd know what to do . . .

I turn, walk to the freezer, take out the vodka, and freshen my drink.

THURSDAY

Gilliana

I left a message for Christopher but he didn't call me back. Okay, that's cheating. The truth is I left a message for Christopher saying things were not good but that he shouldn't call me back because I was going to sleep and I would call him tomorrow, meaning today. So . . .

The doctor's office gave me a list. That's how you find help, you don't even have to walk through the yellow pages, they do it for you. No muss, no fuss, no nothin', as Mollie would say.

We had a little problem about going to sleep last night. It seems Mollie doesn't always want to go to sleep when it's bedtime because Mollie doesn't know it's bedtime because Mollie has no clock. That's what Lew called it.

"What does she know what time it is? In her head there's no clock."

That's what he said to me when we couldn't get her to lie down.

And then this morning Dorothy LaPaglia came over from next door when we were eating breakfast and she had some names and numbers. Let me rephrase that—I was having coffee and aspirins, Lew was eating breakfast, his regular breakfast that he has every day. I even set the table last night so it would be ready for him this morning the way my mother did: the cornflakes bowl, the banana . . . I thought that might make him feel better.

So he cried when he saw the table. Not cried, he sobbed. God knows

I didn't mean for him to cry, that certainly wasn't my plan when I did it, but he fell apart when he saw it all laid out for him on the table and so, of course, I fell apart too, and Mollie just sat there watching us as if she had no idea . . . and she didn't, did she? . . . That's when Dorothy came over with a coffee cake. Not just a coffee cake, one that she had just baked and taken out of the oven, hot and smelling of honey and butter cinnamon and pecans. Maybe that's why their lights go out so early—they eat dinner at three-thirty so they can go to bed at six-thirty so they can get up at four-thirty so she can bake cakes. I wonder what Joe does at the crack of dawn? Work on his car?

Anyway, she also gave me information. A list of people, people who know people who have had problems like this, friends of hers and Joe's who had to get help; she gave me some names and numbers. She must have had the list waiting for a long time; it was wrinkled when she took it out of her housedress pocket. God bless Dorothy, she came over in a housedress, a down jacket, and snow boots with the hot cake in her hands. Of which I ate three pieces immediately without stopping to chew. When Lew left the room, she told me she had wanted to call me plenty of times to tell me about Mollie and how she was getting worse and worse but Lew said no. He said, "Let's wait and see." God knows what he thought was going to happen—Mollie was going to start getting better? God knows.

A couple of times Dorothy lapsed into Italian; when she was crying about my mother, about how she's gotten worse and worse so fast, when she was telling me and she got upset, that's when the Italian came out. Of course, I didn't understand her—oh, maybe a little bit, maybe a word here and there . . . the little I remember from my grandparents, Black Bart's mother and father, Sophia and Alfonzo, and from Black Bart himself, but that's all from years ago. Sophia and Alfonzo died the year Mollie married Lew and we moved to Kansas City; he had a heart attack and she died two weeks after—from what, they said, they didn't know.

"Two heart attacks," my mother told me. "Take it from me; his heart exploded and hers broke because he was gone."

And Julius, my famous and ever-popular father, took a powder soon afterward from me and my life, so that was the end of my Italian lessons.

Except for the Italian I remember from Anthony.

Anthony, my sweet Anthony . . .

Anthony was my second love, that's if we were counting and the first was Tom Johnson . . . but Anthony was really my first. Tom Johnson may have opened the door to possibilities, but Anthony turned on the lights.

He was Italian. That was enough for me. No, thank you!

And he was married, and I, of all people, certainly knew better than *that.* I was not about to get mixed up with another married man. No way, baby, absolutely not, I'm out of here, check please, *nyet.* I wasn't interested and I said no. No.

Emphatically.

No. No. No.

I said no in December of 1970 when I first met him. I was working for Harry Witzer then. I had lasted only three months in Pasadena working for a jerk of an advertising guy who wrote copy that could make you puke. Pasadena could also make you puke, or make *me* puke, to be more exact. I started job-hunting as soon as I could and I landed the job with Harry Witzer through an ad in the L.A. *Times,* which you would think would be next to impossible because it was such a great job.

Harry Witzer was a real character, a New York theatrical agent who had come out to L.A. and opened his own small but prestigious theatrical agency that only handled variety acts. That's what they called them then. Variety acts meant singers and dancers and comics mainly, or, as Harry explained it to me: "I don't handle no jugglers no more, kid, and no monkeys on a thing . . . you know what I mean?"

That was why he was considered prestigious.

I worked specifically for Harry. He had seven other agents in the office but he was the boss. I took his shorthand, typed his letters, and answered his phone. I also laughed a lot—Harry was one of the funniest people I ever knew. Let's put it this way—he played the harmonica in his office. I'm not kidding. Whenever he wasn't on the phone or doing paperwork, he was playing the harmonica. And he could have been famous playing the harmonica because people said he played as good as Toots Thielemans, who most people think is *the* jazz harmonica player, better than Johnny Puleo, who played on "The Ed Sullivan Show" then and was billed as "Johnny Puleo and His Harmonica Wildcats," better even than Little Walter or Larry Adler. Of course, Harry taught me about all those guys; I'd never heard of any harmonica players before. He said the reason he didn't want to work as a harmonica player instead of a talent agent was that he didn't want to go on the road.

"You can't believe the places you gotta stay in, kid; they got bars of soap there that aren't as big as a hangnail after you just had a manicure."

Harry had three really big-deal clients that took up all his time and the rest of the agents handled everybody else. His biggest client was Tony Ronzoni, who was the biggest-deal comic in the business then. That's who I said no to.

"It's just dinner."

"No, thank you."

"But it's Christmas Eve."

"I know that."

"We won't be alone, there'll be lots of people there, it's a big party."

"It's very sweet of you but I'd rather not."

"What are you going to do instead?"

"I don't know . . . decorate my tree . . . buy cookies to put on the mantel for Santa Claus . . ."

"Buy cookies? You're not gonna bake them?"

"Absolutely not. I don't bake."

He laughed. "Do you really have a mantel?"

"Of course I do."

"Are you really gonna have a tree?"

"Of course."

"With tinsel?"

"Of course with tinsel. What do you think?—I don't know how to decorate a tree?"

He laughed again, a rich, deep, low laugh. "Oh, come on, Gilliana, come with me to Barney Fields' party, it'll be boring without you. I promise you we'll have a good time."

"Why don't you bring your wife and kids out from New York? They'd probably enjoy it."

"Because she likes to be with her folks at Christmastime and I have to work every night except Christmas Eve and the little one has the flu."

"I'm very sorry to hear that, tell her I hope she gets better soon. How old is she again?"

"Two. Gilliana, I'm not trying to start anything with you, I promise. Look, it's your first Christmas here . . . I'm here and you're here and you don't know too many people here and I've got to go to this stinking party, so why won't you go with me? It's not such a big thing."

"It is to me. I don't go out with married men."

"It's not going out—it's a Christmas party, it's not a date. There'll be all kinds of people there, maybe you'll meet somebody. How 'bout that? Wait, I got it—you can take your own car. Then if you can't stand me you can leave."

Now I was laughing. "Really, Tony . . . please . . . I can't . . . I really can't."

"Really?"

"No . . . I'm sorry . . . but no."

I said no.

And I said no in July of 1971 when he was in L.A. doing the Hollywood Palace and Johnny Carson.

"What's the matter with you? You don't like Jack's at the Beach? Even Johnny Carson goes there."

"Well, that's the problem. I do like Jack's at the Beach, it's Johnny Carson I don't like. What would I do if he's there? I'd have to go hide in the bathroom."

"You know, you're really funny, Gilliana; you shouldn't be typing for Harry Witzer, you should be writing comedy."

"Oh, I get it, this is your new approach. You're going to try to get to me by offering me a job."

"It's not such a bad idea."

"I could never work for you, I couldn't take the job seriously. I still can't get over your name."

"There is nothing wrong with my name."

"There's nothing wrong with your name? Your name is hysterical. Tony Ronzoni is the silliest name I ever heard."

"It's a good Italian name. Just like yours."

"Ah, but my name is not funny and yours is. That's probably why you became a comic and not a singer, because your name is so funny. Everyone knows Italians are supposed to be the singers, not the comedians."

"You want to hear me sing? Come on, I'll make a deal with you—you come to Jack's at the Beach with me and I'll make a fool of myself at the piano bar and sing for you."

"No, thank you."

"You won't come even if I sing at the piano bar?"

"No."

"Even if I buy you a lobster?"

"Not even if you buy me two lobsters, Tony Ronzoni." I laughed. "See? Look what happens when I say your name—it makes me laugh."

He smiled at me. "What about two lobsters and some cracked crab?"

And I'm laughing again. "No . . . no way. No."

I said no.

And I said no again in the beginning of November of that same year, 1971, when he came out to L.A. from New York to sign some papers and have some meetings with Harry before he went to Vegas to headline for three weeks at the Sands. This time I said no over a cheeseburger. I was in the coffee shop in the lobby of our building having a fast lunch by myself at the counter when he walked in to get a coffee to go.

"Come sit in a booth with me."

"No."

"You won't sit in a booth with me? For godsakes, Gilliana, what could I do to you in a booth in front of everyone?"

"I don't know, you're probably notorious for doing evil things to women in red leather booths in coffee shops in the middle of the day."

"Well, then I'll have to stand right here next to you and drink my coffee standing up."

He stood there smiling at me. He took a sip of coffee out of the paper cup he was holding. He shifted his weight to the other foot.

Everybody was watching us. It was lunchtime and it was very crowded in the Bon-Aire during lunchtime and they were all watching us while he stood there next to me—the customers, the waitresses, the busboys, the two hostesses, and the cashier; even the three cooks flipping burgers and making tuna sandwiches behind the counter were grinning at me.

I picked up my cheeseburger and went to sit with him in a booth. Everybody's eyes in the coffee shop followed us as we crossed the room. Everybody knew who he was; there wasn't any getting around that. Everybody knew who Don Rickles was, they knew who Buddy Hackett was, and they certainly knew who Tony Ronzoni was because he was not only as famous as those other guys, he was the one who was handsome, devastatingly handsome, movie-star handsome, heart-stopping handsome. He looked like the Italian singer that opened for the comic, if you know what I mean. Black wavy hair and big brown eyes with long black lashes and broad shoulders and a lean body and the most incredible mouth—really, a kissable mouth—I can't explain it, really, it was just the shape of his lips that made you want to put your lips on his. As far as I could tell, he was nearly perfect—the only two things I could see that kept him from absolute perfection were: he wasn't tall, he was only about five feet ten, and he bit his fingernails down to the quick. Other than that he was perfect.

"So, can I have a French fry?"

"Okay."

He took one of my French fries and dragged it through the pile of ketchup I had on my plate. I didn't watch him eat it; I was trying to finish as fast as I could and get out of there.

"So, do you have a boyfriend?"

I looked up. "What?"

"A boyfriend. Do you have a boyfriend yet? Has someone discovered how amazing you are in this shallow land of deep waste?"

"You don't like L.A.?"

He laughed. "You're changing the subject, miss."

"I know. Why don't you like L.A.?"

"Well, mainly because it's not New York."

"New York is great, huh?"

"Wait a minute, don't tell me . . . you mean you haven't been to New York?"

"No."

"My God, the child's deprived."

"I'm not a child."

"Okay, how old are you?"

"I'm twenty-five."

"You're a child, believe me."

"Okay, so how old are you, big shot?"

"Seventy-three."

"Come on . . ."

"No, it's true, I'm seventy-three, I just look like this 'cause I live a very clean life. I don't smoke and I don't lie and I'm a strict vegetarian."

"You are, huh?"

"Yep."

"I guess you don't want a bite of my cheeseburger then, huh?"

"I'd love a bite of your cheeseburger."

"You're not seventy-three and you're not a vegetarian."

"Okay. You caught me."

"And you do lie."

"No, Gilliana, that's the only part that's true. I never lie."

I didn't want to look at him so I took a bite of my burger, but it was very hard to chew and worse to swallow—there I was—me, the cheeseburger queen, who'd lost her appetite.

"So, where were we?" I said. "Wait a minute—that means you smoke, right?"

"No, I gave it up." He grinned at me. "Last Thursday."

I was laughing. "Wait a minute, I'm all confused . . . where were we?"

"I don't know, I lost my place too . . . besides, I really don't care what we talk about, Gilliana, I just wanted a chance to finally sit next to you and look in your eyes."

"Oh, Jesus," I said, laughing. "That's gotta be the worst line I have ever heard. Are you telling me you can't do better than that?"

"No, I just thought I'd get it over with fast so you'd realize I wasn't here to make a pass at you and you could relax and eat your lunch."

I looked at him. "Oh," I said. "So you're being serious?"

"I think so, but don't spread it around, it wouldn't be good for my reputation—I'm supposed to be funny, you know. That's why they pay me the big bucks."

"Pay me the big bucks"—that was the first time I'd heard that line. It was Tony who taught it to me. God. In 1971.

"So I guess I'll have to take you to New York."

I laughed. "Aha! Here's the big pass, I knew it was coming."

"This isn't a pass, this is serious. Everyone has to see New York. It's imperative, it's very important for one's . . ."

"One's what?"

"Education. It's imperative that one sees New York before one grows entirely up."

"That's very strange English."

"I can't help it, I'm Italian, you know that."

I laughed again. He was delightful, you had to give him that, he really was. Delightful and funny and handsome . . . and married, with an Italian Catholic wife and two Italian Catholic children.

I wiped my mouth with the napkin and pushed my chair back so fast I nearly knocked it over, grabbed the check, and stood up.

"You're leaving? I thought we were having a good time."

"We were, but I have to get back to work."

"It's only one-thirty, I thought you didn't have to be back till two."

"I don't but I'm leaving anyway."

"Why?"

"I don't know. I think I have to wash my hands or powder my nose or throw up or something."

"Am I making you nervous, Gilliana?"

"Yes, I have trouble eating a cheeseburger in front of a vegetarian. It might give you bad dreams and I wouldn't want to be responsible for that."

"I'm not a vegetarian," he said, smiling.

"I know," I said, smiling.

"Will you come to New York with me?"

"No."

"Will you have dinner with me tonight?"

"No."

He looked at the check in my hand. "Can I buy you your cheeseburger?"

"No."

"Will you still be nice to me when I have to call Harry Witzer to talk business on the telephone?"

"I'm always nice to you, Mr. Ronzoni."

"Yes, you are . . . you're very nice, Miss Ventimiglia, very, very nice."

He was looking at me right in my eyes. This look seemed to have a direct connection to my feet that were intent on getting out of there but had suddenly forgotten how to move.

I laughed to cover this momentary hysterical paralysis.

"So, bye," I said. "Have a good time in Vegas. I'm sure you'll be a smash hit like you always are. Standing room only and all that . . ."

"You want to come and see me?"

"No, thank you."

"I can get you a ringside table—no kidding, I have lots of pull."

I was laughing. "No."

"Even with absolutely no strings attached? I promise."

"I can't, Tony . . . really . . . no."

"No again, huh?"

"Yes."

"Yes?" he said, grinning at me and standing up. "Did you say yes?"

"Cut it out," I said, laughing. "No, I mean no."

No. I said no again. Even everybody in the Bon-Aire coffee shop heard me this time when I said no.

The ticket to New York arrived two weeks later while he was still playing Vegas. I don't know how he got my home address but somehow he got it; he must have coerced one of the other secretaries for it or wrung it out of Harry Witzer. Of course, Harry didn't see the big deal about me going out with him. Harry had been an agent for a hundred years, Harry had seen everything.

"What's the big deal, kid? He's a nice guy, Ronzoni."

"Thank you, Harry."

The ticket was first-class, round-trip: L.A.–New York–L.A. It was for the week between Christmas and New Year's, leaving for New York right after Christmas and returning to L.A. on New Year's Day.

"You've got to go," my roommate, Carole Rose, said, patiently tipping the vermouth bottle so that only a drop fell into her glass of gin. "We need a goddamn shaker, you know that?"

"What do you mean I've got to go?"

"I'm going to Geary's tomorrow and buy us a goddamn sterling-silver martini shaker."

"We don't have money for a sterling-silver martini shaker and I don't even drink gin."

"It doesn't matter, I'll charge it."

"What do you mean I've got to go?"

"You've got to go is what I mean. How many women do you know get sent a first-class, round-trip ticket, L.A.–New York–L.A., with a suite at the Plaza Hotel, no less, to go with it and you haven't even slept with the guy?"

"Carole, I haven't even had dinner with the guy."

"Eating, sleeping—who cares?"

"I care. Come on, Carole, help me out, be serious."

"I am being serious. Who could resist New York at Christmastime? The tree will be up in Rockefeller Center, you can watch the skaters and drink hot chocolate and walk up Fifth Avenue and look in all the windows, especially Lord & Taylor, they have all the moving things in Lord & Taylor's windows, dancing dolls and hammering elves, and at Saks the windows are elegant and the music is piped outside, Christmas carols right on the street . . . and you have to have drinks at the Oak Room Bar . . . and brunch at the Algonquin, corn-beef hash with an egg on top and a Bloody Mary, and you have to go to Bloomingdale's to buy lingerie and . . . take a hansom cab ride through Central Park with a fur blanket on your legs and look into his eyes . . . he's got great eyes, you gotta give him that . . . God I miss New York . . ."

"Carole, I'm not going."

"You're a moron."

"I don't care."

She took a sip of her martini and put her feet up on the coffee table. I was going to say something about taking her shoes off before she put her feet up, but it was actually her coffee table and we also had very strict rules about me being too neat in the part of the apartment we shared. My bedroom and bath looked as if *Good Housekeeping* had given them their seal of approval and Carole's bedroom and bath looked as if they were about to be condemned. Well, no, that's not really fair; they weren't dirty, her things were just kind of haphazardly tossed around—like after a tornado. The rest of the apartment was what she called neutral turf and we tried not to encumber each other's style. It was the only way we could be roommates, and so far it was going pretty well—we were going on seven months. The only time I really had difficulty controlling myself was when she was cooking; she had a penchant for making elaborate dinner parties and using every dish and every spoon and every pot and every bowl in the kitchen and leaving every cabinet door open while she was doing it. I walked through once while she was cooking and tried to nonchalantly close a few cabinet doors, and she nearly hit me with the Pyrex measuring cup she had in her hand.

"Cut it out, Gillian."

"I just didn't want you to hit your head on a cabinet door."

"You touch those cabinet doors and I'll deck you with this cup."

"Excuse me, sorry, I'm leaving."

"Go fluff some pillows or something. Go buy some paper towels."

I was always buying too many paper towels. For some reason, she thought this was hysterical.

Now she took another sip of her martini and looked at me. "So what else have you got going here?"

"What do you mean?"

"I mean, what else is in your life?"

"You know what's in my life . . . nothing . . . well, not exactly nothing if you call dating Alan Steiner something, but I don't."

"No, I don't either," she said.

"And then there's seeing Bill now and then."

"That's nothing, that's just getting laid."

"Carole."

"What? Come on, tell the truth . . . you and Bill aren't ever gonna be anything, are you?"

"No, I guess not."

"So, that's what I said." She laughed. "Of course, you do have the praying mantis. We wouldn't want to forget him."

I'd had a couple of dates with a lawyer who was really very unattractive, to say the least. "Don't call him a praying mantis. He can't help what he looks like and he's very nice and smart."

"Oh, good, thank you for reminding me . . . So let's see . . . what have we got here in your love life? There's Alan, the 'honey, why don't you make something and we can just stay home and watch TV' Steiner, and William, the 'hey, ya wanna fuck, baby, I luv ya but I gotta be going' Kazinsakis and, of course, the praying mantis, in case we need to know something smart. So, what's the big deal if you meet Tony Ronzoni in New York?"

"He's married, Carole Rose."

"Yes, I know that."

"The whole world knows that."

"What else?"

"Nothing. I don't want to get mixed up with another married man."

She put her glass down on the end table and lit a cigarette.

"Read me the letter again."

I picked up the piece of stationery that had come with the ticket. It had been folded into thirds in an envelope tucked inside the American Airlines folder. It was thick, cream, expensive stationery with a thin, black, bold "AR" at the top of the page. Carole Rose and I had already read it about a thousand times. She had already investigated the stationery and showed me that it had come from Tiffany's—if you held the paper up to the light, you could see the Tiffany watermark. Carole Rose knew all about those kinds of things. She was from New York, she was sophisticated, she knew what to serve at cocktail parties and what to wear, and when a certain big shot from a major television network—where Carole Rose also worked—would come out to Los Angeles once a month to meet with his underlings, a long black limousine would appear to carry her back and forth to his bungalow at the Beverly Hills Hotel.

I read:

Dear Gilliana,

This is a ticket to New York as you can plainly see. Think of it as educational, as we discussed. Or think of it as a Christmas present from your Great-Aunt Maude. If you don't have a Great-Aunt Maude think of it as a Christmas present from Santa Claus. Or a New Year's present from the Statue of Liberty. There are no strings attached. Hold up the ticket and look at it. See? No strings. God knows, I hope you're laughing, I'm trying desperately to be funny. Gilliana, it's just a ticket to New York. I want to give it to you. I don't come with it. Hold up the ticket and look at it. See? I'm not attached. I'm being serious here. I want you to see New York. You don't have to see it with me. I won't call you. My phone number at my office is Eldorado 5-6801. Call me if you want to. My secretary's name is Irene McCaffey and she'll find me for you if I'm not there. A limousine will pick you up and take you to the airport in L.A. and a limousine will pick you up at Kennedy and take you to the Plaza and the afternoon of New Year's Day a limousine will pick you up at the Plaza and take you back to Kennedy and a limousine will pick you up in L.A. and take you home. That's a lot of limousines, huh? I just don't want you to have to take cabs or anything.

In the meantime, I've given the concierge at the Plaza instructions that your every wish should be his command. His name is Mr. Jones. Very discreet, don't you think, as should be the name for a concierge. You will find him in the lobby behind an ornate gold-leaf desk with a carnation in his lapel. Red, I think. Unfortunately, he looks a little constipated but maybe that will have cleared up by the time you arrive.

Gilliana, you don't have to call me. I just want you to have a good time, I just want you to see New York. Okay? Okay.

Merry Christmas and Happy New Year
from the man whose name makes you
laugh . . .

Anthony

I folded the letter back into thirds and put it in the envelope. I put the envelope back in the American Airlines folder. I looked at Carole Rose. She looked at me.

She took a drag of her cigarette and blew the smoke out through her mouth and nose.

"Don't you even want to see if Mr. Jones still looks constipated?" she said, smiling. "It might even be better than the hansom cab ride around Central Park."

Somehow, this got to me. I don't know why, but it did. Anyway, as Carole Rose would say, "to make a long story short" I went.

It was a great setup.

I had brunch at the Algonquin and he didn't call me. I looked at all the Christmas windows and he didn't call me. I had drinks in the Oak Room Bar and he didn't call me. I wandered around Tiffany's and pretended I was Audrey Hepburn and he didn't call me. I watched the skaters in Rockefeller Center and drank the damn hot chocolate and he didn't call me. I walked my ass up and down Madison Avenue in the freezing cold and he didn't call me. I went to St. Patrick's Cathedral and the Metropolitan and the Museum of Modern Art and the Whitney and even the damn Frick, which most tourists didn't even know about, and he didn't call me.

It was the fourth day out of the seven when I called him around four-thirty in the afternoon. Miss McCaffey said, "Good afternoon, Tony Ronzoni's office," and I hung up. I grabbed my coat and ran out of the Plaza as if it was on fire.

I went to Bergdorf's to buy lingerie. I know Carole Rose had said to go to Bloomingdale's, but when I hit the street it was sleeting and nearly dark and Bergdorf's was only a half a block away.

I bought a nightgown. Black silk from Italy. It wasn't see-through or anything like that, it was just very slinky and cut on the bias and piss-elegant and demure, something out of a black-and-white forties movie, something Ingrid Bergman would have worn in a movie with Cary Grant loaded with intrigue and mystery. I didn't realize it was from Italy until the saleswoman told me, which, of course, made me laugh. And then I did something even I thought was strange—I had it gift-wrapped. I didn't even know why except that it was so exquisitely beautiful that it didn't seem right for it to get simply folded inside a skimpy piece of tissue paper and tossed into a shopping bag.

He was at the Fifth Avenue entrance to the Plaza Hotel in the back of a hansom cab. It was six o'clock and dark out; the sleet had turned to snow and I was walking fast when he called my name.

The horse was black and his name was Brian, the cabbie's name was Mike and he had a brogue, the blanket tucked around us was Black Watch plaid and just a little bit scratchy. The ride around the park lasted only twenty-five minutes, called on account of blowing snow.

The taxi driver was Mohammed, and as far as I could tell from his language, he had arrived from Jordan that very day; I don't know how he got a cabbie's license so fast. Nick was the maître d' at Frankie and Johnnie's, the bartender was George, and the waiter was Phil. The steak was medium rare, the wine was a velvet burgundy, and the creamed spinach had nutmeg on top. The snow was sticking as we walked uptown, I held on tightly to his arm. The waiter at the Russian Tea Room was Marty and he assured us that the stingers would be divine.

By the looks of things, everybody knew who Tony was, everywhere, except for Mohammed the taxi driver and Brian the horse.

His father had been in construction and his mother had stayed home to cook and clean; he was alive, she wasn't. He had two brothers, both in construction, both married with children, and both living in New Jersey. He was thirty-seven years old, he'd been married to what's-her-name fourteen years—she had been his first girl, he said. His son was eight and his daughter was only three.

I already knew he was sexy and handsome; now I found out about some of the rest of him—articulate, smart, very funny, affectionate, sweet, and kind. He said no one had ever given him a gift-wrapped black silk nightgown from Bergdorf Goodman's before. He also said he thought I looked much better in it than Ingrid Bergman would have looked; I knew it was a stretch but I went for it anyway.

That black silk nightgown from Italy remains one of my treasures locked away in my bureau drawers. If anything ever happens to me, Clare will find it. Maybe she will think I wore it for her father, but I never did, she would be wrong.

Mollie

So, you love a man. You really love him. And you believe in him. And you want him. You know what I mean—in the intimate way, I don't know how they say it now, but you know what I mean—and he wants you. And that's the way it's supposed to be, that's what you wait for your whole life, to find that. I'm sure it's still that way with the young people, that's what they really want after all their big talk. Men and women will never change about those things, that much I think I know.

So you find each other, you're lucky and you find each other, like one in a million, a needle in a haystack, you're so lucky. And then you make a life together, you go through times together, hard times, bad times: you bury a child together, you live through a war together—times that make you stronger, times that make you closer because you've survived them, times that make you think it will always be.

Me and Jule—what could be stronger than us? We were everything. People were even jealous of us because of the look that was still in our eyes; we were still in love with each other after all those years. How could that be? they thought. How lucky we were, they thought. But they were wrong. We weren't lucky, we were doomed right from the start. Sometimes what you think is going to be your Hallmark card can turn out to be toilet paper in disguise.

He was a gambler, my Julie. God help him, he was a gambler, and a gambler can never change. I tell you this with all my heart. No matter what you think can happen or what you hope for, no matter how hard he tries, no matter how much he loves you, no matter anything. And the ones who told me that before I married him were right; the ones on the list that I didn't want to hear from, they knew.

A gambler can never change, all he can do is change everything else—everything you hoped for and everything you dreamed about and everything you cherished—he turns it all to shit. I am not a woman who says such things, I don't believe it's necessary to use bad language and I don't like dirty talk, I never did, but it's the only way I know how to tell you, it's the only word when you look back on it that fits, so that's why I use it here, because everything that was beautiful between us he turned into something foul.

Dell stood at the stove watching the percolator. "If his lips are moving, he's probably lying," she said; "he's probably at the track right now."

"Don't say that, Dell, he's trying."

"He certainly is, he could give you a headache with all his trying."

Mollie looked at her.

"Okay . . . not funny. I'm sorry, kid. Come on, you know I love Julie, I'm crazy about him. It's just that I think maybe it's hopeless. I do, Mollie, he can't stop."

The timer went off. She lifted the percolator from the stove and brought it over to her kitchen table, poured some coffee into each of the cups, and looked at Mollie.

"Eat some stollen."

"I'm not hungry."

"Hey, that's from Lake Forest, that crumb cake, I drove all the way to Clayton to get that for you."

"I can't, really, it sticks in my throat. I'm not hungry, Dell."

"You look like hell, you know? You're too thin."

Mollie smiled at her. "Thank you."

"Oh, shit," Dell said. She sighed and patted Mollie's shoulder, walked past her, and put the percolator on the stove. She came back to the table and sat down, stirred some sugar into her coffee and took a sip. Then she put her cup down, sat back in her chair, and looked at Mollie.

"You probably need more iron or something. Do you get enough iron?"

Mollie looked at her.

"You should eat more spinach . . . more green things . . . leafy vegetables."

"Okay."

"Jesus, I sound just like my mother."

Mollie poured a little milk into her coffee and stirred it, took a sip.

Okay," Dell said. "So, what if you just accept it?"

"What?"

"What if you just live this way?"

"What do you mean?"

"Just accept that he's gonna be like this for the rest of your life and just live with it, you know, like he's got something wrong with him, like he lost his leg or somethin' in the war. Like Hildy Esposito's husband has a plate in his head since Iwo Jima and he has these little fits every now and then."

"But Jule doesn't have a plate in his head, Dell."

"I know, but you could pretend, Mollie."

"I can't do that."

"Why not? So he doesn't have a plate in his head—instead, he's got something missing in his head. It's the same thing."

"It's not."

"Okay." She took a sip of her coffee. "You know he's crazy about you."

"I know."

"He really is, Mol, look how he looks at you."

"I know."

"And he takes care of you and the baby. It's not like he doesn't provide for you and Gilliana, he does. He makes a living and everything."

"I know."

"And you're crazy for him."

"I know."

"So?" She looked at Mollie but Mollie didn't say anything.

"You sure you don't want a piece of stollen? A tiny sliver, maybe?" She took the knife, cut a wedge of crumb stollen, and put it on Mollie's plate by her coffee cup. "Go ahead, Mol, you look like you're hungry."

Mollie didn't say anything.

"Okay. So, tell me, what's the worst part? Tell me, kiddo, it's okay. Mol?" Dell put her hand gently on Mollie's hand.

A small sob came out of Mollie and then a rush of words. "I'm scared,

Dell. What if he gets in too deep with those gangsters, what if he owes them money that we can't pay? What will they do to him?"

"Aw, come on, Mol, they wouldn't do anything to him."

"No, you don't know that . . . and I couldn't take it, Dell, I really couldn't take it if something happened to Jule that he did to himself because of the gambling. Don't you see? It's not like something out of your control, not like Al Esposito getting hit in the head with a piece of shrapnel right out of the sky or your Aunt Ginnie Cocuricci, may she rest in peace, getting hit by that bus like you told me while she was standing there on the corner minding her own business with her shopping bags and her pocketbook in her arms. Those things came out of nowhere, they weren't things they did to themselves. Like the baby, Dell, her little kidneys falling apart like that . . ."

"Oh, God, don't cry so hard, Mol, you're gonna make yourself sick."

"No, listen, I gotta tell you . . . it's like I say to myself, why can't he stop, he knows how awful it is, he knows how it's killing us, so why can't he stop? Doesn't he see my face when I find out that there's money missing again because he bet it on something after he promised and promised, sobbing at the kitchen table with his face in his hands, after he swore he wouldn't gamble again, Dell, even swore on Gilliana's name, swore on our only baby's name—how can he do that and look at me?

"Or when he says he went with John Padrelli to grab a bite because John needed to talk to him and before I can say anything, before I can even open my mouth, he makes up a whole mishmosh story about what John said—the whole thing, Dell—what John said and what he said and back and forth, he tells me before I can even get a word in edgewise, and then when he stops I have to sit there and tell him that John called the house looking for him at the exact time he says this whole conversation was going on, and by then my heart is beating so fast and I'm so dizzy I think I'll fall down because I know he was at the track or playing cards or at a bookmaker's somewhere.

"And what's worse is what happens next, Dell . . . next comes the part where he has to say all the same things again: he didn't mean to, he's sorry, he wasn't going to, he's sorry, he loves me, he's sorry . . . again just like the last time. Again and again and again. Don't you see, it's like a dance, Dell, this awful dance that we have to keep doing because for some reason we can't sit down."

"Oh, God, kid . . ."

"Doesn't he see my face, Dell? Doesn't he look at me? How could he look at me and not stop? I keep saying to myself, if he loved me enough, he'd stop . . . Oh, Dell," Mollie said, sobbing, "I'm just so tired, I don't know if I can do it anymore."

But I still didn't understand. Gambling has nothing to do with love, gambling has only to do with tricks and lies and deceit and worse. Gambling can make people do things they couldn't imagine doing even in their worst dreams.

"What do you mean, the police are coming? What's wrong?"

I was trying to understand Alfonzo, but he was very excited and kept answering my questions in Italian, slipping from English into Italian so fast that I couldn't keep up. Of course, even if I wouldn't have understood one word of what he was saying I still would have known something was wrong; Alfonzo never used the telephone. The telephone was only for emergencies; other than that, it didn't exist.

"I'm coming, Alfonzo, I'll be there," I said, putting down the receiver and picking up my purse.

I left Gilliana where she was—making mud pies with her best friend, Claudia, two houses away. I told Claudia's mother, Hazel, I'd be back as soon as I could—I took the bus to Alfonzo and Sophia's, which only took maybe ten minutes—the squad car was parked out front as I ran up the steps to the porch.

"Ladri in casa, ladri in casa," Sophia was moaning on the sofa, shaking her head and twisting a wet handkerchief in her hands.

"What, what's in the house? What's she saying?" I said.

"We don't know, lady, that's the problem," the younger of the two policemen said to me. "You speak Italian?"

"A little . . . but not really. What happened, Alfonzo?"

"You don't speak Italian?" the policeman said. "Jeez . . . I can't believe this here, Frank," he said to the other policeman.

"È stato rubato," Alfonzo yelled, *"non l'hai perduto!"*

"She lost something, I think," I said to the policeman. "Is that it, Alfonzo?"

"Non l'ho perduto, Mollie, è stato rubato!" Alfonzo yelled at me.

The other policeman, who was sitting next to Sophia, stood up. "Hey, take it easy, old man."

"Don' chu call me an ole man! You an ole man! You go find them!"

"Who?" I said.

"We don't know, lady," the other policeman said, "that's the problem. Something's missing and we don't know what it is and if somebody took it, we ain't got no description or nothin'. All we got here is a lot of Italian, if you know what I mean."

What was missing was Sophia's mother's mother's mother's diamond. There were two of them—one diamond in each earring—Sophia had got one of her great-grandmother's earrings and her sister Gilliana, who had stayed in Sicily, had got the other. Gilliana had passed away the previous October and her diamond had been given to her son Joe, whose real name was Giuseppe and who lived in Cleveland, to be given to his daughter Lucia, who they called Lucy, when she turned sixteen. Sophia's diamond was waiting for our Gilliana, to be given to her when she turned sixteen. When this happened, Gilliana had just had her sixth birthday, I was thirty-eight going on thirty-nine, and Sophia was seventy-two.

This missing diamond was the end of my marriage. *"Ladri in casa"* means thieves in the house. I didn't know that, because I had never heard the word for thief. But what was worse was what I did know—somewhere in between all the yelling and the crying, and in between the English and the Italian, and in between the worries and the fear, it came to me. I didn't say anything out loud, but in my heart of hearts I knew—the thief was my Jule.

Gilliana

LESSONS ON HOW NOT TO BE SEEN WITH HIM—THE FAMOUS MARRIED ITALIAN COMEDIAN—IN HOTEL LOBBIES

Stand very still. Maybe they won't notice you next to him.

Pretend to be a palm tree—hold arms up over head and stick out at right angles—usually only works if you're wearing something green.

Act as if you're with the people standing the closest to you. Say something to one of them as you fall immediately into step with their group. It doesn't matter if they look at you like you're crazy, just smile and keep on walking right along with them.

Pretend to work for the hotel. This requires falling quickly into "hotel dialogue" like "That shower will be fixed first thing tomorrow morning, Mr. Ronzoni, we have no idea why it would be doing that . . ." or "Your return flight to New York has been changed just as you requested, Mr. Ronzoni, and we've ordered you the special vegetarian meal just as you said."

Pretend you are a relative. This is very difficult and requires enormous concentration unless, of course, you also pretend you just got off the boat from Italy and speak no English. But you can also run into a jam here if the people who've come up to him speak Italian. Then you have to faint.

Fainting. This is good because he can come to your aid and look like a good Samaritan taking care of a total stranger. Very good for his reputation. Try to look where you're falling before you fall; you could hit your head on the corner of a craps table, which is not a good thing.

Don't walk with him. Go everywhere by yourself.

Don't go at all. Stay home and just listen to him be funny on the telephone when he calls you from all over the world.

Don't go at all. No, it was too late for that one. How could I not go? There was no way to not be with him. It was everything to me, I had made it all I had. I typed, I shorthanded, I filed, and I waited for Anthony to call. I ate, I slept, I cried, and I waited for Anthony to call. And in between I flew to him. New York, Las Vegas, Atlantic City, San Francisco, even Indianapolis once . . . it didn't matter, I was there. In the snow, I flew. In the rain, I flew. In the heat of the day and in the dead of night. The commuter to Las Vegas, the shuttle to Boston, the red-eye to New York . . . it didn't matter, I was there.

"Hi."

"Howdy, darlin'."

"Aha, you're in Texas."

"Goddarn, you're a smart little gal, aren't you?"

"It's *gol*darn, not goddarn, you guinea."

"Don't call me a guinea."

"Why not? I'm a guinea too."

"Only half of you."

"Oh."

"Well, which half am I speaking to?"

"The top half."

"Oh, that's the Jewish half."

"Really? How do you know that?"

"Your mouth is Jewish, Gilliana."

"Yeah, what about the rest of me?"

"It depends on which parts we're discussing here."

"How about my you-know-what?"

"Excuse me, miss, to what would you be referring?"

"You're having trouble with your English again."

"I can't help it, I'm a guinea, you know."

Laughing.

"God, I miss you, Anthony. I miss you so much."

"Friday. Only three more days now, miss. On Friday in the good state of Nevada in the garden city of Las Vegas in the stunning Star Suite of the Sands Hotel I will inspect you, miss, and we will label all your parts so there won't be any problem with this again."

"How are you going to label my parts, sir?"

"With my mouth, *cara mia,* with my mouth and my breath and my tongue."

Bingo.

I usually stood behind the trombone player. If Anthony was playing Vegas, that is. His contract at the Sands was for the main room, of course, and there was always a big band down front for the singer who went on before him. The band was down front but on the side of the room, and it was dark there when Anthony went on—the lights were dimmed except for his spots. Sometimes I stood in the wings to watch him, but if I did that then I couldn't see the front of him, see his face and his hands as he worked, so I usually stood behind the trombone player.

The band loved him, they laughed their heads off every show, even after they thought they knew his routines by heart. Because he was always different—different and timely and, most of all, personal. That's why he could move the audience into a standing ovation whenever he wanted. It wasn't just that he was funny, he was also sincere and sweet and very real and funny; that's what made him unique. He was every woman's heart-throb and every man's best friend—he told stories about life, but somehow his version touched on yours, his humor was personal to you. No matter who you were, he saw life like you did, and so when you laughed at him you were laughing at yourself—that's what got them to stand. And yell and scream. And applaud until their hands were red. They didn't want him to leave the stage, and some nights if it was the late show, he didn't. He'd go on until they were exhausted from laughing, until nobody could take it anymore.

I could watch him do the same routine a million times and fall down laughing each time as if it was all brand new. I'd watch him do it and still not know how he did it, that's how good he was. Like a magician pulling laughs out of a hat instead of rabbits.

And, of course, I was in love with him. So in love I could hardly breathe. And most of the time, I was without him. He was in New York with "them," I was in L.A. with me. It was awful.

That's the part that they don't tell you about—the lonely part. You only hear about the romantic part when you hear about affairs—the drama—the phone calls, the planning, the airplane rides arriving in far-off cities in the dead of night, the limousine rides to posh hotels, trying to inconspicuously cross a lobby at dawn—you and the ladies with the vacuum cleaners lowering your eyes at each other—up an elevator and down a hall to his room, the number of which you have written on a scrap of paper clenched in your hand, pushing open the door because he left a matchbook wedged in to stop the lock, quietly putting down your carry-on bags, dropping your clothes on the floor, slipping into the bed beside him, into his arms, you smelling like the stale air from an airplane and him smelling like sleep.

If he was on the road, I could go to him but only if what's-her-name wasn't there. It was particularly awful if it was a holiday, 'cause then the older kid was out of school and the odds were she would take the two of them with her and go to be wherever he was.

Las Vegas was the best for me—if he played Las Vegas, it was usually for three weeks and she hated it there so she wouldn't go. She didn't gamble because she was extremely Catholic, she didn't sit in the sun because she burned, and if she brought the kids with her, he said, she refused to leave them in the room with some total stranger baby-sitter, so she'd spend the nights in the room with them and go to bed when they did and wake up when they did; I couldn't understand why anyone would want to go to where her husband was performing and then not watch him perform, but I kept my mouth shut. Meanwhile, Anthony would do two shows every night and then have to wind down, so he wouldn't get to bed till dawn and would sleep till around three the next afternoon, so if she went to Las Vegas she'd hardly even see him—consequently, she didn't go. Needless to say, it worked for me.

I was very busy commuting to Las Vegas from L.A. Not every day but on Friday right after work until early Monday morning before work, and then usually one night during the week. Harry Witzer said I should get a part-time job as a stewardess on P.S.A. or Western or as a waitress in the Sands' Garden Room.

"Think of the tips, kid. You could own a house in Bel Air by now."

There was no way to keep anything from Harry Witzer, he knew right from the first; he had a sixth sense, he said.

"So, Ronzoni finally got you in New York, huh, Gillian? Well, I gotta tell you, you put up one helluva fight."

He said the reason he knew was because my smile had changed.

"It's kinda over to the side now, kid," he said, laughing, "I got it—it's much more Italian now, your smile . . . It's kind of crooked . . . that's how I knew."

Anthony and I never talked about what's-her-name—if he loved her, if he liked her, nothing. There was no picture of her on his dressing-room mirror, he didn't call her on the phone in front of me, he never even mentioned her name. And neither did anybody else, none of the musicians or anybody backstage. It was nearly as if she didn't exist. It was nearly as if I was the one who was with him—except in hotel lobbies, of course.

Besides, it was too soon for us to talk about anything important—lest we forget here, this was still Gilliana and The Famous Married Italian Comedian—The Early Years.

Clare

Amy said the coolest thing today.

We were talking about affection—or, rather, being affectionate, you know—displaying it, as they say. What people do and all. I mean, it all started because of that thing this morning in the newspaper, that article, that's what we were talking about—did you see it?—the one in *The New York Times* about those two losers in New York who went into the Whitney Museum and up to that painting by Roy Lichtenstein called *Curtains.* I've never seen it but, you know, it's a *Lichtenstein,* after all, and the guy—I mean, I don't really know if it was the guy who did it or the girl, because they didn't say in the newspaper, but somehow I figure it was the guy since he put his name first, and besides, it seems to me more like a guy thing to do, you know, to impress her or something—anyway, so the guy takes this black felt-tip pen and he writes "REGGIE AND CRYSTAL" right on the painting. I mean, do you believe it? Right on the Lichtenstein. The newspaper also said that after he wrote Reggie and Crystal he also wrote this obscene message right under the Reggie and Crystal part—I don't know what the obscene message was, *The New York Times* declined to say, but, I mean, who cares—writing on the painting is already obscene.

Anyway, so, Amy and I were talking about it this morning, I read it to her over the phone because we get *The New York Times* at our house and she doesn't at her house—I mean, my mother has to get practically every newspaper and magazine known to man because she's constantly on the search for material for asshole Andy's routines—when she runs out of stuff about her own family, right? Ha-ha. So Amy and I were talking about it and then we got into this really hysterical conversation. She said that this guy, Reggie, you know, he probably thought that writing on a Lichtenstein would be the *pièce de résistance*—that's like an outstanding accomplishment in French, you know—Amy and I talk French sometimes, we've both been taking French since we were two or something, so sometimes we talk in French . . . It's probably really bad French, I certainly wouldn't know, I was only in France once with my dad when I was really little and all I remember about it is hating the food and throwing up a lot and this stupid apartment where we stayed where the bathroom was in the kitchen if you can believe that, not the bathroom, but the toilet, you know? It was really weird. So anyway, I said, no, Reggie probably thought that if he wrote on the Lichtenstein that it would be far better than the *pièce de résistance,* he probably thought it would be the *coup de grâce* for Crystal—a *coup de grâce* is like the final blow, you know, the finishing stroke—that he probably thought that if he wrote on the Lichtenstein, Crystal would be so impressed with him that then he could "have his way with her" and Amy was really laughing about "have his way with her," and then we started throwing all this French around and we got all mixed up with our verbs and then I said something about the whole thing being the *coup de foie gras,* which doesn't mean anything because *foie gras* is this awful stuff they eat in France, this mashed liver or duck yuck *pâté* stuff, which is probably why I was sick when I was there, my father probably gave it to me or something—it was before I was a vegetarian—anyway, we were both laughing so hard that I thought I was going to pass out. I know, you're probably saying to yourself: And she's telling me this because . . . ? Well, the point was that then we started talking about the stuff you would do to impress a person you've got a thing for, and then that somehow turned into a discussion about affection and what people will show to the public and all.

I mean, like I like to hold Scott's hand in public and I like his arm around me, but then Amy and I were talking about how if you see someone's parents doing that, how it's disgusting. Well, her parents, that is, because they're that way with each other; my parents, on the other hand, are not, which is better for me at least. But then I was telling her how my grandparents—Lew and Mollie, I mean, not Kent and Marilyn—how they're affectionate with each other and that doesn't seem to bother me at all. Isn't that strange? It's like it's okay at a certain age and then it's not okay and then it's okay again. I was telling her about how Lew really takes care of Mollie, how you can see that he's doing it, how he's so sweet with her and all. And then I told Amy about how he was when the thing happened with Mollie's car.

What got to me was how Lew didn't make a big deal out of it, you know, how he downplayed it so it was like a regular everyday occurrence or something when it wasn't; it was practically catastrophic. I mean, you figure you get your driver's license when you're sixteen and you drive your whole life, so it certainly was a big deal. Not that Mollie got her license when she was sixteen. She didn't get it until she married Lew and moved to Kansas City—before that she didn't drive, so she didn't get her license until she was in her forties, but when this happened she was already in her seventies, so that's certainly a lot of driving time and certainly a big deal.

The thing was—my grandmother forgot how to drive the car. Actually, she forgot how to turn it on. I wasn't there or anything, I got it secondhand when my mother told my father and me, and then I asked my grampa when I was there and he told me firsthand. And he told me in front of her—I mean, she walked into the living room when he was telling me and sat down on the couch next to him, and he just put his arm around her and went right on.

She was going to the market, just for a few things, you know, in the afternoon, stuff she needed to make supper and all, so she puts on her coat and says goodbye to him and the dog, and she goes into the garage and he's lying on the couch watching TV, actually sleeping and pretending to watch TV the way he likes to do in the afternoons. She kisses him goodbye—they always kiss each other goodbye when one of them leaves, a real kiss, not some little peck or anything—really—and he hears the garage door go up and he's lying there and he kind of nods off and he takes this little nap, you know, and then he wakes up and goes wandering around doing whatever he's doing and then he goes into the kitchen and opens the door to the garage, I guess to do something out there, he's always puttering around in the garage—and anyway, she's still there, sitting behind the wheel of her Oldsmobile with her coat on and all. The motor's not running or anything, the garage door is up for her to back out, but she's just sitting there. My grandmother is sitting there because she can't remember how to turn on the car. Right? This woman who has been driving for thirty-some-odd years is sitting with the key in her hand because she doesn't remember where the key goes, she doesn't remember where the ignition is, she doesn't remember how to make the car go. You get it?

Anyway, it was awful, but he didn't make it awful, you know? He made it like, oh, well, what's the difference, she didn't need to drive anymore.

"Where does she need to go?" he says to me, with his arm around her. "The grocery store, the beauty shop? I'll take her. What's the big deal?"

Then he smiles at her and he says to me, "I'd rather keep your grandmother with me anyway so she doesn't get into any trouble . . . after all, there's still a lot of guys out there who'd like to make my Mollie's acquaintance, you know what I mean?"

And then he winks at her like she's seventeen and his girlfriend, you know, and he leans over and while he's patting her on the shoulder he kisses her right on the mouth. It was so beautiful. Really.

I told Amy I had to leave the living room where I was sitting with them and go into the bathroom because I didn't want them to see me cry. So I say to Amy how that's real affection, you know? And Amy says to me it's like my grampa wrote "LEW AND MOLLIE" on a fucking Lichtenstein, only he did it in invisible ink.

Mollie

Mollie pushed at a piece of hair that had fallen across her forehead, tucked it back up under the bobby pin that held the wave above her right eye. She patted at her upper lip with the back of her hand, scooped up the stalks of celery she'd just cut from the head, and held them under the faucet. She rinsed them, shook them, and laid them side by side on a cutting board; then she splashed some of the cold water from the faucet onto her face. All the windows in the apartment were open but it wasn't helping much—it was noon and already 92 degrees. The two small black iron oscillating fans only seemed to be pushing the tuna smell around.

Mollie picked up a chopping knife, cut the celery deftly into tiny pale-green squares, and scooped the squares into a large white mixing bowl that sat on the counter filled with tuna fish from an open Bumblebee can. She wiped her hands on the sides of her cotton housedress and moved the three steps to the refrigerator door, her high heels making little clicking sounds on the linoleum floor. She was wearing new shoes, brand-new red high-heeled lizard ankle-strap dancing shoes that she'd bought two weeks before with Dell. Before the horror, before the missing diamond, before her life had fallen apart. She'd been saving the shoes for a special occasion and tonight was supposed to be it.

She took a jar of Miracle Whip out of the refrigerator, turned to walk back to the sink, and stopped abruptly as if she'd lost all momentum.

Mollie looked down at the red high heels, slumped into a chair at the kitchen table, and held the cold Miracle Whip jar in her arms as she sobbed.

The telephone rang. She got up, left the jar on the table, wiped her nose and face with a handkerchief she had tucked inside the sleeve of her housedress, and moved to the phone.

"Hello?"

"Hi, kiddo," Dell said.

"Oh, hi."

"So . . . whatcha doin'?"

"Making a tuna salad."

"Well, that's productive. You sound like you were crying."

"No."

"No?"

"No."

"Okay. So, how are you?"

"Fine," Mollie said, and began to cry again.

"Oh, God, I knew it. So what's goin' on?"

"Nothing. I'm just making a tuna salad and I'll eat it with the baby, and then I'll take a bath and do my nails and later I'll get ready and then he'll come home."

"And?"

"And then we'll go dancing."

"And?"

"And what?" Mollie said, wiping the tears with the handkerchief.

"And *everything will be swell,"* Dell said.

"Swell," Mollie repeated.

"Yes, it will," Dell said, "you're gonna get over this."

"Uh-huh."

"Okay, you're not gonna get over this. This is a corker and nothing will ever be the same."

"I have to go."

"Hey, come on, Mol, I'm only kidding . . . of course you'll get over it."

Mollie laughed. "No, really, I have to go, I have to make the baby her lunch."

"Hey, look at that—I made you laugh. What a great friend I am."

"You are a great friend, Dell, truly you are," Mollie said, sounding as if she was about to cry again.

"Hey, cut it out, no more crying. We both know I'm great, you don't have to cry about it, okay?"

"Okay."

"It's enough crying already. So, look, you'll go dancing, the two of you, and time will march on, like it always does, and everything will be hunky-dory again. Let's face it, Mollie, it's got to go uphill from here. Nat says this whole thing is probably a blessing in disguise for Jule—he says, to steal from his own mother, for Jule to hock the very diamond that was going to be handed from his own mother down to his own daughter, well, he can't get much lower than that, so now he's got to change. Right? I mean, Nat's even convinced me and I'm the queen of the skeptics. Right?"

"Okay."

" 'Cause Nat's smart. Right?"

"Uh-huh."

"Okay, good. So, everything will be fine . . ."

Mollie didn't say anything.

"So," Dell said, "you got on the new shoes?"

"Yeah."

"You're breaking 'em in, right? Then they won't pinch you. Well, that's good. Jule will love those shoes."

"I know."

"They're very sexy . . . okay . . . so you okay?"

"Uh-huh."

"Okay, kiddo, have a good time tonight. Everything's gonna be fine now, just remember what Nat says and call me tomorrow, okay?"

"Sure."

"Okay, bye."

"Bye."

Mollie put down the receiver. She walked out of the kitchen, through the narrow hall past the bathroom, and into the little bedroom in the back of the apartment. She walked to the window that overlooked the backyard, sat down on the foot of the bed, and watched her daughter playing outside in the backyard. Mollie leaned over and called through the open window.

"You all right, my Gilliana?"

"Yeah, Mommy, I'm making googleberry-bush pies."

"Well, that's good. I'm making tuna salad."

"With pickles?"

"Of course with pickles."

"It's hot, Mommy."

"I know. After lunch you can take a nice, cool bath."

"With bubbles?"

Mollie smiled. "Okay." She stood up. "I'll call you as soon as it's ready."

"Okay."

Mollie retraced her steps back through the little apartment to the kitchen. She picked up the jar of Miracle Whip on the table, took it to the counter, twisted off the top, scooped out a large dollop with a serving spoon, and plopped that on top of the tuna and the celery in the mixing bowl.

Then she sighed, put down the spoon, and closed her eyes.

"Please, Mary," she said, to no one visible, "if it's not too much to ask, please let it be like Nat says . . . okay? . . . a blessing in disguise?"

She kept her eyes closed and then whispered "Thank you" into the air.

She was whistling "Blue Moon" and chopping sweet pickles when the key turned in the apartment front door. She whirled at the sound and was facing Jules when he walked in. The clock said twelve-twenty; he wasn't supposed to be home until right after six.

Her eyes never left his as he told her he was leaving her, that maybe he never would stop gambling, that maybe he couldn't, that maybe he wasn't strong enough, that he couldn't stand the look in her eyes, that maybe she knew that too, that it was killing him to watch what he was doing to her, that he was no good, that he loved her, that he would always love her more than life itself, but he couldn't stand it anymore so he was leaving. Mollie didn't drop the little paring knife she was using to cut the sweet pickles when Jules told her—not even when he got Alfonzo's old suitcase out of the closet and started throwing things in it and the sleeve of his brown plaid shirt got caught in the locks, not even when the baby came into the room, not even when the baby grabbed his leg and he had to pull her little hands off of him, not even when he went out the door—Mollie didn't drop the little paring knife, she didn't take a step, she didn't even move.

I'll tell you, the nights here are a barrel of laughs. So are the days. I can't even think of what to call the days—if the nights are funny, then what are the days—hysterical?

Christopher called me back this morning. I wanted to say to him, Hey, could you just put the other one of you on the telephone, the one who used to think I was funny, the one of you who isn't my husband, who isn't leaving me—could I just talk to him?

I bet the other one of him knows where I put those postcards. I have this awful habit of stashing away all things of importance, not hide exactly but put away, someplace not readily obtainable by fire or burglary: the letter that Mollie and Lew sent me telling where their safe-deposit box is and their IRAs and insurance papers and their will and everything—that's important, that had to be put away—and the diamond that belonged to my great-great-great-grandmother on my father's side that was given to me on my sixteenth birthday and that I gave to Clare on her sixteenth birthday, but I didn't trust her to wear it yet because she'd probably lose it so I put it away, and this little leather pouch I have filled with silver dollars from my grampa, which I thought was in the box with my black suede Bruno Maglis but it wasn't when I looked, and . . . I don't know . . . actually, the point is, I don't even remember what all I have stashed away. What happens is that suddenly I want one of those things and I have no idea where I've stashed it. If you said you'd give me a million dollars, I couldn't tell you. I have absolutely no idea. I have to ask Christopher, only Christopher knows where I've stashed all those things . . .

"Chris, where are my mother's charm bracelets?"

By the time I bring myself to ask him, I have already torn two closets apart. I hate myself that I can't remember but I've run out of ideas.

He looks up from his *Wall Street Journal,* smiling. "What'll you give me if I tell you?"

Do you think he'll tell me where all my things are before he leaves?

He wasn't too happy with me when he called; he said his mother had been highly insulted by the way I spoke to her when she called here. I guess I might have gone a little overboard, but I always have a problem with Marilyn—she has that voice that comes out of the top of her mouth, calls me "my deah" like she just stepped out of a Gurney play, and as soon as she starts in on me I become my evil twin. She called here yesterday, "And how is dahling Mollie?" and, "Is there anything Kent and I might do?" That's all it took, I turned into the witch from *Hansel and Gretel* and said that instead of putting Mollie into a home I had decided to send Mollie and Lew to live with her and Kent in Connecticut, that I was sending them immediately by Federal Express along with a hospital bed, a wheelchair, and two truckloads of Depends.

"I am trying to understand your sense of humor about this, Gillian. I realize it must be because you're in such pain, my deah."

Okay, so she didn't think it was funny. I guess I didn't think it was funny either. But, of course, I'm not funny anymore.

If I was still funny, I could use all of what's happening here—no editing, no fixing, just let Andy do it as it happens, follow Mollie and Lew and me around with a pencil and just take it all down. Of course, I'll probably only write tragedy from now on, the humor in all this being obliterated by my rage.

After Christopher called to tell me I was rude to his mother, Carole Rose called. She's called every day since I got here, twice, to see if there's anything she can do. I said there wasn't anything except she better start looking for jokes for me to steal because it looked as if my joke days were through. She called me back about three minutes later with a joke about a pretzel she got from Rob Sills, and she said Rob said that because of the situation with Mollie he would give me the joke for just a buck ten, the ten cents being Carole Rose's commission. She said this might prove to be more lucrative than producing her television show. At least she had me laughing—leave it to Carole Rose. Then Andy called from Aspen. He wanted to remind me that Saturday is Christmas, and did I think I could possibly still fly in?

"I'll fly you in for one day, Gill. You from K.C. and the kid and the old man from L.A. One day and then you can go right back . . . after all, it's Christmas, you know."

Christmas. I forgot. I even forgot what day today was . . . Thursday, he told me. "It's Thursday, Gillian, what is that—a joke? Something you're working on, huh? A new routine?" All excited, poor Andy, I didn't have the heart to tell him I will probably never write jokes again, that the odds are he will probably have to find someone else to put funny words in his mouth. Of course, as soon as he heard how bad Mollie was he offered everything. That's Andy's way.

"Who's the best doctor for this, Gill? I'll get him, don't worry. Where is he? New York? I'll fly him in."

Andy, who only wants to fly anybody anywhere, his panacea for all pain.

I tried to explain that it wasn't about doctors anymore, doctors couldn't do anything except throw up their hands and run away.

"So what do you need, Gill? Huh? What can I do for you?"

That was it, he stumped me. I couldn't ask him to fly in and interview some of the people I'm gonna interview tomorrow, I didn't think that was his place. Hey, Andy, how 'bout you fly in and talk to some of the people who take care of some of the people who have lost their way? I couldn't ask him to go to some of the "homes" with me and take a little "look-see." Andy walking around a home doing comedy for people who've forgotten how to laugh, I can just picture it . . .

. . . drumroll . . .

"And now, ladies and gentlemen, coming to you semi-live from the smelly Starlight Roof Cafeteria Ballroom of the beautiful seedy Racka-racka Old Age Home in beautiful downtown Kansas City is the great Andy Minkoff doing his vegetable routine . . ."

". . . and so, folks, I'm lookin' at my mother and I'm sayin' to myself, 'Why, next year she could be a squash . . .' "

Barumpum goes the drum and then the cymbal crash . . .

Oh, God.

I'm so angry.

Tonight was the "washcloth." Today was the *orecchiette al pomodoro* and tonight was the "washcloth," and in between I called my mother-in-law to apologize. She was very gracious to me. She's always gracious; the woman doesn't have a mean bone in her body, and it's insane for me to be such a bitch to Marilyn . . . What am I punishing her for?

So there was the phone call to Marilyn and the two heartbreaks—that about sums up the day. And I don't know which heartbreak was harder, it's probably a toss-up, but what difference does it make?

My mother takes a bath every night, or let's say she took a bath every night when she knew what a bath was. It was important, it ended her day for her, she loved it and it was a ritual, no matter what. It didn't matter how late they got home or how early she had to get up, Mollie took her bath come hell or high water, so tonight I gave her her bath.

". . . Just look at that, folks, the daughter can turn into the mother . . . in one fell swoop they reverse roles magically right in front of your eyes . . ."

How many times, I think, did my mother give me a bath when I was little? How many times? Christopher always gave Clare her bath; I was sure if I did it she would drown. This is the first time I have ever given my mother a bath. I thought it would make her feel good, I didn't know it would break my heart.

The first part went okay. I must admit I was a little uncomfortable about looking at my mother naked, not that I haven't seen various parts of her through the years, but Mollie was never one for walking around naked like I am; she was always partially covered by something—a towel, a girdle and stockings, a shower door—she never just stood there right out in the open. She wasn't embarrassed tonight, she was delighted to be in the bathtub, but I knew that if she knew she was that exposed she wouldn't be comfortable and that's what made me uncomfortable, knowing how she would feel. So, we got by that part and once she was in the water we were doing fine. She knew what you do in the bathtub, you take a bath. She took the plump white terrycloth washcloth off the tile rod and her bar of French hand-milled soap and she's scrubbing her knees and her elbows and I think, Well look at that, those doctors don't know what they're talking about, they're full of shit, because she's fine. I move from sitting on the floor next to the bathtub to sitting on the closed toilet seat. I open the cabinet under the sink and take out an emery board. I file my nails while I watch her. I talk to her. Sometimes she answers me, sometimes she doesn't. Sometimes her answers make sense, sometimes they don't; I decide to ignore the ones that are non sequiturs. Most of the time she says nothing and then she begins whistling, her good whistle, not the one she does between her teeth. She whistles "Ain't She Sweet?" And I begin to sing. Why not? I feel good for a minute, two minutes, three minutes, and so I sing, I file away at my short, stubby nails and I sing:

> *"Ain't she sweet, see her comin' down the street,*
> *Now I ask you very confidentially, ain't she sweet . . ."*

I'm singing and filing and Mollie's whistling and scrubbing,

> *" . . . ain't she nice, look her over once or twice . . ."*

She puts the washcloth on her head. The sopping-wet, soapy washcloth, she plops it right on the top of her head.

"Mom?"

She's still whistling, nothing has stopped for her; there are no bubbles running down into her face, no water dripping off the tip of her nose—she's fine, she's whistling.

"Mom?"

She doesn't look at me.

I drop the emery board, slide off the toilet onto my knees on the floor, and knee my way to the ledge of the bathtub.

"Mollie, what are you doing?"

She's staring straight ahead, whistling. She's gone inside herself, away from me. So fast, this whole thing happens so fast, she's here and then she's gone.

". . . watch this, ladies and gentlemen . . . faster than the speed of light, faster than a locomotive, watch the disappearing lady come and go . . ."

I try to remain calm, which is not easy for me, but I try anyway. I lift the washcloth off her head and wring it out in front of her into the water. I wipe the bubbles off her face, pat the soap off her nose; she doesn't see me, it's as if I'm not there. I look at her.

"Mommy?"

The word "Mommy" slips out because I'm scared, but that's what gets to her, when I call her Mommy she hears; she turns her head and looks at me and then she sees me as if I've just appeared.

"Oh, Gilliana," she says, smiling, "I'm so glad you're here. I miss you way out there in L.A."

It didn't last long, a moment of recognition and then she disappeared again. Took the washcloth out of my hand and started to wash her feet.

Gone.

She was gone.

It just took a moment. One moment, that's all.

She misses me way out there in L.A.? What the hell am I doing way out there in L.A.? What am I doing out there while she's falling apart here?

One simple, tiny moment, just long enough to kill me, like being stabbed in the gut with a fast blade. Boom, one heartbreak.

Anyway, I'm going to bed now . . .

Oh, I nearly forgot . . . the *orecchiette. Orecchiette al pomodoro*—how could I forget?

Orecchiette is the name of a pasta; it's these little noodles that are referred to as "little ears" or "priests' hats." You have to roll the dough into cylinders and then you cut the cylinders into little rounds and you shape each little round into an "ear" by pressing the center with your thumb, and then you press each "ear" well down over the thumb so that it looks like a little round priest's hat without a brim. Mollie and I used to make them together from the time I was little, because I thought they were funny and I would eat them with anything: tomato sauce, cheese and butter, just butter, olive oil, it didn't matter what. She could let them bob around in a bowl of warm milk and I would eat them. I was a finicky eater, so Mollie made a lot of *orecchiette* to entice me to eat. In fact, now that I think about it, the first time I made them was with Mollie and Sophia, my grandmother, in St. Louis, and it must have been when Mollie was still married to Black Bart, because I think I was really small . . . Anyway, it doesn't matter. What matters is that I loved them, I loved to make them with her, but most of all I loved the next part: you have to spread them out on floured towels to dry all around the kitchen. That's the part I thought was so funny, all these itsy-bitsy hats lying around on towels all over the kitchen as if they had been plucked off the heads of little elves . . . Well, I thought it was funny; I was little, after all . . .

Today we're in the kitchen, Mollie and Lew and I. I'm about to make phone calls to set up interviews to look at "homes" tomorrow, and then I decide, how can I do this in front of her—even though I think she doesn't understand what I'm talking about, but what if she does—so I'm going to go make these phone calls from the guest room. I stand up and push the kitchen chair back in place at the table and turn to leave.

"Oh, Gilliana," Mollie says, smiling and reaching out her hand to catch mine with her fingers, looking at me like she always did, "don't go to school today, my sweetheart, stay home with me and we'll make *orecchiette.*"

So normal, so Mollie, so like she was. Stay home and play with me.

I had the only mother in the world who wanted me to play hooky from school to be with her, to make "little ears," to watch the Dione Lucas cooking show on the television, to go to the park and feed the ducks, to try on all of her jewelry, to paint the living room aqua, to wash her car in the driveway with the hose and a bucket of sudsy water . . . sudsy water like in a bathtub.

God, I hate this . . .

That's all, nothin' much, no big deal, just two heartbreaks. Two moments of seeing my mother come and go. It's amazing—she can glide back in and out of her eyes faster than Sonja Henie on the ice.

FRIDAY

stop myself. I mean, when something so shocking happens right in front of you, I think you have to take it as a sign, you have to look at it and see what you get from it, you know? Don't get me wrong, I'm not saying you have to learn a lesson from it or find some deep hidden meaning in it that changes your life. I just think you have to at least take a look at it and stop and think.

You see, this guy dropped dead in the supermarket. I'm not kidding, it really happened and I was standing right there. I was standing in the checkout line with my mother. Ordinarily I wouldn't have even been in the store with her—at first I was waiting in the car and then I remembered I wanted to try the Maybelline mascara, the one in the pink-and-green thing. I read that it was really good, so I went in and she was waiting in the checkout line by then, so I gave her the mascara to get for me, and she says, Watch the cart, will you, I forgot mozzarella, so I'm standing there leaning on the grocery cart looking through this *Elle* magazine that has the tiniest clothes in it on the skinniest models you have ever seen. I'm not kidding, they couldn't possibly ever eat anything, they must live on gum and lettuce or something. Or if they eat, then they get rid of it, you know, bulimia—don't kid yourself, bulimia is rampant, and not just with models and fashion, it's everywhere, let me tell you. In my class alone in my school, which is really small compared to most high schools in Los Angeles since it's a private school, there are for sure three girls I know of who are positively eating and then throwing it up. And that's if they even eat anything. For sure, three of them. And then there's two more of them that I'm not sure about, but I think they are too. One of them, I mean, one of the "for sure" ones, her arms are so thin you can see right through them, right through her skin you can see all her veins and her bones. Really, she looks like an X-ray when she's in the light. And get this, her parents, who think they're so smart and all, they think they know everything, so instead of getting her some real professional help, like an actual shrink who especially deals with this stuff, with anorexia and bulimia, they take her to a nutritionist so she'll know what to eat. As if she's not puking her guts out at every opportunity. Can you imagine? What's the matter with them—don't they look at her? Talk about denial . . . I mean, kids die from this, it's not a joke. What will they say if she dies, these people?—that she had lactose-intolerance and ate too much cottage cheese? Jesus. Sometimes the stupidity of grown-ups makes me sick.

Anyway, so my mother comes back with the mozzarella and I'm about to leave her, you know, go back to the car and wait for her there, and that's when the guy keels over. He's in the next aisle, but ahead of us; he's actually getting his stuff checked out. I didn't physically see him standing there 'cause I wasn't paying any attention, I was putting the *Elle* back in the stand, but then out of the corner of my eye I see him pitch backward and his head hits the metal pole, you know, that divides the people into the aisles, and I mean it hits it like with this big *boing* sound and he's down. Just like that, like my grandma says, and then the grocery store falls into a two-second hush and then a loud roar. I mean, people are practically jumping all over themselves to save the guy, and then the manager or somebody is on the loudspeaker thing paging to see if there's any doctors in the store, and one actually turns up, some lady doctor who's all dressed up, and she's pounding on his chest sprawled on the floor on her knees with her suit skirt yanked up and her hair falling in her eyes and her high heels on, and some guy who was somewhere in the line behind the guy who dropped is now giving him CPR and there's blood everywhere from where he banged his head, but it's clear the head wound is not the problem, the problem is the guy is dead.

Then the paramedics run in, you know, like forty-two of them, really running, and they're all over him and they do those paddles on his chest like in the movies and yell "Clear!" but, you know, it was over, there was nothing anybody could do 'cause he was dead, that's all there was to it, he was through. I can't tell you, it was actually unbelievable in the very truest sense of the word.

They took him out on a stretcher all covered up, and meanwhile everyone in the supermarket is just standing there. Together, you know, everyone: the guys from the meat department with their white aprons splattered with chicken blood and the guys from the back in smocks and the lady doctor on the floor with the CPR guy and the checkers in their uniforms and the baggers and the managers in their short-sleeved shirts and dopey ties, with ballpoint pens in their pockets in those stupid leather things, and the guys in aprons who put the stock on the shelves and the ladies who wait on you in the bakery and the people behind the deli counter and the guys who do the vegetables and the sushi guys with their little hats and the security guards from the parking lot, and all the people who were in the grocery store—you know, the customers—moms with their little kids strapped into the seats of the grocery carts and old people and young people and babies and housewives and gay guys and people off to work and people coming home from work and people in blue jeans and rich people and poor people and people with colored hair and nose rings and straight people and crazy people and lonely people and happy people and sad people—everybody, I mean, everybody is standing there watching this and they're together—it's like suddenly everybody's close, like we know each other, like we're a family, all these people in the grocery store, all these strangers, only now it's like we know each other. Some people are crying and others are saying, "It's okay, it's all right," and one lady has to sit down and this man helps her and people are comforting each other and somebody says somebody needs a glass of water and then, I guess, one of the managers has some grocery carts brought up to the front of the store with bottles of water and orange juice and soda in them for people who want it—you know, for free—and all these people are talking to each other, they've bonded, because they watched this guy die. This guy who brought everyone together—and he's another stranger, right?—the dead guy—I mean, we don't know anything about him—did he have a heart condition already or was he in perfect health, did he have two bags of pork rinds for breakfast or raisin bran, was he single or married, did he have kids or a lover or a job or a dog or a friend, was he a good guy or a scumbag? I mean, we know nothing, absolutely nothing. We only know one thing: he was standing in line at the grocery store and then bam, he was dead. And we saw it, that's what we know.

So here's all these strangers in the grocery store who have experienced this catastrophe and now all of a sudden they're close, but I know that as soon as they leave the store they'll be strangers again, that much I know. I mean, it's not as if they're going to call each other up and meet and have lunch, right? Of course not, this is Los Angeles, they'll go off on their merry ways, get back in their separate cars and be alone. But first everybody says goodbye, you know, when they leave the supermarket, like it's Thanksgiving or something and we've all been together at somebody's grandma's house for three days and now it's over and everybody has to go back home and people are walking out to the parking lot together and some of them are even hugging and waving goodbye and honking to each other as they drive away . . .

And my mother and I—I mean, here we had experienced this thing together—so when we leave the store we actually have our arms around each other, and then on the ride home, I'm sure because we were in shock—you know, the way if you've experienced some horrible catastrophe you can actually make terrible jokes about it—so I said the guy had "checked out" in the "checkout line" and I thought my mother was going to collapse from laughing and fall out of the car. And then she told me about this old expression a friend of hers from New York says, how all these New York guys use it, you know, when one of them dies, they say "He took a cab," and so my mother says that this guy "took a cart," you know, a grocery cart . . . really, I got hysterical . . . I don't know . . . it's just that we were pretty shook up, but we were laughing and we were close, you know? I mean, we were suddenly close like when I was little. We could have talked to each other. I could have told her things inside of me and I could have listened to the things inside of her. Personal things, intimate things, the things that count. We probably could even have talked about what goes on between her and my father, about how lately things have gone from bad to worse. It's like I don't know if they can even see that, how lately it's gotten worse. Sometimes when you're in the midst of things, you can't see how obvious it is, but the people around you do. Especially me—it's not like I'm wearing blinders or anything, and I'm not talking about yelling and screaming, that's not what they do. It's quiet, their warfare, it's like smiling through gritted teeth and everything they say is a double entendre. It's like she goes, "So do you want to go, Christopher?" And he goes, "It's fine with me if you do." And she goes, "But what do *you* want to do?" And he goes, "I don't care either way, Gillian, whatever *you* say." They're both being so polite you want to scream at them, because you know that underneath the politeness each of them wants to sock the other one in the face. In actuality, I'm sure neither of them wants to go anywhere with the other one.

Sometimes I think they should just end it—you know, separate. I'm going away next year and, you know, if they're not happy why should they stay together . . . but then I see myself coming home from Amherst or wherever I go, like next Thanksgiving, and then what?—half of the turkey is at her house and half of the turkey is at his? And God, can you imagine, they could each get a boyfriend and a girlfriend and then I might have to be a stupid stepkid to some stupid jerk . . . I don't know, I mean, I know I'm being pretty shallow the way I'm talking about it, I know the big thing wouldn't be me and where I unpack my luggage or eat my pumpkin pie, the big thing would be about the two of them not being together anymore. And I don't know how I really feel about that. Maybe I'm being shallow about it all because it really scares me. I mean, I don't really want them to get a divorce, not really, I'd just like for them to be okay. Anyway, my mother and I never talked about it or anything else that day, because it's like the whole thing just blew away. I'm not kidding, as soon as we drove into the driveway it was all over, you know? It's like the garage door went up and wiped the closeness away, just erased it, and instantly we were back in our regular lives and before you know it, it's like the thing that brought us close just burst and faded, just evaporated even faster than it took for the guy to die, because she says to me: "Clare, don't forget you have to walk the dog."

Can you imagine? I just looked at her.

Walk the dog? We just saw this guy drop dead together and the first thing that hits her mind is not that we should go into the house together and hang out in the kitchen together and talk about something, but that I should walk the dog? Like I don't walk the fucking dog every day of my life anyway . . .

I couldn't believe it. Suddenly she had to be the mother again, she couldn't wait, so then I had to be the daughter again and that was that, we assumed our roles. By dinner we were annoying each other and not speaking to each other or at least not saying anything that we might be feeling, anything real. It's like the place that was opened because of the catastrophe closed up and it was through—so even though we really were a family, my mother and I, we were back to being strangers again too.

So I guess what I'm saying is, what difference does it make if you're really family if the moments that should count and should change things just fade away and become meaningless before you can even breathe?

And why isn't she talking to me? Doesn't she realize that it might be her mother who's in trouble but it's my grandmother too? My grandmother who I love deeply, my grandmother who I'll never get over if she dies.

I don't want to be that way, I know that. I don't want to be closed off and indifferent. I want to be open and intimate. Of course, maybe I'm being naive, maybe mothers and daughters can never be that way, maybe it's too painful on either side. Maybe if she had continued to be warm to me, I wouldn't have been able to take it and I would have shut my door. The door in my heart, I mean.

Or maybe I really am being naive, maybe everybody starts out being open, and then they get their hearts stomped on and then they're afraid.

Gilliana

March 1972 ~ Las Vegas

"What's that big 'R' there, sleepyhead?"

Tony leaned over and traced the letter "R" with his finger on Gillian's chest above her breasts. She was standing naked next to him at the doorway—he was about to leave the hotel suite to go down and have a talk with the lighting guy who'd been slow with some changes at the second show the night before. She'd fallen back to sleep after he got up to take a shower; they hadn't gone to bed until eight that morning and now it was two-thirty in the afternoon.

"What 'R'?" Gillian said, bending her head down to look at her chest, several dark-brown curls slipping across her face.

"This one," he said, moving his finger against her skin.

"Oh, that one," she said, seeing nothing on her chest and smiling, "that's an 'R' for 'Ronzoni,' I've been Ronzonied, you know."

"And don't you forget it," Tony said, his hand moving to one breast, his other arm moving around her, his fingers encircling her waist.

"No, sir," Gillian said, falling into him.

"And what are you doing naked in my hotel room anyway, lady?" he said, kissing her, his lips moving under her curls to her ear and then across her face to her mouth.

"I was sent by the management, Mr. Ronzoni, to make sure you were happy."

"You were sent by the gods, Gilliana, and I will never let you go."

His lips traveled from her mouth down her neck to her right breast, his tongue softly brushing her nipple as her fingers began to loosen his belt.

"Excuse me, lady," Tony said as he moved her body two steps backward toward the couch.

"I thought you had a date with the lighting guy, Mr. Ronzoni," Gillian said as his hand slipped between her legs and she unzipped his pants.

"Fuck the lighting guy," Tony said, pulling her on top of him on the couch.

"No, my sweet Anthony," Gilliana said, smiling as she straddled him, "fuck me."

And I thought I loved Tom Johnson. What did I know?

You don't know anything about love until it really happens to you and when it does, then you know that whatever happened to you before was really not love, it was nothing. And even if it was more than nothing, it certainly wasn't love. Not this kind of love.

June 1972 ~ Los Angeles

"I'm not gonna be able to come to Indianapolis, Anthony," Gilliana said, switching the phone to her other ear.

"What? Why not?"

"Because I can't make the connections; I can't get to the airport Friday after work until at least seven, so that means I have to change planes in Chicago because they don't have a nonstop from here that leaves after three . . ."

Carole Rose stuck her head in Gillian's room. "You want pizza?"

"Sure. Mushroom."

"With pepperoni?"

"Hey, did you just call me a mushroom?" Tony said, laughing, over the phone.

"No, Carole Rose is ordering pizza."

"Pepperoni?" she said again.

"Pepperoni, sure."

"I don't like pepperoni," Tony said.

"Well, you won't be here to eat it."

"Oh, really? And how do you know that?"

"Because you're on your way to Indianapolis . . . where are you, anyway? New York?"

"Don't get pepperoni on my half."

"Tony . . ."

"Tell her I don't want pepperoni on my half."

"Tony . . ."

"Tell her, Gilliana. Hold the pepperoni."

"Hey . . . I haven't seen you in three weeks and now I probably won't get to go to Indianapolis because by the time I get there I'll have twenty minutes with you and then I'll have to turn around and come back, and you're fooling around with me like you could just come over here and eat pizza . . . you're gonna make me cry."

"I just landed in Los Angeles, my love, I'm about to get in a taxi and come to your apartment, so would you please tell Carole Rose I don't want any goddamn pepperoni on my pizza. Okay?"

"Are you really? Oh, my God, Anthony, are you really here? Really?"

"I'm here, baby. I can only stay until tomorrow night but I'm here."

"Oh, God. I love you."

"I'll be there in half an hour. Gilliana?"

"What, my darling?"

"Don't forget—tell Carole Rose to hold the pepperoni."

"Excuse me, but *I'll* be the only one who holds your pepperoni, Mr. Ronzoni, thank you very much."

"I'm on my way," Tony said, laughing as he hung up.

Oh, God, how I loved him.

September 1972 ~ Los Angeles

"What's that sound?" Gilliana asked him.

"It's pouring here, baby, that's rain crashing against the phone booth."

"Where are you?"

"Sixty-fifth and Madison," Tony said. "There's a suspicious-looking woman in front of the phone booth completely covered in black patent leather trying to flag down a cab—she looks like Himmler in drag—and a sweet, drenched drunk propped against the side of the newsstand drinking something out of a paper bag. It's just the three of us, everybody else in New York is inside."

Gilliana kicked off both shoes and put her feet up on the couch. "You're awfully close to the house, aren't you?"

"It's okay . . . I'm walking the dog."

"Do you have an umbrella?"

"Nope, just a raincoat."

"Does the dog have a raincoat?"

"No, he has an umbrella . . . cutest thing you ever did see . . . Gilliana?"

"What?"

"I miss you."

"I miss you."

"I miss you more."

Carole Rose walked through the living room to the kitchen; she gave a little wave as she passed the couch.

"No, you don't, I miss you more. Carole Rose says hello. Is the dog in the phone booth with you?"

"No, I didn't want him to eavesdrop; he may have a big mouth and tell all the other dogs in the neighborhood about how much I love you. And besides, he doesn't have a girlfriend. I didn't want him to get jealous. Tell her hello back."

"Anthony, what if somebody sees you?"

"Everybody can see me, sweetheart, it's New York."

"I mean somebody who knows you . . . why would you be using a phone in a phone booth when you're so close to your house?"

"I don't know . . . If somebody asks me, I'll tell them I'm calling my bookie."

Gillian started to say something but then she stopped.

"Gilliana?"

"Hmm?"

"Where did you go, babe?"

"I was thinking about a bookie I knew once . . . a big, fat man . . ."

"What bookie?" Tony said. "You don't know any bookies."

"My father used to take me when I was little."

"Where?"

"To the bookie joints with him on Saturday mornings."

"He didn't, you're kidding."

"Yes, he did, he thought it was better for me than Kiddieland."

"Hmm."

"So did I, much more enlightening."

"You never talk about your father."

"I know. He's kind of *persona non grata.* Is that Italian?"

"God, I love you."

"Persona non grata," Gillian said, "a fruit very much like a pomegranate but not as well known as a pear."

Tony laughed but then it was muffled by a big booming sound in the background.

"Jesus," Tony said.

"What was that?"

"Thunder, it's really coming down here. And—oh, my God—will you look at that, the dog just drowned."

Gillian laughed into the telephone. "He did not."

"Yes, I'm afraid so. He's just lying there gurgling in that big puddle at the end of the leash."

"Stop it," Gilliana said, "the dog did not drown."

"I better go, I have to call a mortuary immediately."

"I love you, you're so funny."

"Thank God, that's why they pay me the—"

"Big bucks," Gilliana said with him. He laughed.

"All right, baby, I'll call you tomorrow after the dog's funeral."

"Tony?"

"What, my love?"

"When will I see you?"

"Soon. I promise, Gilliana. I'll think of something. I'll come out or you'll come in or we'll meet in the dreaded middle. I promise, soon."

"I'm wasting away here."

"Don't waste away, there'll be nothing for me to hold on to. Do you want a picture of the dog?"

"Dead or alive?"

"Whichever."

"Dead, I guess. In his casket. Will he be wearing a suit?"

"Pinstripe, I'm sure. Gilliana?"

"What?"

"Will you tell me about your father?"

"What do you want to know?"

"I mean when I see you. Will you tell me everything?"

"Everything . . . well, there ain't much."

"But will you tell me?"

"Okay, but only if I get a picture of the dog."

Tony laughed. "Goodbye, *cara mia,* I love you."

"Bye, Anthony, button up, don't get wet."

The photograph arrived in color and the dog was not only wearing a suit, a thin white pinstripe delicately running through what appeared to be an elegant charcoal flannel gabardine, he was also wearing a white-on-white shirt, a black tie, a gray fedora, and a red carnation boutonniere. I don't know how Anthony got him to close his eyes and lie so still, but he did; the dog must have been very well trained to play dead. All in all, he must have been one incredible dog, because he had a lot to put up with—like his name, which was Samantha, even though he was a boy dog, because that's what Anthony's son named him before he knew the difference, and even though they tried to get him to change it to Sam, the kid was adamant about his puppy being named Samantha after some little girl with red hair who he fell in love with after she threw sand at him in the park. He was two at the time.

Carole Rose loved the photograph so much that Anthony had to send her a copy. She still has hers but mine is gone. So much for all the treasures in one's bureau drawer. But I can still see it clearly in my head and that's all that counts, isn't it?

December 1972 ~ Los Angeles

"How big is your tree?"

"Not as big as the one in Rockefeller Center."

"Is it cold there?"

"Cold and sleeting, it's miserable."

Gillian sighed. "I wish it was sleeting here. Do you remember when we went to see the tree at Rockefeller Center?"

"Of course I remember, I remember everything we ever did, Gilliana. Everything."

"You do? Do you remember the first time you said you loved me?"

"I said I loved you? What? You must be mistaken."

Gillian tucked the receiver into the nook of her other shoulder, pushed the curls off her forehead, and ran her hand across her damp face.

It was three days before Christmas and 92 degrees in Los Angeles. A mean, dry Santa Ana wind was blowing up the dust and there were at least three varying layers of beige smog spread across the sky.

"Gilliana?"

She picked up another strand of tinsel and placed it carefully on a branch of the tiny fir tree.

"Baby, I was kidding."

"I know," she said.

"I remember exactly when I said I loved you. It was April 2nd at approximately eight-forty-five in the evening and we were in Washington, D.C., at that extremely overrated, extraordinarily expensive, fancy French joint and you had a fight with the waiter because you said you wanted something plain. You told him that you didn't want a drop of sauce on anything, and if there was sauce anywhere in your vicinity you would puke in front of him on the very expensive white damask tablecloth, and you told him all of that in a very dignified rich-lady voice and with a very straight face—especially the 'puke' part."

Gillian smiled and moved the strand of tinsel a little to the left and backed up a couple of steps to see the tree in perspective.

"Right?" Tony said.

"Right."

"And the waiter turned red and I told you at that exact moment that I loved you."

"And what did I say?"

"You said that even if I loved you, you still wanted something plain."

"Right," Gillian said, grinning.

"So there," Tony said, "I remember every word. See?"

"Do you believe it's so stinking hot here I'm wearing shorts?"

"Shorts? And what? A bikini top?"

"Nope. Just shorts."

"Hey, lady, where are you? In the bedroom?"

"I'm in the living room putting tinsel on my huge tree."

"What if someone sees you?"

"Who?"

"I don't know . . . some pervert in the alley looking into your window."

"There's nobody in my alley."

"Okay, then, take off the shorts."

"Why, Mr. Ronzoni, how dare you," Gillian said. "I had no idea *you* were a pervert."

Tony laughed. "Oh, yes you did, Miss Ventimiglia, oh, yes you certainly did."

For Christmas he sent me a heavy gold oval disc on a thick gold gorgeous chain from Tiffany's. It was addressed to Holy Gilliana Golightly Ventimiglia. Not Holly . . . Holy. On one side of the disc there was a perfect hand-engraved simple Jewish star and on the other side a perfect cross. He said he wanted to cover all of me. Don't even ask—it's still in my jewelry box wrapped in one of his handkerchiefs.

January 1973 ~ Las Vegas

Gillian stuck the cotton balls in between her toes, perched her feet on the corner of the desk in front of her, and opened the bottle of red nail polish with her teeth.

"You're gonna break a tooth, *cara,*" Anthony said from where he was sprawled across the bed.

"I know . . . don't tell Dr. Melford . . ."

"Hmm?"

She looked at him but he had refocused back to whatever he was scribbling on a notepad.

"I said don't tell Dr. Melford, my dentist."

He didn't say anything. She began applying the red polish to her toes.

"What?" he said.

"What?"

"I thought you said something."

"No, it's okay . . ."

"Uh-huh . . ." He looked at what he was writing, tore off the page, crumpled the paper into a ball, and pitched it over the side of the bed.

The carpet was covered with crumpled paper balls. Gillian smiled. "So, it's a tough one, huh?"

"Hmm?"

"The joke, the story . . ."

"What, baby?" he said, looking at her and frowning.

"I said you're making a lot of paper balls there, mister."

"Oh." He looked around the bed. "Yeah . . ."

"So, what is it?"

"What?"

"Anthony," Gillian said, laughing, "what's the story?"

"Oh, they haven't got it yet, the boys. They just can't seem to get it the way they want it. We've been working on the damn thing for weeks . . . months."

"Tell me." She held the little nail-polish brush out in the air and blew on her toes.

"Okay," he said. He got off the bed and stood in front of her in his boxer shorts as if he was center stage. She started laughing.

"Okay," he said, "so this farmer is walking down a country road on his way to market . . ."

"Yes . . ."

"He's got a pig under one arm, a chicken under the other, and a bucket on his head to carry home the milk."

"Uh-huh . . ."

"So he comes upon this gorgeous farm girl—actually, she looks very much like you, my little sweetheart . . ."

"Go on," Gillian said.

". . . and he asks her for directions and she gives him, you know, a long list of very complicated directions: go straight ahead for two miles and then turn left at the big oak tree and then go right at the strawberry patch and five miles after that . . . you know . . ."

"Uh-huh."

"And then she says, I could show you a shortcut across the cornfield but you'd probably take advantage of me. And the farmer says, *Me? How could I take advantage of you?—I've got a pig under one arm, a chicken under the other, and a bucket on my head.*" Anthony frowned and Gilliana shot back, "And the girl flutters her eyelashes at the farmer and says, *Well, we could put the chicken in the bucket and I could hold the pig.*"

Tony stared at her. "What? What did you say?"

"I don't know—I said, 'We could put the chicken in the bucket and I could hold the pig.' "

"I can't believe it," Anthony said, laughing and picking Gillian up off the chair. "I love you, you little harlot, you fixed the fucking joke."

He did the joke that night at the second show. I didn't know he was going to do it, he didn't tell me, I practically fell on the floor. It wasn't just good, it brought the house down, they went crazy laughing. And it wasn't just the joke, it was Anthony, the way he became the big lug farmer and the way he fluttered his eyelashes when he became the girl, and when he said the last line and the audience went crazy, he turned and blew a kiss right at me where I was standing behind the trombone player in the band.

February 1973 ~ Los Angeles

"But it's Chasen's," Carole Rose said from the bathwater. "Why would you want to give up Chasen's? Is there an overabundance of cracked crab and toasted-cheese bread and butterfly steak with mustard sauce in your life? Hand me that bath stuff, will you? And besides, someone else is paying."

Gillian handed Carole Rose the bottle of bath oil. "I know."

"So?"

"I'm not in the mood."

"How can you not be in the mood for Chasen's? Maybe Frank Sinatra will be at the bar with his henchmen. We can take turns trying to get him to look at us. Come on." She lifted a hand of bath bubbles and blew some of them into the air at Gillian.

Gillian sat down on the tile floor of Carole Rose's bathroom and leaned her back against the wicker clothes hamper.

Carole Rose looked at her. "You can wear that new little black number you just got at Saks. It's great on you."

Gillian didn't answer.

"You like David. Don't you like David?"

"Yes."

"And Eric and Jeffrey . . . good friends, all sharing stimulating conversation together over very expensive red wine and perhaps even Chasen's banana shortcake, all on David's *New York Times* expense account. What could be a better way to start a long weekend?"

"I don't know. I'm just not in the mood, I guess."

Carole picked up the washcloth and a bar of soap.

"You're not in the mood because you're waiting for Mr. Spaghetti to call, right? Where is that bum anyway?"

"I don't know."

"What do you mean, you don't know? The guy doesn't make a move without you knowing. You mean he's missing?"

"Come on, Carole Rose."

"It's getting out of hand, Gillian. You don't go anywhere anymore. You just sit in this apartment waiting for him to call, and it's no good for you. That's not a life."

"I love him."

"I know that."

"Well?"

"Do you think he'd ever leave her?"

"I don't know."

"Do you talk about it?"

"No."

"Does he love you?"

"Yes. I think so. He says he does."

"Does he say he doesn't want you to go out to dinner with friends?"

"No, of course not."

"It's only friends, you know, it's not like somebody's gonna make a pass at you . . . I mean, you don't think David would make a pass at you or anything, do you?"

"No, of course not, I just—"

"—want to wait here so you can get Tony's call . . . right?"

"Mm-hm."

"You're worried about him because you haven't talked to him, right?"

"Yes."

"For how long?"

"Just two days."

"Jesus . . . and you won't go with us no matter what I say, right?"

"Right."

"Okay," Carole Rose said, sighing, "then I give up."

Gillian got up from the floor. She looked at her face closely in the mirror above Carole Rose's sink. "So, what are you going to wear?" she said to Carole Rose without looking at her.

"I don't know, I guess my dark green thing with the suede shoes."

"That'll be good," Gillian said. "It's very Chasen's." She turned to leave the bathroom.

"Hey, I'll bring you back something," Carole Rose said from the bathtub.

"You can't, Chasen's doesn't have take-out."

"It's okay, I'll bring a big purse."

He was with her, he was with me, he was with her, I was alone. Most of the time I was alone—I take that back, nearly all of the time I was alone, living on phone calls and fantasies. He was with her, so as far as I was concerned he was lying next to her, he was making love to her, he was looking at her instead of looking at me, and I was looking out the window at a palm tree, picturing it all in my head. Did he look at her the way he looked at me? Did he touch her the way he touched me? Did he this, did he that—all the things I would never ask him, all the things I kept to myself. I spent a lot of time driving to the ocean and walking back and forth in the sand. Very dramatic, very pathetic, very powerless. I had devoted myself to a man who didn't belong to me and who was three thousand miles away—not exactly the smartest choice, you might say.

April 1973 ~ Indianapolis

"And eggroll, I want eggroll, a hundred eggroll," Gillian says from behind the slick red menu.

"A hundred? How 'bout six?"

"Okay, six . . . and paper-wrapped chicken and kung pao chicken only with cashews, not with peanuts, and shrimp in lobster sauce . . . or is it black bean sauce I like?"

"It's lobster sauce you like. You want all of this *and* beef with broccoli? You'll explode," Tony says, laughing.

"I won't. I'm starving."

"Didn't you eat this week, my darling?" he says, reaching over and pushing down the menu to reveal her face.

"No," Gillian says, "I was waiting to eat with you."

"Oh, you were, were you?"

He leans over and kisses her nose.

She kisses his right cheekbone and moves her lips to his ear.

"I need a rewrite . . . I think 'I was waiting to eat with you' should be changed to 'I was waiting for you to eat me,' " Gillian whispers.

"I see. Well, Miss Ventimiglia, that can be taken care of—would you like that before or after the shrimp with lobster sauce?"

"After, I think, Mr. Ronzoni. After all, this may be a first for Indianapolis: 'Man seen eating woman at Happy Dragon restaurant on downtown Main Street amongst the chicken chow mein.' Oh, shit, Tony, I forgot I wanted chicken chow mein too, now I'll have to leave something else out."

He takes the menu from her, puts it on the table, and takes her hands in his.

"God, you make me happy, Miss Ventimiglia."

"I do?" she says, grinning at him. "Does that mean I can get the chicken chow mein?"

He was wonderful, he was funny, he was delicious, he was mine. Well . . . not exactly.

June 1973 ~ Miami Beach

"They're coming over," Gillian said, putting more mayonnaise on the club sandwich.

"No, they're not," Tony said with his eyes closed. He was lying on a chaise longue by the side of the hotel pool. Gillian watched the couple moving toward them.

"Yep, they've decided that it's really you . . . and . . . yes . . . here they come."

"Shit," Tony mumbled with his eyes still closed. "Tell them I'm sleeping."

"And who am I, the cabana boy? I'm not telling them anything. I'm going." She stood up.

"Come on, baby, don't go."

"She looks very Italian, very made up, lots of hair and lots of gold."

Tony smiled and opened one eye at her. "How does that make her Italian and not Jewish, *cara?*" he said, turning over on the chaise longue.

"I don't know, it's just a hunch. Maybe it's because he's very burly, he looks like he has people squashed under big trucks. I'll be going now, Mr. Ronzoni, I'll be upstairs, come and see me when you're done visiting with your fans."

"Gilliana, at least leave me half the sandwich."

"No way, mister, where I go, the sandwich goes. *Arrivederci,* you-all."

She scooped up the room key, turned and walked away with the sandwich as the people arrived at his side.

"Excuse me, Mr. Ronzoni?" the lady with the big hair said as she touched Tony's shoulder with her hand, "It is you, isn't it?"

* * *

So much for being a palm tree.

July 1973 ~ Los Angeles

"I won't be able to make it, baby. That's why I'm calling at dawn."

"Why?" Gilliana speaks low; the clock next to her bed says it's only five-seventeen in the morning in Los Angeles and she doesn't want to wake Carole Rose, who's sleeping in her bedroom on the other side of the hall. "I'm all packed, I worked it out with Harry and everything . . . Tony? What happened?"

"I forgot something."

"What?" It's still dark outside her window. She puts her hand over her mouth as she yawns. "What did you forgot, babe?"

The New York traffic roars before he speaks. "Someone's birthday," Tony says, and sighs into the pay phone at Fifth Avenue and Sixty-second.

Gilliana turns over onto her right side in the bed and pushes her hair back on the pillow. "Someone . . . oh, Jesus . . . you mean you forgot what's-her-name's birthday? How could you forget that?"

"I don't know."

"What's the matter? You sound funny."

"Nothing."

"Are you upset?"

"No, we'll just have to make it the week after. I'll talk to Harry if you want."

"Are you upset because you forgot her birthday?"

"No, I'm upset because now I won't be able to see you for another week."

"You could see me whenever you want to . . . if you wanted to . . . every minute of every day."

Uh-oh.

Silence.

Silence on the line. Just three buses and probably thirteen taxis, seven cars, and eight trucks go by. No one is speaking.

Gillian sits up naked in the bed in the dark bedroom listening to the traffic on the other end of the phone. The sheet falls away from her breasts into her lap. Her face is pale, she's frightened. She didn't mean to say that, it just fell out of her mouth.

"Anthony?"

Car honks.

"Anthony, I'm sorry. I shouldn't have said that."

"Yes, you should have."

"I'm sorry, I just haven't seen you for so long."

"Don't be sorry, Gilliana. You have a right to say that. You have a right to say whatever you want."

She begins to cry. "It's just that I miss you so much and the weeks go by and some days I'm strong and then there are days when I just can't bear it."

"What am I doing with my life here?"

"What? What did you say? I couldn't hear you."

"I said, What am I doing with my life here? What am I doing with you? This isn't some game with me, you know, I love you. You know that, don't you?"

"Yes."

"I love you, Gilliana. I don't want to hurt you."

"You're not hurting me."

"Yes, I am. I'm hurting everybody."

"Anthony . . ."

"Oh, Christ," he says, interrupting, "I can't believe this . . . it's goddamn eight-thirty; why did I ever say I'd do this thing . . . Look, I'm supposed to be at CBS and I'm still on Sixty-second . . . I'll call you right after . . . okay?"

"I'll be at work by then."

"I'll call you at work."

"I won't be able to talk to you, the phone'll keep ringing and Harry'll be hysterical and . . ."

"I'll call you after work."

"I won't get home till seven, seven-thirty."

"I'll call you."

"But that's ten-thirty your time, how will you get out?"

"Don't worry, I'll call you."

"Oh, God, Tony, I love you."

"I gotta go, babe, go back to sleep, bye bye . . ."

Trucks and cars and buses and the connection breaks. Silence. Gilliana puts down the dead receiver, lies back on the bed, covers herself with the sheet and the blanket, and tries to sob as quietly as she can into the pillow so she won't wake Carole Rose.

Drama. Sadness. Endless lonely weekends. Broken promises. Joy. Tears. Laughter. Heartache. Try perking up your life with some of this stuff. Have an affair with a married man.

July 1973 ~ Los Angeles

"Okay, she knows," Tony said.

Gillian shut the door to her bedroom and sat down on the foot of the bed, pulling the telephone with her.

"Gilliana?"

"I'm here."

"She knows."

"My God, what happened?"

"Not much, very simple. She was standing at the sink putting away the dinner dishes, I went in to get a Coke out of the fridge and when I opened the drawer to get the bottle opener next to where she was standing, she just turned and looked at me and said, 'I know.' "

"My God, Anthony, my heart is beating."

"Thank God your heart is beating."

"Don't make jokes."

"I'm not."

"Then what happened?"

"I asked her what she was talking about and she told me."

"What did she say?"

"She said she knew I was having an affair and that she didn't know who it was with and she didn't care, that she only cared that I wouldn't leave the children, that she was praying that I wouldn't, that she had told Father Maynard about it and he was praying with her. I never liked Father Maynard, that fuck . . . I knew better than to trust a priest with a mustache."

"Anthony . . ."

"And then she said that she was going to sleep in the other room until the whole thing was solved. As if I slept with her, I mean, I sleep with her but you know I don't sleep with her . . . oh, who the hell cares . . . anyway, 'solved,' that was the word she used, like it was a math problem."

"Jesus, Anthony."

"Hell, maybe she was right . . . one man, plus two women, plus two kids, take away one woman and one man . . . sounds like math to me . . ."

"Anthony, are you all right?"

"Yeah, I don't know, maybe not, I had three Bloody Marys for lunch."

"Bloody Marys? You don't drink Bloody Marys."

"I do now."

"Where are you?"

"At the office."

"Then what happened?"

"After the Bloody Marys?"

"Anthony, stop it, after she said that."

"Oh, let's see . . . oh, right, I just stood there holding the Coke bottle."

"You didn't say anything?"

"Nope, I just stood there like a stupid statue, a big stupid statue of a chicken, 'cause that's what I am—a chicken, Gilliana, I stood there like a big chicken and didn't open my mouth. I didn't say all the things I had planned on saying to her, all the things I'd been working on in my head for months, like 'I don't love you and I haven't loved you in such a long time and you know that and this isn't any way for either of us to live and we both need some happiness and what am I here for and I love someone else and I'm going' . . . I didn't say any of it . . . I didn't even cluck . . ."

"Oh, Anthony . . ."

"I just stood there until she wiped her hands on a dishrag and left the room. Oh, and she said she was praying for me before she left the room. She did say that . . . yep, that she was praying for me, that's what she said, all right."

"Oh, baby, you're drunk."

"Yep, I think so. I think I'm drunk."

"What did you eat for lunch with the Bloody Marys?"

"Uh, let's see now . . . I ate . . . the celery, that's right, I ate the celery in the glass. Yes, sirree."

Gillian held on to the receiver tightly.

Neither of them spoke for maybe half a minute.

"Shit," Tony said.

"What?"

"I don't know. Just shit."

Gillian listened to him breathing.

"Anthony?"

"What's the matter with me, *cara*? When did I turn into a chicken? Huh? Did you ever notice I was a chicken before?" And then his voice cracked. "I love my kids, *cara*, have I told you that? Have I told you how much I love my kids?"

"Yes, Anthony, you've told me."

And then Gillian sat quietly on the foot of her bed not moving or saying anything for at least five minutes while she listened to Tony cry.

Whose idea was it that what's-her-name should have God on her side? Not mine, that's for damn sure.

September 1973 ~ *Chicago*

Gillian smacked her pillow a few times, put it behind her back against the headboard of the bed, and sat up.

"You're not going to sleep?" Tony said.

"I'm not sleepy."

"Okay," he said, and rolled over with his back to her.

Gillian sat quietly.

"Do you want the light on?"

"No."

"Don't you want to read or something?"

"No."

"It won't bother me if you turn the light on."

"No, thank you."

"You're just going to sit there in the dark."

"Yes."

"Do you mind if I sleep?"

"No."

"Do you want room service?"

"It's three o'clock in the morning."

"They have twenty-four-hour room service."

"I'm not hungry."

"Sometimes you're hungry at three o'clock in the morning."

"Well, I'm not tonight."

"You could have pancakes."

"No, thank you."

"You love pancakes, Gilliana, maybe they have great pancakes. This is the Ambassador East; the Pump Room is upstairs, after all."

"I don't want them."

"Yes, ma'am, okay, no pancakes."

She stared straight ahead into the darkness.

"Are you mad?" he said.

"No."

"Are you hurt?"

"No."

"What are you?"

"Nothing."

He rolled over and looked at her. "You want to talk about this?"

"No."

"You don't want to talk about this."

"No."

"Gilliana?"

"What?"

She didn't look at him.

"Okay," he said, rolling over with his back to her again, "if you want to get yourself all upset over this, then get yourself all upset over this, but it's you doing it to yourself, not me. I love you. Remember?"

"Fine."

Neither of them moved.

"I can hear the clock ticking," he said.

She didn't answer.

"It's goddamn loud," he said.

"That's not my fault."

"But what's going on is my fault, right?"

"I didn't say that."

"I just said I needed a little more time."

"Fine."

"It's not easy to leave your kids."

"I know that."

"No, you don't," he said and then he didn't say anything.

Gillian bit her lip.

"Well, goodbye, kids, so long, but I must be leaving. Of course Daddy loves you, he's just got to go. You understand, don't you? I mean, you're only five and ten, but you understand. Sure you do. What smart kids you are, boy, oh, boy, what smart kids."

Gillian held her breath.

"That goddamn clock is fucking loud, Gilliana."

"It's not my clock, it belongs to the hotel."

"It's not your clock," he mumbled into the pillow with his back to her. "It's not your clock and it's not your kids."

"That's right," she said softly.

"I love you," he said, "you know that, don't you? You know how much I love you."

"Okay."

"It's just gonna take me a little time."

"Okay."

"It's not easy, Gilliana."

"Okay."

"Okay, okay, okay," he said, his voice rising. "Just give me a little time. Okay?"

"Okay."

He turned over abruptly, reached across her naked body, picked up the alarm clock, and threw it against the wall.

"Okay," he said, "thank you."

"You're welcome," she managed to get out.

We had a great joke in there somewhere, Anthony and I, about "a little time" and "give me a little time" and "here's a little time flying" as the alarm clock flew across the room, but somehow we couldn't get to it, somehow the joke got lost along the way.

September 1973 ~ Los Angeles

"I'm telling you he'll never leave her," Carole Rose said as she brushed her teeth. "He's Italian, Italians never leave them, too much guilt."

"I can't understand a word of what you're saying. And how can you brush your teeth when you're already all dressed up? What if you get toothpaste on your dress?"

Carole Rose turned from the sink and looked at Gillian sitting on the edge of the bathtub. "I said he'll never leave her, Italians never leave them, they have too much guilt."

"Oh, really . . . what about my father?" Gillian said.

Carole Rose stood there holding the toothbrush. "Right, I forgot about your father . . . but wait a minute, he was a gambler, that makes him an exception and besides, he wasn't married to an Italian. It's harder when they're married to an Italian, it's all that Catholic shit."

"Well, that's great, I feel much better now, thank you for telling me that."

"Well, shit. What do I know?"

"I don't know, I always think you know plenty."

"Oh, sure, I know all about men—that's why I'm married and I have three kids."

She smiled at Gillian. Gillian just sat there.

"Hey, come on, Gillian, I don't know anything, I don't even know when to brush my teeth, right?"

The point is Carole Rose was always smarter than I was. I was funnier but she knew more about the important things, especially men.

October 1973 ~ Los Angeles

"So, how are you?" Tony said.

"I'm fine. How's Philadelphia?"

"The same. You know, I'd rather be dead than—"

"—in Philadelphia," Gillian finished with him.

"Right, you know it."

"W. C. Fields. You taught me."

"Yep. I sure did."

Gillian walked around the couch again, twisting the phone cord between her fingers.

"So . . ." she said.

"So, you're fine," he said.

"Uh-huh."

"That's good."

"How long will you be there?"

"Oh, the benefit's tonight, I'll go back tomorrow morning."

"Uh-huh. Well, that's good."

Gillian sat down on the couch and then got up again. She walked around the coffee table and the wing chair. She got her foot caught in the telephone cord and sat back down on the couch.

"So . . ." she said again.

"I love you," he said.

"I love you too."

"This is just a temporary setback, Gilliana."

"I know."

"We'll get through this."

"I know."

"I love you."

"I love you too, Anthony."

"Okay, then. Well, I'll call you from New York."

"Okay."

"Tomorrow, I'll call you tomorrow."

"Okay."

"Will you be there?"

"I'll be here."

"But it's Sunday, maybe you want to go to brunch or something . . ."

"I'll be here."

"Okay. I love you, *cara.*"

"I love you too, Anthony."

"Okay . . . well, then, I'll talk to you tomorrow."

"Okay, bye, have a good show."

"Okay, bye."

Gillian put the receiver back on the hook as Carole Rose came in the room. "Hey, I got the new *Vogue.* You want to look at it, we can pick out all the things we want that we can't afford?"

"Sure."

"What's the matter? You look like you just got hit by a bus."

"Anthony's never gonna leave her."

"Jesus Christ, you mean he just said that?"

"No. I just know."

"No, you don't."

"Yes, I do."

So much for premonitions, intuitions, feelings, and clues.

November 1973 ~ San Francisco

"I'm doing it, Gilliana. I'm leaving her. I've decided, I'm sure."

Gilliana's teeth made a clunk sound against the room-service coffee cup; she was sitting on the closed toilet seat, fully dressed for the airplane, drinking coffee while she watched Tony shave at the bathroom sink.

She lowered the cup from her mouth as tears filled her eyes. She couldn't say anything, she'd lost her breath.

"I am," he said.

He lowered the razor and looked at her. He was naked and still wet from the shower, drops of water ran down his chest.

"I am, Gilliana, it's all I think about." He smiled at her, his face was open and loving, he looked as if he was sixteen years old. "I can't stand this anymore—I don't want you to go, I want to be with you. After all," he said, "I love you—what am I waiting for?"

"Oh, God," Gillian said as she began to sob.

Tony put the razor on the sink, took the cup from her, and placed it next to the razor. He took her hands in his, pulled her to her feet and into his arms.

"I'll work it out with the kids, I'll see them all the time. You'll live in New York, won't you? I mean, it's okay with you to live in New York, isn't it, *cara?* I don't want to be too far from them."

"Oh, God, Anthony," Gilliana sobbed as he kissed her, the front of her taupe suit getting very wet and Palmolive menthol shaving cream melting across her right cheek and on her nose.

I missed the plane. And he didn't leave her. Well, he did leave her but not exactly—we had a little unexpected problem that circumvented the plan just as he was packing his bags.

December 1973 ~ New York City

"I love you, my *cara,*" Tony said, watching the back of Gillian from across the room.

"What did you say, mister?" she said, turning and putting her purse down on the mahogany coffee table, "I didn't hear you. Jesus, this suite is magnificent—is it my Christmas present or what?"

He looked at her.

She smiled and slipped off her coat. "I mean, I don't mind getting a Taj Mahal kind of room for five days as my Christmas present, but I was kind of counting on the car and the diamonds and the emeralds and the yacht and the trip to Italy and the mink coat . . ."

"What kind of car?"

"Anthony, why are you looking so serious? I was kidding, I don't want anything."

"I know. What kind of car?"

"I have a car."

"You have an old Ford Falcon that can hardly make it on flat ground."

"I love that car."

"You need a new one."

"Okay, someday I'll get a new one. Why are you standing way over there?" she said, walking to where he was at the windows.

"I was looking at the view."

"No you weren't, you were looking at me."

"Well, I meant to look at the view but I saw you first."

"I love you," she said, wrapping her arms around him.

They turned together and looked out at the black New York night, at the twinkling traffic lights and Central Park.

"What did you say to me before?" Gillian said, kissing the shoulder of his topcoat. "And why don't you take your coat off?"

"When?"

"When we walked in, you said something . . ." She turned from the window and looked at him. He stayed perfectly still facing the window. "What's the matter, Anthony? What's wrong? Why won't you look at me?"

"I'm gonna buy you a new car."

Gillian laughed. "I don't want a new car. Is that what's bothering you? My car?"

He blinked, his eyes stayed straight ahead, glued to the night sky outside the window of the Plaza Hotel.

"Anthony?"

"And we'll go to Italy before it's all over, that's where we'll go. I'll take you."

"Okay, we'll go to Italy. Before what's all over? What's the matter?"

He didn't answer her.

"Anthony, please, you're scaring me. What's wrong?"

He turned and looked at her.

"I have a melanoma, *cara,* I have a deep, thick, black melanoma embedded in my back below my left shoulder blade, and the odds are I'm going to die."

Well, Merry Christmas, Gillian. Maybe that will teach you not to fool around with a married man, maybe that will teach you once and for all.

Clare

My mother called and asked me if I believed in God. Can you believe that? First she won't talk to me and now she calls and wants to talk theology. I say "Hello?" and she says, "Clare, do you believe in God?" I mean, it wasn't as if I had time to prepare.

I know what she's doing, she's trying to make her peace with everything—you know, about my grandmother—and there was a part of me that wanted to say yes, because I knew that would make her feel better, but really, I don't know how a person can believe in God with what goes on today. I can believe in Him about the life part, like creating the world and all, and maybe even creating us from Adam and Eve and, of course, I do say His name for stupid stuff—like, please God, have Scott call me, or please God, let me get an A—but that's not believing, that's just, like, who else are you gonna say it to?

The part that stops me is the death part. I mean, how can anybody believe in Him about the death part? It just doesn't add up. Like how does He decide who to take if He's really up there? The angels bring Him a list and He goes eeney, meeney, miney, moe? Or He looks down from His throne where He sits on this big white fluffy cloud and says, oh, goody, there's one, he looks good, I'll take him, and He points a thunderbolt and that's it, the guy's gone? I mean, it's so random. It's not like He only takes the bad guys. As far as I can tell, the bad guys seem to make it, it's the good guys that He takes. Even in my life if I think about who I know that's already dead, and I'm only about to be seventeen . . . I mean, even in my life, it makes no sense.

The first guy I knew that died was when I was just in junior high, seventh grade, I think, or maybe eighth, I don't remember exactly, but we'd gone to the same elementary school. He got killed riding his bike. Now, why would God want him, huh? I mean, you try to come up with an explanation; he was only—what? fourteen? God needed him for some special function? Anyway, some hit-and-run dick ran over him and just left him dying there in the street next to his bike. They never even found out who did it. He had this complicated, long Israeli name like Elliyahoo or something, but we just called him El, and he had dark hair and dark eyes and was kind of reckless, not that I knew what reckless was when I was only eleven or twelve, but he was reckless, as I remember, and he could really ride his bike. He was from the Valley. That's this part of L.A. that's over the mountain, you have to cross Mulholland Drive to get there—Mulholland Drive is kind of famous, that's where everybody races around on these curvy roads way up high with skinny edges; lots of people probably died flying off of there but I don't know any of them—anyway, on the other side of that is the Valley. El lived in some flat neighborhood in the Valley, you know, where everybody rides their bike from the time they can walk or something and El practically lived on his bike, he was like "one" with it, if you know what I mean. Anyway, he was the first person I knew who died and I felt bad, you know, but when it happened I hadn't seen him for maybe three years, since he was three years ahead of me, and by then we went to different schools. So I felt bad about it, but that was nearly all. Bad and kind of stunned, I guess. I mean, that somebody could actually be there and then be gone, you know, just not be there anymore. It's amazing, not only the first time you think about it, but always. It makes no sense. But El was the first time I had to really think about it. I tried at the time to conjure up some special memories of him to keep in my head, but I didn't have too many. After all, I was only eleven or so, how many memories can you have stored up at eleven?

And then my friend's mother died, which was really pretty freaky since she was also killed by a hit-and-run driver, and in the Valley, if you can believe that. It seemed to me then that there must be all these hit-and-run drivers running around the Valley smashing into people and driving away. Really. And I was going to school in the Valley at the time. Anyway, they did catch that guy. He was drunk, so drunk that he didn't even know that he'd hit a real person, he thought he'd just hit some stationary object when he ran into her, like a building or something and not my friend Karen's mother. Can you imagine how drunk you would have to be to think that?

Anyway, she was my first funeral, I went with my parents. It was in this little chapel kind of building in the Valley and they said some prayers and people got up and talked about her; my mother even got up and talked because she knew my friend's mother from before either of them were married, long before Karen and I were even born—they were secretaries together somewhere. Luckily, my mother was not embarrassing, she just kind of talked to my friend Karen from the podium and reassured her how much her mother loved her; it was actually okay. The hard part for me was looking at Karen and not knowing what to say to her, so I just gave her a hug and kind of patted her shoulder. I mean, what was I supposed to say to her, "I'm sorry your mother's dead"? Anyway, I didn't go to the cemetery, I went back to school.

The only time I've gone to a cemetery is with my mother to visit Harry Witzer. She used to work for this guy she really loved named Harry Witzer—she worked for him when she first started typing in L.A. until she wasn't a secretary anymore, until she started writing comedy, if you can call it that. Anyway, he was a major influence in her life and helped her and she really loved him. I don't mean romantically or anything, he was much older, but anyway, she really misses him. She has these pictures of him all over her office and she really wants me to remember him. She'll say, "Don't you remember when you were little and Harry would do pratfalls up the steps from the living room to make you laugh?" Which, of course, I couldn't remember since I was maybe only one and a half at the time, but I do remember him from when I was a little older and we went to eat in some Italian restaurant and I remember how I was standing next to him while he was sitting and I put my arm around his shoulders and he was so skinny his bones were sticking out and it scared me—that's about all I remember. Oh, and that he played the harmonica—at least I think I remember that, but maybe it's only because my mother has told me about a million times. Anyway, he was supposedly this really great funny guy from what they tell me. I mean, even my dad says how great Harry Witzer was, and I guess besides really missing him my mother would like him to be here so they could talk about her work. Because he really believed in her—that she could be something someday—so sometimes she actually goes to the cemetery to talk to him. I don't mean she's crazy or anything, I think she goes there because it's peaceful and she can concentrate and I guess he always made her feel good about herself so that's why she goes there, to kind of put herself back in touch with herself and clear her head. You know, like sometimes when you need a new perspective when everything gets muddled up? Anyway, every now and then I go with her. I kind of clean his stone off and sometimes we plant flowers in these pots. But I specifically remember the first time.

He's buried in a really little cemetery tucked behind a lot of tall buildings in Westwood—that's this area in L.A. with big office buildings and lots of movie theaters and stores and restaurants and all—it's right next to U.C.L.A., so there's always a million college kids roaming around. Anyway, hidden in the middle of all this is this little cemetery. Really, you wouldn't believe it. All this green grass and trees with leaves swaying and flowers blooming behind all the traffic and shit. Marilyn Monroe is buried there. Well, actually, she's not buried, she's kind of shoved into a drawer in the middle of a marble wall with a lot of other dead people. But, you know, in the front of her drawer is the long-stemmed red rose that that famous ballplayer guy still has put there for her fresh every day. Joe DiMaggio. So, anyway, that's this cemetery's claim to fame—Marilyn Monroe in a marble drawer.

Anyway, Harry's not in a drawer, he's in the ground, but it's really only his ashes in the ground. Of course, I didn't know that the first time I went there. Really, I couldn't believe it, I got out of the car with my mother and she says, "He's over here"—actually, it's kind of nice where he is, he's under this really leafy low pepper tree that's all wispy and beautiful—so I'm following her and I say, "God, Mom, you have to step on people to get to him? Excuse me, I think I'll wait in the car." And she's kind of laughing, but it's true, they don't have standing headstones at this cemetery, they're all flat on the ground and they're really close together so you have to like tippy-toe around to not be stepping on someone. So I'm following her and then it dawns on me that these people must all be very short or something, or else how do they all fit? I mean, the stones are very close together and if you look at how they're all placed you realize that Harry Witzer was either a very, very short man or the lady in front of him has her feet on his nose. So I see this and I get hysterical and I'm really laughing, you know, the way you do when you can't help yourself, and my mother starts laughing too because she can't help it either. Anyway, it was maybe one of the nicer moments I've had with my mother since I'm a teenager. I don't know, maybe not, but I think so, the two of us falling all over each other laughing at Harry Witzer's grave. I mean, at one point we were both actually kind of sprawled on the grass laughing so hard we couldn't get up. I'm sure the cemetery people saw us, but my mother didn't care. She even said Harry would have loved it. Actually, the reason the plots are so small there is that there's only people's ashes buried under the grass in urns or whatever, not their actual bodies in one piece, so they don't need a lot of space.

I guess the best part about what happened was that she didn't use it, you know? I mean, knowing my mother, she could have turned it into some routine for asshole Andy and that would have killed me, but she didn't; she refrained, thank God.

So, look, see?—I used Him—I mean, I said "thank *God,*" but that's an expression that people say without thinking, you know, it's not like they believe in Him when they say it, it's just like they're pressing their luck.

It's like I think, How can you believe in God when you see what goes on in the world today? I mean, do you watch the news? People dying the way they did in Rwanda that time, tons of people just toppling over like when you hit a stream of ants with Raid—like they were nothing. And all that shit between those people in Bosnia, both sides shooting the shit out of each other for a million years—and for what? I mean, who cares who's right or wrong? It doesn't make any difference anymore, there's hardly anybody left. Shooting at kids trying to get a drink of water, babies in their mother's arms while they stand in line waiting for a scrap of bread. Jesus. I mean, is God behind that shit?

And cancer, how about kids dying from cancer—what did they do? something wrong before they were born?—look at an angel cross-eyed or something? I mean—what?

And getting shot at by gangs in the street—I mean, a little kid can be standing in a school yard playing ball and somebody drives by in a fast car with a big gun and boom, he's dead. A four-year-old spread-eagled on a playground with the ball still in his hands while blood is spilling out of his guts turning his tennis shoes red.

And airplanes. Something called a "wind shear factor" comes out of nowhere from behind a pink sunset and the next thing you know, what used to be a big silver DC-10 airplane is smithereened into chunks of scrap metal on the ground, and body parts are hanging all over tree branches and spread across lawns and driveways from two hundred-and-something dead people who were just watching a movie and eating vegetarian lasagna up in the sky. I mean, how can you believe in somebody who would do that? Is that God? Well, if it is, then I can't buy it.

Maybe you have to be born Catholic; then it gets ingrained in you right from the start. The Father, the Son, and the Holy Ghost. I mean, it sounds good, but of course I don't know anything about it. I know some kids who were born Catholic and a few of them go to church, but I don't think I know anybody who goes every Sunday the way people used to. I mean for Christmas, maybe, if you're Christian, and Easter Sunday, and Yom Kippur if you're Jewish, and I don't know what you do if you're Buddhist; I know one guy who's Buddhist and I think he celebrates Christmas, but I don't think they go anywhere, his family—like to a church, I mean. Maybe nobody goes to church anymore. I mean all faiths. Maybe that's what's wrong with the world today.

I was thinking that maybe they should bring church back, make it mandatory for everyone. Of course, that would mess up people's sex lives 'cause you weren't supposed to do it then until you got married, and people didn't have babies out of wedlock and gay people were in the closet and it would change everything—drinking and drugs and music and how we dress and what we say and what we do—it would all go backward and then where would we be? I don't know, it's very confusing.

Maybe in the old days when people went to church there wasn't as much bad stuff going on, maybe that's why they could believe in God. I mean, I don't want to eliminate people's freedoms or bring back olden-day morality or anything, but something's definitely wrong in the world today with all this random violence. Maybe the world could change and it could be like this magic cycle, you know—like everybody could go to church again and everybody could believe in God again and then maybe He would fix things and make the world a better place the way it was before. But how would you get everybody to go backward? I mean, really . . . it would be impossible. It's hard enough for most people to just go on.

Anyway, at this point, I don't think I believe in God, so when my mother asked me, I said no.

Mollie

I put on my hat and gloves, took the bus downtown, and got a job.

Not at first—at first I tried to pretend that Julie was overseas, I tried to go on like I did when he was in the war, but that didn't last long because he wanted to see Gilliana. How could I picture Jule marching up a storm in a uniform in Germany when he was standing like a stranger looking at me in our living room?—or not looking at me—each of us not looking at the other, me looking at the side of his face or down at my feet in my shoes or both of us only looking at Gilliana so we wouldn't see each other's eyes. It was too hard to look at him or not look at him, it was too hard to see him at all.

So I decided it would be better if he'd pick her up at Sophia's. I would take her there and leave her and he'd pick her up and bring her back there and then I'd go pick her up and bring her home. That way I wouldn't see him. Such a *meshugas,* you don't want to know. Julie and I moving Gilliana around like she was a red checker on a checkerboard. A *meshugas* in Yiddish is a craziness, and I use that word because when I saw what I was doing there I realized it was a craziness and I had to stop.

I was hiding behind a maple tree down the street from Sophia's in front of the Costellos' house watching Julie and Gilliana, studying the back of him as he put her in his car, his hand on her shoulder, his hand locking the door as he put her in, watching his stride as he walked around to the other side of the car, his shoulders, his back, holding my breath standing there watching him from behind the Costellos' maple tree, looking through the green maple leaves as if I was Mata Hari looking through a green veil, and when I turned around Georgina Costello was staring at me from her front steps with her arms crossed over her chest and with a look on her face like I had lost my mind. What could I tell her?—I'd become a spy? That's when I realized what I was doing was a craziness and if I didn't stop they'd put a straitjacket on me . . . So, the very next morning, it was a Monday, I put on my hat and gloves and took the bus downtown.

I found a job doing the exact same thing I'd done before I knew him—a bookkeeper in a dress factory. Only, the difference was that before Jule I couldn't wait to finish the day to get away from all the numbers, and this time they were a gift to me. When you do numbers, that's all you can think about, you have to write them clearly in black ink in perfect ledger columns, the accounts receivable and the accounts payable, you have to make sure everything is exactly in order to get them to balance, that's all you can think about—the numbers—which means, of course, you can't think about your husband leaving you. Only the rest of the time you can think.

When I got dressed, when I attached my stockings to my garter belt, when I put on my lipstick, brushing the red color inside the line, when I made Gilliana's lunch, cutting the crusts off her peanut-butter-and-jelly, brushing her hair, reading her a story, when I sat on the bus going downtown, when I made supper, turning the salmon croquettes over in the pan, hearing the sizzle as they hit the fat, mashing the potatoes, seeing the butter melt yellow in the middle of the white, when I took a bath or read a magazine, all I could see was his face, in the aisles of the grocery store, coming toward me from across the street, on the pillow next to me in the bed. Jule.

And then the months went by and then it was a year later and little by little I found my way. I picked up the pieces, as Dell would say. Of course, I still loved him—that had nothing to do with it—you don't live with a man for so long and feel the way I did about him and then that's that—but little by little I got stronger. Even though I had a big hole in me, I went on. And by the time he asked me if he could come back, I knew it was better for me to stay the way I was, so I said no.

Who would have thought such a thing could happen?—Jule asking to come back and me saying no? Nobody would have believed that I could do that, not in a million years; everybody would have thought I'd take him back on a bet. Even I would have bet on it. Even my Jule would have bet on it; he would have been positive that a bet like that would have been better than what he called "a sure thing"; he would have been positive that a bet like that would have been what he called "a lock." But he would have been wrong, like all gamblers are, because they forget that even the surest thing can still turn out to be a sucker bet.

"I love you, Mol," Jule said.

Mollie stared at his hands on the steering wheel, the dark-olive skin as if he'd just been sunbathing, his square stubby nails, his wedding ring. She turned her head away. It was nearly dark, the streetlights flashed on, the houses on the Hill now suddenly bathed in amber light.

"I know," she said. She watched their neighbor Mr. Spano rake the last heap of colored leaves into the big pile he'd already moved into the center of his yard. He was wearing work pants and boots with just his undershirt on—he had taken his other shirt off and hung it over the wooden fence that separated their yards. Mollie kept her eyes focused on Mr. Spano's navy-and-dark-green plaid shirt as it flapped around in the October twilight.

"I'll always love you," he said.

"I'll always love you too."

He put his hand on her knee. "Mollie, look at me."

She turned her head to his.

"I want to come back, it will be different now."

"It won't, Jule."

"Yes, it will, I told you, honey, I don't gamble anymore."

"Maybe for now you don't, but you will."

"No . . ."

"You will, Jule, you know you will. It's just a matter of time."

"I won't, I promised you."

Mollie looked down at Julie's hand on her knee. She moved her own matching wedding ring unconsciously around her finger with her right hand.

He leaned forward and kissed her lips but she didn't kiss him back. It was the first time in her whole life that Mollie hadn't kissed Jules back.

He moved his face back from hers; his eyes were filled with tears. Mollie turned her head away.

"I miss you, Mol, I can't do it without you."

Mollie watched Mr. Spano set fire to the leaves, she watched them catch and burn, dark-orange flames rising against the navy sky. She watched the flames burn with Mr. Spano as he leaned solidly against his rake and wiped his face and neck with a white handkerchief.

"Mollie?"

"I can't do it again, Jule, I'm too afraid."

"I won't gamble, I promise."

"You can't help it, you will."

"I won't."

"Oh, Julie, yes you will. You'll promise you won't and then you will and we'll argue and you'll promise and then you will again. And every time it will be just like the lamps."

"What lamps?"

"And then eventually I'll hate you. I don't want to hate you, I couldn't stand it if I hated you."

He reached across the front seat of the Plymouth and took her in his arms. He held on to her tightly. "You could never hate me, Mol," he said, his face close to hers. "You'll always love me. And I'll always love you. We were meant to be. Don't you know that?"

His eyes were very brown as he looked at her. He kissed her again and she kissed him back. She could feel herself melt into him, all the old feelings coming back.

"Remember how we made it through Sandy together? Remember how I came back to you after the war? There'll always be us, Mol," Jule said into her hair. "It's got to be."

It was as if a soft air suddenly surrounded her, an invisible cushion protecting her from the rest of the world that she always thought of as Jule's love—she could feel it slide around her and entwine her like his arms around her waist. She loved him and he loved her—maybe this time, maybe it could work, she knew it could . . .

Mollie kissed Jule hard and held on to him, and then as she felt herself slipping down on the seat with him, she could see Sophia's face the night of the diamond.

She pulled away from Jules, out of his arms.

"I can't," she said.

"I won't gamble, Mollie."

She opened the car door fast as she slid across the seat from him.

"Please, Mollie, don't do this."

She opened the car door, put one foot on the pavement, and she ran.

"Mollie, I love you!" Jules yelled.

She didn't even shut the car door, she just kept going; one foot and then the other, running in her new brown suede pumps across the front walk of Mr. Spano's house, through the gray smoke in her new cocoa sweater and skirt—she could feel the wool against her stockinged knees—across the grass of her own yard, up the front walk and the three steps and inside. Mollie didn't look back, she just ran.

Dell was standing at the living-room window looking out at Jule's car when Mollie unlocked the front door, slammed it shut, locked it, and stood there breathless.

"So, what happened? What was the big deal that he had to see you to talk?"

"He wanted to come back. Where's Gilliana?"

"Jules asked you if he could come back?"

"Uh-huh. Where's the baby?"

"In the bedroom, making something with a lot of Elmer's glue. Mollie, wait a minute—he asked you to come back?"

"Uh-huh."

"And you said no? You, who've been waiting for this day to come for over a year? Who's bought a brand-new outfit you can't afford? Who's been putting on 'Bravo' lipstick since twelve o'clock this afternoon? You look like you're gonna throw up. You said no?"

"Uh-huh."

"Jesus, Mollie, I thought you wanted him back."

"I did."

"So what are you doing?"

"I don't know . . . is he still out there?"

Dell turned and looked out the window. "He's sitting in the car behind the wheel."

"I'm going to help the baby."

"Jesus, Mollie, you're just going to leave him out there?"

"I'm going to help Gilliana with her project for school."

"Mollie . . ."

"Leave me alone, Dell. I have to do this."

Mollie turned and walked quickly out of the living room and down the hall.

Dell stood at the window and watched Jule's Plymouth idle in front of the Spanos' house for forty-six minutes. Her eyes became transfixed by the exhaust from the tailpipe as if it held her captive at the glass. She smoked three cigarettes and bit two fingernails off her right hand until Jule swung the car out from the curb and drove away. Then she poured herself a large scotch, drank it in four gulps, went to the telephone, and called Nat to come and take her home.

So I would be alone, it would be better. And besides, I wasn't alone, I had Gilliana.

There was only one bedroom and Gilliana had always slept in that bedroom while Jule and I slept on the hide-a-bed sofa in the living room, but when I knew for sure that Jule wasn't coming back I moved into the other twin bed in the bedroom with her. We became roommates, my Gilliana and me. Maybe that wasn't a good thing, putting all of my love into a little girl, maybe it was too much for her, but I didn't know any better so that's what I did.

For my fortieth birthday I got a divorce. And I became a *shandeh* twice.

Gilliana

My hair needs coloring. The gray ones are suddenly overtaking the brown ones . . . it probably all happened today.

I went to three homes this morning. The first thing I learned is that they don't call them that, a "home," they call them anything but that: a "nursing facility," a "convalescent center," a "care center"; one was even called a "guest residence," which I thought was pretty funny—as if you were a guest who could leave when your holiday was over—and these words are always coupled with the pretty words like "garden" or "terrace" or the name of a flower, as in the Fountain View Gardens, the first place I went, which actually does have a fountain in the middle of "the grounds," a stretch of brown yard that runs around three sides of the place; the lady in charge proudly pointed out the fountain to me, which, of course, isn't turned on now because it's too cold.

Next was the Briar Oak Terrace Facility; now, here they have succeeded in working a specific tree into the name of the place and not just an oak but a briar oak, which I assume is better somehow or at least more visual to the people moving in if they are conscious enough to know. How the briar oak works with the terrace, I don't know.

And then there was the Mariposa Guest Residence—is that a tulip? A tulip in Spanish? Or a butterfly? I don't know. Tomorrow I go to the

Shalom Courtyard—they don't mind that I want to come on Christmas, probably because they have Shalom in their name.

The second thing I learned is you have a choice of how to behave upon leaving these places; while you're there you behave like a lady, which isn't difficult to do because you're stunned, but once you leave you have a choice, you can either gag or yell. And you can do this either before you get into your car or during the drive to the next place, it doesn't matter which. Oh, I'm sorry, three choices, I left out crying and sobbing, which is actually one choice and should be written with a slash or a hyphen since it's hard to cry without sobbing and vice versa. I guess one can only do these things when one is alone. Lucky me, I was alone.

Tomorrow is Christmas, Mollie's birthday. Should we have a cake? Would she know what a cake is?

Oh, God.

The three places have all blurred into one for me and only certain things remain: the putrid smell of bad food and urine and old people—that was in all three. It didn't matter how clean each looked or how nice each lobby was, which turns out to be very important since the lobby is where you enter and it is your first impression, so they do a lot with their lobbies—lots of fancy couches and chairs and magazines and ficus trees. The lobbies all have discreet closed doors that open onto long corridors, which is where the fun begins.

At the Mariposa, the man in charge, Mr. Billingsly, who had a humiliating problem with clicking dentures that I pretended not to hear or see, explained how they allow *their* guests to bring their own furniture with them when they move into their rooms so they can feel more "at home." You can bring your huge mahogany dresser and your overstuffed wing chair with you and cram them into your private room for $117 a day or into your semiprivate room for $95 a day. This means it costs $22 a day extra if you don't want to share. I could not ask Mr. Billingsly how they came up with that figure; I believe I had my hand clenched over my mouth at the opportune moment.

He was gracious enough to show me what he was talking about. Mrs. Annie Moskowitz, who thought I was her Aunt Soochie, has a lot of her living room and bedroom stuffed in with her around her hospital bed: a soiled olive corduroy club chair and ottoman that she reminded me belonged to Michael (Mr. Moskowitz, I assume), a six-drawer heavy dresser with clawed feet, two end tables with china lamps and filthy fringed lampshades, and possibly a hundred photographs, framed. The photographs are propped up everywhere, on every available surface in the room. Since Mrs. Moskowitz thought I was her Aunt Soochie, I am sure she has no idea who the people are in the frames. I yelled after I left the Mariposa.

At the Briar Oak Terrace Facility ("facility" makes it sound like a jail, doesn't it?—a jail with briar oak trees) they have two separate sections, Mrs. Boyer, the head matron, pointed out to me. Excuse me, I mean head lady, not head matron, don't I? One section for the people who are really sick and one section for the people who are not so sick. I believe the difference is whether or not you are tied to your chair. At the Briar Oak I was able to sample the food, and then Lew couldn't understand why I didn't want to eat anything when I got home. Silly Lew. Actually, I had driven to Winstead's to make myself feel better and eat what I used to eat in high school, but for some reason my legs didn't feel like working so I just sat in the car.

And then I called Christopher from a phone booth, but unfortunately I got Clare. I say unfortunately because I tried to talk to her, but I wasn't in the best of moods and before I knew what happened we were having a big fight about God. This, of course, was not my intention but nearly everything that goes on between Clare and me is never what I had planned. It's as if we're each speaking a different foreign language. Was it that way between Mollie and me?

We will keep Mollie at home. I don't care what it costs, I will sell my soul. Or the house. Or ask Andy for the money. Or ask anybody—who cares . . .

And then this afternoon I met Mrs. Minnie Jane Jones Pomerantz, who came to visit from the First Choice Home Care Nursing Service. Quite a mouthful. I assume the First Choice Home Care Nursing Service employs only the first-choice nurses in town.

Mrs. Pomerantz is a practical nurse. She can take blood pressure, give shots, medicine, or a bath, she cooks and feeds her "ladies"—that's what she calls her patients because, as she explained, she "doesn't take care of no gentlemens no more"—she also changes her "ladies' " diapers and does their laundry. She keeps their areas tidy, she said. She does not do for anybody else in the house, just for the people in her care, "nothin' for nobody else," she said. When she said that, she looked at Lew but he didn't say anything back. Neither did I. Mrs. Pomerantz had just said the word "nothin' " exactly like my mother did; I was riveted to the chair.

Mrs. Pomerantz is a large semisweet-chocolate-colored woman with deep-set brown eyes and gray braids. The braids are coiled around her head in a style somewhat similar to Princess Leia's in *Star Wars* but with little curly wisps of gray popping haphazardly out of the braids, creating a kind of silver halo effect around Mrs. Pomerantz's brown face. Her hands are big. I believe that with a minimum of effort Mrs. Pomerantz could pick Mollie up and chuck her hard against a wall. She wore a white uniform, spongy white nurses' shoes, and white hose. She didn't have a lot of time to visit with us, she said, what with it being Christmas Eve and all.

Mrs. Pomerantz can work through the First Choice Home Care Nursing Service or not. If she works through them, she gets $13.50 an hour during the day hours on weekdays and $14.50 during the night hours and on the weekends. If she doesn't work through the First Choice Home Care Nursing Service, she will make you a "deal," but only if you pay her cash. That's if she likes the "lady."

In my head I try to add up the $13.50s and the $14.50s and if it's only so many hours a day or if it's twenty-four hours a day, but I can't do it, I need paper, because it couldn't be that you would be paying someone $400 a day to be in your mother's house and take care of her . . . that would be how much a week? Two thousand a week for just the weekdays? That can't be.

"Oh, yeah, it can, missus," Mrs. Pomerantz tells me, "that's why they gots to change the health care, because the Medicare, it don't pay. If you stays in the hospital it pays, but if you goes home, it don't."

My fingers are holding on to the chair I'm sitting on because I feel I'm going to fall off. Mrs. Pomerantz smiles at me. Lew is very pale. I smile back at Mrs. Pomerantz.

"And how much would a 'deal' be?" I ask graciously.

"It would depends on the hours I keeps and how sick the lady be," Mrs. Pomerantz says.

"I see."

Up till now Mollie is being held captive in the bedroom by Dorothy LaPaglia. I decide we should let them meet. I have fallen for Mrs. Pomerantz. I know it is because Mrs. Pomerantz has said the word "nothin' " just the way my mother does and I know that that is the stupidest reason in the world, but I can't help myself. I know it couldn't be possible that Mrs. Pomerantz could be the one—the angel who has been sent to help us with Mollie couldn't possibly be the first person who walks in the door. I know that would be next to impossible, but what the hell . . .

I stand up. "Maybe you should meet my mother, Mrs. Pomerantz."

Mrs. Pomerantz stands up. "Maybe that would be best, missus, and then we shall sees what we shall see."

A lot of what happens next is a blur for me, but I know clearly how it began. Mrs. Pomerantz and I went into Mollie and Lew's bedroom. Lew did not join us; he stayed put in his chair. Maybe he fainted, I'm not sure. Dorothy LaPaglia was on the edge of the big bed and my mother was in a chair. Not tied, just sitting, it occurred to me, which somehow made me want to dance around the room laughing and singing, but I didn't. I didn't do anything and nobody said anything to anybody, we just walked into the room.

Mrs. Pomerantz went directly to my mother; she stood in front of her and looked at her until Mollie raised her eyes.

"Hello," my mother said very politely to this large brown stranger.

"Hello, Mommy," Mrs. Pomerantz said to my mother, and held out her hands, "how 'bouts you come with me?"

Mollie smiled, put her hands in Mrs. Pomerantz's, and stood up.

"Where?" my mother said.

"How 'bouts we takes us a little walk around this house?"

"All right, Jules," my mother said brightly.

Oh, no, Mollie's gonna blow it, she called Mrs. Pomerantz Jules . . . I take a step toward them as if I had a way to signal Mollie to try to behave normally, but neither of them pays any attention to me.

"It's okay if you wants to calls me that, Mommy," Mrs. Pomerantz said gently to my mother. "My name is Minnie Jane Jones Pomerantz, but for you I could be Jules."

We will make a deal with Mrs. Pomerantz; I don't care if she's a serial killer, we will make a deal.

I tried to explain about her and everything that happened today when I finally got Christopher on the telephone, but he was having a great deal of trouble understanding me—that's what happens when you sob and cry and talk at the same time, it's difficult for people to hear.

Clare

My father wants me to go to church with him. I mean, I'm going, it's Christmas Eve. He asked me so sweetly I couldn't say no to him and I wouldn't say no, I hardly ever say no to him. We have to get there early because it fills up fast—it's like nobody goes to church forever and then everybody remembers they'd better go to church on Christmas Eve. Not my father, he actually goes to church every now and then. I don't mind going, I like the carol part. First are the carols and then the service, because the big deal if you're Episcopalian is to not get to the Communion part of the service until after midnight so it will actually be Christmas when you're taking Communion, you know? Not that I take Communion, I don't take anything. Anyway, I've gone before.

It's really interesting to me how well I get along with my father, because I really don't get along with my mother at all. It's like we're each speaking a different foreign language, you know? I mean, I know part of it is hormonal, mood swings and all, but that's only a part of it. I have my own theory.

I think a lot of it is jealousy. I mean, just think about it: I'm in essence starting out and she's in essence ending up. Not that she's over the hill or a hundred years old or anything, it's just that my hormones are probably running around my body raging to break free and hers are probably lying down in her ovaries taking a nap. Did you ever think about that?

That's probably the root of all the evil madness that goes on between mothers and daughters—the jealousy thing. I mean, I know it's only my theory but look at it—one is getting her period while the other one is making some horrid descent into the dreaded menopause. Really—think of the jealousy that must be involved. I know we're not supposed to think our mothers are jealous of us, I know we're supposed to think that when they fight with us about doing something or going somewhere, it's basically because they're trying to protect us, not thwarting our growing need for independence, but don't you think there could just be the tiniest amount of jealousy going on in there? Just look at it—here's this daughter standing in front of this mother wanting to go out with this boy and the daughter's all excited because she knows what could happen with her and the boy, but the mother says no because *she* also knows what could happen with her daughter and the boy. I mean, where does the protection leave off and the jealousy begin? Don't you honestly think that part of it is because the mother can't do that anymore? I mean, really, how many forty-something-year-old mothers do you see running around madly in love? All excited about seeing someone? Or kissing someone? Or, God, touching someone? You know what I mean? They have to be jealous, don't kid yourself.

And then there's the independence thing. You know—roots and wings? Mothers have a terrifically shitty time with the wings part. They probably should have split it up, because when the daughters are little the mothers are perfect for the roots part—you know, like mashing up those cooked peas and feeding it to them with those sweet little spoons, and changing their diapers and washing their hair with baby shampoo and making sure it doesn't get in their eyes and coloring in the lines and reading the same story over and over a trillion times and driving them back and forth to school year after year and making their witch costumes for Halloween and fixing up their rooms—all that stuff, you know, that comes with the roots part, but then comes the wings part and look out, the mothers just fall apart. I think only the fathers should be allowed to do the wings part. I mean, really, my father would let me go anywhere. I'm serious. It's like he doesn't care. I mean, I know he cares, it's just like he's accepted it; he knows I'm gonna go, I know I'm gonna go—why make such a big deal?

That's what always happens if I ask and they're both there; she says no and he says yes and then it's a fight, each of them stating their pros and cons to each other, not only like I'm not there but like it's some federal court case or something . . . really, it's so boring, I just go to my room. I'm telling you, me wanting to go somewhere can turn into World War Three with those two. I mean, I'm not saying it's easy to be a parent. You can't just let your kid run off with some maniac or go berserk somewhere, but somehow I think they make it more complicated when they turn it into their fight instead of mine. Anyway, if I'm lucky I work it out so that I ask my dad first, and then it's already done; she doesn't even get into it. I mean, if he says yes she can't very well change it. Well, I guess she could, but that would really not blow over so easily.

Sometimes I think it's because she doesn't trust me, as if she knows what I could do even though I haven't even thought about it yet, and then sometimes I think she doesn't know anything, like she's lived in this vacuum all her life. I mean, I know she had a life. I even know she had this lover before my father and my mother were together and their relationship went on for a long time and it was all really dramatic, but even though I know about some of it—not the details, thank you, God—even though I've heard about some of it, it's like I can't imagine it was *my* mother. I mean, how could the woman I know who's always moving my shit around my room and putting it all back in the wrong place and then saying she didn't do it and telling me no a thousand times that I can't have her precious car and walking out of a discussion throwing things, with her face all pursed up like that and looking at my father sometimes as if he couldn't mean more to her than some big piece of cheese—I mean, how could that be the same woman who was once having some mad, hot love affair?

I mean, is it possible that she could have once felt like I do? I mean, excited about her life? The way I feel about Scott? In her body and all? I don't know . . . you know, tingly in anticipation or something . . . I mean, it's not possible, is it? My mother, the fierce queen of the one-liners—could she actually have ever felt like I do when Scott calls or when he rings the front doorbell or when he kisses me? Could she have ever felt like that?

Really. I think it's got to be impossible. I've thought about it a lot. Because if she did, then what happened to her? Was it all so much for her that she got cold? I don't know . . . maybe it's because she's with my father. I mean, maybe she never got over the other guy.

Gilliana

A person can die when they're only thirty-nine. And before they die they can disintegrate. That is the hardest fact I have ever had to accept in my life and I had to accept it because it came true, but that doesn't mean I believe it, I only accepted it—I will never truly believe Anthony is dead. Even after all these years since 1974—in my head he's not gone, he's just away on tour.

The other thing I had to accept is that someone can die no matter how much you love them, no matter how much you're sure that a love like that can exempt the two of you from the mundane. Guess again, sweetheart, nothing's sacred. Watch this.

Right in front of your eyes you see him fade and you can do nothing; you're helpless—a funny, vibrant, powerful man turns into a funny, weak, desperately sick man and you're helpless to stop it. No matter how much you beg God, no matter how much you plead and beg and try to bargain with Him, God doesn't hear you. He's unavailable, He's in Jerusalem on business, He's out to lunch.

Your own life dies right alongside this man, this man who only had to hold you or look at you or talk to you and you lit up like the Chrysler Building and knew you were meant to be. Now you stand there like a piece of soggy eggplant trying to get it through your dim pea-brain that this is really happening and you are powerless to stop it. There is not one thing that you can do.

Okay, I take that back—there are a few things you can do—you can laugh hysterically at his jokes because that might make him feel good if he's not in too much pain, or you can smile like a million-dollar-an-hour cover girl when he looks at you because then maybe he'll think he's doing better than he really is, and all the rest of the time you can hold his hand. Even when he's sleeping you can hold his hand, and then you will come to find out that you're not always holding his hand to make him feel better; most of the time you're clutching his hand to make *you* feel better because you're so scared you can't breathe. You can also hold on to a lot of sinks in hospital ladies' rooms splashing water on your face because you're sure you're gonna pass out in the corridor; you can spend a lot of time putting on extra Blush-on so you don't look like shit in front of him, and you can try to stop biting on the hole you've already ripped in the fleshy part of the inside of your cheek. Other than that, you can't do anything but cry and stare into space looking for some cockeyed answer that doesn't exist out there, or you can pray. But try praying without bargaining . . . see how far you can get. I didn't get farther than out of Manhattan for ten days when he was adamant about taking me to Italy, but those ten days were pretty much touch-and-go; three of them were spent in a hospital in Rome—not exactly the romantic holiday we had planned.

When they removed the melanoma from Anthony's back, it had already spread to his lymph nodes and, as my mother would say, that was that. They cut a big piece of flesh off the back of his thigh and sewed that onto where they had hacked away the melanoma and most of the surrounding tissue—which also happened to be most of his back around his left shoulder blade. It was like a cavern in his back, a festering cavern of hell was actually how I thought of it when I changed the dressings.

"How does it look, *cara*?"

"Fine . . . much better . . . it looks fine, sweetheart . . ."

I wouldn't come around to the front of him until I was sure there was some color back in my face.

They also cut away the lymph nodes—I have no idea what they did with those. I must say at one point I pictured them floating around in a large Hellmann's mayonnaise jar like the black-and-white brain samples in Dr. Frankenstein's movie lab.

After they cut away the evil lymph nodes and half of Anthony's back, a trail of fancy specialists danced in and out and did a lot of head-shaking and frowning and stammering, but all that really amounted to was different forms of "I'm so sorry, Mr. Ronzoni, there's nothing we can do for you, you're going to die." All the doctors seemed very upset and, of course, they had reason to be—here they'd finally gone and met the famous Tony Ronzoni and now they'd be able to get the best seats in the house wherever he performed, but it was clear he'd never perform again so they were screwed.

There was talk of experimental radiation then, which someone actually dared to call deep-heat treatments—if you can believe that—and there was talk of experimental chemotherapy, but the consensus was that there was nothing anyone could do, no experimental anything, because it was all too late.

I don't know how it got to be so late. He had a mole that he'd been born with, the same sweet brown mole that was on his back when he was a little boy, that was under my hands when I held tight to him when he was deep inside me, that was under the soap when I washed his back in the shower, the same dear mole that I touched lightly with baby oil when I straddled his backside naked and gave him a rubdown. One day that mole woke up and decided to kill Anthony, and suddenly everything was all too late.

We had six and a half months after the diagnosis—that was it—from December until the end of June—that's all we got to say goodbye. So he and I and what's-her-name began living some kind of gothic novel or maybe it was a futuristic novel, because the setup was unheard of . . . Anthony had found an apartment for us to move into when he was going to leave, but once the melanoma beat us to the moving date we had to let it go. How could he leave if he was dying? How could he move out? And, of course, he wanted to spend as much time with the kids as possible and that meant being with her and, after all, they'd been together sixteen years and even though he'd decided to leave her, she still loved him . . . so what could I say? And besides, what would I say? Nothing. He should be with his kids until he couldn't; as much as I wanted him to be only with me, that much I knew. In the face of death, watch your priorities change.

Anthony got me a suite at the Wyndham and our new life began. Him and me and what's-her-name—both of us loving him, both of us being polite, both of us graciously taking turns as we watched him die—we became the most unlikely threesome anyone could have ever come up with. I know we were enough material for several comedy routines and probably even one of those condensed novelettes in the back of *Redbook—The Man, the Wife, and His Mistress Face Death Together in Room 701*—but I couldn't write it, I was too busy being in it, I was too busy trying to hold on. There was always that outside chance that if we held on and ran fast enough we could leave the cancer in the dust. Ha-ha-ha.

January 1974

"Because I'm gonna quit, that's why," Gillian said, across the table from Tony in the Rose Room of the Algonquin. He frowned and leaned a little sideways in the chair. "Are the bandages on your leg bothering you?"

"No, they're perfect," he said. "I'm fine."

She looked at him hard—he grinned at her, winked, and took a sip out of his coffee cup. "I'm fine, sweetheart. Stop looking at me like I'm under a microscope."

"I'm gonna quit, Anthony."

"No, you're not," Tony said. He acknowledged the couple across the room who had recognized him with a smile and a nod of his head. "Aren't you going to eat your bacon?"

"No."

"Why not?"

"I'm not hungry."

"I never saw you leave bacon on your plate. Are you sure you're not sick?" He reached his hand across the table to touch her forehead. "Do you have a fever?"

"Anthony, please, I'm trying to talk to you . . ."

"Okay, okay," he said, his fork poised over her bacon. "You sure you don't want this?"

"I don't want the goddamn fucking bacon and I'm gonna quit."

"My, my, my . . . such language, madam," he said, stabbing the bacon. "What's the matter with you?—you want to give Witzer a heart attack? It's bad enough what it's gonna do to him when he hears that I'm dying, losing all those ten percents; you'll really kill him if you quit, he can't dial a number without you, the man can't function, he can't find his shoes . . ."

"Please don't say that, I can't stand it when you say that."

"What? Talk about Harry's shoes?"

And then her head was bent and she was sobbing.

"Gilliana, you're crying on your French toast."

"I don't care."

"Well, it's not very nice to get it all wet like that, it's very expensive French toast."

Gillian didn't say anything. Tony put his fork on his plate, reached across the table over their breakfast, and gently raised her chin with his fingers.

"I'm dying, *cara,* what does it matter if I say it?"

"I can't stand it, that's all."

"Okay, I won't say it if it upsets you. What should we call it?"

"You're not gonna die, you're gonna beat it."

"Okay."

She looked at him and he smiled at her.

"I'll only beat it if you eat your breakfast; it worries me that you're not eating, you don't want to make me worry, do you?"

Gillian sighed and wiped her face with the big white Algonquin napkin. "Okay, I'll eat my breakfast," she said, sticking her fork into a wedge of French toast.

"You can't quit, it isn't good for you . . . How 'bout we ask Harry to transfer you to the New York office, you can work here . . . part time, while you take care of me . . . how would that be?"

"Why can't I just quit?"

"Because you'll need to work later . . . afterward . . . when I'm—"

"—on the road," Gillian said quickly, finishing his sentence, "doing club dates." She looked at him.

"Right," Tony said, smiling at her, "okay . . . that's good, baby . . . you'll have to work later when I'm on the road."

That's how we started the tour thing. Sometimes even now I look up at the sky and I see all the stars and I think, Anthony must be killing them tonight in Botswana, they must be rolling in the goddamn aisles.

February 1974

"I'm awfully glad 'melanoma' isn't an Italian word."

"Anthony, don't start with me; I don't want to talk about melanomas. We're in Rome having a wonderful time. Where are your gloves? It's cold out."

"In my pocket. That's why it's on my mind . . . you know, Rome . . .

Italy . . . Italian. Actually, the word is New Latin, New Latin versus Old Latin from the Greek word *melas,* which means black . . ."

"You're trying to get a riff going on melanoma so you can say something funny."

"Me? Be funny? Don't be ridiculous."

The elevator doors opened to the lobby and he held his hand out for Gillian.

"After you, madam. All I was saying was there's a big difference between Latin and Italian and that ain't nothin' compared to the Greeks since the word stems from the Greek—"

"Anthony, if you don't stop with this melanoma shit, I'm going to hit you right here."

"Where?" he said, putting his arm around her, bending and kissing her neck inside the collar of her red wool coat where it touched her hair.

Gillian looked up at him, her eyes wide. "My God, your lips are hot. Do you have a fever?"

"No, I just have hot lips, you know that."

"Come here," she said, moving her hand to his face, "let me feel you."

He ducked away from her. "*Cara,* cut it out, I'm fine, we're going to St. Peter's in a carriage."

"It's too cold to go in a carriage, have you lost your mind? It's snowing out."

He stopped fast in mid-stride, faced her, and put his hands on her shoulders.

"Stop it, Gilliana. Don't treat me like a baby. I'm going to St. Peter's with you in a carriage because that's what I want to do, and no matter what we say out loud we both know I won't ever get another chance and I don't give a fuck if there's a blizzard out. Do you understand?"

His face was white. Other than that he practically looked the same, still devastatingly handsome, a little bit thinner perhaps, a little strain showing now in a white face, which only made his eyes look bigger, his very brown eyes that were staring at her.

So I shut my mouth and we went to St. Peter's in a carriage, which was quite a feat for February in the middle of a snowstorm and I don't know what it cost him for the carriage driver and his frozen horse that skidded us across the ice of the Piazza San Pietro, but Anthony was right that we should go—it was breathtaking and it was wonderful; it was one of the most extraordinary days in my whole life. Of course, the next two days we spent trying to break his fever in the Fate Bene Fratelli Hospital, which Anthony thought was very funny because in English "Fate Bene Fratelli" means the "Do-Good Brothers," and I told him that sounded like a bad lounge act from the Sands.

March 1974

"That's a crock, don't bullshit me," Gillian said.

She dropped the spoon and it clattered on the countertop. She picked up the mug of instant coffee and took it with her out of the tiny kitchenette into the living room of her suite. Tony sat on the sofa in front of the windows, backlit by a New York day so clear and bright she could hardly see him, only his outline, a charcoal shadow in the yellow light. She handed him the coffee cup and flopped down beside him. A million dust particles rose from the sofa pillows into the sunbeams. "Jesus," she said, waving at them with her hand, "somebody ought to dust around here. You know, I can call the corner and get real coffee delivered. You don't have to drink that shit."

"I like this shit," he said, "and don't try to change the subject. How come you always change the subject when we're talking about your life?"

"Because it's boring."

"Listen to me, Gilliana, I'm serious. You're funny, you could write comedy."

"I'm telling you that's bullshit—being funny doesn't mean I could write comedy. You just think I can do anything because you love me—I don't know anything about writing comedy, I only know how to type. How about I type comedy?"

"You see? You're doing it."

"I am not."

He grimaced and moved on the pillows.

"What's the matter?"

"Nothing."

"Are you all right?"

"Goddamn it, Gilliana, don't change the subject. I'm telling you you can write comedy."

"I can't. I don't know anything about writing comedy."

"What about the farmer joke?"

"I don't know, it was a fluke—it's 'cause I'm from the Midwest, I have an affinity for farmers that just comes naturally."

"Oh, really? And what about the Mary Magdalene joke? Is that from the Midwest? And what about the gargling of the holy water? And the one about the guy with the mustache in the truck?"

"I don't know . . ."

"I am telling you, Gilliana Ventimiglia, you can write comedy."

"Okay, I'll write comedy. Do I have to do it now or can we make love?"

He laughed and then he grimaced again. She kissed him.

"Hey," he whispered, "I'm wise to you. This is just another way of changing the subject."

"Ah, but such a clever way, don't you think?" she said, her face up close to his. "So . . ."

"Okay," he said, leaning forward and then standing up. "You're not listening to me and I want to get serious here, this is important."

"Hey, where are you going?"

"I'm just changing chairs, sweetheart, that sofa is too soft for me."

He walked slowly to the desk chair and sat down; he was thinner now and it was difficult sometimes for him to get up and move. Gillian could see that, she watched his every step while she held her breath and bit her lip.

"Come here, *cara.*"

She got up and went to him at the desk, smiling brightly as if she was about to be photographed. "So, what do you want? Paper? Are we going to write comedy?"

Tony looked up at her from the chair as she stood in front of him, his eyes on hers as he slid his hands up the backs of her legs under her black gabardine suit skirt, pulled her to him, and put his face against her sweater under the swell of her breasts.

"I don't think so," he said into her skin as he lifted the black cashmere away from her body with his mouth, "it's up to you."

Gilliana shivered. "God, I don't know . . . I've always wanted to write comedy, you know . . . it's been my life's dream . . . and you said you'd teach me . . . and . . ."

"And?" Tony said, moving his lips across her stomach and then lower while he undid the right garter from her right stocking, running his fingers lightly around the top of the flesh of her leg until he touched the silk of her panties between her legs. "And?" he said again.

"And . . ." Gillian said as her breath caught, "and . . ."

"And?" Tony said, his head bent, his lips and his teeth and his hands pulling her panties down.

"And . . . I think I'm falling, Anthony . . ."

And somewhere she thought he said "I've got you," but she didn't know because her panties were gone and his lips were on her and his tongue moved ever so gently and she held on to the back of his head as she bent back, her ass cupped in his hands as she got wet and Tony kissed her there and softly sucked her and she forgot everything except his mouth.

God bless the Wyndham. Anthony went back and forth between me on West Fifty-eighth between Fifth and Sixth and what's-her-name and the kids on East Sixty-sixth between Madison and Park. I usually got the nights and the mornings and they'd get the afternoons; he'd go there and rest and then do after-school time, and children's suppertime, and read-a-story time to the little one and do homework with the big one and then they'd go to sleep and he'd come back to me. In the afternoons I would go to Harry's New York office and pretend to work; the idea of me working then was pretty funny, I was having trouble even getting dressed. Anthony hired a stunning driver named Mr. Smith, a very muscular, very strong, very black man who'd been a prizefighter in his earlier days and now was very elegant in a suit and tie and gold cuff links, and drove Anthony back and forth in a midnight-blue Lincoln Continental as tenderly as if he was a soufflé.

March 1974

Gillian turned left off Fifth Avenue and practically ran down Fifty-third Street dodging people; she was twenty minutes late. She spotted them right away when she entered Paley Park, the little girl's back in a navy-blue coat as she stood close to the waterfall and Anthony seated next to her in a white plastic chair. The park wasn't crowded; it was nearly four-thirty and getting dark. Gillian walked forward. She saw Anthony see her—he smiled a big smile and then turned his head. She came closer until she was right next to them and sat down in a chair one chair away from his.

"It's only a hot dog, Daddy," the little girl said as she turned.

"I know, sweetheart, but it's awfully close to your suppertime."

"So?"

"So how will you be able to eat your supper if you're all filled up with hot dog?"

"I'll give my supper to Samantha."

"You will, huh?"

"Sure," she said, smiling, "Joey does it all the time."

"He does not."

"Yes, he does, when Mommy's not looking he does."

She was beautiful. She looked like Anthony—dark hair and pale skin—but her face was in a heart shape, which was not like his, and her eyes were blue.

"Basset hounds are not supposed to eat people's suppers, they have their own suppers to eat."

"Well, I happen to know, Daddy, that Samantha likes people food much better than he likes dog food."

"Oh, does he now?"

"Yep."

Gillian laughed out loud—she couldn't help it. The little girl looked at her and smiled. Gillian smiled back.

"So?" she said to her daddy.

"What?"

"So, can I have a hot dog, please?"

"I don't think so, maybe next time, but you can have a Coke."

"Okay, deal."

She held out her hand for the money and skipped over to the man behind the refreshment cart.

"Hi, there," Tony said to Gillian.

"She's so beautiful, Anthony."

"Joey had basketball, I forgot."

"It's okay, next time."

He took her hand and squeezed it.

"I love you," he said. "I just wanted you to see them."

"Oh, Anthony . . ."

He let go of her hand.

"Hi," the little girl said to Gillian.

"Hi."

She sat down in the chair in between Anthony and Gillian. She took a sip of her Coca-Cola and swung her legs.

"I like your shoes," Gillian said.

The little girl looked up at her. "They're saddles."

"I know, I used to have some."

"You did? Did you go to Marymount?"

"No."

"If you go to Marymount, you have to wear them or you can have loafers, but my mommy says loafers aren't good for me because my ankles are wobbly."

"Oh."

"When I'm older I can wear loafers, she says."

"Well, that'll be good."

"Were your ankles wobbly?" She leaned over in the chair and studied Gillian's ankles.

"No, I just liked saddle shoes."

"You did? I think they're yucky. I have to wear a uniform too. See?" She flipped open the bottom of her coat and patted her charcoal-gray jumper skirt. "It's disgusting to have to wear a uniform, that's what my friend Mary's big sister Lea says, she says it's *très* disssgussssting, she speaks French."

Gillian laughed.

"This is my daddy," she said, pointing to Anthony. "Otherwise I wouldn't be able to talk to you. I'm not supposed to talk to strangers, you know."

Anthony grinned at Gillian over the child's head.

"My name is Rosie," she said.

"What a beautiful name."

"It's really Rose but I like Rosie better."

"So do I."

"You do?"

"Absolutely."

Rosie leaned closer to Gillian. "You know, you could get a hot dog here except it's awfully close to suppertime."

"I know. That's why I'm not having one, I wouldn't want to ruin my supper."

"Oh, me neither," Rosie said.

Anthony stood up. "Well . . . speaking of suppertime, we really should be going . . ."

Rosie stood up and slipped her hand inside Anthony's.

"Goodbye," she said to Gillian.

"Goodbye," Gillian said.

"Maybe I'll see you someday when I have loafers," Rosie said.

"Sure," Gillian said.

Her eyes filled with tears, but she kept smiling as the two of them turned and walked away. As they left the park and turned east on Fifty-third Street, Anthony lifted his fingers to his lips and then held them out to Gillian behind him in the air.

I never did talk to Joey in person. I saw him a couple of times from a distance but never up close. As much as I wanted to, it was probably better that I didn't—grown-ups can pretend they don't know each other in front of a six-year-old, but in front of an eleven-year-old, I don't know. I also don't know what time I finally left Paley Park that day except it was very dark and very cold and I had to take a scalding bath to get my hands to thaw. Unfortunately, the hot water did nothing to stop my shivering. Nothing at all.

April 1974

Gillian stood in front of the building. The doorman had already tipped his hat and tried to open the door for her.

"Oh, no, thank you . . . I'm just waiting," she said, smiling.

"Yes, ma'am," he said, smiling back at her and resuming his stance.

She did a little pivot turn and walked in the opposite direction toward Madison. When she got to the end of Anthony's building she did another turn and walked back toward Fifth; the doorman smiled at her again as she passed in front of his awning.

"Would you like me to buzz someone upstairs for you, ma'am? I'd be glad to."

"No, thank you."

"Yes, ma'am," he said. He looked very official—a freshly pressed hunter-green uniform, gold and white braid on his shoulders and hat, white gloves buttoned, his name beautifully written in gold script across the left side of his chest: "Whitney," it said in gold letters, with a curlicue at the beginning of the "W" and a curlicue at the end of the "Y."

Gillian turned and walked back toward Madison. As she passed the building, Whitney was helping an older lady in a pale-blue suit into a cab. Her shoes and her handbag were also pale blue and so was her hat, Gillian noticed, and her hair. Gillian laughed.

"What's so funny?" Anthony said.

Gillian turned.

"Hi, there," she said. He was wearing a tan sport jacket and tan slacks that were a little too big for his frame now and a beige shirt, one side of the collar up and the other side down.

"Hi, there," he said back. And they stood for a minute not moving, just looking at each other in the middle of the sidewalk.

"So," she said, "is everything all right . . . upstairs?"

"Yep."

"Would you like a taxi, Mr. Ronzoni?" Whitney said.

"No, thank you, Whitney," Tony said, without taking his eyes off Gillian.

"You don't want a taxi?" Gillian said. "You told me to tell Mr. Smith we didn't need him until five."

"No . . . I don't want anything, I think I feel like walking," he said, grinning at her. He took her hand and they walked side by side. She could feel his eyes on her, and she turned.

"What is it?" she said. "Anthony, why are you looking at me like that?"

"Because you're beautiful," he said, "you're so beautiful, *cara,* and I can't believe you're mine . . ."

And then she moved into his arms on the corner of Sixty-sixth and Madison, down the street from the building where he half-lived with what's-her-name and their children—Tony Ronzoni and an unknown young brunette woman, standing there, kissing, oblivious to everything but each other while the movement and the noise of New York City just went right on.

It was a perfect day, pale blue and fuzzy yellow, very spring, with a soft, light breeze and puffy white clouds that looked as if they'd been painted on the sky. He felt good, and because he felt good I was floating. We actually walked for quite a few blocks, only stopping for a Yoo-Hoo and a hot dog that Anthony insisted on eating, no matter what I said, from the man under the Sabrett's red-and-yellow umbrella on Madison and Fifty-fifth. Anthony said it was common knowledge that you could eat from a street vendor only if it was a Sabrett's, that the rats wouldn't dare touch a Sabrett's cart, they knew better because a Sabrett's hot dog was kosher and clean. I was so happy that he felt good that I went along with everything he said. Of course, when he told me that Whitney, the doorman, was related to the Whitney of the cotton gin, I drew the line.

May 1974

"I look like shit, I don't know why I'm going."

"You look gorgeous," Gillian said; she caught Mr. Smith's eye in the rearview mirror of the car. "Doesn't he look gorgeous, Mr. Smith?"

"You look very nice, Mr. Ronzoni, very nice indeed."

"You see?" Gillian said, tucking her arm inside Tony's and snuggling closer to him, "Mr. Smith says you look very nice, so there."

"You're both crazy, I look like shit—my skin's yellow, for crissakes . . . and what do I need with a bunch of comics toasting me? Let me ask you, do I need that? No. That fucking Witzer ought to be shot for talking me into this. And you too, *cara* . . . goddamn it."

Gillian smiled at him. The collar of his shirt was too big for his neck and she was trying to ignore that, so she straightened his tie. "And I love this tie," she said, and she kissed his chin.

"You love it 'cause you bought it for me."

"No, I didn't."

"Of course you did, you bought it for me last Christmas at Sulka's."

"No, I didn't, baby," she said.

"Gilliana, don't fuck with me, you bought me this goddamn tie. I remember the goddamn shiny holly wrapping paper and the goddamn green bow and the goddamn box." He brushed her hands away, pushed at the knot in the elegant burgundy silk tie, and looked out the window.

She held her hands in her lap and didn't say anything.

Mr. Smith maneuvered the car to the curb, jumped out, moved quickly around the Lincoln, and opened Tony's door.

"The Friars Club, sir," he said, extending his hand.

Tony turned to Gillian. His eyes were soft and full of pain. "I'm sorry, *cara,*" he said.

"It's all right, my darling."

He frowned. "Are you sure you didn't buy me this tie? Don't lie to me, tell me the truth. Did you buy it?"

"I will never lie to you, Anthony," she said softly. "No, I didn't buy it."

"Well, that's great," he said as he grabbed Mr. Smith's hand; the big man helped him out of the car as Gillian scooched across the seat and got out behind him. A tiny but still audible moan escaped Tony's lips as he straightened his back. Gillian looked down at an imaginary something on the sidewalk so he wouldn't see her watching him while he was in pain. Mr. Smith let go of Tony's hand but stood quietly right next to him, shoulder to shoulder, as if he was a solid yet invisible brace.

Tony looked at Gillian and smirked. "So, isn't that great, baby? Isn't that just wonderful? Now, on top of everything else, I'm losing my mind."

He *was* yellow. Sometimes he was white, sometimes yellow, sometimes even pale green. I tried to ignore it. Sometimes he made jokes about it, even awful Oriental ones: about how now that he was yellow he was going to change his name to Tony Ro and open a Chinese restaurant on the East Side called Ro's Sun Luck Palace Gardens of the Melanoma Panda . . . don't ask . . . he could come up with them.

He was also forgetting things, and confusing things, and having horrendous headaches and blurred vision. One of the headaches was so bad he smashed his fist into a kitchenette cabinet at the Wyndham and splintered the wood. He said the only thing that was good about the blurred vision was that instead of looking like a cracked Picasso he was now beginning to resemble a Monet. The sore I had made biting the inside of my cheek was worse; all I tasted, no matter what I ate, was blood.

June 1974

"I love you, Gilliana," he said. He was drifting in and out, talking and then sleeping and then talking again.

"I love you, Anthony," she said from behind him. "Now go back to sleep, it's nearly morning."

He was on his right side; his "free side," as he called it, as in "melanoma-free." As sick as he was, Tony had not given up working on his melanoma routine; just that day he had been trying to come up with words that rhymed with it, but Gillian refused to help him. She said he was sick and he said, well, that was the truth, and she said she didn't mean that, and then they were laughing and he laughed so hard he practically keeled over from the pain.

Gillian was lying behind him on the bed; her knees were tucked into the backs of his knees and her right hand touched his hair, but the rest of her body didn't touch his. Even the slightest pressure of her nipples grazing against the skin of his back now caused him pain.

"I loved you from the first minute I saw you. You were sitting on the desk outside of Witzer's office on the phone, and you were wearing orange . . . and you leaned across the desk to get a pencil and I could see your legs clear up to your thighs and I thought, Well, that's for me."

"What do you mean—I was wearing orange?"

"Orange, you were wearing orange."

"I was not."

"Of course you were; it was an orange dress or something, I remember . . ."

"Anthony, I have never had an orange dress. Nobody has ever had an orange dress, nobody in this whole world wears orange."

"They don't?"

"No, absolutely not."

"Then it must have been your aura."

"Oh, sweetheart, is my aura orange?"

"Yeah . . . I think so . . . will you be here later?"

"Of course I'll be here, where else would I be? Bloomingdale's? You better go to sleep, Mr. Ronzoni, before I spank you."

"And then you were in the lobby . . ."

"What lobby?"

"I was going to lunch with Witzer and we were walking through the lobby as you were coming in through those big glass doors, and the light was behind you and I could see all of the outline of you through your dress . . ."

Gillian laughed. "You could not."

He patted her softly with his hand on her left thigh. "Oh, yes I could, you hussy . . . and you did it on purpose . . . this whole thing is your fault."

"No, it's your fault, you kept asking me out to eat."

"Uh-huh," he said. "Well, I was hungry . . . Do you still think my name is funny?"

"It's the silliest name in the history of time and what you don't know is that I'm writing a sketch about it, but I can't tell you because it's so dirty. Now go to sleep, goddamn it."

"A dirty sketch? . . . That's damn good . . . that's my girl . . . On Tony or on Ronzoni?"

"On both, of course. Didn't you teach me to use everything?"

"See? Didn't I say you could write comedy? . . . Tony . . . phony . . . bony . . ." he mumbled and then his body jerked.

"Anthony?" she said but he didn't answer her; he was asleep again.

Gillian's eyes were wide open in the dark. The tears flowed freely down her face but she didn't make a sound. The clock on the bedside table said 4:14. She knew it was one of the last times she would sleep with him unless they would let her climb into the bed with him at Sloan Kettering. She knew he couldn't make it much longer without being on morphine day and night. She stroked the hair at the nape of his neck and inhaled his scent.

"Oh, Anthony," she whispered, "how will I live without you?"

"Hmm?" he said. "Who what?"

"I said you need a haircut."

"Oh," he said, "well, that's good . . ." And then he was quiet.

She tried to memorize every inch of him so she could remember: the exact width of his shoulders, the silk of his skin against hers, the fingers of his left hand resting on her thigh, the little ridge on the side of his thumb where he told her they'd had to sew it back together when he cut it on a Coca-Cola bottle when he was four . . .

"Cara," Tony whispered, "tell me the truth—are you crying?"

"Of course not, what would I have to cry about?"

"I don't know . . . I thought maybe the sketch on my name was so funny you laughed until you cried."

And then as he tried to move on the sheets, he yelled out loud, "Jesus God, Christ, this hurts!"

So we went to the hospital. On June 8th. We left from the Wyndham and even after we were all ready for at least an hour, with Mr. Smith standing at the door watching "his" Mr. Ronzoni like an armed guard, I couldn't get Anthony to leave the suite. He kept saying, "I just want to look around a little bit more." I thought I was going to throw myself out the window.

June 1974

"Do you want me to send you up something?" what's-her-name said quietly from the door of the hospital room.

Gillian turned from the window. "What? I'm sorry . . ."

"I said do you want something from the cafeteria before I go?"

"Oh, no, thank you, if I eat anything else from that cafeteria I'll have to bomb the place for sure."

What's-her-name smiled.

"Even the red Jell-O nearly killed me," Gillian said.

"I'm sure Mr. Smith wouldn't mind going to get you a hamburger, would you like me to ask him? He could take me home and then bring it back to you."

"God, no . . . really . . ."

"He could go to P.J. Clarke's." She looked at Gillian for a second and then frowned slightly, "I'm sorry, isn't that where you like hamburgers?"

"Yes . . . uh-huh . . ."

"Tony told me . . . I don't remember why . . . I'm sorry . . ."

"It's okay. I don't mind if you know where I like hamburgers."

What's-her-name stood there. "So, would you like one?"

"Oh, no, really, I'm not hungry . . . thank you."

What's-her-name looked over at Tony asleep in the bed and then back at Gillian.

"You'll call me if anything—"

"Of course I will. You know that."

"Okay . . . I'll see you in the morning."

"Okay . . . tell the kids hello . . . I mean . . . from their daddy, you know."

"Of course, yes," she said. She looked at Tony again, took a step backward, gave Gillian a little wave, and walked out the door.

Gillian turned. She put her hand over her mouth and took a breath.

"Oh, my God, is this really happening?" Gillian whispered to the window.

She walked to Anthony in the bed and looked at him. He was lying on his back, his cheekbones were very prominent and there were pale-lavender smudges under both eyes. She straightened some red roses in a vase on the bedside table. She picked off one leaf, tore it into thin shreds, and let them flutter to the floor. She thumbed through the first two pages of a magazine and put it down. She looked at him. She smoothed the collar of his pajama top; he refused to wear hospital gowns—he told the hospital if they wouldn't let him wear his own pajamas he would leave Sloan Kettering and go to die at Columbia Presbyterian and then they would lose all that free publicity. Gillian smiled, remembering. She sat down on the chair at the side of the bed and bit her lip. Then she put her hand very gently on top of his hand on the blanket. She watched him for about twenty more minutes and then began to doze.

"Hey, mon, were you lookeen at me?" Tony said thickly, in a very bad Puerto Rican accent.

"Absolutely not," she said, blinking awake. "Did you just wake up?"

"I don't know, I think so—did I miss something?"

"No," Gillian said, yawning. "Except for that little escapade that made the nurses so mad."

"What?" He was trying to look at her, but his eyes kept closing he was so drugged.

"Oh, you know . . . I don't know why they got so pissed—really, it was nothing." Gillian leaned forward and kissed him: "I just went down on you under the covers."

He laughed a little. "What do you mean, it was *nothing,* madam?"

She took his hand. "How do you feel, baby?"

"Oh, just great," he slurred, "but I think I'm a dope addict."

She laughed.

He squinted his eyes to keep them from closing, "Do morphine addicts have to go to A.A. like alkies do?"

"Absolutely."

"Well, shit, then I'll have to take the seven-step program."

"It's twelve steps, Anthony."

He looked right at her. "I don't have time for twelve steps, *cara.* Don't get mad, but I don't think I could make it to four."

My teeth hurt from clenching them. We took turns, what's-her-name and me: she would go home to the kids and read them stories or whatever mothers did—I didn't know then—and I would go home to the Wyndham and scream in the shower. I realized that in a way I was lucky—I didn't have to put on a face for anybody, I was alone. I realized that in a way she was lucky—she had the kids, who were a part of Anthony I'd never have, and she wasn't alone. And then I decided it was a toss-up. She loved him, I loved him, we were both losing him—neither of us was lucky, we were both doomed.

June 1974

"It won't be much longer now," Dr. Okuma said to the two women across from him.

"What is that?" Gillian said, frowning. "Is that supposed to make us feel better? I don't get what that means."

"He's just trying to help us," what's-her-name said.

"Oh, I see . . . how silly of me, I didn't get it," Gillian said, getting up off the black leather couch. "Look, why don't you just let him help you? It's clear to me that I'm too stupid for all this help."

She walked to the door of the doctor's office, threw it open and ran out, ran to the elevator, pushed the button, waited for it to come, got in when the doors opened, pushed seven, got out when it hit seven, moved quickly down the hall, grabbed the handle on the door to Anthony's room, but didn't open it. What was she going to do?—discuss it with him? "So he said it won't be much longer now, darling, and then you'll be dead. Isn't that wonderful? How perfectly grand!"

Gillian walked down the hall and into the ladies' room. She was sitting on the tile floor under the towel rack when what's-her-name walked in.

"Are you all right?" what's-her-name said.

"Yeah . . ."

"You can tell me if you're not, you know."

"Well, of course, I'm *not* all right. How could I be all right? Are *you* all right?"

"I think so." She looked at Gillian steadily as Gillian stared at her.

"Aren't you angry?" Gillian asked.

"No."

"How can you not be angry? You love him, I know you love him, I see that."

"I have my faith."

"You have your *faith?* Oh, that's a good one . . . that must make up for a lot of things . . . God knows, I'd rather have my good ole faith than Anthony any ole day."

"Does it help you when you're sarcastic?"

"Oh, shit," Gillian said. She put her head down on her raised knees. "I'm sorry, I don't mean to put down your faith," she mumbled from between her legs.

"What?"

Gillian raised her head. "I said I didn't mean to put down your god-damn faith! Oh, shit," she said, lowering her head again. "I'm sorry, really, I am . . . I just can't seem to find a place for this."

"There's nothing we can do. We just have to love Him and accept it."

Gillian raised her head. "Which him? The big Him or the little him?"

A small smile crossed what's-her-name's face. "Both of them, I guess."

"Uh-huh . . . well, you can love the big Him but it just don't work for me . . . I'm having a problem with acceptance, I'm just not ready to accept Anthony being dead."

"Would you like to come with me to the chapel?"

"Are you kidding?"

"No."

Gillian looked at her. "No, I don't think so."

"All right."

What's-her-name stood there, one shoulder of her pink Chanel summer suit near the bathroom wall but purposely not touching it, her beige leather handbag over one arm, her beige pumps at right angles like a model at the foot of a runway; Gillian sat there, the back of her T-shirt touching the wall, the seat of her white palazzo pants on the dirty tile floor, her Keds firmly planted among the wads of crumpled paper towels that had missed the trash can. Neither of them said anything for a minute or so.

"Do you want to know what Dr. Okuma said?"

"No. I wouldn't believe what he said anyway." Gillian laughed, and then began crying. "Anthony said we shouldn't trust an oncologist who can't say the goddamn thing right."

"What?"

"The fucking killer mole," Gillian laughed, the tears rolling down her cheeks.

What's-her-name blinked at Gillian. "I'm sorry, I don't understand."

"The mole," Gillian said, laughing, trying to catch her breath, "the mole that was on Anthony's back . . . the famous Okuma can't say it . . . don't you see?" Gillian keeled over on her side on the dirty tile floor, laughing hysterically. "Okuma calls the goddamn thing a 'me*rr*anoma.' "

She didn't get it—or, rather, she got it but she didn't think it was funny. I don't know if she ever thought anything was funny, I never saw her laugh. I also never did understand what Anthony was doing with her; I never asked.

Anyway, I did not go to the chapel with her. I went to the Plaza Hotel. First I spent an hour trying to find Mike the Irish hansom cab driver and Brian the horse; I thought maybe I would pray riding through the park with them, but it seemed they had disappeared forever. So I wound up praying alone at the Oak Room Bar.

It was probably as quiet as the chapel since it was only ten minutes to nine in the morning. I sat at the bar, had one coffee and two stingers, got instantly drunk, and prayed that they would take him. I did not pray to God or Jesus or Buddha or any of those guys; I prayed to the comics. At first I tried to pray only to the dead ones but then I decided it didn't matter, and besides, since I was tanked, it was hard to remember who was alive and who was dead. And then I decided Anthony would want me to pray to the best ones, the ones he had taught me about, the ones he had learned from, the ones he said were genius. And what did it matter where they were?—a comic was a comic, alive or dead.

I told them in my head, because I don't think I said any of this out loud, but of course we'll never know; the only reason I think I was quiet was because the bartender never said a word. Then again, bartenders probably have to put up with a lot of babbling women drinking stingers before noon.

I told them that I had a message for them, that it was their turn, I was throwing in the towel: I couldn't save Anthony, not even with all my love. I told them how he had awakened in torture the night before, sat straight up in bed, his eyes filled with such pain I thought that *I* would die, and said clearly and distinctly without a trace of morphine slur, "Okay, boys, that's it, this isn't funny anymore."

So it's up to you now, I said, he must have been talking to you guys—he's one of yours—you take him out.

I astounded myself. I prayed to the comics to help Anthony die. If anyone had ever told me I would do that, I probably would have shot them. And I not only asked them to help him die, I asked them to please help him die *now*.

I prayed to all the ones I could remember him especially loving: Ben Blue and Joe E. Brown, Jack Benny and Ed Wynn, Ed Brophy and Laurel and Hardy and Abbott and Costello and Billy DeWolfe, Harold Lloyd, Bert Lahr, Gene Baylos, Jules Munshin and Fred Allen and Phil Silvers and Myron Cohen and Ernie Kovacs and Red Skelton and Henny Youngman and Bob Hope and Lucille Ball and Bea Lillie and Milton Berle and Chaplin and Harpo and Chico and Zeppo and Groucho and even the fifth Marx brother—I prayed to him the most because Anthony said the reason nobody ever could remember his name was that he was always out of town on the road on tour.

June 1974

"Gilliana," Tony said from the bed, "where are my pants? I gotta go."

She sat up abruptly, she'd been asleep in the chair by the window. It was dawn now, the sun had just popped up, and the sky was making a monumental painting of itself streaking gold and red across its black and blue.

"What?" she said, moving to him.

"I gotta go check the room out . . ."

"What room, sweetheart?"

"I want to do some of the new stuff . . . you know . . . get the feel of it . . . before the dinner show. You want to go with me?" His eyes moved around the room. "Where's my pants?"

"Anthony, look—it's morning."

"Oh," he said, turning his head on the pillow toward the window. "God, will you look at that," he said, gazing at what the sky was doing with the dawn, " . . . so fucking beautiful . . . " and then he took her hand.

"Uh-huh," she said, but by then Anthony wasn't looking at the sunrise, he was looking at her.

She turned her head back from the window and caught his eyes.

"You like the new stuff?" he said.

She fixed the pillow under his head, stroked the hair off his forehead, bent down and kissed his nose. "Absolutely," she said.

"Good."

They stared at each other.

"Do you want some water?"

"I want you to be happy."

"I am happy. Do you want some water?"

"I want you to always be happy."

"You do, huh?"

"Yeah . . ."

"Well, then, okay, I will."

"Thank you, madam."

"And thank you, Mr. Ronzoni."

"And thank you, madam," he said, smiling up at Gillian, ". . . and two hard-boiled eggs."

He died three hours later, he never said another word.

I was amazed. I thought it would be so much more dramatic, so significant—twenty-seven violins coming out from behind the curtains, a death scene to beat Rodolfo throwing himself over dead Mimi's body in *La Bohème,* Anthony's last words being something about how much he adored me and worshipped the very ground I walked on—but leave it to my Anthony that his last words would be from a Marx brothers' routine. Of course, that part I loved.

After all that pain and torment and agony and suffering, my darling man just closed his eyes, fell back to sleep, and died. I couldn't believe it. I didn't even know it had actually happened, I thought he was just asleep until the nurse came in and told me no.

Just for the record, I did not throw myself across his body, I didn't even cry. I just sat in the chair like a zombie and waited for what's-her-name. And after she came I sat in the chair and after she left I sat in the chair, and then they wanted to take away his body and I sat in the chair . . .

June 29, 1974, and my life stopped.

It was Witzer who finally got through to me; he'd been in New York since Anthony got so bad and he came right to the hospital—I never even knew who called him. Somehow Witzer knew that June 29th was St. Peter's Feast Day and he made a big deal about how since St. Peter has the keys to the Kingdom of Heaven and since it was his Feast Day, he figured Peter would be in a pretty good mood.

"Don't worry, kid—he's got it made, your Anthony—Pete won't even ask to see his I.D., he'll just open up the gates and wave him through. Of course, that's if you believe in that kind of shit," Witzer said.

It was his last line that finally broke me and I began to cry, and Witzer held me until I could get out of the chair.

I did not go to the funeral. I promised him I wouldn't. He didn't want a funeral; he said he would have preferred all the guys saying how funny he was over a Dr. Brown's and a pastrami sandwich at the Carnegie Deli, but there was no way he could talk what's-her-name out of it, that she would want a High Mass and a Low Mass and a medium Mass and God knows what else; he said that she would probably need that for herself and the kids to make her peace with it and there was nothing he could do.

He also made me promise I'd never go to the cemetery.

"How can you go see me in a cemetery if I'm on the road on tour, *cara?*" he said, smiling.

And so I've never been.

August 1974

"Gillian, I need you to come outside now!" Carole Rose yelled from the door.

Gillian ran out of the bedroom; she was barefoot and wearing a pair of underpants and one of Anthony's old T-shirts. "What's the matter?"

"I hit somebody!"

"Jesus, are you all right?"

"I'm fine, come on!"

"Well, wait a minute," Gillian said, hopping around, trying to get her legs into a pair of jeans, "what happened?" Jamming her feet into a pair of tennis shoes, she ran out of the apartment and chased Carole Rose down the hall and into the elevator.

"You hit somebody or a car?"

"A car, a car," Carole Rose said, banging the lobby button with her finger. "Shit, come on, come on!" she yelled at the doors until they finally slid shut and the elevator went down.

They ran through the lobby and outside.

There was no accident, it was just Carole Rose's way of getting me outside. Since I was hardly getting dressed or going anywhere, imminent disaster was probably the only way she could get me to go outside.

It was sitting on a flatbed tow truck in front of the apartment. It was completely gift-wrapped in white paper, with gold ribbons and gold sparkles and a huge gold bow on top. Carole Rose and the guy driving the flatbed had to help me get the paper off because I was crying too hard.

It was a Stingray, a 1974 top-of-the-line Corvette Stingray with shiny alloy wheels and soft fawn-colored leather interior—which, at the time, the Chevrolet company called "saddle"—and the latest T-bar convertible roof on top. It was loaded, it had everything available you could put on a car then.

It also had a custom paint job. I would guess it was the only Corvette Stingray that had ever been painted the color of someone's aura—it was orange. The card on the dashboard was in Anthony's handwriting:

My darling cara,
Burn the Ford Falcon.
I will always love you,
A.

Mollie

"Oh, *tzatzkeleh,* what can I tell you," my mother said gently, "there's no way to explain it . . . it's just that"—she shrugged one shoulder—"there's love and then there's love." She was smiling at me but with an expression so hopeless, as if there was no way to explain it even if she had the words.

I sat in a chair pulled up close to the side of her bed at the FeeFee Road Sanitorium, my coat buttoned up to the top, my woolly gloves on, a scarf tied around my neck, a cloche hat pulled down over my ears, talking to my mother in whispers so the other women couldn't hear us while our breath came out in little white puffs like from a choo-choo train. They kept all the windows open in the sanitorium, it didn't matter how cold it was—they thought then that tuberculosis patients needed fresh air to help them breathe no matter that it was winter, so when you went to visit you had to stay all bundled up or you would freeze. You were bundled up and the patients were bundled up and there were actually icicles hanging from the sills of the open windows and big gusts of wind blowing around the room. It would have been funny if only everybody hadn't been so sick. I was sixteen years old, it was 1930 and I was sixteen and my mother was thirty-four, only thirty-four years old, but she was dying. Of course, I didn't know she was dying, it never occurred to me that she could actually die. When you're sixteen, nobody can die, especially not your own mother and not when you love her as much as I did—it was an impossibility in my head.

The sanitorium was really just a big old stone house in the middle of some fields outside of St. Louis, and the women patients were on the first floor and the men patients were upstairs. My mother was in a bed in a room that had probably once been the dining room in the house; she was in a bed in the middle of nine other women—I had counted them—some lying down, some sitting up, some coughing, some sleeping, all of them as pale as my mother, all of them dying of TB.

She had been there for a week and it was the first time I could get there to see her since my father took her there because I had school every day. It was way far outside of St. Louis in the middle of nowhere, and I had to take three streetcars and then walk three-quarters of a mile, so this was the first time I could get to her. It was a Saturday and I had left the house at dawn.

My father had been a crazy man before he took her there, because the doctors had told him that where she really needed to go was out West. West was where the air was cleaner, they said, West was where my mother needed to live to breathe.

"*Vos meynstu* West?" my father had yelled, stomping around the kitchen, "*Ich hob nisht keyn gelt* for West!"

He had no money for West, he was screaming right in front of her as if she wasn't the one who was making things more difficult for him, as if she wasn't the one who was sick and was going to die. My mother lay motionless under blankets on the sofa bed in the kitchen and watched him carry on and throw things while she calmly tried to help ease his tantrum. She lay quiet except when she attempted to soothe him and he stayed loud, his face red and hers white, and I sat frozen at the kitchen table like a statue in the middle of their words. It seemed to me that my father was always yelling, always angry, always stomping off and slamming doors, and she somehow knew that he had to do that and didn't let his tirade fall on her.

I was asking her how she could love him, how could she love my father when he was so mean to her, and she was trying to explain it to me, but I understood nothing; after all, I was only sixteen—what could I know?

"It's just the way he is."

"But he's terrible to you."

"No, Malya, he's terrible to himself, not to me."

"No, he's terrible to you, Mama."

"I love him, *kleyna.*"

"But why? Why did you pick Papa when he's so mean?"

I clutched her pale-pink mittened fingers with my cherry-red gloves and shook my head in wonderment and disapproval. How could somebody love somebody who was no good for them?

"It's like I said . . . there's love and then there's love . . ." and she patted my hand with hers. "You'll understand someday, Malya, I promise you—when you're big."

Jule had been gone two years and we were officially divorced. My life was just walking through the days then; I walked in and out of life as if I was in the middle of a big fog. I went to work, I came home, I played with Gilliana, I saw Nat and Dell, once a week Gilliana and I went to Sophia and Alfonzo's house to eat; that was it—in one day and out the other—the main thing, I thought, was just to keep on going—after all, as Dell pointed out to me, Jule and I hadn't been together for two years and lo and behold I was still alive. Just keep on going, Mollie, I told myself, like a horse with blinders, don't look, just go. It was as if I was in a trance then, moving but not feeling anything, like being in the middle of a big cotton fog.

"I think I'll have a drink," Dell said.

She was pacing around on the grass in Mollie's little backyard. Mollie opened her eyes; she was sitting on a lawn chair in the sun.

"You mean a drink drink?"

"Yeah."

"What's the matter with you?—it's only four o'clock."

"Yeah . . . but that makes it five in New York, it's the cocktail hour, the shank of the evening, dahling, and besides . . ."

"What?"

"I need one."

"What's the matter?"

"I have to tell you something and I don't want to, so this way I can have the scotch first and it will make me brave."

"But now you've already told me that you're gonna tell me."

"I know. Because I've been here at least ten minutes and I never could last very long with a secret, you know that."

Mollie laughed. "You want to tell me before you go inside?"

"No. But I'll bring you a drink too. Scotch and water?"

"Why don't you just tell me, Dell?"

Dell paused on the grass, one hand propped on her hip.

"Okay. God. Shit, I hate this. Okay. Julie's got someone."

Mollie didn't say anything. Her chin lifted slightly and her shoulders raised, but she didn't open her mouth or move in the chair.

"A redhead," Dell said, and she pursed her lips. "She works in a photo store, la-de-da. That's all I know." She stared at Mollie. "Are you okay?"

"Sure."

"I'm sorry, Mollie, but Nat heard it from Jack Rubin at Protzel's this morning buying bagels, and he just told me about an hour ago. I said, Why didn't you tell me this morning as soon as you found out, and he said he forgot and what was the big deal anyway since you guys were already divorced. Can you believe him? I'm always re-astounded by how stupid men are."

"It's okay."

Dell sighed. "Okay. Shit, I hate this."

They looked at each other.

Dell laughed. "So, should we have a drink or should we just go over there?"

"Huh?"

"It's only four o'clock. We could go and see what she looks like. You know, go to the photo store . . . kind of saunter in and look around . . ."

"Dell, we can't do that."

Dell put her other hand on her other hip.

"We can't? *Why the hell can't we?* I've got a car."

Red hair, cut right below her ears and parted in the middle with two dips over the eyes and a full green skirt and a cream blouse and black high heels and a pink beaded sweater thrown nonchalantly over her shoulders like I could never do and pink lipstick to match.

"Pink and green with black shoes . . . what is that? *Haute couture?* Let me tell you, kiddo, her taste is in her mouth."

Dell hadn't stopped since we left the place.

"And can you imagine to spend all that money to have your nose fixed and it comes out like that? Long and pointy with that little bump on the top, did you notice that?—the little bump? She should have sued the ass off that cheapo doctor, and God, her eyes are small, aren't they?—much too small for her face," Dell said, driving the car while she swiveled her head back and forth watching me and the road. "Why, her eyes are practically beady, don't you think, Mol?"

Her eyes were blue, was what I knew, and her lashes were long and she had put her mascara on perfectly and then she must have separated each eyelash from the other one with a straight pin so when she opened and shut her eyes it was like little black spider legs going up and down.

The photo store turned out to be in the Scruggs, Vandervoort & Barney Department Store, where people sat for those horrible portraits to be done that were in color and looked like bad oil paintings, and then they'd spend a lot of money to blow them up real big and put them in fancy frames and hang them in their living rooms over their fireplace. Dell got prices for portraits in every shape and size.

I didn't say much while we were there; maybe I didn't say anything and I know I didn't say anything for most of the ride home. I was trying to stay upright; all I could see in front of my face was Julie smiling at those eyelashes and that red hair.

"And her accent is 'halushious,' " Dell said. "Bea Carducci comes from the Bronx, not from Manhattan, Mollie, I don't care what she says . . . Manhattan, my ass."

Her name was Bea Carducci, and, of course, she was Italian. That's what hurt the most. I felt as if somebody had put a big hole right through me, like I'd been shot right through my middle and my insides were going to fall out and make a terrible mess all over the gray upholstery seats of Dell's car.

The trance was over; it was as if Jule had just walked out the door, not two years before but then, that very minute, and it hit me so hard that he was really gone that I practically fell down and then I couldn't stop crying. I don't mean a little crying because this was different—this wasn't regular crying, it was crazy crying. I cried every day for two months, I'm not kidding, every single day from the day Dell told me and we'd gone to the photo store to look at her. I cried in the bathtub and on the bus to and from work and in the middle of the night, I cried at my desk at work until I couldn't see the numbers, I cried pushing the cart in the grocery store and putting the clothes in the washing machine; I couldn't stop, I cried all the time where Gilliana couldn't hear or see me. It didn't matter if anybody else could hear or see me, I didn't even know they were there. I was a crazy person. I cried more than I cried when my Sandy died or maybe I was finally crying for that too, maybe I was crying for everything that had been taken from me—my mother, my baby, and Jule. It didn't make any sense to me that because there was suddenly a redhead I should cry, but that was how it was for me; another person in the picture made all the difference then, her mere existence made me know Julie and I were really through, it was really over and I was alone. The fog lifted as if somebody had yanked the blinders off my eyes and I could feel everything. I was in such pain I could hardly move.

"Hi," Mollie said quietly into the telephone.

"God, you're up early, kiddo," Dell said. "Is everything all right?"

"Uh-huh. What are you doing?"

"Well, since it's dawn, I'm boiling water," Dell said, looking at the kettle on her stove. "I figure I can either have a baby or a cup of tea." She laughed.

Mollie didn't say anything.

"Okay . . . a cup of coffee?"

Dell waited.

"That was a joke, Mol . . . boiling water . . . a baby or a cup of— You were supposed to laugh."

"Oh."

"Oh? That's it?—oh?"

"I walked around the apartment again all night."

"Well, that's good for you, that's healthy. Now what are you doing?"

"I'm sitting at the kitchen table."

"Uh-huh . . . Where's Gilliana?"

"Sleeping."

"Uh-huh."

There was silence on the line.

"Mollie, it's enough already, what are you gonna do about this?"

"I don't know . . . nothing."

"You're just gonna sit there?"

Mollie didn't answer.

"Are you still crying?"

"Uh-huh."

"A lot? I mean, the way you were?"

"Uh-huh."

"Oh, Jesus, honey, this ain't good."

"I can't seem to stop, Dell, I don't know why."

"Okay, it's okay . . . Mollie, honey, listen to me—do you want Jule back?"

"No . . . oh, God, I don't know . . . I don't think so, but then I do."

"Undecided, I believe, is your best answer."

"Oh, Dell."

"Okay, listen to me, kiddo, you could have Jule back if you wanted."

"How do you know?"

"Is that what you want?"

Mollie stared at the kitchen table. She brushed some toast crumbs into a tiny pile at the side of her coffee cup.

"You have to decide, Mol, if Jule's what you want. It's up to you."

What you want. What you want is not necessarily what you need or what is good for you, but of course you don't know that when you start. When you start, you could walk right into anything like a fireman into the fire. But when you have a hole of pain in you, you have to look at all the consequences and weigh all the odds and then sometimes you still don't want to know. I didn't want to know from nothin' when it came to Jule. If I would have, I would have listened to what everyone said about him right from the start. Why would a person love a person when they know that person is no good for them? The question I had asked my mother all those years ago, and now I knew. It's when a person can't help it, when they can't stop themselves, when it's one of those kinds of loves that seem unstoppable no matter what you do. My mother couldn't help it that she loved my father no matter if he was mean to her, just like I couldn't help it that I loved Jule; there's no explanation when it's a love like that, there's no asking, there's no reasoning—it overtakes you like the wind.

All I know is that if the "something" hadn't happened to me, I probably never would have stopped crying, I probably would have gone crazy from that love. But I was one of the lucky ones; the thing that happened to me broke me from the spell. It happened two days after I'd talked to Dell. In the meantime I was still crying.

Gilliana was in the house so I was crying in the shower, sobbing in there where she couldn't hear me, with my hands over my face and the water coming down hard on my head—trying to decide what I should do—should I call him?—should I see him?—would it be just like it always was? And then suddenly I wasn't in myself. That's the only way I know how to say it, I wasn't in myself because I was up above. Just like that, one minute I was me in the shower crying and the next minute I was up above looking down at me like I was someone else. Like witchcraft it happened, like a force from beyond. I don't know how else to tell it, but it's as clear to me now as if it happened a minute ago.

I could see myself in the shower, see me crying, I was watching me, and then suddenly everything was very clear. I knew that in my life I was teetering as if I was perched way up high on a flagpole, that my love for Jule was making me crazy, that it was pushing me to the edge. If I went back to Jule, I would always be crying, I would always be frightened, and I would never be safe. And then it was clear about the falling, that there were two ways to fall—we always forget that when we're in the middle of it, we forget we have a choice. If I fell one way, I wouldn't have to worry about anything because then I would be crazy and they would take me away in an ambulance somewhere and I could just sit in a chair and look out the window at the sky—that was if I went back with Jule. And if I fell the other way I wouldn't be crazy, but I would have to do everything, I would have to live, but it would have to be without Jule; I would have to give him up for good and start fresh and alone. And it was very simple to me all of a sudden that I had a choice which way to fall.

That was it, the whole thing in a nutshell.

It only took a few moments, the thing that happened, and then I was back.

I wanted to fall the other way, of course. I wanted to be taken away and not have to worry about anything—who wouldn't—what a way to live, to not have to worry about anything. But if I fell that way I would be crazy and I knew I couldn't let that happen because I had Gilliana. I was a mother, after all, and that was more important. I had Gilliana to look after and I couldn't do that sitting at a window somewhere looking out at the sky.

So I stopped crying and I got out of the shower and, like they say, that was that. I gave up Jule in my heart and I lived my life.

And later when I thought about it, I realized that it *was* Mary who had saved me after all. You see, all those years I was praying to Mary to help me with my husband and his gambling, but what I forgot was, first and foremost Mary was a mother—she was married to Joseph, but that wasn't her most important thing; her most important thing was being the mother of Jesus. So that's what she could teach me, that's what she showed me when I prayed to her for so long; she sent my soul out of my body and up above me so I could see—my life wasn't just about loving Jule, it was also about loving my child, and loving Gilliana had to be the first and foremost for me because even though it was different from how my mother meant it, it was still the same—there's love and then there's love in everybody's life; the tricky part is that each person has to figure out which love comes first.

SATURDAY

Clare

Merry Christmas, Grandma Mollie and the baby Jesus.

I got three really nice old cashmere sweaters from my mother—antique ones like I wear. I was really surprised that she actually went and found them, because it's not like just going to Bullock's and walking into the sweater department; you have to drive to Melrose or Third and go in and out of all these vintage clothing stores to find them. Anyway, I don't know when she did it but she did it before she went to Kansas City, and had the box all hidden away in her closet wrapped really pretty with antique ribbons and gorgeous Christmas paper and a card that sort of looks like her and me, you know, two women like a mother and daughter both with dark hair, it's a Mary Cassatt painting—anyway, the sweaters are really nice ones. I can't believe that she actually found them . . . a black cardigan with little black pearl buttons and two pullovers, a gray one and a light blue and really soft, just the way I like them.

Dad gave me this book. So I take the paper off and he's standing right there watching me and I think, Oh, God, I'll never read this, why did he get me this, what is it? And he's got this funny little smile on his face and then I get it, see, it's not a book at all, it's this beautiful ancient antique leather box that looks like a book but it has a tiny golden lock that you don't see at first and that opens and you can put things inside. He says,

"You can put in things you want to save, Clare . . . from whoever, from who's-it—"

"*Scott,* Dad, not who's-it."

"Right, Scott," he says, pretending to frown.

"Scott," I say, laughing, and then I hug him.

Anyway, as Scott would say, I did good. He gave me—Scott, I mean, or who's-it, as my father likes to call him when he's teasing me—

You know, that's interesting, isn't it? I mean, look at what I did there—when my father does it, I call it teasing, but when my mother does it, I call it annoying and I get all pissed. Not calling Scott who's-it but something like that—when she does something like that, it's definitely annoying to me, not charming . . . isn't that weird?

Anyway, Scott gave me this butterfly necklace. I know that sounds strange, but it's absolutely beautiful. All these tiny hand-painted enamel butterflies hanging from a fragile gold chain and it's old so all the colors are dull and faded. I can't tell you, I just adore it, I think it's Chinese. He came over at practically dawn this morning to give it to me, and then the three of us made Christmas breakfast, Scott and me and my dad, and Dad called him who's-it the whole time we were cooking. Scott doesn't mind, he thinks it's funny, and I guess since we were having such a good time scrambling eggs and shit, I thought it was funny too.

Anyway, it's Christmas. We made a fire in the fireplace even though it's 82 degrees outside. I mean, really, there has to be some tradition even though we live in L.A., and a fire going with the windows open is kind of beautiful if you think about it, and Dad put Handel's *Messiah* on, but I didn't mind, it was actually right for the day.

You know, sometimes I think my father is more free when he's around me than when he's around my mother, more comfortable or something. It's like when my mother's around he gets all uptight, and considering he's already not an extraordinarily loose guy, it just gets worse. And then she's always making this snappy dialogue, you know, jokes. It's like they're on different wavelengths. How can you be married and be on different wavelengths? When does that set in?

Sometimes I don't even understand what they're doing together in the first place. I mean, they look okay together, it's not that, it's just that you can feel the lack of something between the two of them and the constant threat. Like one of them could tell the other one to go fuck themself without a blink. Not that they do that or anything, but sometimes I feel it would be better if they did instead of the perpetual pressure they always put each other under that's always waiting to explode. I realize I may be the only one who sees this shit, I don't know . . . but it's not like I'm gonna have a discussion with their friends to see if anyone else notices.

A lot of my friends' parents have split up. Not Amy's, they're together . . . and Chad's . . . but Lisa's parents have been divorced since she's a toddler. Of course, that makes it easier—all she remembers is living her life going back and forth, Christmas at her mother's, Easter at her dad's. It's not the coming and going so much that I hear my friends complain about, it's when the two parents start dating, and then if one of them gets married, then the shit can really begin. Peter's mother got remarried, to this guy, and actually had a baby. Really, last year—she was packing Peter off to Stanford and wiping spitup off her shoulder at the same time. I was there, I saw it. Peter was holding the baby while he was drinking a beer. Let me tell you, it was a little strange. But, of course, it wasn't awful, it was just kind of sweetly embarrassing. Now my friend Susan got stuck with "awful"—her dad married this bimbo. I'm not kidding, a skinny, blond, big-busted bimbo like a joke, and she tells everybody that she was a dancer, but if you ask her where she danced she sort of laughs and looks at him. And he's fifty-two years old, Susan's father, you'd think he'd know. Susan always tries to come down with the flu or something when it's her weekend to spend with him and the bimbo. And then Julia Regan got stuck with this really embarrassing stepdad. I mean, you can't imagine, her mother actually married a clown. I mean, a real clown, his name is Buffo, he does kids' birthday parties and things, but the worst part is that when you go over there to hang out with Julia, he's always wearing a part of his clown costume, like just his red nose or his orange hair, with his regular clothes and doing things, you know, like having things fly out of the cookie jar at you when you lift the lid, or when he opens the door he asks you to smell the flower in his lapel and you have to do it because how can you say no, and then this big disgusting rubber bug comes out of the flower—he thinks this stuff is really funny, and Julia just wants to die and her mother won't even discuss it with her because she's so madly in love with him it's like she's blind. I mean, the last thing I heard is now he wants Julia's mother to be his assistant, you know, to go with him to the kids' parties and hand him his top hat and his bunnies and things. Julia says if anybody refers to her mother as "Mrs. Buffo," she is definitely leaving home.

Okay? So, you see what I'm talking about here? Besides all the heartache that goes on if your parents actually split up, there's still the worse stuff that can come after, like who they could end up with . . . I mean, that would probably be my luck, my mother would marry a clown. Or worse . . . oh, God . . . she could marry asshole Andy! God, that's probably what would happen; asshole Andy is divorced from his fourth wife and he can't live without my mother—he'd probably marry her.

Maybe what I should do is try to push them together. My parents, I mean. Is that possible? I wouldn't know where to begin. What would I say? "Gee, Mom, look how cute Dad is, don't you agree?"

I couldn't. I just couldn't.

I was trying to remember when they were okay with each other or even loving. I mean, not that I want to see them be loving—please, spare me—but, you know, like just look at each other or something. Anyway, I can't remember. I mean loving over nothing, not when a bad thing happens. People are always coming together when there's bad times, but that's not what I'm talking about, I'm talking about just looking at each other across a room as if you just love the other person. I don't know, but I don't think I can remember ever seeing them do that. Maybe I was just too young when they did.

Gilliana

THE REMAINS OF THE AFFAIR BETWEEN GILLIANA VENTIMIGLIA AND THE FAMOUS MARRIED ITALIAN COMEDIAN

One five-inch-tall porcelain statue of a little girl with pigtails and ribbons wearing a nightgown and clutching a teddy bear that he bought me at some little shop on Madison Avenue—one arm slightly crooked where she was glued back together imperfectly by Clare, who was in a hurry to fix her before I got home after Murray the dog crashed into the table where the statue was standing when he dove under it to get his tennis ball.

One oval gold scratched St. Christopher medal that he bought for me in St. Peter's in Rome.

One black nightgown from Bergdorf Goodman's, previously discussed.

One gold necklace from Tiffany's, previously discussed.

One powder-blue, soft straw summer hat with a wide brim that is slightly unraveling at the crown, which we bought together at De Pinna's before De Pinna's went defunct.

His old gray cashmere turtleneck from Sulka's that I used to wear when I was cold. The sleeves and the turtleneck part have since been cut off by Clare; the Sulka label remains intact.

A plastic, perma-plaqued three-column glorious review he got in *Variety* when he opened at the Sands in May of 1972.

One round gold cuff link with a block-letter "R" engraved on the top that I still carry around in my coin purse with my change.

One box containing a thousand of the 8 × 10 black-and-white glossy head shots of him that were used for fan-mail requests. He is wearing a tuxedo, a frilled evening shirt, a satin bow tie, and a large grin.

One birthday card to me that is signed, "I love you, *cara,* forever, your, Anthony," in his handwriting, and seventeen florists' cards that say variations of that same statement in seventeen different florists' handwriting.

A lock of his hair. One beautiful black curl from the top of his head snipped off by me when we were fooling around in the bathroom of a bungalow they had put him up in at the Beverly Hills Hotel. It lies in a plain white letter-sized envelope in the third left-hand lower drawer of my dressing table, along with other envelopes containing Clare's baby teeth.

A large open hole in my gut.

So I went back to L.A., but I did not stay in the apartment with Carole Rose and I did not go back to my job with Harry Witzer. I couldn't. Everywhere I looked in either place there was too much Anthony; I had to move. I got a little apartment in a little building on a street behind Saks and I. Magnin's in Beverly Hills that had a lot of hardwood floors and a lot of sunshine, and Harry got me a job as a baby staff comedy writer on "The Carol Burnett Show." This was not exactly easy then since no one had ever heard of me as a comedy writer and, second, I was still in my twenties and everybody was sure then that you couldn't write comedy unless you were older and you had some history in your head, and, third, I was a girl. That was the worst part, being a girl. There were no girls writing comedy then. All right, wait, there were a few girls—maybe there were three or maybe four, tops, but I'm talking about in the whole world, not just in Hollywood. A "gal" who can write comedy? A "gal" in with "the boys"? A "gal" who's under thirty and has never done this before? What are you—kidding me? But there was the farmer joke—and by then everybody knew Ronzoni's farmer joke—and the Mary Magdalene joke and a lot of other material that Anthony had been doing that was mine; what I didn't know was that Harry and Anthony must have called the whole world to make damn sure everybody knew that material was mine.

A joke is a surprise, it has to be something that will catch people off guard—if you can put any two things together that are unlikely and make it work, you will probably have yourself a joke, and for some reason I could do that and Anthony knew. It wasn't just that he loved me, he believed it was something I could do. So the other thing that should be added to the list is that my darling Anthony gave me my new life. I was going to be a comedy writer, no matter what.

I had a new job as one of "the boys" and a new apartment. I had no furniture, no money, and a top-of-the-line orange Corvette. Oh, and the hole in my gut, I did have that.

I met Christopher William Hall seven months later at a black-tie charity event in the grand ballroom of the Beverly Wilshire Hotel that I went to only because no one else on the show wanted to go and we had the tickets and I was low man on the totem pole so they made me go; he was the stranger to my right. There was no one on my left because I had gone alone—dragged myself there alone was more like it. He had someone on his right that he introduced me to, but I was paying absolutely no attention and she blended right in with the waiters and the band. He did something with money that I didn't understand, he had sandy hair and light eyes—maybe green, maybe blue, I didn't know—he was a little stiff but very polite and very attentive even though I'm sure I was rude.

"The chicken's good," he said.

"Oh, they do a very good job here with rubber chicken," I said, pushing a dead chicken breast around the plate with my knife.

"What?" he said, laughing.

"Rubber chicken, haven't you ever had rubber chicken?"

"I don't think so."

"Well, you're not supposed to eat it, that's why they serve it at charity affairs, because it doesn't cost them anything; they just wash it off and put it back on the plates, maybe two, three times a week."

He was laughing again.

"You're not eating it, are you?"

He was still laughing.

"Where did you grow up?"

"Connecticut," he said, with a big smile.

"Oh, well, that explains it, chicken is much too mundane for Connecticut. At the charity dinners in Connecticut, they probably only serve rubber pheasant or rubber small game hen."

He was hysterical. I looked at him closely. It didn't matter what I said, the man was laughing. I thought I would never be funny again, but he thought I was funny; Mr. Hall thought I was funny, whimsical, and enchanting, and certainly not his type. We were married six months later.

He was madly in love with me, I don't know what I was.

I moved my worldly possessions from my new apartment into Christopher's—it wasn't much to carry: me, one small flowered couch and matching wing chair I'd bought from W & J Sloane's with the first money I'd made from "The Carol Burnett Show," one exquisite antique iron double bed with brass finials and white porcelain turnings hand-painted with tiny purple and yellow pansies that I'd bought from Ita and Saulie Hermann, who had to move to New York and couldn't afford to take it with them, two sets of pale-blue sheets, three sets of pale-blue towels, one Portuguese needlepoint pastel flowered rug Carole Rose insisted she buy for me for my "new life" when the Design Center was having a parking-lot sale, four lamps I'd had made from Chinese ginger jars, three cooking pots, two sauté pans and assorted kitchen stuff, one set of restaurant-supply plain white dishes, one set of plain silverware, my clothes, makeup, hair stuff, toothbrush, and the list of "remains" mentioned above. Christopher's apartment was larger than mine and had even more hardwood floors and more sunshine. I parked my orange Corvette in the second space which was allotted to him in his building, made a lot of jokes about everything, let him love me, and tried not to think.

Can one be comatose but still be functioning? Perhaps. A whirlwind courtship, you might call it. Oh, right, and I was also pregnant, pregnant with Christopher's baby from the very first time we did it, when I held my breath and kept my eyes screwed shut so I wouldn't see Anthony's face, and Christopher said I was the most extraordinary woman he'd ever been with. Funny, I nearly left that part out.

So as far as I was concerned, this "hole in my gut thing" could all work out—I could fill it with hardwood floors and sunshine and a baby, right? Why not?

* * *

"Of course Christopher likes you; he just doesn't always laugh when you say certain things because he doesn't understand you're being funny. He just doesn't understand your sense of humor, that's all it is. So, where are our drinks anyway?" Gillian looked across the Polo Lounge for their waiter and ate the olive off the toothpick in her hand.

"How can he understand your sense of humor and not understand my sense of humor? It's the same fucking sense of humor, for crissakes," Carole Rose said. "What's the matter with him?"

"I don't know . . . nothing, he's just different from us."

"You can say that again. And so are you. You're not the same person since Tony died—you know that, don't you?" She turned from Gillian as the maître d' crossed in front of their table. "Dino, can you have that nit-wit waiter bring us another round of drinks already and some of that stupid cheese in the bowl with the crackers?"

"Of course, Miss Rose," Dino said, smiling and nodding, and then he noticed Gillian.

"Ahh, Miss Gilliana, ahh, I didn't see you for such a long time . . . *come va?*"

"I'm just fine, Dino, and how are you?"

"Just fine, just the same." He frowned slightly. "I'm so sorry, Miss Gilliana . . . about Mr. Ronzoni . . . You know how much I like him, such a nice man, such a—"

"Yes, I know, thank you," Gillian said, interrupting him.

"Such a tragedy, such a gentleman, so young, so handsome, so—"

"*So* everything," Carole Rose interrupted, watching Gillian's eyes fill up, "so how about some of that *'so'* cheese, Dino, huh?"

"Ahh, the cheese, yes, Miss Rose, I get it right away."

"Great." She turned to Gillian as Dino left the table. "You better not tell Dino you're marrying what's-his-name, he might throw himself under a train."

Gillian looked at her empty drink and pushed an ice cube around with her finger.

Carole Rose shook her head. "You know you shouldn't be doing this . . . you have absolutely no business marrying this uptight piece of white bread. I don't care how nice he is, he's absolutely not for you, and if Tony hadn't died and you hadn't gone crazy, you wouldn't have ever given Mr. Hall the time of day."

"Carole Rose . . ."

"No. I'm dead serious. This is a mistake, Gillian, I promise you."

"Thank you for your encouragement . . . It's always good to know your best friend is behind you when you're about to make one of the biggest decisions in your life."

"Hey, listen, if *I* don't tell you, who's going to tell you? Witzer? Your mother? Witzer wouldn't say a word to you 'cause he's afraid you'll shatter like glass, and your mother's so happy you're getting married already she wouldn't care if you married a baboon. I'm telling you he's not for you, Gillian, he's not. You should be having an abortion and putting him behind you. Chalk him up to someone who got lucky and snagged you because you had too much grief in your eyes to see."

She took a swig from her empty glass. "Goddamn it, where's my martini?"

She frowned at Gillian. "You're not through grieving over Tony, Gillian—this is not the time to get married, let me tell you."

Gillian folded the cocktail napkin into tiny squares. "Christopher is a very nice man. He's very good to me."

"Oh, Jesus . . . Well, that's great, *good* to you—oh, well, now I understand."

"I'm not getting an abortion, Carole Rose."

"Okay. Okay, I can go for that, you don't want an abortion, then don't have an abortion. Have the baby and bring it up. I'll help you, everybody will help you . . . just don't marry the guy."

"Why?"

"Because you're not ready, Gillian. You're not ready for somebody else."

"Maybe I'll never be ready."

"Maybe. Maybe you won't."

They looked at each other. Gillian stared at Carole Rose. Then she took another sip of her melted ice cubes and put the glass down.

"Okay . . . well, then, I'll just make myself ready. Okay? You watch me. I'll just make myself goddamned ready. I'll marry him and have his baby and live a regular life . . . like everybody else does . . . a regular life, regular and plain—no pipe dreams and no fancy romance and no running all over the world and meeting like teenagers and no wild heartbeating and none of that stuff that breaks you up and kills your insides, okay? I'll learn how to be regular—iron and sew and make piecrust and I don't know . . . what the fuck . . . jam . . . How 'bout that, I'll make my own goddamn jam in little jars, Carole Rose, with little labels that say 'from Gillian's kitchen' and paraffin on top, okay? I know about that shit, I know about paraffin and all that stuff. Hey, I could even wear an apron, couldn't I? How 'bout that, me in a fucking apron with little ruffles and a big bow . . ."

Carole Rose watched Gillian dissolve against the back of the red leather booth sobbing, her hands over her face.

"Okay," Carole Rose said quietly. "Okay . . . Jesus Christ, Gillian, okay."

There were a lot of wonderful things about Christopher besides the fact that he was good to me and was a very nice man; unfortunately, at the time of that conversation the only one I could think of I wasn't willing to part with and tell Carole Rose—it was one of those things that you know will lose in the translation, one of those "you had to be there" endearing things.

We were standing in a field. We were on the way to spend a weekend in Ojai, which is this sweet little town up the coast from L.A., and I had asked him to stop the car because I was queasy; he got out of the car with me and we were just standing next to each other in this field of wild grass by the side of the road.

"You okay?" he said, looking at me.

"Absolutely," I said, smiling.

"Good."

"I'll be fine, we're going to have a great time."

He looked at me. "A happy time," he said seriously. He wasn't smiling, his face was solemn, and out of nowhere he began to sing:

> *"Now someone said they just came back from somewhere,*
> *A friend of mine that I don't even know,*
> *He said there's lots of fun if we can get there,*
> *If that's the case, that's the place, the place we want to go . . . "*

I was staring at him. He was singing right there in the middle of this open field, Christopher William Hall. Singing.

> *"We gotta get goin', Where we goin', Whatta we gonna do.*
> *We're on our way to somewhere, the three of us and you . . . "*

It was "Cuanto le Gusta," Carmen Miranda's song, the one she used to sing with the bananas on her head, the one my very own mother used to sing when she was dusting the living room.

"What'll we see there, Who will be there, What'll be the big surprise,
There may be caballeros, With dark and flashing eyes . . . "

I was astounded. He started to do a little samba around me in the grass. I was laughing so hard I nearly fell over.

"We're on our way, pack up your pack,
And if we stay, we won't come back,
How can we go, we haven't got a dime,
But we're goin', and we're gonna have a happy time—Sing, Gillian
Cuanto le gusta, le gusta, le gusta . . ."

I sang. We sang and sambaed around the field. He not only knew the verse, which I didn't know and he taught me, but he even knew the last chorus about I'll take a train and you take a boat and I'll take a plane and you ride a goat. It was amazing. Christopher singing "Cuanto le Gusta" in a field. I couldn't tell Carole Rose; somehow I thought she might not get it. No, that's not it . . . she would have gotten it, she probably would have cried. I didn't tell her because somehow it was just too personal.

Carole Rose was my maid of honor and Harry Witzer was my man of honor, if there is such a thing. They both wore dark blue and neither of them stopped shredding Kleenexes from the beginning to the end. A judge who was a friend of Harry's married us at high noon on a September Sunday in the living room of Harry and Lil Witzer's sprawling house in Bel Air. The entire wedding party fit in between Lil's grand piano and the brocade club chairs by her French doors: me, Christopher, Carole Rose, the Witzers, and Judge Isenberg. There were no bishops, no ministers, no rabbis, no "nothin'," as my mother would say, and my mother and Lew and Christopher's parents were not invited, because Christopher asked if I would mind if we could just please make this whole thing very low-keyed. I said I didn't mind, it was fine with me, low-keyed—it was so low-keyed it practically didn't even open, to say the least.

The only things I remember about the wedding were that the white Bible my mother sent me to hold was shaking, and that behind the judge and the French doors there was one squirrel making a hell of a lot of racket in an avocado tree, the hors d'oeuvres were overcooked and lousy, the cake was too sweet, and the sprinkler system turned on during Harry's champagne toast to us and wouldn't go off. The plumbers arrived as we were leaving. That was about it, and I was pronounced married to someone I hardly knew.

Gillian could feel Christopher watching her. She'd read the same page three times to avoid his eyes. She moved her back slightly against the pillows on the little flowered couch.

"Are you all right?" he said.

"Mm-hm," she said, not looking up but smiling as if everything was okay. It was not okay. It was more than not okay. She was spotting. Well, it probably wasn't what you'd call spotting anymore, you could probably refer to it by now as actual bleeding, since she had two pads on and she could feel them nearly saturated, even though she'd barely moved. She'd been sitting in the same spot on the little flowered couch with the book in her lap for at least two hours.

"You know we can call the doctor again even though he said to wait."

"I know."

"Gillian?"

"Mmm?"

"Look at me."

She raised her eyes. He was kind of half-kneeling in front of her; he put his hand gently on her knee. "I love you, Gillian."

"I know."

"We'll have other babies . . . I mean, if this baby doesn't make it . . . you know, we'll have other babies . . . we have time."

"I know. Eight babies . . . maybe twelve . . ." She cocked her head at him: "Ten? . . . How 'bout ten?"

"It'll be okay," he said, smiling at her. Then he bent forward to kiss her forehead, leaned back and looked at her. "You sure you're okay?"

"Yep."

"Are you . . . bleeding?"

"Yep."

"Jesus. A lot?"

"I don't know, I think so . . . I don't know what a lot is, I've never done this before."

"Jesus, let's call the doctor."

"No, let's do like he said, let's wait, okay? And you know, you better watch it, you're saying an awful lot of Jesuses for a high Episcopalian—you could get in big trouble with the Church."

"Gillian, you're sure?"

"Absolutely, if you see a bunch of bishops following you around with their bishopy robes on but with fedoras pulled down low—"

"Gillian—about waiting to call the doctor."

"Yep, let's do it the way he said."

Christopher looked at her and smiled. "I love you, you know. Very much."

"I know." She shook her head and sighed. "Boy, this is some honeymoon you're having here, Christopher—instead of three weeks in Maui snorkeling, you get three weeks watching a woman lose a baby on a couch; talk about a raw deal . . . I'd put in for an annulment if I were you."

"We didn't lose the baby yet, Gillian."

"Okay."

"We might not."

"I know."

"It might hold on, Gillian."

"Okay . . . let's not talk about it, shall we? Okay?" She smiled weakly and lowered her eyes back to the book.

Christopher stayed where he was in front of her for a few minutes, but when she didn't look at him, he stood up, walked around the coffee table, and across the living room.

"You want some juice or something?"

"No, thank you."

"A glass of milk?"

She raised her eyes to his. "I hate milk, Christopher. It makes me gag."

He laughed. "Oh, right, I'm sorry, I forgot."

"It's okay."

"I'm sorry, really."

"Chris, really . . . please . . ."

"Okay."

What was I doing? I was having the wrong baby from the wrong man or maybe it was the right baby from the wrong man. Actually, I wasn't "having" anything even resembling a baby anymore, because by then it had stopped being a baby. It was just clots and tissue and blood coming out in my underpants—the most dreadful, appalling, frightening, sickening, sinking feeling I had ever had. Pieces of this baby coming out of me, pieces of a baby I felt I had nothing to do with, as if I hadn't even been there, pieces of a baby I had made with a man I didn't even know, a man who also happened to be my husband. My what? Earth to Gillian, come in Gillian . . . hello?

And how was I behaving? Who was this nice, quiet, sweet pliable person making jokes? Where was the Wild Woman of Borneo, the dancing, laughing "whore-madonna" woman who Anthony said should probably best be kept tied up most of the time? Did she die with him? Was she gone? And who cared? Not me, of course, I was walking around practically anesthetized.

Of course we lost the baby. I should have known.

White lights, white walls, cold bright white light, freezing white, steel table, steel, metal, metal cold, cold icy metal, freezing white bright blinding light, who was putting stockings on my legs?

"Anthony?"

"Okay, let's just move you over here," the voice said. "Come on, just move your body a little more; that's it, Mrs. Hall."

Mrs. Hall? Who was Mrs. Hall? One had my shoulders and the other had my bottom half . . . aliens, I'd been abducted by aliens and they were moving me . . .

"Cold," I said.

"It'll all be over soon and you'll be nice and warm."

Who did they think I was—a four-year-old? The next thing you knew, they'd be bringing me toast and jam and hot chocolate and a stuffed rabbit to squeeze.

"Okay, Gillian, you won't feel a thing now, just count backward for me."

Man's voice. Deep, solid, grown-up . . . who the hell . . . the captain of the ship . . . the head alien?

"Come on, Gillian, count for me . . . one hundred . . . ninety-nine—"

". . . bottles of beer on the wall," I said.

Laughing. Somebody was laughing. I heard that. See? I told you I was funny.

"Come on, Gillian . . . ninety-nine, ninety-eight—come on, count for me."

"You already know it, you do it, what do you need me for?"

"Hey, she's funny."

Who said that?

"Come on, Gillian, ninety-six, ninety-five . . ."

"Ninety-four, where's Anthony?"

"Good girl, that a girl, come on . . . ninety-three . . ."

"Ninety-two . . . fucking no-good silly baby couldn't hold on."

"Ninety-one . . ."

"Son of a gun . . ."

"Eighty-eight . . ."

"Lay them straight . . ."

"Eighty-seven . . ."

"The baby's in heaven. Oh, that's good, the baby can be with Anthony . . . in heaven on tour . . . oh, God, my Anthony . . ."

"Who's Anthony?"

"I don't know—maybe that's what she called the baby."

"Come on, Gillian, don't cry, there's nothing to cry about, just count for me . . . come on, Gillian . . . don't cry."

Just step right up here, folks, just count backward and you too can have a D and C. Dilation and curettage. Bread and butter. Shuck and jive. We'll just scrape away at that uterus wall until it's as good as new. Any traces of that disintegrating baby left in there? No, sir, clean as a whistle in here, sir. No baby here. No baby left indeed.

"Oh, I'm gonna be sick."

"It's okay, kid, I'm holding the pot."

"Oh, I'm sorry . . . Carole Rose . . . oh, God . . ."

"It's okay, Gillian, what are friends for? Whoops . . . that's good . . . there you go."

"Is she all right?" Christopher said. He was pale and looked devastated but was standing back about three feet from the bed. He hadn't taken a step closer to Gillian since they'd brought her up from the recovery room. "Is she okay?"

"Sure she's okay," Carole Rose said, smiling at him and crying at the same time. "She's fine, absolutely fine. She's just had a baby scraped out of her and now she's puking her guts out. We women do this all the time."

So Carole Rose said I hadn't finished grieving for Anthony and she was right, but now I had two "babys" to grieve for—the one I would always love and the one I never even got a chance to meet. Not exactly the most helpful way to start a new marriage, one might say.

Mollie

So I started my life over and then my father came back—out of nowhere, as if he'd seen a big billboard on Lindell Boulevard announcing that Julie was really gone. He hadn't said a word to me since I'd married Jule except when the baby died, and then I don't know what he said because I wouldn't look at him at the cemetery, and that was already years before and I hadn't seen him since.

He'd never even seen Gilliana; he never even got in touch with me when she was born. As far as he was concerned, as long as I was married to the *Talyaner* I was dead and gone.

And then there was a knock on the door on a Sunday morning and I opened it and there he was. He took his hat off, held it in his hands, muttered something that I couldn't hear, and scowled. I didn't say a word, my head was spinning to see him standing there, and then Gilliana came up behind me—she was eight, she'd just had her eighth birthday—she ran up behind me, smiled at this stranger in a suit and tie who was her grandfather, and said, "Mom, where's my green sweater—the one I wear with my blue jeans? Claudia and I are going to the Parkmoor and to the show."

"Dos kindt kickt oys vi dem mama," my father said in a low voice.

"Yes," I managed to whisper.

"What?" Gilliana said, giggling.

"Ir oygn," he said, looking at me.

He was right, Gilliana's eyes were just like my mother's, big brown eyes with long eyelashes and thick brows. My mother's beautiful brown eyes laughing out of my daughter's face.

"What?" she asked again. "What did he say?"

"I say," my father said to her in his thick Russian accent, "det you are loking like your grandmother, specially in de eyes."

"I do?" She looked at me, and back at him. "You think I look like Sophia? But she has gray eyes, my grandmother, and mine are brown."

His face got dark, he made a gesture with his hand as if to disregard Sophia, as if she did not exist. "Not whoever you say. *Ava,* you haf *Ava*'s eyes," he said firmly.

It was just like him; he arrived with no warning and before he even got his foot in the door he was going to have a fight.

"Come on in, Pa," I said.

So he was back, my father, with all his righteousness and all his stubbornness and his reluctance to ever say he was wrong. It was simple—the whole thing was my fault because I had married an Italian, that's why he had to turn his back on me, and as far as he was concerned, look how it had turned out, so he was right. The only thing I got out of him about all the missing years was a quiet but passionate *"Ich bin shuldik,"* which was "I'm sorry" about Sandy dying. Of course it wasn't I'm sorry that I didn't come to you when you lost your child and let bygones be bygones like a father could; the only thing he would give me was I'm sorry that she died, and that was that. But this was my father, and I already knew from him; I knew not to expect too much, that way I wouldn't have too much to lose.

He was back and he taught Gilliana checkers and dominos and he bought her a dog. I wanted to kill him about the dog but, of course, he bought it and brought it over to her so she could fall in love with it before he said a word to me. That was also my father; there would be no discussion, he would do what he wanted to do, with or without your approval.

"*Tzvantzik tollah* and wit de bed, Malya—such a bargain, who could pass up?"

At least it was a little dog; the place was hardly big enough for me and Gilliana, much less a dog. It was a six-week-old white puppy with brown spots that my father had bought for twenty dollars from a lady with a box of six of them in front of the A & P; it seemed that the final negotiating point in the deal included her also throwing in a dog bed. When Pa bought the puppy, she fit in the palm of Gilliana's hand, and Gilliana fell madly in love with her and named her Dot. Just what I needed then, my father back and a Dot.

Jule was supposed to see Gilliana once a week and I mostly stayed in the other room during the picking up of her and the bringing back. He was supposed to take her with him to spend every Sunday and sometimes he did and sometimes he didn't.

"Stay out of it, Mollie. If he wants to be a good father he'll do it, and if he doesn't he won't," Dell said.

So if he made a date with her and broke it I tried to keep my mouth shut. My father, on the other hand, was another story.

"A hundred percent no-goodnik," he said, sipping his tea.

"Okay, Pa . . ."

"Hab zi in drerd."

"Pa, that's enough."

"Oh? A lie, I'm saying? A man, he has no time for his child, dis is a goot ting, Malya, wot?" He took another sip of tea, the spoon inside the glass grazing his cheekbone by his eye.

I looked at him and he looked back. "Wot? Wot, Malya? It's a lie I'm saying here?"

"Just let it go . . . please, Pa, okay?"

He shook his head and put the glass down.

"So . . . you have a piece cake, maybe, for someone, could be me?"

He came over three, four times a week, always unannounced; you never knew when he'd show up or how long he'd stay, and already he was mixing in with my life.

I wasn't seeing anyone, which was fine with me, but every now and then I would go out. Every now and then I would go to anything, mainly because I had nothing else to do and Dell was always pushing me.

"You'll meet someone."

"I don't want to, I have to wash my hair."

"You washed your hair last night."

"So I'll wash it again."

"Mollie . . ."

"What?"

"You'll meet someone."

"I don't want to."

It went on and on. Her theory was *not* that you would necessarily *like* the someone you would meet, but that the someone you would meet might possibly introduce you to someone else—and that someone else could possibly turn out to be the good one. It seemed like a lot of rigamarole to me; who wanted to get all dressed up to meet the someone who wasn't going to be the someone? Not that I wanted a "someone" anyway—I didn't. But Dell was always pushing me to go, so every now and then I went—to anything—a lecture, a social, a dance where you were supposed to meet people, it didn't matter, I just went so she would let up on me. And I didn't look for a somebody when I went—I went, I sat with my pocketbook in my lap, and I came home.

But no matter what I did or where I went, if I met someone or got introduced to someone and they took me out, even if it was for a nothing—a cup of coffee, a picture show, it made no difference—no matter who the someone was or what he did, to my father he was no good.

"So, who is dis fellah?"

"Who?"

"Some person, I heard."

"Pa, there's nobody, stop it."

"I heard from a bird maybe, you went somewhere."

"I went to eat, that's all."

"Wit?"

"With nobody."

"Wot?—he was a *sheygetz, efsher?* Dat's why you don't want to tell me?"

"Pa, he wasn't a *sheygetz,* he was a nice Jewish man from Chicago that works for Barad Lingerie."

He smirked. "So, tell me, wot kind of a man sells underwear, Malya? Huh? You tell me. Wot kind of a man?"

You had to laugh sometimes, he was so impossible.

A year went by . . . and another . . . and I started seeing a man. Just seeing, that was all it was. His name was Paul Fredericks, a very nice man and very sophisticated, a semiretired older businessman who lived in Atlanta and also worked as a public speaker. I met him when I went to a social for the Jewish War Veterans one night; he was the speaker. The only reason I even spoke to him that first time was he asked if anybody knew where all those good St. Louis Italian restaurants were and someone said, "Oh, ask Mollie," and he did, and then he said, well, could he take me and I was going to say no and then I figured, why not? Dell would let up with me if I went out with him so I let him take me to Ruggeri's and

I ate fried ravioli and he was very nice. From then on, whenever he was in town speaking, I let him take me out.

"Fredericks is a Jewish name?" my father asked. He was sitting at the kitchen table watching me iron.

I put down the sprinkler bottle. "I don't know, I already told you that."

"I don't tink so."

I moved the iron around the cuff of my blouse. "Why don't you turn on the radio?"

"It's not a Jewish name, I'm tellink you. If it was a Jewish name, I would know."

I put the blouse on a hanger, hung it on the back of a kitchen chair, and buttoned up the front. Then I turned on the radio and found some music, unrolled another damp blouse from the pile, and picked up the iron.

"He probably changed it to pull a fast one."

I whistled "Stardust" with Nat King Cole and worked the iron up and down a sleeve.

"Dat's wot dey do, you know . . . is okay to be Jewish but not all de way . . . just in case someone should know who wouldn't like it."

"Listen to how nice he sings, Pa."

"Who?"

"Nat King Cole."

"Dat's not a Jewish name either."

"He's not Jewish, Pa."

He gave me a look. "Dat's wot I said, Malya, whoever heard of a Jewish Cole? No one. A King maybe, but not a Cole."

I had to put the iron down, I was laughing so hard.

Of course, I knew my father was up to something, but there was no way I could ever have guessed he would have gone that far. It was a week later and he'd shown up one night after supper. Gilliana was taking her bath.

"So wot are you lookink? You don't know wot I'm talking here?"

He raised his voice, as though if he spoke louder I would understand him, and went on. "A *lantzman,* Malya, a friend . . . from de old country . . . from Berdichev, where I was born."

"I know what a *lantzman* is, Papa."

"So, wot are you lookink funny on me?"

"I'm not looking funny at you, I just never heard of this man before."

"Of course you did, my whole life I know him, I speak of him many times."

"Not to me, Pa."

"Of course, Malya."

"No, I don't think so."

"Yes, Malya, I speak of Sam Shapeskovsky many times."

He took a loud sip of tea from the glass, but he didn't stop looking at me. I moved the knife through the poppy-seed stollen and put a piece on his plate.

"Tank you, *kleyna.*"

"Mm-hm."

"So, wot I was sayink here?"

"I don't know, something about Sam Shapes-something."

"Shapeskovsky, Sam Shapeskovsky, my goot friend from de old country, his son."

"Mm-hm."

"His son, det's wot I'm tellink you, he's living close to here."

"Mm-hm."

"Wot's all dis 'mm-hmming'?"

"Nothing, I'm just listening."

"Goot, I'm glad you're listening. So, he's comink."

"Where?"

"Here."

"To St. Louis?"

"To St. Louis, to dis apartment on Shaw Avenue where you live in a neighborhood filled with *Talyaner*s—I don't haf to tell you, you should move already—for coffee. Sunday."

"What?"

"Sunday."

"This Sunday? To my house?"

"Mm-hm," he said. "See, I can make 'mm-hmming' too, Malya."

"Pa, you invited him here? Some stranger?"

"*Vos meynstu* a stranger? Dis is de son of my *lantzman,* is not a stranger."

"Pa, I don't want somebody I don't know coming here for coffee."

"Wot's de matter, you're so busy all of a sudden comink Sunday?"

"It has nothing to do with being busy, I don't know this man."

"Neither do I, we meet him together when we haf the coffee. And you'll buy a nice cake too, Malya. Maybe chocolate . . . something for special, maybe wit flowers in icing."

I looked at him. "Why, Pa?"

"Because he is the son of my *lantzman* Sam Shapeskovsky, like I'm tellink you, is why. Wot's de matter wit you, Malya, you don't speak English no more?"

His name was not Shapeskovsky, my father's old friend's son Bill. His name was Bill Shapell. It must have been changed when he came over from the old country. I have no idea how he got the name Bill, I had never met a Jewish "Bill" before, but I didn't say anything to my father, who was having a wonderful time entertaining in my living room.

"More coffee *efsher,* Bill? Malya, maybe he wonts more coffee."

I moved my hand toward the china coffeepot on the table.

"Oh, no, thank you, really, Mr. Kramer, I'm stuffed." He put his hand horizontally in front of his face, level with his eyes. "To here."

My father nearly had a fit laughing. It was clear he thought Bill Shapell was very funny. I didn't. I thought that was also clear from the way I was behaving, which was to practically not speak to either of them. I was furious that I'd allowed myself to get roped into this, furious with my father for setting it up, and even furious with poor Bill Shapell, who was sitting across from me sweating in our hot apartment with his jacket still on. His jacket was checkered and probably very fashionable but a little too loud for me. So was his tie, it had orange flamingo birds on it. And his very gold pinky ring had lots of flashing diamonds. He made awful jokes and smiled too much, and was wearing brown shoes that had been shined so brightly they were like lights coming out at the ends of his pants. Bill Shapell turned out later to be a very good person, but that afternoon I wanted to hit him with the china coffeepot.

He did not live in St. Louis or even anywhere near it; he lived in some city I'd never heard of called St. Joseph, which was all the way across the state of Missouri and then north. I had no idea what he was doing in my living room except that my father was up to something and, knowing my father, it was probably no good.

"So, you were married a long time, Mollie?"

"Yes."

"Too long," my father said. I looked at him and he averted his eyes.

"And where's the beautiful daughter your father told me about?"

"She's with her father."

"Oh, I see. How old is she?"

"Eleven," I said.

"He takes her nowhere, her no-goodnik fadder, let me tell you . . . to a park to stand and do notink, dat's where he takes her, nowhere."

I drank some more coffee so I wouldn't say anything.

"So . . ." Bill Shapell said.

I kept my eyes on my cup.

"So," my father said, "and wot do you do, Bill?"

"Oh, tires, Mr. Kramer, I'm in tires, I own a Goodyear tire store—a franchise, you know."

"Goodyear, well dat's a big name, Goodyear."

"Oh, yes sir, Mr. Kramer, it's the best."

"Bill is in Goodyear, Malya, wot do you tink of dat?"

"That's very nice."

"It's better den nice," my father said, "it's Goodyear, it's da best."

Better I should hit my father with the china coffeepot.

Bill had never been married and was five years younger than me. He explained that he never found "the right girl" to settle down with; I wanted to make it clear that I also was not "the right girl," but I kept my mouth closed. He drank coffee and ate bakery chocolate cake with icing roses for three hours and a half, and then he stood up and said it was time to go. Pa tried to talk him into staying a little longer, but when he said he had a long drive ahead of him Pa said he understood.

"So, Malya will walk wit you to your machine, Bill."

"Excuse me?"

"Wot—excuse you?"

"He means your car," I said.

"Oh, right, of course, my machine. Like in Russian, right?"

"Your car, your car . . . sometimes I make a little slip wit my English and out come de old words, but I'm an old man, wot can I do?"

Bill Shapell laughed. "You're not an old man, Mr. Kramer."

"Well, young you couldn't call me exactly . . . young I'm not."

Bill Shapell laughed some more. "Well, no, but you look like you're in pretty good shape to me."

"Like dey say, not bad for an *alteh-kocker.*"

Bill Shapell laughed again and so did my father; I stood there like a doorstop and didn't say a word.

* * *

My father watched from the window, he didn't hide behind the draperies or try to make himself less noticeable, he just stood there watching me and Bill by the door of Bill's sparkling white Cadillac Eldorado convertible parked in front of my apartment. The tires were black with white sidewalls, and you could read the word "Goodyear" on each tire as if he had scrubbed the letters with Colgate and a toothbrush.

I extended my hand and he shook it.

"Well, it was very good to meet you, Bill."

"Likewise, I'm sure," he said, smiling.

"And have a good trip back to St. Joseph."

"St. Joe, we call it St. Joe."

I smiled. "Well, have a good trip back to St. Joe."

He smiled. "Well, I'd like to call you if that's okay, Mollie. Or do you prefer to be called Malya?"

"No, Mollie is fine."

"Mollie."

He had a few chocolate cake crumbs on the lapels of his jacket. It occurred to me that the brown crumbs matched his shoes. I could feel my father's eyes staring at the back of my head.

"So how 'bout it, if I call you?"

"Bill, you're a very nice man . . ."

"Thank you."

"You're welcome, and it's very nice that you want to call me, but I really want to be honest with you."

"Of course, and I want to be honest with you too, Mollie. Honesty is the best policy, just like they say. It's the way I am in my business and in my personal life."

"Of course."

He smiled and I tried to go on. "You see, I, I just—"

"You don't want me to call you because you wouldn't want to go out with me?"

"Well, it isn't that I wouldn't want to go out with you, it's just that I—"

"You don't think I'm for you."

My mouth actually opened.

"I like to get right to the point, Mollie."

"I see."

"It's the way I am. I hope I haven't offended you."

"No, of course not."

"Because if you don't think I'm for you I understand why you wouldn't want to go out with me because it would just be a waste of your time"—he smiled again—"and mine too."

"Uh-huh."

"Okay, then, I guess we should call it a day." He smiled again, shook my hand like we'd just made some big deal, and opened the door of his car. I took a few steps backward, but then he turned and snapped his fingers as if he'd just had an idea. "Hey, you know, Mollie, now that I think about it, it would be a shame to let a sweet woman like you get passed by . . . You know, I have these two friends who live in Kansas City—actually, they're brothers and they're both single—maybe you might like one of them . . . since you're not interested in me." He laughed. "They're both very nice fellas . . . gentlemen." He laughed again. "Not scholars exactly, I'd have to say, but certainly gentlemen . . . How 'bout they call you up and take you out?"

I was so shocked I didn't know what to say, I just stood there staring. I thought he might roll up his sleeves like the Texaco man in the advertisement on the television and sing, "We are the men from Texaco, we work from Maine to Mexico"—doing whatever they said—"to your car."

"Huh? How 'bout I give them your number?"

"Well, I . . ."

And then his smile turned into a big salesman's grin, "Might as well give it a chance, Mollie—it's like they say, what have you got to lose?"

That's how I met the Grimm brothers. Of course, that wasn't their name, that's what Dell called them. Actually, she called them the brothers Grimm, only not Jacob and Wilhelm, she called them Tweedledeedee and Tweedledeedum Grimm.

Mollie shook her head at Dell. "No, that's what he called it; he said, we'll drive in and have a visit."

"Which one?"

"I don't know, whichever one I was talking to when they called."

"This is too much, kiddo, you're importing men from Kansas City to St. Louis, and brothers yet—now this takes the cake."

"Dell, don't start, this wasn't my idea, you know."

"I know, I know, I'm only kidding you."

"I just couldn't tell them they couldn't come when they acted like it was arranged already. I'm telling you, I'm fit to be tied with this whole business. I could wring Pa's neck, and do you know, on top of everything else he actually had the nerve to accuse me of messing it up with Bill Shapell."

"What?"

"Oh, you should have heard him; he said I probably told Bill I had been married twice and that scared him away."

Dell laughed. "Hey, it's okay, Mollie, the Grimm brothers might turn out to be swell guys."

"Oh, sure, I can just picture it."

There was no way to picture it.

They were sweet and kind and short and quiet and practically dressed alike and wore hats that they took off and put in their laps for the first hour they were in the apartment. They wore dark suits and white shirts and plain ties and black shoes, and they hardly said a word. Gilliana and Dell and I tried to make conversation but it was very one-sided. Dell didn't do anything out of line, she was a perfect lady, but it was so obvious to me what she was thinking that it was hard for me to keep a straight face. I could hear the jokes as if her eyes were talking.

Their names were Keith and Gary Rubin, neither of them had ever married; one was a furrier and the other was in "small appliance repair," that's what he called it, and that's what changed everything that afternoon, because as soon as he told us what he did for a living, Gilliana told him about the problem we had with our toaster and Gary Rubin said, oh, he would be happy to take a look at it right then and there to see why it wasn't popping up correctly, and everything changed. Before I could say a word, his hat was off his lap and perched on an end table, his jacket was hung over the back of a chair, his tie was loosened, and our toaster was sitting in a million pieces on the kitchen table and he was explaining in detail to a fascinated Gilliana every part of it and how it fit. Suddenly he talked. And then so did the other Mr. Rubin, because Dell asked him one little question about a fur coat that used to be her mother's and he proceeded to totally win her over by spelling out to her "the goods" and "the bads" of owning a coat that was made of sheared beaver versus one that was made of Persian lamb and, by the way, how she would look like "a million dollars," he said, blushing, if she didn't mind his saying so, in either one.

The Rubin brothers were lovely men; they just weren't for me. The good thing was that they knew it, I didn't have to tell them, and that was such a relief. They both so wormed their way into our hearts that by their third visit to St. Louis to us, when the older one, Keith, proposed his idea, I never even thought to say no.

"You see, Mollie, we had a sister."

"Bess," Gary said.

"Bess," Keith went on, "a beautiful girl . . ."

"A strawberry blond," Gary said.

"Gary."

"Sorry."

Keith nodded, "A strawberry blond like you couldn't think was imaginable—like gold, her hair was, and with very white skin and freckles. She had freckles all over her face and her hands . . . everywhere," he said, and then he stopped; you could tell this was very hard for him.

"Neither of us has freckles," Gary said, continuing for his brother, "as you can see, it was kind of a rarity."

I shook my head; my eyes had filled up with my baby Sandy's face, her white skin and the smattering of little freckles across her cheeks and nose.

"She was the youngest, after me, and—" Gary said, and stopped.

I looked at him and then at Keith.

Keith shrugged his shoulders and nodded his head a little, "So, she was our baby sister and she followed us everywhere and we loved her and then she grew up and got married . . ."

"And she was very happy," Gary said.

"Very happy, yes, she was very happy—" Keith stopped again; he looked at his brother.

"And then," Gary said, ". . . she died."

"My God," Dell said.

"Cancer," Gary said softly, frowning, "very fast . . . everywhere . . ."

"She didn't know what hit her," Keith said.

"And neither did we," Gary said.

Keith shrugged again and made a little grimace. "I guess we still don't."

"And it's four years ago, come May."

"May 1st," Keith said and shut his eyes.

We sat there, the four of us. Gilliana had already gone to bed and Nat was working late or he would have been there too.

"My God," Dell said. "What a fucking tragedy."

Nobody said anything, the brothers shook their heads.

"Pardon my French," Dell said.

"It's okay," Keith said. "I feel the same way."

"I'm so sorry," I said. "It's terrible."

"God," Dell said. "Let's have a drink, shall we?" She got up from the sofa. "How about a scotch, Keith?"

"Okay, that would be okay—a little one, with water."

"I'll have one," Gary said, "neat."

"Okay," I said, getting up.

"Stay put, Mollie," Dell said. "I'll fix 'em," and she moved to the cabinet where I kept the liquor. I looked at the brothers. Keith shrugged again and then smiled at me.

"So, Mollie, I have to tell you, the reason we brought this up, you see, is we have an ulterior motive."

"You do?"

"Say it louder, I don't want to miss anything," Dell said, banging an ice-cube tray against the kitchen sink.

"He said they have an ulterior motive for telling us about their sister."

"Bess," Gary said.

"Bess," I repeated.

"Yeah?" Dell said, dropping ice cubes into glasses and pouring scotch.

"Yes, we want Mollie to meet Bess's husband."

"What?" I said.

"What?" Dell said from the kitchen. "I missed that."

"Bess's husband, our ex-brother-in-law. Of course, we don't feel that way about him—like he's an ex, I mean—we're still very close to him."

"He's a great guy," Gary said, "we see him all the time."

"What?" Dell said, standing in front of us with four drinks on a tray.

"We want to introduce Mollie to our ex-brother-in-law," Keith said. "We think she might like him, we want Mollie to meet Lew."

So that's the story of how I met Lew, my dear sweet Lew, my "Mr. Security," as I always called him, my third and final husband, as he always called himself, because my father, against my will, made a coffee date for me with the son of his *lantzman,* his friend from the old country, except that none of it was true.

My father had no *lantzman* named Sam Shapeskovsky from Berdichev, Russia, where he was born. The truth was, my father put an advertisement in the newspaper, the *Jewish Daily Forward*; he put an advertisement in the personal section of the newspaper for someone to come and marry me.

I never knew the words he used, I never saw the actual ad or heard how he worded it or what it said. I never even knew he did it until a year after Lew and I were married and Pa was dying, which was why he told me, but he refused to say what the ad said.

"Wot difference?" he said, looking up at me from the pillows. "I did it, and look what you got from it, dat's all dat counts."

Leave it to my father, making sure even when he was dying that he got credit for doing something good. I guess he figured he needed it on the list of goods and bads before he died. He was also crazy about Lew; he liked to tell everybody his Malya was nothing until she had Lew—typical of my father, God forbid he should compliment me for anything.

So all these years I wondered, How did he put it in the newspaper? What could he have said? My Gilliana says that, knowing her grandfather, he probably wrote:

ONE WOMAN WITH A FEMALE CHILD
NEEDS A HUSBAND—COME QUICK.

God knows how he put it. All I know is that a stranger named Bill Shapell from St. Joseph, Missouri, answered the ad and came to St. Louis to meet me, and from him came the Rubin brothers from Kansas City, and from them came the best thing that ever happened to me: from them came my Lew.

Gilliana

It's Christmas and my mother's birthday. It's also snowing out and very cold. I took a long walk this morning all around the neighborhood.

This is not the neighborhood where I was when I was a teenager. When Mollie married Lew and we moved to Kansas City from St. Louis, we lived on Seventy-third Street between Holmes and Cherry; I was fourteen and I went to Southwest High School on Wornall Road. They still live off Wornall Road but now a little farther south; Mollie and Lew haven't ventured too far from their beginnings, but everything around them has changed. Even me. Even Southwest High School, which was very la-de-da then, now I think it's second-rate, I think now all the la-de-da schools are on the Kansas side. Going to school in Missouri is probably déclassé; they probably have to smuggle the la-de-da kids over the border in a plain brown bus.

I took the walk in Mollie's mink coat. I know it wasn't politically correct, but I couldn't help it; I didn't bring my own foul-weather gear, leaving L.A. the way I did in a huff. That was a car, wasn't it? I think so. I should write it down, look it up, do a piece on it, a huff . . . might be good for a few laughs. If I ever laugh again. Ha-ha-ha.

Actually, me in Mollie's coat is good for a few laughs. The sleeves are too short for me and my arms and my hands dangle out like a gawky fur monster. I took a pair of her gloves out of that glove drawer. I decided since it was Christmas I would be festive, so I took a pair of black leather ones that reach clear up above the elbows, with black bugle beads sewn on the knuckles in a kind of fleur-de-lis motif. The rest of the outfit was my old Levi's, my cowboy boots, my stained T-shirt, one of Lew's old alpaca sweaters monogrammed with his initials, and one of Mollie's scrumptious Chanel silk scarves—multicolored red-and-white peonies with green leaves on a black ground—over my wet hair. Very Christmassy. The whole thing got soaked in snowmelt.

I had to take a walk because I had to get out of there.

It all started because I played the game with Mollie this morning; I got suckered in because she was actually coherent for maybe three, four minutes, and the impact of me assuming that that could be reality nearly did me in. Take yourself for a walk, Gillian, get yourself some air, Gillian, soak your fucking head, Gillian, grow up.

I had been flipping through *Vogue,* not really looking at anything, just turning the pages in front of my eyes. I'd bought it to look at on the airplane, but I never did. I was in her bedroom and she was in the bed. Breakfast was over, the kitchen was spotless, the presents were all opened, the torn ribbons and ripped wrapping paper in the garbage . . . oh, shit, we forgot to have presents, didn't we? How could that have slipped my mind? What's Christmas without presents? . . . Oh, shut up, Gillian, shut up.

The house was peaceful. Lew was puttering in the basement doing God knows what he does, Mollie and I in the bedroom doing nothing . . . I'd already looked at everything on her dresser, skimmed my fingers across the surface of all the things I'd grown up with—Mollie's things that were always on her dresser top. The dresser top in St. Louis became the dresser top in Kansas City without a change; my mother could change men and cities but not dresser tops, dresser tops remained the same: the crystal perfume bottles on the flowered porcelain tray, the rose satin handkerchief box, the three-tiered glass jewelry case with the curved filigree handles and the gold claw feet, the snapshots under the glass top, my face at various stages in my life looking back at me from under the glass, four thousand pictures of me and three of my sister, Sandy, because all that's left from her eight short months of life are three.

I picked up *Vogue* and walked to the window. I was leaning against the wall by the window that looks out on the peach tree and the LaPaglias' side yard, just turning the pages, and she was lying there quietly—I didn't think asleep but her eyes were closed.

"Anything good, sweetie?" she said to me.

I looked up.

"What?"

She smiled. "You want to play the game?" she said.

My knees began shaking. "Okay."

She actually patted the bed where she wanted me to sit down next to her. She put her hand on my leg while I turned the pages until I found something. It was astonishing; I was having trouble getting my breath.

She looked up at me.

"Okay," she said in anticipation.

"Okay," I said, looking at her and reciting the way we always did. "If I had all the money in the world, what would I buy?"

"If I had all the money in the world, what would I buy?" my mother said with me. Mollie, my Mollie. The same Mollie with the washcloth on her head said the words perfectly.

She was still there. She was actually there in her eyes, the way she always was since we'd been doing this together, since I was maybe sixteen. She nodded her head, waiting.

And then I read from the *Vogue,* in a kind of shaky voice, since I could hardly speak: " 'Distressed meets delicate, mixing as a raw-edged shearling peacoat gets tossed over a flowing velvet skirt, Calvin Klein collection, skirt about $1250.' " I held the magazine up for her to see.

"Nah, the skirt's too long," she said. "You'd get it caught in the car door."

I laughed. There were a few tears running around my eyes because this was even happening, but I laughed and turned the page.

"Go on," she said, and she squeezed my thigh with her beautiful fingers.

"Okay," I said, "let's see . . . how 'bout this, Mom? 'Ellen Tracy's extravagant swirl of duchesse golden satin . . .' "

She patted my leg and I looked at her.

"We can't wear golden, Gilliana, golden is yellow no matter what they call it and we're too olive. We can't wear yellow, we'd look like we passed away."

"Passed away," she said. I could get hysterical here. I turned the page.

She began to whistle "Young at Heart."

I looked at her to make sure she was still there, and she smiled and winked at me while she was whistling.

"Mom?"

"What?" she said, stopping.

"Nothing, I just . . . like that song."

"Frank Sinatra," she said.

I was having trouble breathing. I assumed she had made a miraculous recovery while we were playing the If I Had All the Money in the World game. Stupid me, if only I had played it earlier we could have avoided all this *Sturm und Drang*.

"But he can't sing anymore," she said.

"He can't?"

This was a conversation we were having here, a real conversation with long sentences between two adults.

"No, Lew bought a tape and I listened. His voice is gone now, it's crapona."

I laughed. "Mom, it's 'crapola,' not 'crapona.' "

She looked at me. "Well, that's what you call it out there in Los Angeles; here in the Midwest we say 'crapona.' " She tilted her head and squinted her eyes like she always did when she was going in for the punch line. "And we know crapona when we see it," she said, grinning, "even if we just hear it we know."

I thought I was going to fall off the bed.

"Keep looking, sweetie," she said, and patted my leg again.

I picked up the magazine. "Okay . . . hey, here we go, Mom, listen to this: 'Erasing the boundaries between day and night dressing—crisp wool coats team up with sheer and elaborately flounced evening dresses, Prada, Charivari, New York.' How 'bout this, Mollie, you love this rich, dark red."

I held the magazine out to her and she scanned the outfit.

"Bravo red," she said, smiling, "perfect . . . like a maraschino cherry."

"That's right, like a maraschino cherry," I said, laughing. "Well, should we buy it? Let's see . . . how much is this thing anyway?" I scanned the words . . . "It's probably ridiculously expensive . . . where the hell is it?" I looked at her, I was so happy. "It probably costs more than a car . . ."

She was gone. I didn't even have to say anything, it was so clear. Her hand was dead on my leg, the fingers loose and limp like a dead salmon, the light had dimmed from her eyes . . . going, going, gone . . . back into her other life away from me.

"Oh, Mollie, wait a minute . . ." I wiggled the magazine at her. "Look, you like this one . . . please . . . wait . . ."

Nothing.

"Mom?"

Nothing.

"Come on, Mollie, we're playing the game here."

Nothing.

"Mommy?"

Nothing. I couldn't believe it.

I wanted to slam her back into reality but I didn't think I could even touch her, my hands were shaking too hard—the *Vogue* was flapping around on the bed in front of me as if it was being yanked on a string. I clenched the pages and studied the text under the glossy photograph of the blood-red gown.

I looked back at my mother. I looked back at the magazine.

Come on, Gillian. You can do this. Bring her back, like the Mounties.

I read from the description: "Erasing the boundaries between day and night dressing . . ." And then I stopped. "Well, that must be it, Mollie, you don't need this dress because you've already got something that erases the boundaries between day and night dressing, don't you?" Loud, I said it, clearly and distinctly, but most of all loud. And bitchy.

I touched the shoulder of my mother's soft pink flannel nightgown.

I could get her. I would make her mad.

"This little number does that for you, doesn't it, Mollie? It surely erases the boundaries between day and night dressing."

That's it, Gillian, come on . . .

"Of course, you also have the distinct advantage of not knowing whether it's day or night. Don't you, Mom?"

My voice was raised, each word clipped . . . This would get her . . . come on . . .

Nothing.

Come on, Mollie, get me; come on, Mollie, come on . . .

"Right? You don't know nothin' at all, do you, Mom?"

Good, Gillian . . . that'll get her back . . . here we go.

"Right, Mom?"

I gazed into her eyes. She didn't blink, she didn't do anything.

"Right, Mom?"

Come on . . . I put a hand under my mother's shoulders, I raised her upper body off the stack of flowered pillows beneath her head.

Nothing. Oh, God, I know she's in there . . . let her come back to me . . . I can't live with this coming and going. Goddamn it, if it doesn't kill her it's going to kill me.

I shook her by the shoulders.

I did. I shook my own sweet Mollie.

Her head rolled loosely. Her long hair that I had tied earlier freed itself from the ribbon at the nape of her neck.

"Mom? I need you, Mom. Please, listen . . ."

Nothing.

"I'm talking to myself here, Mom!" I yelled in my mother's silent bedroom.

Silence. Just silence. I put her little body back on the pillows, I straightened her nightgown, smoothed her hair under the ribbon, and retied the satin into a perfect bow. I fitted the blanket all around her, folded the top sheet over the satin border, and put her beautiful hands on top of the fold.

And then I hurled the magazine. It flew across the room, smashed hard in the middle of one pale-rose wall, and fell to the carpet with a loud thud. I stood up and was about to crash everything on her dresser top when I decided I'd better take a walk.

You know, I was looking at all the decorations in people's windows and on top of their houses, and I was realizing how stiff they look in the daytime, how cardboard-cutout and phony when the red and green lights aren't twinkling and flashing against the black night sky . . . and I was thinking about going back to Mollie and Lew's and having a stinger in honor of it being Christmas and my mother's birthday . . . and then I was thinking, Maybe it's time to pray to Anthony, to pray to Anthony and Henny Youngman and Ben Blue.

Mollie

Pa insisted upon standing up for me so I let him. What could I do? I had Gilliana on my right, Pa on my left, and Nat and Dell kind of over to the side, and Lew had Keith and Gary and Bill Shapell—even though he wasn't that close to him, he said he figured he owed him. "After all, Mol, without Bill Shapell there would be no you."

We got married in a judge's chambers in St. Louis. Judge John Alexander Ward married us; he was an old war buddy of Nat's, they were in the Navy together in the Pacific and had stayed friends. He was tall and skinny, had a booming voice, a shock of white straight hair, and a tattoo of an anchor on top of his hand. I don't remember much else except it was a beautiful room, his chambers, with lots of mahogany and lots of books on shelves; the whole thing probably took less than twenty minutes from the moment we walked in till it was through. My father wept the whole time.

I wore toast, a burnt caramel, more-to-the-taupe toast color. I wore white when I married Larry because it was the first time, and I wore rose when I married Jule, and I wore toast when I married Lew. Slightly off-the-shoulder draped chiffon that crossed over the bodice with a tea-length, very full skirt, dyed-to-match plain pumps in peau de soie, pale stockings, and no corsage. I didn't want one. I carried orange roses, not orange exactly, more-to-the-coral—they looked very nice with the toast. The name of the rose was Tropicana—look at that, I remember the name of a flower. Dell and I didn't buy the dress in the garment district this time; we paid retail at a little shop called The French Corner on Clayton Road. Lew wore a charcoal suit and a white-on-white shirt and a very expensive Countess Mara dark-floral tie. My Gilliana wore a deep-coral polished-cotton dress that looked beautiful with her skin; it also matched my roses. That's about all I remember except that I was very happy, maybe really happy for the first time.

It was a small affair. I mean, the wedding. It was never my way to do anything like that with anybody before I was married to them. We got married, left Gilliana with Nat and Dell, went to Hawaii for ten days on a honeymoon, and that was that. I was no longer Mrs. Julius Ventimiglia, I was Mrs. Lewis Allen.

We packed up the little I had in St. Louis and took it with us and Gilliana and Dot the dog and moved to Kansas City into the two-story house Lew had bought with Bess when he came home from the war. I didn't mind that it was their house, I didn't mind one bit. Her dying so young was a terrible tragedy, and all I wanted to do was try to make Lew happy after he had lived through so much pain. I figured wherever she was, she would see that I had good intentions, and if she was still worrying about him, she could finally relax and rest in peace. It was the house they were supposed to have babies in, but no babies had come and then she died and Lew had lived there all those years alone. The poor man went from living in a quiet, almost empty house to a noisy, running-over house with a new wife, a new teenage daughter, and a rambunctious jumping toy fox terrier.

He said he loved it; he said Gilliana was the only reason he was marrying me because he'd always wanted children and most of all a daughter. I said it was the least I could do. From the moment he proposed to me and I said yes, he walked around singing, "Just Mollie and me, and baby makes three, we're happy in my blue heaven." It made no difference to Lew that that wasn't the way the song began or that he didn't know any of the rest of the words, it made no difference to him one bit, and back then he didn't just hum, he sang. "Just Mollie and me," Lew would sing and put his arm around me, and that was that. He insisted that the third time would be a charm for me; he insisted he would be my Mr. Security and everything would be wonderful for us, we would be a family—he was so positive, what could I say? I kept crying, I was so happy. It's a lot different crying from happiness, let me tell you, a lot different than crying from sad. Even the dog was happy; at last she had a backyard to run around in that was bigger than a box top.

And my Gilliana had a father, a real one who was consistent. One who went to work after breakfast and came home for suppertime. One who was around on Sundays, one who helped her with her homework and taught her how to use a lawn mower and have a paper drive and play softball, one who praised her and disciplined her depending on what was needed, one who paced and waited up with me when she started dating, one who taught her how to dance the box step and drive a car. One who held on to me and told me it would be all right when she grew up and moved away. A father who told her she could do anything. Who said she was funny. And smart. And beautiful. Who loved her as if she was his own daughter. A father who was there. A forever father like on the television was my Lew.

And I had a real husband for once in all my three marriages, a real husband who wasn't running anywhere, who just wanted to love me and stay by my side. No ballgames, no hoops, and no ponies. No "here today and gone tomorrow." No "What happened to the savings?" And most of all, no lies.

I'm not saying things were perfect. Things are never perfect even when you think they are. There were adjustments, many adjustments, but the bottom was there, if you know what I mean. It wasn't up for grabs anymore. I wasn't walking around on eggshells and thinking today was the day. The bottom wasn't going to fall out, is what I mean. Because I was never looking for anything dramatic, I wasn't looking for moonbeams, I was just looking to be a married woman with a husband having a life.

Lew was normal. How can I tell you? I don't mean boring and I don't mean simple and I don't mean plain. I just mean normal. Normal as in sane and good and honest and reliable, gentle and soft-spoken and genuine, sweet and righteous, and fine. Fine like a diamond, only not one that sparkles. You had to be with him a while to see his shine. Sometimes what you think is a diamond is really a rhinestone—you get taken in by the flash and the sparkle, but you're left with something that wouldn't cut the mustard, much less the glass. For once, I had a diamond and I knew it. I knew the difference because of what I'd been through. If I wouldn't have loved Jule, I wouldn't have known Lew was a diamond.

I'm not saying Jule didn't want to be a good person, he did; he just couldn't because of what really meant the most to him—himself. And what made himself the most happy was gambling, and because that was number one to him it could never change. A person can't really be a good person if they're number one in their own priorities. I'm not talking about believing in yourself and having confidence, I'm talking about when push comes to shove. When push comes to shove, Lew would always be there with me; when push came to shove, Jule walked out the door.

So when I say it was the first time I was really happy, it's because I believe it truly was. I'm not saying I didn't love Jule, I loved him with my whole being, but what I didn't know is you can never be happy when you love a man like that because the happy is always tinged with torture and pain. What I didn't know then that I learned when I loved Lew is that true happy doesn't make you afraid.

We dated and then we went steady and then we got engaged. He came to see me in St. Louis lots of times, and sometimes I drove to Kansas City with Dell or with Nat and Dell and Gilliana to see him, and sometimes he flew to St. Louis and sometimes I flew to Kansas City or took the train—back and forth and back and forth—and then he came to Kansas City and asked me to marry him and I said yes. I didn't bat an eyelash.

I told him the only thing was, I had to discuss it with Gilliana before I could give him a "one hundred percent for sure" yes.

She looked at me. "Okay, I guess so."

"It's okay with you?"

"I don't know . . . I guess so . . . I can't really imagine living in Kansas City—do you think the kids there wear cowboy hats and ride horses to school?"

"Gilliana, you've been there, you know it's not like that."

"Yeah, I know, I was just teasing, Mom."

"Don't tease me, this is serious. So?"

"I like Lew."

"I know that."

"I'll miss my friends . . ."

"I know that too, sweetheart, but it's a good time to move, just starting high school."

"I don't know . . ."

"The new kids there will like you too."

"How do you know that?"

"I just know."

"What? It's one of those 'mother things' that you just know?"

"Uh-huh."

"Mom . . ."

"I think it would be good for us, Gilliana, for both of us."

"Are we taking Dot too?"

"Of course we're taking Dot, I wouldn't leave her, neither would Lew. He says he's marrying all three of us, you and me and the dog; he says he always wanted three women in his life, but he says the real reason he wants to marry me is that he always wanted a daughter, he says the real reason he's marrying me is you."

She looked at me. "God, Lew's smart, isn't he, Mom?" she said, laughing.

So we married him, the three of us; we moved to Kansas City and changed our lives.

The only thing hard about leaving St. Louis was leaving Nat and Dell. Dell and I had been friends since the first day of fourth grade, when she transferred into my school from New York and told me a filthy dirty joke. She was outrageous and wild, and in the beginning I was even a little bit afraid of her, but there was no way for us not to become best friends. We understood each other, and as much as we were different from the outside, from the inside we were the same. Dell said it was destiny, Nat said it was because we were cut from the same piece of cheese. Nat always had his own way of putting things, and from the moment she fell for him he became a brother to me. No questions asked and we were inseparable, Nat and me and Dell. Dell and I were like links on a bracelet, our arms wound around each other moving through the years: grade school and high school and jobs and husbands—one for her and three for me—babies—none for her because she had female problems and two for me, and then only one for me. We'd buried my baby together, and my mother, and her parents when they were killed in a train wreck coming back from a wedding in Cleveland, Ohio; we'd sent our husbands off to war together and waited together for them to come home—years and years of daily life, that's what we'd had, and that's something you can't ever imagine giving up, you can't imagine leaving your best friend.

Leaving Nat and Dell was truly the only bad thing that happened to me when I married Lew, because in the end, even though I was only 252 miles away, I might as well have been in Timbuktu. We talked every other week on the telephone and in those days that cost plenty of money, let me tell you, and we wrote maybe a hundred thousand letters over the years, but it was never the same as being together; you can't remember to tell each other everything, and little by little your lives go separate ways. Dell and I were always best friends, but we never got over the change.

Leaving my father was another story. Because our relationship had not always been so hunky-dory, in many ways to not be in the same city with him was just as well.

And that left the only other hard thing to do, which was to say goodbye to Jule.

I thought he might make a fight about me taking Gilliana. I had discussed it with Lew and I had made myself really nervous about it, that even though it was only 252 miles from St. Louis to Kansas City, Jule could still be upset that I was taking Gilliana away from him. I had worked out what I was going to say to him, how it would be better for her, how he could come and see her anytime, how we would drive her to him if need be, but none of that happened, he never even brought it up. What happened instead was much better than I could have dreamed.

What did I have in our little tiny apartment? A couch, a couple of chairs, a kitchen table, a dying sofa bed—there was no reason for me to schlep any of those things to Kansas City when Lew had a fully furnished house. My Gilliana was finally going to have a room of her own, I was finally going to have a kitchen big enough where I could take two steps and turn around without bumping into a chair. So I called Jule and told him he should come and take whatever he wanted before we left. I was packing when he got there; Lew had taken Gilliana and all of her school friends to the Parkmoor for a goodbye lunch, but they weren't back yet when Jule knocked on the door. It was a sunshiny Sunday at twenty minutes past two.

He looked very handsome. Of course, he never changed much through the years, he never was one to put on weight, he always kept himself nice and trim, and even when his hair began to turn gray it was like God painted it, first the temples and then the wave, a few gray hairs in his mustache, a few sprinkled here and there, still like Clark Gable. He had on slacks and a nice sport shirt and a jacket and good shoes. Jule always had a thing for good shoes.

"Hi, Mollie."

"Hello, Jule."

He smiled his smile at me and I smiled back. I can't tell you I didn't still like to look at him; there was no way to look at Jule and not feel good.

I never knew if it was the way he looked at me or if it was just me looking at him, but I still liked to look at him, I always did.

He glanced at the boxes. "Some mess, huh?"

"It makes me crazy."

He laughed. "I know, Mol, I remember how you hate messes."

"I'm packing things in the bedroom—why don't you just see what you want out here?"

"Go ahead, finish, I'll watch you."

"No, it's okay, I can finish later."

He laughed. "No, go ahead, Mol, I know how you hate everything lying around. You fold, I'll talk to you."

It seemed so silly being uncomfortable with him; after all, I'd lived with the man all those years . . .

"Okay."

He followed me into the bedroom. It looked like it had been hit by a cyclone: clothes on every surface, open boxes, sheets of tissue scattered everywhere.

"Maybe I'll finally learn how to pack a jacket so there's no wrinkles when you take it out."

I laughed. It was a thing with us, folding a jacket. "It's not hard, Jule."

"Not for you it isn't."

He moved some things around and sat down on the edge of the bed. I stood at the dresser, took my gloves out of a drawer, and put them in a suitcase. He lifted the lid of my handkerchief box and moved his fingers through my hankies. We didn't speak for a few minutes.

"Maybe we should have had another baby," he said.

I stopped fixing things in the suitcase. "What? What did you say?"

"Another baby, Mol, how come we didn't have another baby?"

"Jule, what are you talking about?"

"Didn't we want to?"

"I don't think so, it never came up."

"Maybe we should have."

"Why? It wouldn't have changed anything."

"You don't know that."

"It wasn't about babies, Jule. We had our Gilliana, *she* didn't change anything. And why do you want to talk about this now?"

He shut the handkerchief box and stood up. "Do you love him?"

"Yes."

"I don't think so."

"What?"

He took the two steps to where I was standing at the dresser. "I think you still love me. I know I still love you, Mollie."

"Don't do this, Jule."

"Why not? It's the truth."

"I don't want to hear it."

He put his hands on my shoulders. "Why not? Does it scare you?"

I tried to back away but I was up against the dresser, there was nowhere for me to go.

"Please, Jules . . ."

"What? I love you, Mollie. What difference does it make to me if you married him, I don't care."

And then he tried to kiss me and I tried to back away.

You wouldn't have thought his doing this would have turned out to be such a big deal with me. It wasn't like it lasted long or that it was violent or like they discuss now on the talk shows—he didn't try to overpower me or hit me, that wasn't what happened—Jule just tried to kiss me and I tried to back away, but he kept trying and I had to keep backing and there was nowhere for me to go. I was trapped and he kissed me. His arms went around me just like always and he held me just the same, but the backs of my legs could only feel the cold wood of the dresser, and for some reason that hit me—a hit like somebody had knocked me over the head with a hammer, that's how I knew.

I'd always felt trapped with Jule, always, I just never put it together before—walking around on eggshells, waiting for the other shoe to fall, knowing there would be more bad news, waiting for the whole thing to explode. And now I looked at him and I finally knew that—and what was even better was that I knew I didn't want to feel that way anymore. Jule had no idea his trapping me up against the dresser would release me. Who could have known that? I'm sure he thought he would kiss me and I would be his again, and I would have thought that too, but that wasn't what happened. If I had any doubts about really being finished with him, the doubts were over, and I knew at that very minute looking at him that Jule and I were finally through.

Gilliana

I forgot to get Christopher a Christmas present. How could I do that? I got Clare's sweaters in plenty of time and wrapped them; they were ready long before I left, and I was going to get Christopher something but I hadn't figured out what . . . so instead, I didn't get him anything. How sweet of me. He said it was okay on the telephone, but that's probably because I'd just told him about my harrowing morning with Mollie and how I'd wanted to smash everything in her room. I didn't tell him I shook her; I'm having enough trouble telling myself.

I'm sure it hurt him plenty that I didn't get him a Christmas present. When I opened my suitcase the first day I got here, I found the blue Tiffany box, but I didn't open it until this morning, until Christmas; I'm very spooky about presents not being opened until the day they're meant for, so I didn't yank off the red ribbon until today, even though I was more than curious. Inside was the silver bracelet I'd oohed at in the catalogue, a heavy silver link bracelet with a dangling silver heart. I didn't even know Christopher had heard me oohing, I didn't even remember he was in the room . . .

The only catch is that the heart is still blank, no engraving, no "I love you, darling," no "mon amour," no "to Gillian from Christopher," no anything; I assume he bought it before he decided he was going to leave me. Maybe he was even going to return it and then for some reason he stuck it in my suitcase when I decided to come and see my mother . . . maybe he was going to have Tiffany's engrave "I'm leaving you, Gillian" in block letters across the silver heart but he didn't have time . . . "So long, Gillian" or maybe just "See ya" . . . or "Adios." Or how about "Do the words May 19th mean anything to you?" Don't be funny, Gillian, I asked you not to.

I did not mention that when I thanked him on the telephone, I did not mention that the blank heart on the bracelet made my own heart turn cold. That it scared me. That this whole thing is scaring me, this thing with my mother and this thing with him . . . I didn't say that, I just said the bracelet was beautiful and I was surprised and thank you and I was sorry I didn't have anything for him and he said it was okay.

Is everything I do okay with him? No, that can't be . . . If everything was okay how could he be leaving me?

And why is he leaving me?

And then there's that little thing I thought of in the shower, that little thing I tried to push down the drain with the water; my hands were full of shampoo and it walloped me so hard I nearly fell to my knees.

Am I one of those wives in a bad play—everyone knows but her, everybody's talking about it but she's too dumb to see?

Does he have someone else—Christopher? Is that what this is? Are there two Tiffany bracelets and the other one is beautifully engraved?

Oh, God, I don't want to know, don't tell me.

But that couldn't be what's happening, could it?

Think hard, Gillian, think hard . . . Is that why he's leaving you? Men never leave to go *nowhere,* they always leave to go to someone else. I know that, I've read *Ladies Home Journal,* I know the score.

Don't make jokes, Gillian, this isn't funny. Think.

So we were married and then we had the miscarriage and then it was less than a year later and I was pregnant again. Only, this time I wasn't spotting; I was gloriously healthy and growing as big as a horse—or maybe a house would be more accurate. That's when I met Andy Minkoff; he was doing a guest shot on Johnny Carson and I was writing for the Carson show then. Andy and I were both New York types who were really from the Midwest—everybody always thinks I'm from New York no matter what I tell them. "Kansas City?" they say, squinting at me; "Is that a joke? It's a joke—right, Gillian?" Nope. Well, Andy was born and raised in

Iowa. I know it's shocking. Andy Minkoff, with all that New York moxie and attitude, to think that he actually came from Iowa with straw sticking out of his brain; straw, corn, hay, it makes no difference, it's still Iowa no matter how you slice it. Maybe that's why we got along from the very beginning, our Midwest mentality, two kindred spirits drenched in barbecue sauce as if we were ribs.

It was a fluke that I even met him. Staff writers on Carson wrote in the daytime, and guys doing guest shots came in at the end of the afternoon to tape at night, so you rarely ever saw each other. I just happened to be there killing time at NBC because I was going to meet Christopher for dinner someplace in the dreaded Valley and I didn't want to go back and forth over the hill. I was walking down the hall in front of the greenroom where Andy was pacing and talking to himself when he backed into me. Did I hurt you and hello, hello, and who are you and I'm doing a guest shot and oh, are you Andy Minkoff, I like your stuff, and who are you, I'm on staff here and oh, God, I need someone to hear this, thank God you're walking by here, do you think this is funny? That was the first thing Andy asked me; he told me a gag he'd just thought of and wanted to put in—do you think this is funny, he said, and I said no.

Comics are extremely fragile; if they ask you if something is funny, you never say no. Never. You think of another way to tell them, but you never, never, ever say no. But I was hugely pregnant, my ankles were swollen and my face was swollen and my hands were swollen, and he had just stepped on both my feet and I wasn't in the best of moods.

"What? You don't think that's funny?" He had turned white and looked as though he was going to pass out.

"No."

"Oh my God, oh my God, oh my God . . ."

"Okay, wait a minute, maybe it is funny, maybe it's just me. It's not like I'm at the top of my form at this particular moment."

"What?"

"Well, I'm pregnant—didn't you notice?"

"Of course I noticed, you look like the *Hindenburg*."

I could feel my face get hot. "The blimp? You're saying I look like a blimp? You don't even know me, and you're saying I look like a *blimp?*"

"The *Hindenburg* wasn't a blimp, it was a dirigible. A dirigible you look like. I would never say you look like a blimp."

That was it. I couldn't stop laughing, I had to sit down on the floor.

"Now *that's* funny," I said when I could finally speak.

"Thank God," he said, sitting beside me in the hallway, holding my hand. I think we both thought I was going to have the baby right there.

That was the beginning of me and Andy Minkoff. I wrote for him until I left the Carson show to write for him full time. Me and four other crazies—we called ourselves the Minkoff Five. And in between, Christopher met Andy, which was kind of like listening to a Greek guy who only speaks Swedish talk to a Dutch guy who only speaks French. Or how can I put it more simply?—the two of them are not only *not* apples and oranges, they're more like apples and chairs. Pudding and Chihuahuas? They don't understand each other, but they get along. It's enough for me, I don't need them to be brothers, I just need them to get along.

And before I went to work full time for Andy Minkoff, I had Clare.

Back labor—you don't want to know from it, as Mollie would say, but it's hardly even mentioned in the Lamaze classes, as if it was nothing, an aside . . .

"Yes, there is this thing called back labor, but hardly anybody ever gets it . . ." So why bring it up?

I thought I was going to break like a chicken bone, my carcass cracking right up the back of me, bones splintering like a ship mast; the foremast, the mainmast, the mizzenmast, all cracking at the same time—here we go, boys, in the middle of a hurricane and we're fucking going down.

"Breathe, Gillian."

"Whuh, whuh, ahwhuh, ahwhuh, hha, hha, hha . . ." My lips pursed, my cheeks puffed up.

"That's it, that's it . . ."

"Fuck you, whoo, whoo, whoo, hha, hha, Christopher . . ."

"That's it . . ."

Another wave subsided, leaving me panting on the shore.

"Hha, hha, I can't do this anymore, Christopher, phha, phhoo, phhee, please, please . . . let's go home." Kind of like a beached whale gasping for breath.

"You're doing beautifully, you're beautiful, Gillian."

"You call this beautiful? I'm gonna smack you . . . oh, no, here it comes . . ."

Sheets flapping like the mainsail in the wind.

"Breathe, Gillian."

"I'm breaking in half! *You* breathe, I'm getting outta here . . . ow, ow, ow, ha, ha, ha, howww . . ."

"That's it."

"Tell them to get this baby out of me, you big shit, whooo, hooo, whoooohowwww . . ."

I couldn't believe her. I couldn't believe her fingers, I couldn't believe her toes. I couldn't believe her eyelashes. I couldn't believe the smell of her or the sound. I couldn't believe she was real, this little baby breathing on top of me when they pulled her out, actual breath going in and out of her baby nose. I couldn't believe any of it. The little gap where your thumb fit where her head connected with her neck in back, the cottony hair on her head like duck's down. Her knees. Her shoulders. Her mouth, her eyes. I never wrote one word about having Clare, not one gag, not one joke, ever—I couldn't, it was too personal, it was more than intimate; it was holy, the whole experience was sacred, not something to make jokes about. I had a daughter, I had Clare . . . and just the way Lew sang, now I could sing too: "Just Mollie and me and baby makes three . . ." The only problem was that for me it wasn't exactly blue heaven, because Mollie had taken to motherhood like a general to his army and I wanted to go AWOL.

What had possessed me to have a baby? I couldn't hold her right; her head flopped and looked like it would give way. I didn't know how to bathe her, I was sure she would drown. I couldn't clip her tiny fingernails. I couldn't clean her ears. I couldn't get her to burp. I couldn't get her shirt over her head. I couldn't get her into the car seat. I couldn't even get her goddamn fucking stroller to open. I couldn't do anything when it came to Clare. I let Christopher do everything, I was too afraid.

"Why isn't she walking?"

"Because she's not ready."

"She's supposed to be walking, Christopher, that's what it says right here in this book."

"Babies don't work on schedules, Gillian."

"But these guys are from Yale."

"She's not ready to walk yet, honey. I promise you, there's nothing wrong with her."

Gillian throws the book across the room.

"Gillian, stop it."

"Okay, but she'll have to be a Harvard man, I'm not letting her go to Yale."

* * *

I always thought there would be something wrong with her, God forbid, that one day right in front of my eyes she would suddenly show signs of some devastating disease.

"Gillian, don't go in there, you'll wake her up."

"But it's nine-thirty already, why is she still sleeping?"

"Maybe because she's tired."

"What?—she had a hard day doing subtraction? Since when does a seven-year-old get tired? Oh, God, Christopher, there must be something wrong with her."

Christopher laughs, pats Gillian on the shoulder, and walks off down the hall. Gillian stands mumbling in front of the door to Clare's room.

And if I didn't think there was something physically wrong with her, I was sure someone or something would do her in.

"But the kid threw sand on her, I saw him."

"You're supposed to leave her at nursery school, Gillian, you're not supposed to stay and watch."

"I was leaving, I was leaving . . ."

"Honey, you can't fight her battles for her."

"Why can't I? She's only three."

"I'll take her from now on."

"Okay, you take her, but I want you to know I'm buying her a sword."

I couldn't stop . . .

"No, you can't go."

"But why not, Mommy?"

"I don't know, because you're not tall enough."

"Of course you can go, Clare—just make sure you hold on."

"Oh, thank you, Daddy!" Clare shrieks with delight, hands her father her cotton candy, and runs off with her friends.

"If anything happens to her, I'll kill you."

"That's a nice thing to say to me."

"Well, you know it was a joke, I didn't mean it."

"How would I know that? Everything's a joke with you, Gillian, how would I know how you feel about anything?"

* * *

What? How would I know how you feel about anything? Is that what he said to me? Wait a minute here . . .

Okay. So we were married and we had a baby and the years went by. And we got along. Didn't we? Of course we did.

I was working full time for Andy and it was a lot of work since he was hell-bent on becoming a household word by Tuesday. He was all over the place doing standup back then: from Vegas to the Westbury Music Fair, from the big hotels in Atlantic City and Miami to Wolf Trap in Virginia and every small town and every college in between. There were five of us who wrote for him, four of "the boys" and me. It's hard to explain about writing comedy, what it's like sitting in a room throwing ideas and gags around at each other like tossing coins . . . Of course, it's not for normal people if you ask me, and then there's the scary part, like being an airplane pilot and everything's on automatic and then suddenly somewhere over the ocean the left wing makes this abrupt dip and you lose your fuselage . . .

The phone rings again.

"That's too big," Clare says to Gillian, who is cutting her steak into tiny squares. "I'll still be able to taste it, Mommy."

Gillian yells over her shoulder, "Christopher, can you get that?" She looks down at Clare. "What do you mean too big? They're minute, these itsy-bitsy pieces, they're diminutive, they're infinitesimal, these teensy, tinesy pieces of delicious, nutritious steak."

The phone rings again.

"Shit," Gillian mumbles. Clare looks up at her. "You said a bad word, Mommy."

"Thank you for pointing that out to me, I forgot it was bad."

"No, you didn't."

Christopher comes into the kitchen. "Gillian, it's for you, it's Andy." He smiles at Clare. "Whatcha eatin', punkin?"

Gillian looks fast at the clock. "Andy? It can't be Andy, it's five past nine in Boston—it can't be Andy, he's on stage."

"Nope, he's on the telephone."

"I'm not eating it, Daddy, it's *meat.*"

"I've had enough of this *shit* with meat, Clare, you're gonna eat it, it's good for you," Gillian says as she grabs the phone.

"Hello? Andy?"

Christopher grins at Clare. "How about we drown it in ketchup? We can drown it till it tastes like spaghetti sauce."

Clare looks at her father. "Okay."

Gillian closes her eyes; she can hear the band playing Andy's entrance music and the crowd roaring over the phone. "Andy?"

"Hey, Gillian!" Andy yells into the receiver. "It's snowing like hell here . . . freezing and snowing like hell . . ."

"Yeah?" She picks up a pencil.

". . . big flakes, about a foot a minute . . ."

"Yeah?"

". . . so gimme something about snow."

"Uh-huh . . . snow . . ."

"Yeah . . ."

"Snow . . ." Gillian turns her head and stares out their kitchen windows—light plays across the blossoming orange tree and the purple bougainvillea on the garden wall—"uh, so much snow that, uh . . . on the way to the theater . . . a kid hit me with a snowball, it had a Volkswagen in it."

Andy laughs. "A Volkswagen . . . yeah . . ."

"And it's so cold . . ." She chews on the pencil eraser.

"Uh-huh . . ."

"So cold out there that . . . uh . . . when the cabbie dropped me off, he held out his hand . . . I thought he wanted a tip, he just wanted me to blow on his fingers."

Christopher laughs as he drowns the tiny pieces of Clare's steak in ketchup.

Gillian turns away from the windows, Clare is watching her.

"So cold . . . uh . . . they tell me it's thirty below out there," Gillian says. "We don't know below what, the thermometer is on its way to Florida."

"Florida, yeah . . ." Andy says.

"The incredible *Andy Minkoff,*" Gillian can hear the announcer yelling over Andy's blaring music and the deafening applause.

Christopher smiles at Gillian, Gillian smiles back.

"Andy," Gillian says into the telephone.

"Yeah."

"Andy, it's so cold out there," Gillian says, "I saw a mink wearing a fat lady."

Clare is giggling, "That's funny, Mommy."

"The baby likes that one," Gillian says to Andy.

"That's one smart baby you've got there," Andy says, and hangs up.

That's what I mean about losing your fuselage over the ocean. The band is playing and he should have walked on already and he's calling me to come up with a joke about snow. In thirty seconds. You could have a heart attack right there in your own kitchen. And there's no way to not come up with it; you come up with a gag about snow or else. Let's put it this way, I'm the only person I know who had a beeper in 1980. Andy made it clear he had to be able to get me no matter where I was. Christopher thought that was very funny.

"What do you mean, he has to get to you?" he said, laughing. "This is not brain surgery you guys are doing here, it's more like brain deadery than brain surgery, if you ask me . . . or brain dredgery . . . brain surgery, brain durgery . . . " And he's working on this and he's still laughing and it's not even good.

"Honey, please don't try to make jokes, okay? Leave the joke-making to me."

Of course, sometimes he didn't think it was so funny.

"But why don't you want another baby?"

"I just don't."

"That's not good enough, Gillian. This has to do with me too."

"You want another baby, you have another baby, Christopher."

The beeper on the end table next to the bed starts beeping. Gillian reaches for it, picks it up, and looks at it. She reaches for the telephone. "It's Andy in Vegas, I knew I should have answered the phone."

"Is that all you're going to say to me?"

"Yep."

"You're just going to cut me off? You're going to call him when we're trying to discuss this here . . ."

Gillian dials a number. "You know I have to call him, and what difference does it make, Christopher? . . . There's no discussion here, we've discussed it a million times—you want to have another baby, you can't have one with me. I'm not having any more babies, I've told you that before."

Christopher swings his legs out from under the blankets, stands up, and walks out of the bedroom.

* * *

I was busy, I was working, I couldn't have another baby, I was becoming a star.

Okay, so it wasn't me, it was Andy, but I was the words that came out of Andy's mouth, wasn't I? Doesn't that count for anything?

Okay, wait a minute . . .

Maybe it wasn't because I was too busy working, maybe I didn't want to have another baby because I was afraid. It's not like you get guarantees with babies, don't you know that? . . . Something could happen . . . what if something happened?

Of course something would happen, I knew that, I knew all about the too-much-happiness business; the whole thing was too good to be true anyway, and I better not tempt my fate. And not just in the baby department: don't make waves in anything, Gillian, don't ask for anything, don't change your life in any way, and keep your mouth shut. Maybe then the boogeyman won't be able to find you.

And what? I was going to tell Christopher that? Not on your life.

"You're not serious." Gillian looks up from what she's typing; he's standing at the window, his back to her.

"Chris? You're kidding, aren't you?"

He turns.

"No, I'm not kidding, I'm serious. This would be a great opportunity for me."

"Florida? You want to move to Florida? What about my hair?"

"Gill, please, I want to discuss this."

"Do you realize I'd have ringlets? Frizzy ringlets? I'd look like Shirley Temple only without the smile."

"Gillian."

"And I can't tap-dance the way she could."

"Gillian."

"What?"

"This is important. It's a great offer."

"Everyone's old in Florida, Christopher, they wear white loafers and have false teeth and blue hair, the food's greasy, Clare would develop a Cuban accent, and then there's my hair . . ."

"Stop it."

She sighed, took her fingers off the typewriter keys, and folded her hands in her lap.

"Okay. Tell me."

"This is a great opportunity for me—I'd be the head consultant, the major decisions would all come from me."

"Why can't you do it from here?"

"Gillian, I can't invest a conglomerate's money without being there."

"Why not?"

"Because I have to be there, you know that. I can't invest a company's money and not be there. What are you talking about?"

"I can't believe this."

He moved away from the window and stood in front of her desk.

"Why can't you write in Florida?"

"What? Retirement jokes? For old people with blue hair?"

"You already mentioned the blue hair, you already mentioned it in your list."

"Well, well, well, I didn't know you liked my stuff so much that you memorized it as it came out of my mouth."

"Gill . . ."

"Christopher, I can't write for Andy from Florida. I have to be here with the boys."

"You could still write some stuff, you could send him your own stuff every now and then."

"What do you mean 'every now and then'?"

"I mean, why do you have to work for Andy? Why do you have to work full time anymore? We don't need the money."

"Without the money I made we'd be back in our two-room apartment with the baby stuffed in a bureau drawer."

He turned and took a step away.

She stood up from the chair. "Chris, I didn't mean that."

"Yes, you did."

She came around the desk. "No, I didn't."

"That was a while ago—"

"I know that," she interrupted, "I'm sorry."

"We could have made the down payment on the house with what I made then—it just would have taken us another year or two."

"I know that. I didn't mean it, I'm sorry."

"Gillian, we have to consider this."

She put her arms around him and kissed him, she nestled her head against his chest. "Christopher, please don't make me move to Florida. I think I'd die."

He tucked his chin back away from her forehead and looked at her. He lifted her hands up and off from around his neck and backed out of her arms.

"Well, I guess it's settled then. I certainly wouldn't want you to die."

He turned and walked out of her office and shut the door.

"Oh, Chris . . . wait," Gillian said, but she didn't go to him; she stayed where she was.

Okay, so I didn't want to go to Florida. Who in their right mind would want to go to Florida once they understood the meaning of the word "humidity"? And I didn't want to stop writing for Andy. It was true that Christopher was making good money by then and if I stopped working we would have been fine, but I loved writing for Andy, I was great at writing for Andy—why should I have to change?

Okay, so I was afraid. Change is scary, but don't they tell you it's okay to be afraid of it, isn't change one of the acceptable things on the list? What's on that list, anyway? . . . death, moving, a new job . . . change . . .

And besides, it was just a job offer and he got an even better job offer that he took a year later, right in L.A.

It was just a job offer and he got over it. Didn't he?

"We can go the weekend after."

"No, we can't," Christopher said, putting his fork down. "The weekend after is the carnival at Clare's school."

"Then we'll go the weekend after that. No, wait a minute, the weekend after that Andy opens in Vegas, I'll be crazy . . . We'll have to go the weekend after that."

"It's okay, Gillian, we can go some other time."

She looked at him over the chicken salad. "I just have to get a better blackout for the car sketch and I won't be able to do it if I go away."

"It's just a hotel reservation, don't make such a big deal."

"But I want to go to Ojai with you, I do."

He wiped his mouth with the napkin and put it on the table.

"Chris . . ."

He stood up from the table and pushed his chair back in place.

"It's okay, Gill, we'll go another time, it's fine."

"Chris . . ."

"Hey, what did I say?"

Shit.

Christopher stands at the car door; Gillian sits behind the wheel with the motor running, waiting to back out of the driveway if she can get him to move away from the car.

"Gillian, goddamn it, we have to talk about Mollie."

"Why? Let's talk about your mother, my mother is fine."

"Your mother is not fine."

"Who says? Let's talk about how much your mother drinks."

"Come on, Gillian, there's something wrong with Mollie—stop fucking around."

"Christopher, such language."

"Gillian, for crissakes . . ."

She slams her hand against the steering wheel. "There is nothing wrong with my mother, leave me alone!"

"What were the slips of paper doing in the serving pieces?"

"To remind her what to put in them."

"Salad? Your mother had *'salad'* printed on a piece of paper in her big wooden *salad* bowl? What else would she put in a big wooden *salad* bowl but *salad?"*

"I don't know, rice pudding . . . she's very creative . . . I have to go."

She steps hard on the accelerator, Christopher jerks himself away from the Corvette as the tires squeal, and Gillian burns rubber as she backs down the driveway.

Is the destruction, collapse, and breakdown of one's mother on that list of things you're allowed to be scared about? Or how about just the discussion of it with Christopher; are you allowed to be scared about that recurring nightmare?

"Gillian."

"What?"

"You can't run away from this."

"What now?"

"We have to talk about what happened when you left the room."

"We talked about it three times already, Christopher. I don't want to talk about it anymore."

"You left the room, and when Mollie noticed she said, 'What happened to the other one?' "

"So?"

"She called you 'the other one,' Gillian, she didn't know your name."

"Don't be ridiculous."

"Gillian, don't do this. Mollie's your mother, this won't do."

"Don't tell me how to take care of my mother, goddamn it, you take care of your own goddamn mother, you take care of good old Marilyn and leave Mollie alone."

"What are you so afraid of, Gillian?"

"God! Just don't talk to me! Okay?"

Well, now, that wasn't very funny, was it?

Or have I been afraid about everything since Anthony died? Jesus. Could that be true?

Clare's coming here—Christopher just called again. He said he would put her on the plane first thing in the morning, nonstop on USAir; I have to pick her up around noon. He said he thought that she should be with me. I didn't say anything except okay; then I hung up and cried. I'm glad she's coming, I never even thought of it—he did—but I'm glad, because if I tell myself the truth, I want her here with me.

And if I really wanted to tell myself some truth, I'd like Christopher here with me too.

"Hey, why don't you come with her, Christopher?" I could have said that, you would think, such a little sentence, I could have squeezed it in between the silences where he wouldn't have even noticed until it was right there in the telephone line, but I couldn't, I just couldn't ask him, and he didn't offer, so instead we had one of those little holes in the conversation where you stand motionless with your hand sweating on the receiver and you wait for the other one to say something while you both listen to the air.

"Well, okay, then," says Christopher.

"Okay," says me.

"Well, okay, then—goodbye, Gill," says Christopher.

"Okay . . . goodbye," says me.

"Mr. Watson, come here, I want you." That was the first complete sentence transmitted by the inventor on his miraculous invention, the telephone. If only I had the courage of Alexander Graham Bell.

Clare

I'm going to Kansas City in the morning. I asked Dad if I could come back here for New Year's Eve and he said he didn't know. He said he really thought I ought to go there and see what's going on with my mother and my grandmother and not worry about New Year's Eve.

Part of me wants to go and knows I should go and part of me doesn't, not the part of me that doesn't want to leave Scott for New Year's, because even if we had gone to asshole Andy's we were still going to be back here for New Year's, but I'm talking about the part of me that wants to see my grandmother and the part of me that doesn't want to because I don't want to remember her the way she is now, I want to remember her the way she was. I mean, if it's true that she really doesn't know anything and my mother's not exaggerating, because it's hard to know with my mother. I mean, for a hundred years she's been acting like there's absolutely nothing wrong with my grandmother, you know, like she's got her head stuck in the ground, and now suddenly she says my grandmother is *gone.* Amy says that's what I should write about—about the going and the staying and about what's happening with my grandmother and all. She says that would show who I am without really saying. See, we have to write this thing for college that goes with all the entrance applications and all that other shit you have to send in, and it's really making me crazy because it's due; I mean, the U.C. schools you already had to send it in—I'm not applying to any U.C. schools, I'd rather die than stay here and go to school in California—anyway, it's due and has to be written and mailed over Christmas and I'm not sure what to say. The thing is majorly important—it's not something you can just bullshit or I would.

Amazing, isn't it—me actually going to graduate in May and going to college next fall—me, the baby Clare, the youngest in her class. Really. Talk about life's changes. Hello, I'm ready, thank you very much.

Anyway, this thing I have to write is supposed to be about me, like who I am and what I want and how I'm different from all the other millions of people applying, you know? Anyway, it's a little different for each college, but it's really all the same idea. They want to know the "who you are" that's not seen on the question-and-answer stuff on the application. Not how well you did in French but how you feel about the death penalty or women's rights or something. I mean, not that exactly, but something personal in you, you know, your personal feelings about something that isn't readily available by looking at your test scores and grades. Anyway, it's hard. I mean, I've written about thirty-two beginnings, but they were all so stupid that I could hardly read them to myself, much less let some entrance person at Yale see them. The truth is, I have really good grades and I'm applying to really good schools and I have a really good chance of getting into maybe three of them, so this is really important to me, you know?

But what am I supposed to say? The truth is, my head is flooded with lots of things that are important to me, my personal views about parts of my life and all, but how do you narrow it down to something that is big enough to be recognized by some person reading twelve million applications? I mean, what are they really looking for?

Actually, it reminds me of the Miss America Pageant, you know, where those girls never stop smiling with all those white teeth flashing even while they're twirling a baton or playing Chopin poorly and they all look like giant interchangeable Barbie dolls with cotton candy coming out of their brains, and then after the twirling and the bathing-suit competition where they walk around in string bikinis and three-inch heels, no less—I mean, these girls have never seen a Birkenstock, let me tell you—then, when they get to the serious part and they bring them out one at a time and ask them what they really want to do in life, well, then it's just amazing, because every single one of them wants to help underprivileged people or teach kids how to speak who are drooling and have no arms and legs, or they want to work in Rwanda fanning the flies off the dying or follow in Mother Teresa's footsteps no matter where she goes. These girls who are the dead ringers for the ones on the billboards where you call in for phone sex. I mean, really, it's amazing.

The point is, I don't want to lie, you know? I mean, I could make up something really great about what I want to do with my life that would be dramatic and yet humble and significant and momentous, but it would be a lie because I don't have the tiniest clue as to what I want to do. And anyway, I guess it's not really supposed to be about what you want to do as much as it's supposed to be about who you are—you know, your inside stuff that you don't show to the world. And that's tough too, because that means you're actually sharing some of your inside stuff with some stranger you'll never lay eyes on who's sitting behind a desk somewhere deciding if they should let you into their school. I mean, it really sucks, no matter how you look at it.

Of course, some people prefer to confide in strangers, don't they? Like people who talk to bartenders or share their innermost secrets with some guy next to them on the plane to Boston. I don't know . . . I'm not like that. I don't tell my innermost things so easily. The only person I ever really discussed stuff with was my Grandma Mollie, and of course that will be over now. I mean, if it's true that now she won't even know me, much less what I'm talking about.

Amy is writing about a particular moment that she had and I don't even know if I can tell it or if you would think it was significant enough, but when she tells it you just get it, you know, and you can see by the way she describes it who she is inside, the parts of her that are so special and why you'd want her to go to your school. I don't know . . . I don't think I have any moments like that yet. I mean, maybe she's right and I should write about what's happening, but I don't know . . .

I mean, I was thinking . . . it's not like I don't have anything at all, but somehow most of my moments seem funny or pathetic or maybe even funnily pathetic. Like most of them aren't exactly about me—it's as if I'm a participant but not the star.

For instance, I was thinking about some of the stuff that happened with me and my grandmother before—you know, stuff that happened when she was still okay; actually, when she looked like she was okay but then she'd do these crazy things that would totally shock you. Like this one time they were visiting us in L.A. and my mother drove the three of us to the grocery store, my grandmother and my mother and me, but my mother was on the telephone in the car in the middle of some big hoohah conversation with asshole Andy, some major act they were working on. I mean, he calls her no matter where he is, night or day, like he owns her brain. So my Grandma Mollie and I went into the store to get the few things we needed for supper and left my mother out there gabbing on the car phone looking ridiculously embarrassing . . . I mean, I am never having a car phone, I don't care, people sitting there blabbing while they're driving and running into things—it's ridiculous. So we get the milk and the wine and the broccoli and we go to the checkout line and she's fine, you know, my grandmother, we're talking about school or something, and then when it's our turn—bang! She just steps behind the checkout stand, like she's the checkout lady, you know? Behind the cash register! Of course, the actual checkout lady is also standing there, her name is Jean—I don't know her, but it says "Jean" in white stitching on the pocket of her Gelson's uniform—and she smiles politely at my grandmother, but of course she can't figure out what this beautifully dressed, stunning older woman is doing behind the register with her. I mean, it's not like my grandmother looks like a bag lady or anything, she was wearing a black elegant pantsuit with a gorgeous pin on the jacket, you know, and great shoes—anyway, my grandmother glares at Jean, the checkout lady, because she wants her to move, like she's in Mollie's way, like Mollie is supposed to be there and Jean isn't, and before I can do anything, Mollie says, "Well, now, you just get out of here!" to Jean. Boy, you should have seen her face. Well, actually both of their faces, because Jean's mouth opens she's so stunned, and Mollie looks like she's gonna hit Jean, and I say, "Grandma?" But she doesn't even look at me, she just gives Jean a push to get out of her way. A real push, I'm not kidding. Jean tumbles back away from the register and onto the railings behind it, and my grandmother kind of takes her place behind the register, smiles sweetly at me like I'm some teenage girl she doesn't know, and puts her hand on the milk carton and moves it across the checking thing. I mean, like a real checker, you know, like she's done this for forty years, and then she moves the bottle of Chardonnay and then the whitefish and the broccoli and she's smiling and doing her thing and Jean starts yelling for the manager and I kind of lose the moment right there 'cause that's when my mother comes in. It was something, let me tell you.

So, that's a moment, right? I mean, I have specific feelings about it because it's my grandmother and I love her and it's funny and it's sad, but it's not really about me, you know? It's not my moment, I was just kind of there.

And then I was thinking about a particular moment I had with my dad . . . If you had seen it you would have just laughed, because it looked like such a silly thing, but not close up, close up it was a real eye-opener. It happened a while ago, you know, before I drove. We were coming from the orthodontist's office one day after school. My dad always took me to all my doctors' appointments, my mother always said she couldn't, she said it made her crazy to think that anything could ever be wrong with me, but I'm sure that wasn't it, I'm sure she just never wanted to leave her office when she was in the middle of writing some big gag. Anyway, he's taken me to all my doctors' appointments since I'm born. I realize it's kind of unusual. I mean, all my friends have always commented, you know, that I'm the only person who ever went to doctors and stuff with their dad.

So we were walking up Bedford Drive, which is this street in Beverly Hills where a lot of doctors' offices are, we were going back to the parking lot after the orthodontist's office, and I'm drinking a strawberry milkshake I got from this coffee shop I like that's called Terry's that's in one of the doctors' buildings—they make it with these really big pieces of real strawberries that keep getting caught in the straw and it's really good, and my dad and I are talking about something while we're walking and he's got his face turned toward me, and at the same time this woman comes racing out of the bank building and crashes into me, and the milkshake goes flying everywhere, but the straw, which is in my mouth at the time, gets smashed up into my gums and my braces, which, of course, the orthodontist has just adjusted, and one little piece of the plastic breaks off under one of the new brackets and I'm lying on the ground and the lady is all over me, you know, saying like, "Oh, my God, I'm so sorry, are you hurt," and my father is bent over me seeing if I'm okay, and then they help me get up together and then he looks at her. I mean, my dad actually focuses on this lady for the first time since she's crashed into me, and his face and his body totally freeze. It's like the music starts. Really, I'm not kidding, like Muzak comes pouring out from behind the bank building, gushy music like the kind where some guy sings and snaps his fingers in a tuxedo with greasy hair. And it's suddenly loud and clear to me not just that my father knows this woman, but much more than that, it's like in one tiny second everyone on Bedford Drive must see that my father slept with her, like it's coming from a loudspeaker somewhere: "Attention, Beverly Hills Shoppers, stop shopping and look at this; these people did it once a long time ago"—really—the looks on their faces are that loud, that blaring. Once upon a time this guy, who is my father, was in this lady's life. You can see it like it's some corny movie in black and white and my father, who is Mr. Polite about introducing people, has actually lost his voice; he's just standing there staring at her and she's staring at him and I'm standing there with my gum bleeding all over my face and this piece of plastic straw very attractively sticking out of my mouth stuck in the bracket of my braces, and they're paying absolutely no attention to me. I mean, none whatsoever—it's like I'm not there, it's just the two of them with this imaginary orchestra and probably Frank Sinatra or one of those guys singing just to them.

Well, the moment itself was funny, the visual of the moment—funny and pathetic—but that wasn't what made it so memorable. What made it so memorable was that that was the exact moment I grasped that my dad had been a person before my mother. Or not a person, but a guy, who had this other life, a before life, before he was a father, before he was married; he was a guy who slept with somebody he didn't marry. I mean, there were probably lots of women he slept with, but it had never occurred to me before, and now all those years later here was one of them looking at him as if all those years weren't gone—I'm not kidding, you could see that he had been important to her, and I look at my dad and he suddenly looks young again. I mean, nothing's changed, but it's like I'm the one who's changed, because I'm looking at him with new eyes, this lady's eyes, and in her eyes he isn't married and he doesn't have a daughter, especially not one with a plastic straw sticking out of her face, it's like no time has passed—and you could see it, you could see everything. Really, like they were young again and in love or whatever they were, right in front of you. Like a freeze-frame or a giant billboard on Sunset Boulevard. It absolutely freaked me out. It's like I wanted to say, What happened with you and this lady? Who was she? Who were you? How did you get hooked up with my mother, of all people? Did she ever look at you that way? Of course, I didn't say any of those things because we had to go back to Dr. Harry and have him pull the straw out of my teeth.

But that's a moment, right? I mean, that's an incredible moment.

And that's exactly what I want to tell Vassar, right? Or Amherst.

"Hey, you Admissions People, did you hear the one about my dad and this lady and how I knew they did it while I had this straw sticking out from between my teeth and blah, blah, blah . . ."

See what I mean? It's not like I don't have some moments, I mean, I've had more, I could go on . . . but it's like they're not *my* moments. Not moments about *me,* you know? Not yet.

I feel like this girl kind of waiting for life to take off—you know, begin. As though I've been in a holding pattern, like I'm this big empty 747 going round and round above Kennedy waiting to land and fill up with people and things. I mean, things have happened to me, but they're not my things; this is probably the year the momentous things for me will begin. After all, it's the year I will graduate high school and get to leave my parents and go away to college and be completely on my own and it's probably the year I'll have sex for the first time unless, of course, I decide not to, but I don't think I will . . . I mean, I think I will have sex with Scott, especially since we'll never end up going to the same college; we probably won't even end up on the same side of the world, considering my grades and his. I mean, my S.A.T. scores are like somewhere between good and genius, you know, like around fourteen hundred and something—that's their terms not mine, I certainly wouldn't call myself a genius, God knows—and Scott's S.A.T. scores are not even reaching a thousand, which falls into the bad category according to them, so we probably will not only not get into the same schools, we probably will break up, because that's what other kids have told me. You know, the ones who have graduated already—they say that if you're a couple and one goes to school in one place and one goes in another, it's like over as soon as you go because no matter what you do or how much you love each other and no matter how many letters you write or phone calls you make or how you hold your breath waiting for Thanksgiving or Christmas break to see him, there's just no way to stay together when you're that many miles apart. I don't know . . . but that's what they tell me. Anyway, I'll probably have sex with him before I go. Really.

And as awful as it is to say this and as much as I don't even want to think about it, this is probably the year I'll have to bury my grandmother, which would be the first time in my life that a person I love would die—I mean, God forbid, but from the looks of things, it probably will be. I mean, it's not like anybody's said that, it's just a feeling I have inside of me—so when you even take just those three things into consideration, it's like I have to write about me when none of the significant things have even occurred. You know? I mean, college and sex and death, those are momentous things. Right?

I don't know . . . somebody ought to tell those people that it might sound interesting but it's really a fucked-up idea because I want to write about *my* things, not use other people's things the way my mother does when she's stealing from everybody's life for an asshole Andy routine, and it's like I'm not ready, like I'm this batter that hasn't quite become a cake.

I mean, they want me to write about me, but as far as I'm concerned I haven't happened yet, you know?

Gilliana

Wait a minute.

What if Christopher really has somebody? What if the Tiffany bracelet wasn't for me in the first place? If he was leaving me, he probably didn't have a Christmas present for me—why would he?—and then when suddenly I was going home to my mother's and he had to come back for Clare, he probably felt bad and took the goddamn bracelet that he had bought for what's-her-name out of the goddamn closet and threw it into the suitcase for me. How would I know? It's not engraved, is it? No. It doesn't say anything and there was no card . . .

Oh, my God. I said what's-her-name.

I haven't said what's-her-name since . . .

Oh, my God. But if it's true, then that would mean I'm the what's-her-name. Is that what's happening here? Have the fates turned and the winds changed and what I dished out will now all come back to me?

Oh, Anthony, you wouldn't let that happen, would you? I always thought you were out there looking after me.

Oh, my God.

But I love Christopher. I do. I love him.

Then why didn't I have a Christmas present for him if I love him? Huh? Why do I always put Chris last?

Wait a minute . . . he wouldn't really leave me, he wouldn't do that to

Clare. He adores Clare, he worships her . . . how could he do that to her? Half of her at my house and half of her at his . . . He wouldn't do that, not Christopher . . . maybe he just wants to scare me so I'll behave differently . . . so I'll behave how? . . . What? What does he want from me?

He'd be putting her where I was. If he left me. Us. If he left us. Because that's who he would be leaving. No, that's not true, he would never put Clare where I was. I don't believe that for a minute. Christopher would never take a powder the way Jule did; he'd always be with Clare.

The truth is, he'd be putting *me* where I was.

Abandoned.

Alone.

I'd have to find a Lew. Like Mollie did.

But Christopher is a Lew, isn't he? Isn't Christopher my Lew?

What happened to being furious? For two hours the whole world has been sleeping and I was too furious for sleeping . . . Now all I feel is that somebody's kicked me in the gut.

SUNDAY

Gilliana

Snow.

No, that's not what I hear; I hear a shovel scraping against cement, scooping up snow. I open my eyes. Is that what woke me? The little clock on the table reads 6:37. It must be dawn outside, but it's still dark in the room. I lie there and listen.

Is Lew shoveling the sidewalk? At six-thirty in the morning? That can't be. I get out of bed and go to the window and push aside the flowered draperies.

Yes, Lew is shoveling the sidewalk. I should have known; doesn't everyone shovel their sidewalk at six-thirty in the morning?

I smile and tap on the glass, but he doesn't look up so I stand there and watch. I could go out and try to help him, but I already know he would say no—my stepfather would never relinquish his shovel to a female even if I wrestled him to the ground. It makes no difference that he's going on eighty; as far as he's concerned, shoveling is a man's job. Also changing tires. Not changing the oil in a car—he taught me how to change the oil in his Oldsmobile as soon as I was his, but not tires. Tires are a man's job, Gillian, he said. Oh. Okay. He also taught me how to change spark plugs and the filter on a furnace . . . and hammering or nailing—that you could do, Gillian, he said, I'll teach you, I'll teach you everything. And he did. He really did. That little man out there shoveling the sidewalk and throwing salt.

My eyes fill up even though I'm smiling. For my twenty-first birthday, Lew gave me a brand-new fandangled electric drill with about three million drill bits, an all-steel hammer, and four coffee cans filled with different-sized nails.

"What kind of a present is that to give your daughter on her twenty-first birthday?" Mollie said, appalled.

"I love it, Lew," I said, kissing him.

He smiled and hugged me.

My mother shrugged. "I never did understand the two of you," she says.

It occurs to me how cute he looks, even dapper—and for shoveling, yet he's perfect, as she would say—galoshes and blue jeans and a big thick down jacket in tan and a tan hat with flaps, and brown leather work gloves with fur inside and a cashmere scarf around his neck in tan, gray, and brown plaid. Look, it's Lew Allen, stepping out of the pages of *Esquire* in the most appropriate attire for shoveling snow. Lew and Mollie, always the best-dressed . . .

"God, look at them, they look like little salt and pepper shakers, they're so sweet," Carole Rose said the first time she saw them. I had to do a double take; "sweet" is not a word in Carole Rose's general vocabulary, "sweet" is probably a word she had never said before.

My breath is frosting up the window. I blow on it and make a smiley face with my finger and then wipe it away. Squeak, squeak. For some reason I feel good . . . I feel peaceful . . . how could that be? My mother has lost all her marbles, my husband wants to leave me, and my daughter wishes I would go away. This is not the time to feel peaceful, Gillian, take it from me. Maybe it's the sound of the shovel scraping on the concrete, maybe that's what's making me feel good, like the way people talk about how certain foods give them a special feeling—comfort foods: meat loaf and mashed potatoes and little green squooshy peas, vanilla pudding and oatmeal, tomato soup with grilled cheese . . . or maybe it's just watching Lew.

I rest my forehead against the cold glass, I watch the puffs of breath come out of his mouth like train exhaust as he shovels snow to his right and his left. I think of all the things Lew taught me:

How to ride a horse.

How to field a grounder and catch a pop fly.

How to shoot a basket from the foul line, overhand, like a boy.

How to ride a motorcycle, causing Mollie to take to her bed.

How to drive a stick shift, and I nearly put him through the windshield the first time he showed me and he didn't even get angry or raise his voice.

How to make a really good salami sandwich, which requires hot mustard on both slices of the bread.

How to tinker in a garage or in a basement—but in L.A. there are not a lot of basements, you're mostly limited to the garage. When Christopher and I bought the house, it was Lew who built the workbench for me in our garage.

How to play the piano, but only one song. I'm not kidding; he only knows how to play "Canadian Sunset," but he can play it brilliantly, like a famous jazz pianist, and that's how he taught me. I sit down and play "Canadian Sunset" brilliantly and then I get up and everybody says, Oh, God, Gillian, that's wonderful, we didn't know you played the piano, play some more, and I say, as if I'm very bored, Oh, no, I gotta go, sorry . . . Lew taught me that.

I laugh to myself at the window and watch him sprinkle salt.

He even taught me how to do the box step when I began to go to dances, which was hard for him because dancing was not something he did with ease . . .

Lew stops, leans on his shovel, and looks up at the sky.

I can't hear him through the glass but I know he's humming.

That's when I start to cry, thinking about Lew humming while he taught me all those things, and now I'm crying so hard at the window that I can't see him because the glass is all steamed up.

Where was my father all this time? Huh? Where was my real father? The biological one? Where was good old Jule? After all, he was the famous dancer, wasn't he? He could dance rings around the box step, the *bons vivants.* He was the one who took Mollie dancing, leaving clouds of Old Spice wafting around my bedroom, flashing his cuff links and winking at me as he walked out the door . . . where was he when I needed him, the big shot . . . Where was he when I had to learn how to drive a car? Or go dancing? Where was he when I got my first kiss or had my first date or did my first anything?

I drop the edge of the draperies and turn away from the window.

Maybe we should have sent the Mounties to find my father.

I get back in the bed and pull up the covers.

I think of all the things Lew taught me. I write each thing lovingly down on a list I make in my head.

I think of all the things Jule taught me.

Oh, my goodness, would you look at that—the list is pretty lopsided, isn't it?

What Jule taught me I would never want to teach to anyone. And it's only one thing. He taught me how to leave, go, take a powder, take a hike, vamoose, get lost, walk out, and disappear; how to relinquish, end, and finally abandon, in full and forever. "So long, baby, and *arrivederci,*" I whisper.

I turn over in the bed, my face down in the pillows.

All Jule taught me was goodbye.

We left St. Louis when I was fourteen. You'd think at first there would have been a flurry of phone calls—"How ya doin', Babe? How's school? Did you make some new friends? Are you okay?"

Nope, no phone calls. Two postcards in the first three months. "Hello, Babe. How are you? Love, Dad." Seven words. No phone calls, no long letters, no driving to Kansas City to see me, only—Hello, Babe, how are you, love, Dad. Seven words, I knew them by heart, shows how interested he was in my life, huh? Wait, it gets better. He did not come to Kansas City until a year later.

Gillian waits breathlessly at the window in a new dress, new shoes, her little heart doing flip-flops to finally see her dad . . .

He only stayed three hours, said he had to get back.

I found out years later that the real reason he came to see me then was not to see me at all but to borrow money from Lew. I guess he thought he might do better if he asked in person. Charming, huh? Lew never told me, it slipped out of Mollie's mouth one day when she was mad. Now that's what you call *chutzpah*—which is "guts" if you want to say it nicely, but it's really "balls"—this man drives to Kansas City to borrow money from his ex-wife's new husband, who is not only taking care of his ex-wife but also raising his child—lest we forget, my father never sent my mother one lousy nickel to take care of me. Now that's what I call *chutzpah,* folks, that's "balls."

Then we have a few more postcards and maybe one phone call for Christmas and then my mind can't help going to my Sweet Sixteen birthday, Gilliana Ventimiglia's Sweet Sixteen Disaster, brought to you by her father, Jule.

He said he was coming. If he wouldn't have said he was coming, everything would have been fine. A Sweet Sixteen luncheon for eleven girls at Eddy's, which was a nightclub in Kansas City where you went in the nighttime if you were a grown-up to hear the Four Aces or the Four Freshmen or the four anythings. But if you were a kid you could go on a Saturday to have lunch and see a show. This was not something you did ordinarily; it was only for something special, like a birthday, like a Sweet Sixteen lunch.

He said he'd be there, so I kept my eyes on the door. Through the fruit cocktail or the shrimp cocktail (you had your choice), the hamburger steak or the roast chicken with French fried potatoes and LeSueur baby peas, the French vanilla ice cream topped with strawberry or chocolate sauce . . . no Daddy . . .

Through the "Happy Birthday to You" and candle blowing and cutting of the cake . . . no Daddy . . .

Through the opening of the presents and the shrieking and holding up of each and every gift . . . no Daddy . . .

Even through the singing of the four somebodies, the goodbyes, and the paying of the check . . . no Daddy.

You'd think I would have given up, but I didn't. Four and a half hours of torture—you'd think I would have had a neck ache from keeping my head angled toward the door. And that ain't the half of it, because it went from bad to worse; he not only didn't come, he didn't call, and I made Mollie call him because I was hysterical because I was sure somewhere along the way he'd crashed. Big mistake. Jule didn't crash, I did, because the truth was my father couldn't be there because he forgot. Plain and direct and simple—he forgot.

Happy Sweet Sixteen birthday, Gillian.

I turn over and punch the pillows. The room is light now; I'm lying on my back.

And who was there while I cried? Sitting quietly in my room while Mollie held me? Lew. When Jule didn't show up for any of my birthdays or even send me anything, when he didn't call on Sunday mornings week after week when he'd promised to, when he continually disappointed me until he eventually disappeared, who was there saying "It'll be okay, Gillian"? Lew.

* * *

I pull the covers up to my chin.

I have to get up and make some coffee. I have to find the courage to look at my mother and see if she's inside herself today. I have to take a shower and get dressed and go to the airport and pick up Clare. I have to call Christopher and ask him not to leave me. I have to go back to sleep.

I turn over and push my face into the pillows.

It suddenly makes sense to me why Mollie warmed Lew's pajamas. And if we would have sent the Mounties to St. Louis to find my "real" father, they would have been shit-out-of-luck. Jule Ventimiglia was somewhere hiding in St. Louis, but my real father is outside shoveling snow.

Clare

This whole thing is very confusing. Or maybe "confusing" isn't the right word, but I don't know what is.

I mean, I got here and my grandmother's eyes are blank. I talk to her and there's nothing there and at first I couldn't really believe it, it's like she was teasing me and this was all some big joke. I know it's not, I'm not a child, but it's just so eerie to have somebody be sitting right there in front of you but not really be there at all. She looks at me but she doesn't see me—it's like I'm trying to connect with her from behind a veil. And she's not talking, she's only whistling. Well, she does talk sometimes, but what she says doesn't make any sense. I mean, it makes sense but it's all out of context, it's not what's going on in the room or what anybody else is talking about or anything—but that's if she says anything, and like I say she's hardly talking, she's hardly saying anything at all. The only thing she said to me had nothing to do with anything. I was sitting there talking to Mrs. Pomerantz, who's the nurse who's helping with my grandmother, and in the middle of us talking about colleges and she's telling me that her daughter went to Syracuse, my grandma says, "It's okay, Dell, I'll hold your hand."

She doesn't know who I am. My grandmother, I mean, not at all. When I got here, she didn't even want to look up at me. She was all busy with some black-and-white photographs she had in this hatbox on her lap, but it wasn't even like she was really looking at them because she wasn't, she was just moving them around inside the box, and my mother kept saying to her in a loud voice as if my grandma had lost her hearing, "Look, Mommy, Clare's here," and "Look, Mommy, it's Clare." God, it was so awful. I mean, I wanted to stop both of them; I couldn't bear hearing my mother call her mother "Mommy," it just made me crazy. I wanted to jump up and put my hand over my mother's mouth so she would shut up, and I wanted to grab my grandmother and shake her and tell her to be the way she used to be . . . or not at all. I know it's awful to say that but I can't help it, it's how I felt and it was true.

I got here at lunchtime, my mother picked me up. She looks as though she hasn't slept since she left L.A., I'm not kidding, really awful, and I think she must have lost five pounds. My mother can't afford to lose any weight and certainly not five pounds. We stopped for lunch at this hamburger place my mother used to go to all the time when she was in high school, this place she loves called Winstead's, and she always gets the same thing when she goes there, a double cheeseburger, and she devours it in practically two minutes right in front of you, I'm not kidding, and today she just picked it up and held it and then put it down. I said to her, "Mom, you're not eating," and she says "What?" to me like I'm some stranger from a strange land.

Anyway, so I asked Mrs. Pomerantz—she's done this before, she told me, so I figured she would know—so I asked her what was really going to happen with my grandmother and she said, "Whatever's gonna happen's gonna happen, there's nothin' you can do." My grandma is going to get worse and worse and there's no stopping it. So I thought, Well, what am I supposed to do with that information? How am I supposed to feel?

I sat at the dining-room table with her, I took all the photographs out of the hatbox and put them in front of us and I tried to get her to tell me about them—you know, like, "Who's this, Grandma?"—but she didn't answer me or most of the time even look at me; she only wanted to make piles with them and move the piles back and forth on the tabletop as if she was playing solitaire, so eventually I just started to look at the pictures myself. I don't know most of the people in the pictures—I mean, of course, I know some of them: some of them are of my mother when she was little and my grandma and my other grampa, you know, the one that I never met, not Lew; but a lot of the pictures are before that, my grandma in places in St. Louis wearing a lot of different hats and gloves. At first I was only looking at the pictures superficially, you know, thinking about how funny it is that everybody was always all dressed up like that and they never even heard of jeans or only wore them if they were a farmer or something, and then I was looking at the pictures closer and, you know, thinking about how it's so sweet. I mean, here's my grandma standing around in a park somewhere in a soft little summer dress, or in the middle of these piles of snowdrifts all bundled up in a suit and a coat with a fur collar and these high-heeled galoshes they wore then and a hat with a feather and gloves. But then I started really studying the pictures, how she's smiling and she looks so young and hopeful, and then I looked at her next to me at the table and she's like really into *dealing* these snapshots, you know, really fast, like she's in the middle of this hot card game with a bunch of guys smoking cigars. And at first I felt really awful because, you know, she's the same person, but of course she isn't, she's like gone. But then, I don't know, this thing happened . . . it's like I was looking at the pictures and I was seeing my grandmother, but I was also seeing me and I'm not just talking about how we kind of look alike, you know, with the dark hair and the dark eyes—I'm talking about how somehow we're really the same person—do you know what I mean? Like when you watch the Olympics and those guys race around in a relay and they have to pass back the baton, back to the one who's waiting with his hand all stretched out—well, that's what hit me; it's as if my grandma will pass the baton back to my mother and then someday my mother will pass the baton back to me. I don't know . . . when I thought about it, it made me feel better. Of course, then I thought about it some more and it seemed so stupid. I mean, it must be my mood, because it certainly isn't like me to think of anything as cheesy as baton-passing . . . Maybe I'm just looking for something to make me feel better, like I don't want to really face what's going on here. You know, denial . . . because then I thought about it and you have to realize what's in the middle there. I mean, if you go along with the cheesy baton-passing—in the middle is my mother, not me. You know? I mean, my grandma would have to pass it to my mother and then my mother would pass it to me. You get it? It would be different if I could get it from my grandma, but I would have to get it from you-know-who.

Maybe one of the reasons I'm confused is because she's acting pretty normal. My mother, I mean . . . well, not normal, because, you know, she's upset and all, but normal toward me. Well, not even normal, really, because she's acting differently, she's acting as if I'm not her daughter all of a sudden but like I'm just some other woman in this dilemma with her. I mean, we actually had a real conversation about an hour ago. Actually, it was even more than a conversation, it was . . . well, I guess you'd have to say it's like we were having this really nice private moment. I mean, I know it's hard to believe it but it's true. See, we had eaten dinner and I had washed the dishes, and I made the kitchen all perfect and spotless, you know, neat, like they both like—I mean my grandma and my mother—but actually it made me feel pretty good. I folded the dishtowel over the edge of the sink on the left side the way my grandma used to, and I propped the sponge up next to the Ivory in this pretty tray she has next to the faucets . . . I don't know, I guess it sounds stupid, but it made me feel pretty good when I looked back at the kitchen from the doorway. Like she was okay or everything was okay even though it wasn't, you know? Anyway, so my grampa was watching television and kind of dozing the way he does on the couch, and I was kind of wandering around. Not that it's a big house, I mean it's little, it's only got two bedrooms . . . Anyway, I didn't know where my mother was and I walked by my grandma's room and the door was halfway open, and my grandma was sleeping on the top of the bed with this quilt tucked all around her and my mother was just sitting on this bench at the foot of her bed, not doing anything, you know, just sitting there, and she just kind of stared at me in the doorway and so I went in. I sat down on the bench next to her and she just started talking to me real quietly. She told me about going to look at all those horrible places, those homes, where she might have had to put my grandmother and how she was so thankful that she was working, because the money she makes from asshole Andy will help keep my grandma in her house for as long as possible; it will pay for Mrs. Pomerantz or whoever helps my grampa, and my mother was being so okay with me that I didn't even refer to him as "asshole Andy" because I somehow didn't want to piss her off for no reason, and then she told me that asshole Andy had even offered to help her, which is so amazing to me because he always appears to be such a dick.

And then she whispered, "Hey, do you want to see what I found?" and she got this box out of my grandma's closet and it was filled with all these gloves. I mean, you couldn't believe it, they were the very same ones from the pictures that I had just been looking at, and we started trying them on. Really.

I mean, here's my mother and me trying on all these gloves, long ones that go up to your elbow and short ones with these little beads, and you know, we're like whispering to each other so we don't wake up my grandma, and it's like suddenly we're the two daughters having fun at the foot of my grandmother's bed. It's all so mixed up and confusing and it's more than just the fact that I was having this really good time with my mother—which is pretty confusing anyway, since I was—but it's like, talk about role reversal; it's like I'm the daughter and my mother is the mother, but then my mother is also the daughter to my grandmother and my grandmother is the mother to her, but then look what happens—suddenly, boom, my grandmother has turned into another daughter for my mother. I mean, let's face it, my grandma's kind of helpless, right?—so look who's taking care of who. You see what I mean? It's like my mother and my grandmother have switched roles, right? Okay. But then you have to get to the really scary part, which is that someday it will be me. I mean, think about it, because I certainly am.

Someday, no matter what I do, my mother will turn into the daughter and I'll be the mother to her. I will be the one who's lost at least five pounds and looks like she hasn't slept in six days and is checking out homes. I mean, there's no way to not see that, so I keep looking for the bigger picture, you know, the point to the whole thing, because there has to be a point to it. I mean, after all, this is the big stuff we're talking about here, and I'm sure there's more to it than just continuation, some greater meaning than we mere shallow mortals can see, but I guess you have to be more evolved to really get it, not older necessarily but more spiritually evolved, which maybe I am just not yet. It's like I know it has to be more than just continuation, because if that's all it was it wouldn't have to be me and my mother and my grandmother, it could just be the box of gloves. You know what I mean?

I don't know . . . maybe I'm just too tired . . . I mean, it's like I'm trying to read this book we're supposed to read over winter break, but the words keep getting all blurry because I can't concentrate. I was thinking that maybe I should just get a Diet Coke and veg out watching television on the couch with my grampa, but it's like, my mother's still in there, you know, sitting in the room with my grandma, so maybe I'll just go in and see what's up with her.

Mollie

My Gilliana moved to Los Angeles. It didn't matter that it was Los Angeles, it could have been Timbuktu—it didn't matter where it was, except that it was away from me. Somehow I never expected that; that we could be separated was not in my head.

I knew someday she would go away to school, but you go away to school and then you come back. You live in your mother's house until you find someone and then you get married and you have babies. In the same city as your mother. In my head, Gilliana and her husband and the babies would come to my house every Friday night for supper and Lew and I would baby-sit whenever they needed us and we'd take care of the babies when they'd go away on a trip and I'd make all the holidays at my house and Gilliana and her husband and her babies would be in my dining room sitting by my table eating by me. Everything hunky-dory, that's the way I predicted, the way any mother predicts no matter what they tell you—not that their child, their only child, is going to grow up to go off and live in Los Angeles, which, as far as I was concerned, she might as well have been going to live on the moon.

You have a child and you forget. All the ways you know your own life didn't go perfectly you forget, and for your daughter you are sure it will go perfectly, no matter that in your heart of hearts you know that life doesn't follow anybody's plan. What I didn't know was that my daughter moving to Los Angeles would turn out to be the easy part; first was the affair with the married man.

No, first she graduated from high school, went to college for six months, came home, and made an announcement that school wasn't for her, she wanted to get a job. Okay, I said. As much as I wanted her to go to college, I knew if I pushed her it would only backfire; you can't make somebody go to college if they don't want to, that much I knew. She got a job as a secretary in an advertising firm downtown. She got a little car. She had lots of friends. She came and went. She was happy, I was happy. It was too good to be true.

He worked in Gilliana's office. I found the little round thing of birth control pills, I nearly had a heart attack, and I knew. And then right away it was over and she wanted to move, and as much as I didn't want her to go, Lew said it would be a fresh start for her. He said I better make my peace with it because she was going to go no matter what I said, so in my heart I told myself: Let her go, Mollie, and everything will be good. We made a little goodbye party, even Dell and Nat drove in from St. Louis to say goodbye to her, and my only child moved to Los Angeles.

The second time Gilliana fell in love, the man wasn't just married, he was married and he was famous and, on top of everything else, he was a *Talyaner* just like Jule.

You raise a child and you teach them right from wrong and you expect them to understand, and I know mothers have had to live with much bigger pains in their hearts than their daughter having an affair with a married man, but I couldn't believe my Gilliana would do such a thing. To this day there's still a piece of me that's amazed. When I found out, I tried all the other things in my head to make it not so bad: thank God she didn't shoot anyone, thank God she isn't a murderer, thank God she isn't a thief—but it didn't matter, you can't put yourself in the other mother's shoes, you can only know from your own.

I know there were a lot of years in between from when we moved to Kansas City until these times I'm talking about, but in between everything was good, and when you look back and things were good you don't see particular pictures but more like a comforting blur. The only things that change are the differences in how I remember her: shorter, taller, with braces, without braces, without breasts, with breasts, and on and on—a blur of my baby growing up and getting bigger. And then out of nowhere she's not a baby anymore, she's a big shot living in Los Angeles and in love with a married man. As far as she was concerned she was all grown up, and as far as she was concerned she knew everything about everything, and somewhere along the way as far as she was concerned I didn't know a thing. That's what happens with daughters—overnight everything you might have experienced or learned from what you did in your life is, like they say in French, passé. And there's no talking to her, the same child that used to look at you as if you were everything is now looking at you like you should go jump in a lake. And there's no reasoning with her no matter what you say, because the answer to everything you try with her she answers with "I love him, Mother." That's all she says because that's all she knows, she doesn't see the good or the bad or the right or the wrong, she doesn't see that the odds are that it will never go anywhere, that she's going to be hurt; all she could see is blinded by her love for him but she doesn't know that, only you know.

"But Gilliana . . ."

"I love him, Mother. You wouldn't understand."

I wouldn't understand? The same me who wanted to follow Jule off to war? Who walked around while he was gone smelling his shirts? The same me who nearly killed myself over loving him? Who wound up flying around over my own head in a shower?

"I do understand."

"Mother, you couldn't. Nothing you could have ever done could have possibly been like this."

So what was I going to do? Tell her my life story? Try to explain to her how I knew?

First of all, a daughter doesn't want to hear all that. As far as a daughter is concerned, a mother is only supposed to be a mother, not a woman who ever had passions and desires. A mother is for holding and tucking you in, a mother makes your supper and sews your name tags in your camp clothes, a mother wears a housedress and maybe a little lipstick; a mother is not someone who could turn her life upside down for a man, and even if she did, the daughter doesn't want to know. Did I want to hear how my mother loved my father or what they did? No.

But unfortunately I forgot that; unfortunately when you're the mother and you're confronted with something your daughter is going through—that you think you know all about—you try to talk to her and she doesn't want to listen to you and the whole thing goes from bad to worse. Lots of terrible phone calls where your heart beats too fast and neither of you says anything until you say too much. Me, I was always the one who was saying too much.

"So, how long are you going to go on with this?"

"Please, Mother, just let it be."

"Okay, all right . . ."

Silence on the phone, just airwaves and a little static until I clear my throat and I say to her, "So, how are you, sweetheart?"

"I'm fine."

"Uh-huh. How fine could you be? Have you seen him lately?"

I couldn't stop myself.

"Mother . . ."

"Gilliana, what about his wife?"

"Mother, please . . ."

"But how many years are they married?"

"Mother, I can't discuss this with you."

"Why not?"

No answer.

"Gilliana, please think about what you're doing . . . please think about what you're doing to his wife and his children. I can't believe this is you."

"Mother . . . I have to go . . . please . . . really."

I was always the one saying too much, it was always me. Lew told me to stay out of it, to leave her alone, but, oh, it was so hard for me. Dell said it wouldn't matter even if I put my head in an oven, Gilliana was going to do what she was going to do. I knew they were right, but I couldn't stop myself. We fought on every phone call until there were no more phone calls, because she stopped talking to me at all. She would only talk to Lew. I was beside myself. It was the first time there had ever been anything bad between Gilliana and me. I wanted her to listen to me, I wanted to protect her, I wanted to make her understand she should stop loving him and find someone else who was free. I wanted to call him up and tell him to go away, to leave my baby alone. I wanted to fix it before all the pain came, but you can't do that—no one can do that, not even a mother. So instead of fixing it, I couldn't keep my mouth shut. I became her enemy and we were through.

And in the long run the pain that came to my Gilliana was much worse than the pain I was trying to stop that could have come from just a love affair, because the man she loved, the handsome comedian that was so talented—I'm sure you've heard of him, Tony Ronzoni, may he rest in peace—he got sick with cancer and he died. Gilliana went to New York to be with him and the three of them were together through the whole thing—Gilliana, Tony Ronzoni, and the wife—a situation I couldn't imagine, the three of them together at the hospital, the wife and Gilliana taking turns watching him get worse and worse—who could imagine such a thing? Of course, I never got to hear any of the details, because even then she wasn't talking to me, she would only talk to Lew. When Tony Ronzoni died, Gilliana couldn't even go to the cemetery. She said she didn't want to go; she told Lew that she never wanted to see him that way, but I didn't think so. I think the wife didn't want her to go there. After all, how would it look? A wife buries a husband, not a girlfriend, after all.

She came to us for two weeks before she went back to Los Angeles. Lew told her she should come home to sleep, that's what he told her, I heard him on the telephone.

"You'll come here and you'll sleep and you'll rest and we won't bother you. You don't even have to talk to us, Gilliana, it will be good for you to come home."

And she came. Lew told me that if I said one word to her about how wrong I thought it was that she had an affair with Tony Ronzoni, may he rest in peace, that he would never speak to me again. He was serious, my Lew. The same man who had never demanded anything, he finally made himself a demand.

"Let bygones be bygones, Mollie, she loved him and don't you open your mouth."

I didn't.

Most of the time she was home she was sleeping, and when she wasn't sleeping I tried to get her to eat a little, and the rest of the time she talked about Anthony—she didn't call him Tony, she called him Anthony—and we listened and I never said one word. She talked about how funny he was and what a good man he was and how sweet and how brave and how kind, and how she had never met anyone like him, how he was so good to her, how much he believed that she could write comedy, how much he loved her, and how much she loved him. I didn't ask a thing, I just listened. I don't know if he ever would have left his wife and children to marry her, who knows what might have been? All I know is, at the end of the two weeks of her talking and me listening, I said I was sorry.

"You have to let me live my life, Mom."

"I do."

"No, you don't, you want to tell me how to live it."

"I just wanted to help you."

"Mom, we can do this two ways. You can ask what's going on with me and I can tell you, or you can ask what's going on with me and I can lie."

When did she get to be so tough, my daughter?

"No, no lying."

"Then if you ask me you have to be ready to hear my answer."

"And what? I can't disagree with you?"

"Of course you can disagree; you just can't disagree like a mother, you can only disagree like a friend."

"What? Your friend Carole Rose thinks having an affair with a married man was such a good idea?"

"Mom, this has nothing to do with Carole Rose."

"Okay, okay . . ."

"Okay what?"

This was very hard for me.

"Mom?"

"Okay."

"What?"

"I'll disagree like a friend."

"You're sure?"

"I said okay, didn't I?"

"Okay."

She put her arms around me and hugged me and kissed me.

"Does this mean you're going to call me Mollie now? I won't be Mom anymore?" I didn't hear the answer, I was crying too hard.

She went back to Los Angeles and changed everything—a new apartment, a new career, she started to write comedy for all the big shows. I never dreamed that she would know how to do such a thing, but she did.

When she started taking up with Christopher, I disagreed like a friend. Not at first, at first I didn't say anything, I just listened when she told us about him on the telephone. I listened and I was happy that she was seeing someone. Then Lew and I went to Los Angeles for a visit and we met him, and then I disagreed like a friend. I pointed out that he seemed very nice, but wasn't she getting serious a little too fast? She said no. I pointed out that he seemed very nice, but it didn't look like she was in love. She said yes she was. I pointed out that he seemed very nice, but was she really over Anthony? When she said, "Mom, you don't understand," I shut my mouth. She married him.

I always wanted a daughter, I never wanted a son. I never understood women who said they wanted a boy, I always thought they were lying. Who knows what to do with a boy? With a girl at least you can understand, even if you disagree. Gilliana was my everything, I was not about to lose her. If she wanted to marry Christopher, I would make it okay. It was clear that he was in love with her, you could see how he looked at her, you could see in his eyes how he cared. In Gilliana's eyes you couldn't see anything, so I turned my head away. When Lew and I went to Los Angeles to visit them, he was wonderful; when they came to Kansas City to visit us, he was wonderful. I asked her what was going on with her when we talked on the telephone and she said everything was fine. What was there not to like about Christopher?—nothing. It wasn't that I didn't think he was wonderful, it was that I didn't know if Gilliana thought he was so wonderful, but it wasn't anything I could put my finger on, it was just a feeling, so what could I say?

She got married and they were both working—too hard, I thought—and then they bought a house somewhere way far out near the ocean that they fixed up like if you were walking into a magazine and Gilliana got pregnant and then she had my Clare . . .

Mollie opens her eyes. She's lying on her back on the bed, she looks up at the pale-blue ceiling of her bedroom. Her fingers touch the quilt on her chest; she knows which quilt it is without looking at it. She lifts her head slightly up off the pillow and focuses her eyes to the foot of her bed to see Gilliana and Clare. They're sitting next to each other on the brocade bench. They have their backs to Mollie. She can't see what they're doing but she can hear them. They're laughing.

Mollie smiles.

She opens her mouth to say something but no words come out.

She pats the quilt gently with her right hand, lowers her head back to the pillow, and closes her eyes.

Gilliana

My mother was dead and I didn't know it. Can I say that? Dead? How can I say that?

My mother is dead, my mother died, my mother passed away . . . who gives a fuck how I say it . . . my mother is dead. My Mollie. My sweet Mollie, my mommy . . .

Gilliana reached for the vodka bottle. She poured two inches of vodka into the juice glass and drank it down. She moved her ass a little on the cold kitchen floor, flexed her back, which was up against the refrigerator door, and placed the bottle on her lap with one hand.

I don't feel she's dead, I feel I forgot something, that's how I feel . . . like I lost something . . . that panicky feeling you get when you realize your car keys aren't in your pocket as you're waltzing down the cereal aisle and you reach for the bran . . . or in your mind you can see your wallet where you left it on the counter when you took out your VISA card, only it's three hours later the next time you open your purse . . . and, look, there's your heart where it fell on the floor when it occurred to you that perhaps your mother was dead when your daughter pointed out to you that your mother had been in that position for, boy-oh-boy, a very long time, hadn't she, but you didn't notice because you were in never-never land. That's what I feel like, like I forgot something and I can't remember what it was. Then I remember. My mother is dead.

Gilliana picked up the vodka bottle and took a swig.

I didn't know she was dead. I don't even know exactly when it happened . . . she was asleep . . . I thought she was asleep. What did the guy say on the telephone, the paramedic talking to the hospital?

"We request permission to pronounce the patient dead."

Shit, he looked like he was twelve years old.

Maybe that's why he had to request permission, maybe he wasn't old enough to pronounce her dead all by himself. Of course, he could have asked the other paramedic; the other one looked much older, the other one looked at least twenty-three.

"No response to verbal or painful stimulation."

The two of them in their uniforms, mustaches, and muscles, they looked like *Beach Blanket Bingo,* pinching Mollie hard in that place between her neck and her shoulder, pinching my mother hard and yelling at her, *"Hey, Mollie! Hey, Mollie, are you okay? Mollie, can you hear me? Answer me, Mollie! Hey, Mollie, hey!"*

Hey, boys, don't pinch my mother—that's my mother, hey . . .

The refrigerator clicked off and the enameled steel door behind Gilliana's shoulder blades stopped humming. She closed her eyes.

"No visual look of breathing, no pulse."

Of course she wasn't breathing. Even I, the layman moron fucking daughter, could see she wasn't breathing. Why the hell did they think I called them? Because I thought she was breathing? No way.

Gilliana blinked.

Watch your mouth, Gillian. It's enough cussing for one day. And night. Shit. Is it still night? It is still night, isn't it? Please let it still be night.

She turned her head and squinted at the window over the sink.

Dark . . . that's dark out there, isn't it?

Yep . . . dark . . . It looks black to me, baby. But not entirely, is it? . . . Maybe a little navy . . . Oh, God, is it dawn? Don't let it be dawn, please . . .

I can't see the clock from here.

She lifted the bottle to her lips but didn't drink.

"No cardiac or respiratory function."

The young one blowing air into my mother, muscles bending over my little mother in her nightgown as she lay on the floor . . . his mouth on and off hers . . . It looked like they were kissing, didn't it? I wanted to laugh until I saw Clare's eyes.

Why was Clare still in the room? Why didn't someone think to make her go away? Clare shouldn't have seen that.

"Mom, what's wrong with Grandma?"

"Nothing, why? She's still sleeping . . . why?" Whispering, we were whispering at the foot of her bed.

"I don't know . . . Mom . . . Mom, look at her . . . how long has she been lying there like that?"

Moving to her, shaking her . . . "Mom, Mommy? Oh, Jesus, no, please, God, Mollie, come on . . ."

"Mom, what is it? Mom? Mom? *Mom?*" No more whispering, Clare was yelling at me now.

Hey, don't turn to me, kid, I'm not the mother. There's the mother over there, that's Mollie, she's the mother, that sweet lady with her eyes closed. I'm not the mother, I'm Gillian, the girl. Oh, God, sweet Jesus . . . don't let my mother be dead.

Well, my mother would have known not to let Clare see that, Mollie would have known . . . Oops, too late, Gillian. Mollie can't help you now, she's dead.

Gilliana laughed and then put her hand over her mouth. "Shut up," she whispered, "you'll wake the whole house . . ." She took a swig out of the bottle. "Vodka for breakfast, anyone?"

Hey. I'm an orphan.

I'll be goddamned.

I am, aren't I?

It's true, I am am orphan . . . Cute, Gillian—not *am* orphan, *an* orphan. I mean, if you don't count Lew and of course I count Lew, but in the truest sense of the word, I am an orphan since the famous Jule is dead too.

Ha. Here's to you, Gillian, you orphan . . .

* * *

She held the bottle out in the air in the dark silent kitchen. She toasted the oven door of her mother's stove and took a drink.

Oh, Mollie . . . what will I do without you?

"The police unit has been called, ma'am . . . Uh, where would you like us to place her?" said the baby paramedic.

Gee, I don't know, blue eyes, why don't you *place* her back on the goddamn bed where she was when you found her? Before you put her on the floor and hit her with your mouth-to-mouth and whacked her with your fucking paddles . . . Mollie's little body flying off the pale-blue rug of her bedroom . . . Hey, that's my mother you're zapping there; she wouldn't like that, you boys better put those things away.

"The EKG indicates asystole."

"What is that? What is he saying?"

"It means a straight line, ma'am," said the brown eyes and the mustache over the perfect white teeth.

"It means no cardiac activity, ma'am," said the baby paramedic with the eyes of blue.

"It means zip," Gilliana whispered in the kitchen.

Zip, my Mollie's zip.

The police? Did he say the police?

"You need a legal release from the coroner's office, ma'am. The police will have to speak to your mother's doctor and make a record of her history. If the doctor concurs and will sign the death certificate, then the police can get a legal release from the coroner's office and they can release your mother's body to the family . . . uh . . . to Mr. Allen and . . . uh . . . to you, ma'am."

Lots of releases there, huh?

Well, of course, that makes sense.

What? What makes sense? What the fuck did he say to me? My mother's history? What fucking history?

And who the hell else would they release my mother's body to except to me and Lew? The Smithsonian? The Museum of Modern Art? The Louvre?

"Meet me in St. Louis, Louis . . ." Gilliana sang softly.

And dear Lew, sitting on the bed next to her, holding her hand and stroking her hair as if she was just asleep. I had to leave the room.

Gilliana reached up and grabbed the handle on the door of the refrigerator and held on to it as she hauled herself up to her knees. "We will dance the hoochie-coochie . . ." She grasped the handle and stood up.

". . . meet me at the Fair . . ."

She bent over at the waist to pick up the vodka bottle, lost her balance, and fell in a heap back down to the kitchen floor.

"Whoops . . . shit . . . well, hello there, Gillian . . . it seems to me we're having a little trouble here with our feet."

She got back up on her knees and grabbed the handle of the refrigerator door again. She giggled as she tried to get to her feet and collapsed back down.

"Well, where are those fucking paramedics when you need them? That's what I say. Where are those boys?"

Gillian crept across the cold linoleum on her hands and knees like a soldier in the infantry; then she stopped abruptly, turned over, and lay motionless on her back in front of the sink.

"Oops . . . too much movement here . . . let's not let the kitchen go around like that . . ."

She closed her eyes and quickly opened them, folded her arms across her chest, and clasped her hands.

Not a pretty picture . . . Focus, Gillian . . . Come on, girl, focus here.

She took a deep breath.

That will teach you to open things that don't belong to you.

C'mon, Gillian, let it go.

No, better yet, hold on to it, hold on to it and fuck you.

All Mollie's beautiful handbags in her closet in a row. Each one smelling of Estée Lauder as you click open the clasps and peek inside, and you're smiling because they're so beautiful, the handbags, so like your mother, a part of your mother, and then in between the little mirrors and the little coin purses and the little tortoise combs and buried deep inside the tissue you find all the little notes. Folded neatly and written in Mollie's perfect penmanship, but also a part of your mother—not the beautiful part, not like the handbags—and they puncture and wound you as you read:

"Lew says I'm not keeping up."

Take that, Gillian.

"I forgot how to drive the car."

And that, Gillian.

"I don't know what's happening to me."

And that.

"Maybe I'm losing my mind."

And that and that and that.

Gillian rolled over onto her stomach and laid her cheek on her folded arms, the tears running across the backs of her hands and dropping to the floor.

"Oh, Mommy . . . I'm so sorry I didn't want to know about you."

"Mom?" Clare stood motionless in the dark kitchen, staring at her mother on the floor. "Mom, what are you doing in here?" She moved across the linoleum and crouched down. "Mom?"

Gilliana opened her eyes and saw the toes of Clare's thick white socks in front of her face on the floor. "Curses . . . the sock police," she mumbled into her arms.

"What?" Clare said, sitting down next to where her mother was sprawled on her stomach. "What did you say? Sock what?"

"Nothing."

"Sock police? Is that what you said?"

Gilliana didn't answer.

"Mom, really, what are you doing in here? Didn't you go to sleep? Mom?"

"Hmm?"

"Aren't you going to turn over?"

"I don't think so."

"What? I can't hear you, you're talking into your . . ."

Clare lay down on the floor next to her mother. "Mom," she said, looking straight into Gilliana's eyes, "Mom, please . . . what's wrong?"

"They took my mother away in a truck."

"What? A truck? Is that what you said? It wasn't a truck. You know that. It was the van from the funeral home . . . Oh, God . . . what are you doing here, Mom? You're not making jokes, are you? Please don't make jokes . . . I couldn't stand it if you made jokes . . . Mom?"

Clare moved closer to Gilliana. "Hey, Mom . . . what? Are you crying? Hey, Mom?"

Hesitantly, Clare put her hand on her mother's back, she patted Gilliana on the shoulder as she moved closer, closer, until her body was touching Gilliana's, until she put an arm around her mother's shaking shoulders, until she was holding her mother as they lay next to each other on her grandmother's kitchen floor.

"Come on, Mom, it'll be all right," Clare said, beginning to cry too as she held the sobbing Gilliana. "It's okay, Mom, I'm here."

MONDAY

Clare

So I found my mother drunk this morning. I mean, there's no other way to put it, because she could hardly stand up and had finished, I guess, most of a bottle of vodka. I mean, I don't know where it was when she started, but there was like this little drop left in the bottle when I found her on the kitchen floor. Not that I was upset about it or anything, because I certainly wasn't. She certainly had a right to get fucked up, but the whole thing was just, you know, a trip. I mean, not just finding my mother like that . . . I mean, the whole thing. It's like I don't even know where to start.

See, my grandma died. That in itself I can't even begin to talk about yet or even think about with any of the details, because really, I don't want to remember them, I don't want to go over them and possibly engrave them in any way on my brain. She died, and there was this whole business with the paramedics and the police department and then the funeral parlor people who came to take her away. It was gruesome and dreadful and totally unreal, like none of it was actually happening. I mean, there was this part of me the whole time that kept wanting to laugh.

It all started after dinner, I guess like around seven or seven-thirty, and by the time it was over I don't have the slightest idea what time it was. When I went to bed, my mother was in the kitchen. She was sitting at the kitchen table wearing her jeans and an old T-shirt and having a drink. And

I said Mom are you going to sleep soon, and she said yes and that was it, and I wasn't sure if I should sit with her, you know, because I had this feeling like she needed her own space, especially after all the chaos, and then dealing with my grampa because when they took my grandma away, he just totally lost it. It was as if everything he'd been holding inside of him the whole time she was sick just poured out of him when they carried her out the door and he couldn't stop crying, my grampa. I mean, he really couldn't. He'd try to collect himself and then he'd start again. It was awful. My heart was breaking for him. My mother finally made him lie down on the bed, and we just sat on either side of him and let him cry. I don't think he ever would have stopped if he hadn't just fallen asleep there. Anyway, so the house was quiet and I thought maybe I should leave her alone.

I was out of it as soon as I hit the pillow, I don't even remember closing my eyes. And when I woke up it was still dark but it was morning, you know the way you know without looking, that time right before the sky is about to turn into dawn, and I don't know what made me get up because I certainly could have just turned over and closed my eyes and gone back to sleep, but I didn't. I knew my mother hadn't slept in the bed next to me because that side was still perfectly tucked in, but of course she could have slept on the couch in the living room or, I don't know, in a chair.

I found her in the kitchen; she was lying on the floor on her stomach, and I thought, What is this? Is she sleeping? I went in and then, you know, she like fell apart crying, which was really hard for me to deal with because I've probably only seen my mother cry twice in my life, so I fell apart too and we were both crying, and then it was clear that she was loaded, you know, which was pretty shocking to me. I mean, I've seen her have a drink, you know, or wine with dinner, but it's not like I've ever seen her even tipsy, much less drunk. And so I'm trying to take care of her because she's having trouble even standing, and then it comes out that she hadn't called my dad yet. I mean, she hadn't called to tell him about my grandma, I couldn't believe it.

That was the first thing I made her do after I got her up and sitting at the table. She was actually trying to convince me that it was too early, since it was still the middle of the night in Los Angeles, and I said what difference does it make in the light of why you're calling him? I mean, really, what does my dad care about what time it is if she's calling to tell him my grandma died? Who cares about time? And anyway, he's got to get on a plane to come in for the funeral, which will be tomorrow, Tuesday.

And she says, Well, maybe he won't come in. And I say, What are you talking about—of course Daddy will come in. And then she starts carrying on really crazy, and it was hard for me to understand what she was talking about at first, about how she never lets Dad in, and she didn't even let Grandma in—when it came to Grandma being sick—and how she's been a shitty wife and a shitty daughter, and then she starts saying that she's been a shitty mother too, because she doesn't even know what's going on with me. And then she starts asking, "So, Clare, how are you?" and "How do you feel about Scott and going away to school?" I mean, in some ways it was actually funny. I said, "Mom, you're being ridiculous." I mean, all of a sudden she's gonna try to talk to me after all these years and while she's fucked up, you know?

Anyway, I made her call Dad. I couldn't believe it, that she was really that scared. I mean, like a kid. It's astonishing to me sometimes how the ones who are supposed to be the grown-ups behave. She's sitting there with her hand on the receiver and she won't dial the phone. So I said, Well, why don't you just tell him you're sorry—you know, that you've been afraid. And she like looks at me.

"How do you know I'm afraid?" she says.

And I say, "Well, gee, Mom, it's kind of obvious."

"Obvious," she says.

"Yeah," I say.

Anyway, she called him and of course he's coming, but you would not believe the conversation. I mean, it's not like I would have chosen to hear it, but in a way I'm glad I did. Not that I had a choice, of course, because through the whole thing my mother was actually clutching my hand, like if I had let go of her she would have gone down for the count or something—just fallen back on my grandmother's kitchen floor . . . and I've never seen my mother like that, because she's always a tough guy, you know?

So she's telling him she's sorry she woke him and I guess he says that it's okay, and then she gets hysterical sobbing and she says, "Oh, Chris, my mother be's a dead duck," which, of course, is not the normal way you tell somebody that your mother died, but "be's a dead duck" is this expression my grandma always used when she talked about when she would die, and my dad knows that, so he understood what she meant.

Then I guess he said things to try and make her feel better about my grandma, because she kept saying, "I know, I know . . ."

And then out of nowhere she blurts out something about this silver bracelet and if it was really meant for her. And I think, Huh? What is she talking about? But then I get it, what she's asking is if this silver bracelet was for her or for another person, another *woman,* is what she's asking, okay? Well, I nearly fall on the floor with that one, because I knew they were in trouble but I certainly didn't think it had gone that far. I mean, I can't imagine my dad with another woman while he's still with my mom . . .

And then I guess he must have said that he needs *somebody,* because she says, "But you do have *somebody,* Christopher . . . you have *me.*"

And then I guess he says he doesn't have her, or he doesn't feel like he has her, because then she says, "Oh, Chris, you know how you say I only cry at the movies and never at real life, but this isn't the movies, is it? This is real life," and she's really sobbing by this time and then she says that so is he. Her life, I mean. She says that my dad is her life.

And I don't know what he says back to her, because he talks for like a whole two minutes and she's listening and shaking her head and crying, and then my mother looks at me with her eyes glued right into mine and she says *what I told her to say to him;* she says, "Christopher, I'm sorry, I've just been afraid."

Anyway, I don't know what he says back to her because he talks again and she just listens and then she says, "Please, Chris, could we just *try* to fix it? Please? Could we just *try* until"—and she can hardly speak she's crying so hard when she says it—"until May 19th?"

And then he starts laughing, I mean I could hear him since I was standing practically on top of her, she was holding my hand so tight, and my dad is laughing, and then she starts laughing with him even though she didn't stop crying because she didn't, she cried through the whole thing.

Anyway, he's coming here, my dad, and it doesn't really matter if I get what's going on with them, because I guess the only important thing is that they're going to try. I mean, what more can I ask for, even if you just look at the whole thing from my point of view, right?

She's sleeping. *Finally.* I made her take three aspirins and I even sat with her until she fell asleep.

Then I made Grampa breakfast and I ate with him. I think he'll be all right. I mean, I know he'll be in shock a while and he'll never be the same again without my grandma, but I told him that, you know, he was really one of the lucky ones, because they not only had this really incredible love together that everybody dreams about having from the time they're old enough to know they can fall in love, but the most important part of it is that they *knew.* And I said that all I want is to someday have a love like that and how lucky I was that they had showed me that a love like that can even be. Of course, let's hope that I can remember that when it happens to me, if it happens; let's hope I'll know if I walk into one of those loves, because it seems to me no matter how smart you think you are, you don't always know. I mean, it's not like a sign lights up or something. You could walk right by the right person and not even know it. Or you could be with someone for a hundred years and forget how much you love them, how much they mean to you.

Later, when my mother gets up, we have to figure out what clothes to take over to the funeral parlor—you know, what clothes they're going to put on my grandmother to bury her in, which I assume will be funny. I mean, the whole thing is so unbelievable anyway, the idea of my mother and me choosing an outfit that my grandma's going to be buried in, and considering what my mother's like, the whole thing will probably be funny because that's how my mother is. And, you know, it's weird, but I was thinking that maybe that's one of the good things about her. I mean, I always put that part of my mother down, how she's always making jokes about everything, but maybe it's just the way she handles things and maybe there's nothing wrong with that, because somehow as of this morning it seems to me that maybe it's easier to deal with the hard stuff in life if you can laugh.

I don't know . . . it's just that I see that life isn't always what you think it's going to be. I mean, I could sit here and plan out the whole thing and be sure that I'll be the smart one, that I'll know exactly what I want and not let anything stop me, but then it's like I think . . . who knows?

PERMISSIONS ACKNOWLEDGMENTS

Grateful acknowledgment is made to the following for permission to reprint previously published material:

Donaldson Publishing Co. and *George Whiting Publishing:* Excerpts from "My Blue Heaven" by Walter Donaldson and George Whiting, copyright © 1927, copyright renewed 1955, by Donaldson Publishing Co. and George Whiting Publishing. International copyright secured. All rights reserved. Reprinted by permission of Donaldson Publishing Co. and George Whiting Publishing.

Peer International Corporation: Excerpts from "Cuanto le Gusta" by Ray Gilbert and Gabriel Ruiz, copyright © 1948 by Promotora Hispano Americana de Musica, copyright renewed. Administered by Peer International Corporation. All rights reserved. Reprinted by permission of Peer International Corporation.

PolyGram International Tunes, Inc.: Excerpt from "Do Ya" written by K. T. Oslin, copyright © 1987 by PolyGram International Tunes, Inc. All rights reserved. Reprinted by permission of PolyGram International Tunes, Inc.

Arthur Schwartz Music Ltd. and *Warner Bros. Publications Inc.:* Excerpts from "Something to Remember You By" by Howard Dietz and Arthur Schwartz, copyright © 1930 (renewed) by Warner Bros. Inc. (ASCAP), and Arthur Schwartz Pub. Des. All rights reserved. Reprinted by permission of Arthur Schwartz Music Ltd. and Warner Bros. Publications Inc.

Warner Bros. Publications Inc.: Excerpts from "Ain't She Sweet" by Jack Yellen and Milton Ager, copyright © 1927 by Warner Bros. Inc. Rights for the extended renewal term in the U.S. controlled by Warner Bros. Inc. and Edwin H. Morris & Co., a division of MPL Communications Inc. Canadian rights controlled by Warner Bros. Inc. All rights reserved. Reprinted by permission of Warner Bros. Publications. Inc.

A NOTE ON THE TYPE

The text of this book was set in Fairfield, a typeface designed by the distinguished American artist and engraver Rudolph Ruzicka. This type displays the sober and sane qualities of a master craftsman whose talent has long been dedicated to clarity. Rudolph Ruzicka was born in Bohemia in 1883 and came to America in 1894. He has designed and illustrated many books and has created a considerable list of individual prints in a variety of techniques.

Composed by The Haddon Craftsmen, Inc.,
Scranton, Pennsylvania
Printed and bound by Quebecor Printing,
Fairfield, Pennsylvania
Designed by Dorothy Schmiderer Baker